MORE PRAISE FOR
LITTLE GREEN MEN

"The real pleasure of this book lies in its fun-house reflection of the real world—distorted, but all too hilariously recognizable."
—*Newsday*

"Buckley takes two subjects that might have seemed beyond parody by now—weekend political chat shows and abduction by aliens—and whips them into a fine comic confection."
—*The New Yorker*

"Cleverly written, replete with witty asides and acerbic insights. . . . You won't put down *Little Green Men* without a sigh of regret."
—*San Jose Mercury News*

"A bright, good-natured entertainment."
—*Cleveland Plain Dealer*

"Buckley spins a graceful and witty tale. . . . The combination of absurd plot and droll delivery makes this book uniquely entertaining. . . . Unless you are comfortable with staring

strangers, don't read *Little Green Men* in a public setting. The writing is too good, the laughs come too often. This book is too much fun to be able to hold in."
—*Denver Post*

"In a time when hating Washington has become a national blood sport, every half-baked humorist attacks the capital. But few can match the ammunition at the disposal of veteran journalist Christopher Buckley, a congenital Beltway insider. Familiarity may breed contempt, but it also breeds fine satire, and in his fourth novel, *Little Green Men*, Buckley's Washington teems with expediency and ego, hypocrisy and hype—and truth enough to make it all resonate."
—*Chicago Tribune*

"Christopher Buckley's knowledge of the ruling class and its whimsical ways is what grounds *Little Green Men* and makes you smile the whole time."
—*Washington Post*

"Christopher Buckley's withering farce, *Little Green Men*, sends up, or rather, beams up, the Washington inside-the-Beltway crowd, anti-government zealots, the media, the U.S. space program, UFO enthusiasts and, for good measure, high profile lawyers."
—*San Diego Union-Tribune*

"Give thanks, then, for Christopher Buckley, whose thoroughly delightful new novel, *Little Green Men*, brings to life a few prisoners of Washington's drear and lets us laugh at them as the drear gives way briefly to events of high excitement."
—*Vogue*

Also by Christopher Buckley

God Is My Broker (with John Tierney)
Moby Dick (with Herman Melville)
Wry Martinis
Madame Bovary (with Gustave Flaubert)
Thank You for Smoking
Campion (with James MacGuire)
Wet Work
The White House Mess
Steaming to Bamboola

LITTLE
GREEN
MEN

LITTLE GREEN MEN

Christopher Buckley

HarperPerennial
A Division of HarperCollins*Publishers*

HarperCollins books may be purchased for educational, business, or sales promotional use. For information please write: Special Markets Department, HarperCollins Publishers Inc., 10 East 53rd Street, New York, NY 10022.

First HarperPerennial edition published 2000.

Designed by Mercedes Everett

Library of Congress Cataloging-in-Publication Data

Buckley, Christopher. 1952–
    Little Green Men /Christopher Buckley.—1st Perennial ed.
      p. cm.
    ISBN 0-06-095557-0
     1. Unidentified flying objects—Sightings and encounters—Fiction.
2. Alien abduction—Fiction. 3. Washington (D.C.)—Fiction. I. Title
PS3552.U339 L58 2000
813'.54—dc21   99-055682

---

00 01 02 03 04 ❖/RRD 10 9 8 7 6 5 4 3 2 1

For Caitlin

The exercise took place in the early 1960s . . . and involved launching fictional UFO sighting reports from many different areas. The project was headed by Desmond Fitzgerald of the CIA's Special Affairs Staff (who made a name for himself by inventing harebrained schemes for assassinating Fidel Castro). The UFO exercise was "just to keep the Chinese off-balance and make them think we were doing things we weren't. . . . The project got the desired results, as I remember, except that it somehow got picked up by a lot of religious nuts in Iowa and Nebraska or somewhere who took it seriously enough to add an extra chapter to their version of the New Testament."

—Former CIA officer Miles Copeland,
quoted in Above Top Secret: The Worldwide UFO Cover-Up

[President Clinton] said, "Hubb, there are two things I want you to find out for me: One, who killed JFK? And two, are there UFOs?"

I actually did go to NORAD (North American Aerospace Defense Command) when I was in Colorado Springs and asked them about UFOs. Of course, they denied it.

—Former Associate Attorney General Webster Hubbell,
in USA Today

PART
ONE

ONE

"Ten seconds."

John O. Banion stared unblinkingly into the TV camera's cyclops eye, keeping his famous cool under the baking glare of the Videssence lights. It pleased him that he was more at ease than the person seated opposite him, who as it happened was the most powerful man in the world.

"Five seconds." The technician counted down with an outstretched hand. With his huge headset, he could have been a crewman on an aircraft carrier signaling for the launch of an F-14.

"Three, two . . ."

The theme music was cued, a variation on a Handel trumpet voluntary with echoes of Aaron Copland. The TV critic for *The Washington Post* had called it "Fanfare for the Self-Important Man." Still, nothing like a few bars of brass to get the Establishment's hemoglobin pumping on Sunday mornings as it sipped its third cup of coffee and scanned the newspapers for mentions of itself.

"*Sunday . . .*"

A satisfying opener, implying, as it did ownership of the entire day, and the Sabbath at that. The announcer's voice was familiar. It had taken four meetings between Banion, his producers, and the sponsor, Ample Ampere, to settle on it.

Ample Ampere had wanted James Earl Jones, but Banion said that he couldn't hear the voice of James Earl Jones without thinking of Darth Vader, hardly an appropriate tone setter for such a high-level show as his. Ampere countered with Walter Cronkite. No, no, said Banion, Cronkite, the beloved former TV anchorman, was too avuncular, too upbeat. The voice must have such gravity as to suggest that if you missed the program, you were not a serious person. Only one would do—George C. Scott, the voice of General Patton.

"... *an exploration of tomorrow's issues, with today's leaders. And now* . . ."—Banion had dictated the slight pause in the manner of Edward R. Murrow's wartime "This . . . is London" broadcasts—"*your host . . . John Oliver Banion.*" The *Post* critic had written: "Drumroll, enter praetorians, household cavalry, concubines, elephants, rhinos, captured slaves, eunuchs, and other assorted worshipers."

Banion looked owlishly into the lens through his collegiate tortoiseshell eyeglasses. He seemed perpetually on the verge of smiling, without ever giving in to the impulse. He was in his late forties, but could have been any age. He had looked this way since his second year at Princeton. He had a round face that was handsome in a bookish sort of way. His graying blond hair was unstylishly cut, on purpose. He disdained salon haircuts as marks of unseriousness.

"Good morning," Banion said to the camera. "Our guest today is the president of the United States. Thank you for being with us this morning."

"My pleasure," lied the president. He had loathed John O. Banion ever since Banion had corrected him on a point of history at a White House dinner, in front of the French president. He would much—much—rather have stayed at Camp David, the presidential retreat in the Catoctin Mountain Park outside Washington, on this Sunday morning. He chafed at being told by his press secretary that Banion insisted on a live interview *in the studio.* What was the point of being the most powerful man on earth if you had to grovel before these assholes, just because they had their own TV—

"Sir, it's the top-rated weekend show. And it looks like he's going to be moderating the debates this fall."

"All right, but you tell him, no commercials. I won't sit there twiddling my thumbs while they break for commercials every five minutes. It's unpresidential."

"Mr. President," Banion said, "I want to ask you why, in light of your administration's below-par performance in a number of areas, you haven't fired at least two-thirds of your cabinet, but first . . ."

It was a trademark Banion opener: establish the guest's inadequacy, then move along to the even more pressing issue. The president maintained glacial equanimity. For this he had gotten up early on Sunday and helicoptered all the way back to Washington. The press secretary would suffer.

". . . let me ask you about something else. We have a report that NASA, the space agency, is planning to advance the launch date of the final stage of the space station *Celeste* to right before the presidential election this fall. Would you call that a triumph of American aerospace engineering, or of politics? You can take credit for both, if you'd like."

The president smiled, suppressing his desire to pick up the water pitcher and smash it against the forehead of this supercilious twerp. But inside his brain alarms were sounding like those on a depth-charged submarine. How did Banion know about the launch date? They'd gone to pains to put in so many buffers between the White House and NASA on this exquisitely delicate matter that no one would be able to trace the decision to the Oval Office.

"John," he began, in his slow, overly patient tone of voice that suggested he wasn't sure English was your first language, "the credit for *Celeste*'s dazzling success has to go, first and foremost, to hundreds and thousands of men and women who have worked their hearts out on this project from the very beginning. . . ."

Banion looked over his glasses in the manner of a disappointed schoolteacher and jotted notes on his clipboard. He did this not because any of the drivel exgurgitating like foam from the presidential mouth warranted recording but because it made his interviewees nervous.

". . . to make sure that America will not only be number one here on earth but number one out . . . there."

"Before we return to whether the timing of the launch was politically manipulated," said Banion, "let's talk for a moment about the wisdom of spending so many billions of dollars on a space station. So far all it seems to have accomplished is to provide a platform for studying the effects of weightlessness on copulating fruit flies."

"That's—"

"Three and a half years ago, only days after a disastrous and, if I may, ill-advised military operation in North Korea, you gave a speech at an aerospace plant in the Mojave Desert in California in which you called for completing an orbital space station. You called this 'an urgent national priority.' Some cynical voices at the time suggested that, like President Kennedy, who announced the man-on-the-moon initiative right after the Bay of Pigs fiasco, you were trying to get people's minds off the Korean debacle. But leave that aside for a moment—"

"Let me—"

"If I may? And leave aside the fact that *Celeste*'s biggest contractors are in California and Texas, two states you almost *lost* four years ago and which you desperately need to win this time. Let me ask you, after four years of cost overruns that would have made the emperor Caligula blush crimson, what does the nation have to show for this celestial boondoggle, aside from three-point-four-million-dollar zero-gravity coffeemakers and one-point-eight-million-dollar toilets?"

"With all due respect, I'm sure there were some people in the court of King Ferdinand and Isabella who objected to the cost of the facilities on Columbus's boats."

"I don't recall that there *were* facilities on the *Niña, Pinta,* and *Santa María.*"

"My point is that you can't really put a price on the future."

"With all due respect, whenever a politician says you can't put a price on something, you can be sure it's going to be a whopper. The fact is that you can put a price on anything. In this case, it's twenty-one billion dollars and counting, as they say at Cape Canaveral. This is a huge sum of money. What's more, it's being said that your reelection committee should report this as a campaign donation by the American people."

"Fine," said the president, "but let me tell you what *I* hear when I travel around this country in support of *Celeste.* I hear people saying, 'This is excellent. This is something we can *all* be proud of.' "

"Fine. So what *are* the American people getting for their billions?"

The president pressed play and, straining against the weariness of reciting it all for the two hundredth time, began to tick off the bountiful spin-offs that *Celeste* would bring to earth: glorious advances in—you name it—machinery lubricants, long-distance telephone networks, sewage treatment, robotic wheelchairs, insulin pumps, pacemakers, research on cures for osteoporosis, diabetes, uh, radiation-blocking sunglasses, energy-conserving air-conditioning . . . too numerous to mention, really.

Banion listened to this life-enhancing litany with the chin-quivering air of a man at pains to stifle a yawn. Sensing that he had better come up with something more millennial than *Celeste*'s contribution to the field of ultrasound scanning, the president gave a gripping description of what the AOR—atmospheric ozone replenishment—module, part of the launch package, would accomplish once it became operational, namely squirting ozone back into the atmosphere to cover the O-Hole, which now stretched from the Falklands to Madagascar, wreaking havoc on plankton and emperor penguins alike.

Still Banion looked faint from boredom. The president dragged out the LAWSI module, the ultimate—if slippery—argument for *Celeste's* relevance. If in doubt, refer to the large asteroid warning system indicator, which theoretically could detect whether some astral death star this way was heading. The top people at NASA and the Pentagon had been cautioning him from becoming too evangelical on this particular aspect of *Celeste*. It was tricky business, getting the citizenry in a lather over the prospect of death-by-gigantic-meteor, especially this close to the millennium, when every fruitcake in the pantry was screaming Apocalypse.

"But what," Banion said, "are we supposed to do if we find out that there *is* an asteroid coming our way?"

"Well, in the unlikely event . . . we'd want some sort of warning."

"I wouldn't. If the world's about to end, I don't want *any* warning."

"No one is saying the world is going to end," said the president, trying to smile. "This is about beginnings, not endings."

When he began to extol the racial and cultural diversity of the astronauts being launched, Banion interrupted him.

"We'll be right back with the president, after this."

The studio filled with the sound of Ample Ampere's theme music. The commercial showed a basset hound sitting staring hopefully through the glass door of an oven, inside which a juicy roast was baking. The president gestured to his press secretary to approach with his miserable, inadequate excuse as to why he, Leader of the New Millennium, was being made to endure a homey commercial message about the joys of electricity.

A makeup woman, modern-day medic of the TV battlefield, sprang forward to touch up glistening foreheads.

Banion, overhearing a snatch of perturbed presidential conversation, leaned forward and said, "I asked them myself if we could bank the commercials at the beginning and end, but"—he smiled dryly—"it seems I am as helpless as you, sir, in the face of the exigencies of Mammon."

BANION'S WIFE, BITSEY, REACHED HIM IN THE CAR ON HIS way to brunch at Val Dalhousie's in Georgetown. The interview had made her nervous. After all, the president was coming for dinner, next week.

"He's going to cancel now."

"No he won't."

"They'll make it sound like a last-minute thing. I've spent the whole *week* with the Secret Service."

"Bitsey, he's only a president." She would understand. She was fourth-generation Washington, a cave dweller.

Banion hummed along Rock Creek Drive, fairly throbbing with contentment over the entrance he would make at Val's. The car, made in England, had a burled walnut dashboard that shone like an expensive humidor. He could actually make out his reflection in it, and he liked that. He'd paid for the car with two speeches—one of them on how to revitalize the U.S. auto industry—and he hadn't even had to leave town for them. More and more, he hated to leave town. Everything he needed was here.

It was a bright, clear June day. He felt devil-may-care. He had just stuck it to the president of the United States in front of all the people who would be at Val Dalhousie's brunch: senators, Supreme Court justices, editorial-page pontiffs, bureau chiefs, an ambassador or two for seasoning, perhaps the papal nuncio, or at least a tony bishop. They added such nice color in their robes. It gave him a little thrum of pleasure that Bitsey was anxious. Dear thing—didn't she understand that presidents came and went?

"You were great," the press secretary said to the president as soon as they were inside the vibrating cocoon of *Marine One,* the presidential helicopter, en route from the *Sunday* studio to Burning Bush Country Club in suburban Maryland for eighteen holes with Prince Blandar. The chief of staff pretended to be preoccupied with his PRESIDENTIAL ACTION folder. "Your line," the press secretary tried again, "about how this is about beginnings, not endings. A home run."

The president, changing into his golf togs, tossed his suit jacket at his Filipino steward.

"I go to his studio on a Sunday morning, because John Oliver Banion does not *do* remote interviews, and I get half an hour of abuse interrupted by *three* commercials showing toasters that talk to you and people smiling—smiling—as they're being fed into MRI machines. I've had an MRI, and you do not *smile* while you are having it, let me tell you. It's like being stuffed into a torpedo tube while waiting to hear whether you have cancer. You're not smiling. You're pissing down your legs. Why don't Ample Ampere's commercials show people being electrocuted in their new electric chair? That's it. No more *Sunday* with John O. Banion." He flung his pants at the steward. "I don't care what his ratings are. 'Exigencies of Mammon.' Prick!"

The chief of staff's rule was never to interfere while the president was shredding the self-esteem of another member of the staff, but it was his job to save the president from himself. He looked up from the secretary of transportation's urgent memo about a bridge over the Mississippi that was about to collapse, halting all commerce on the river.

"Is Banion moderating the debates?"

The press secretary gratefully picked up the cue. "I talked to Jed Holcomb at the League of Gay Voters, and he says it's a done deal. This is their first time hosting the debates, and they're going out of their way to have as straight a moderator as there is. Banion's nothing if not straight."

"How did the League of Gay Voters get to sponsor the debates?" the president asked. "For Christ's *sake*. Where does it end?"

"It was their turn."

"We have no say in the moderator?"

"Theoretically. But if we veto him, it'll get out and we'll have elevated him into the Man the President Is Afraid Of."

"Afraid, my ass. While he was playing squash at Harvard—"

"Princeton."

"—my unit was taking thirty percent casualties in the A Shau Valley. I am not 'afraid' of some pipe-sucking, bow-tied talk-show host whose idea of hell is finding grit in his Wellfleet oysters."

Marine One was circling Burning Bush, preparing to land. The president was lacing his spikes.

The chief of staff said, "Of course we're not scared of him. But why give him a career boost by vetoing him in the debates?"

The president looked out his window at the small army waiting to receive him. "Aren't Laura and I supposed to go to his house for dinner next week in honor of someone?"

"The British ambassador."

"Schedule something for right before the dinner. Something that might run late. Really late. CIA briefing on the Russian situation."

"Okay," said the chief of staff. "But wouldn't it be cooler to smother the bastard in honey? What's the point of pissing him off?"

"When did these people get so goddamned important that the president of the United States has to suck up to them? Someone tell me."

They were saved from having to answer by *Marine One*'s landing.

"All right, but you let him know: I'm not doing his show again. You *tell* him."

The press secretary nodded.

The president stepped out onto manicured grass and was immediately engulfed by entourage.

A staff car was waiting to take the staff to the White House. The press secretary lay back against the seat with his tie loosened and the thousand-yard stare of a freshly reamed presidential aide.

"What are you going tell Banion?" the chief of staff asked.

" 'Great show, Jack. The president really enjoyed himself. He wants to do it again. Soon.' "

The chief of staff nodded and went back to his IMMEDIATE ACTION folder.

The president sliced off the first tee into a stand of sycamores, narrowly missing the skull of a congressman. The ball made a loud *thok* before disappearing into poison ivy. Prince Blandar, desirous of the president's support with respect to congressional approval for the purchase of fifty shiny new F-20 jet fighters for his desert kingdom, urged him to take a mulligan.

VAL DALHOUSIE, PLUMP, TWO FACE-LIFTS INTO HER SIXTIES, voluptuous and billowy in a Galanos caftan, thousands of dollars of diamond-studded gold panthers chasing each other around her wrists, beckoned the late-arriving Banion into her Matisse-intensive parlor.

"I'm not sure any of us *dares* be seen with you." She gave him a peck on each cheek in the European manner. She whispered, "If I had known you were going to be so *feral* with him, I wouldn't have invited so many of his cabinet."

Val had been a stage actress years ago. Before that, it was said that she had been in a different line of entertainment. She had married up the food chain, eventually reaching the rung occupied by Jamieson Vanbrugh Dalhousie, adviser to presidents, heir to an immense steel fortune, and twice her age. Jamieson had died ten years ago, leaving her a half dozen houses, a number of alarmed heirs by his first wives, a tidy collection of Impressionists, and $500 million in walking-around money.

Jamieson was a humorless old grouper with bad breath and hairy ears whom official Washington revered for reasons no one, if pressed, could really explain. He had advised President Roosevelt that Joseph Stalin was really, deep down, a decent sort. Another president had wittily put him in charge of the Vietnam peace negotiations, resulting in years of negotiations about the shape of the negotiating table and a peace that quickly went to pieces.

Before Val entered his life, his houses in Georgetown and Virginia were temples of parsimony and gloom. Guests entering his dining room mumbled to themselves, "Abandon hope, all ye who enter here." The wine could have been mistaken for cough syrup; only the most determined alcoholic could swallow it without wincing. Over this grim mahogany domain, Jamieson Vanbrugh Dalhousie ruled, treating his guests to endless monologues on such riveting topics as Russia's projected uranium needs in the next century and Konrad Adenauer's struggle against fluctuations in the deutsche mark during the postwar era. Jamieson's untimely death at the age of eighty-eight, after stepping on a garden rake, was treated by the Establishment as the end of an era and the passing of a national treasure. In his eulogy at the National Cathedral, the president said how much he would miss his wise, dependable counsel.

Val, by contrast, loved to spend money—by the fistful, by the armful. She practically used it to mulch her Georgetown garden. She sent helicopters to fetch her guests for weekends at Middleburg, in Virginia. She hired Pavarotti to sing for them, fed them caviar and quail eggs, flew in foie gras and truffles from France. She spent money on presidential contenders the way others bet on horses at the track. One of them was bound to win, after all. One of her horses eventually came in, and with it an ambassadorial appointment to the Court of St. James's. You could hear Jamieson moaning at the expense in his grave. *Thirty million? You could have gotten Italy for half the price.*

Val took Banion by the arm and led him into the parlor, bursting with peonies and reeking sweetly of perfumed candles. Banion scanned the room for his wife. It was a fairly typical Val Sunday brunch: two cabinet secretaries; several more former cabinet secretaries; one declared presidential candidate, one undeclared; a movie star (in town to testify before Congress against a stylish disease); Tyler Pinch, curator of the Fripps Gallery—ah, there was Bitsey, with him—a quorum of senators; the Speaker of the House, majority whip; the managing and foreign editors of the *Post;* ah yes—Banion was pleased to see these two: Tony Flemm and Brent Boreman, hosts of the other Washington weekend shows; a brace of Op-Ed pundits, one readable, the other un-; a husband and wife biographer team, a Nick and Nora pair, rather exotic; a former presidential mistress (several administrations ago) now heavily involved in the symphony; looming above them all, suave, immense, baritone-voiced Burton Galilee, lawyer, lobbyist, friend of presidents, who had turned down a Supreme Court appointment rather than give up, as he had actually put it to Banion, a confidant, "God's greatest gift to mankind—*pussy.*" Who else? The State Department's new chief of protocol, what *was* her name, Mandy Something; the French ambassador, the Brazilian ambassador, the Canadian ambassador, the Indonesian ambassador, who was gamely trying to explain to the other diplomats his government's recent decision to "pacify" another ten thousand East Timorians; that architect and his wife Banion couldn't stand because she had announced to him that she never watched television.

A butler appeared with a tray bearing Bloody Marys, champagne, white wine, sparkling water with limes. Banion chose a sparkling water and took up his position, waiting for the homages to begin. He waved away the watercress sandwiches; too awkward, receiving compliments with a mouth full of verdure.

Bitsey reached him first, trailing Tyler Pinch. She was smartly turned out in a double-breasted suit, pearl necklace, gold earrings. Bitsey was petite, angular, pretty, in a slightly toothy sort of way, with large eyes conveying a permanently startled look. She had southern roots, as many Washington cave dwellers do. Her father could bore a man to death at a hundred yards tracing the family tree back to the Precambrian era.

Banion and Bitsey had met twenty years back when they were both summer interns on Capitol Hill taking part in an Excellence in Futurity program in which America's young leaders were brought to Washington to stuff the envelopes of the power elite. Banion, shy and bookish, had never been very successful with women, but he was attracted to her. At a time when women took pains to look their worst so that men would take them seriously, Bitsey always looked her best, arriving each morning fresh, in pumps, stockings, and smartly pleated skirts, smelling of a perfume (White Shoulders) that Banion found intoxicating. He finally worked up the nerve to ask her out. To his amazement, she accepted.

That night, after the symphony at the Kennedy Center, they sat on the marble steps by Memorial Bridge and he told her in excited tones, in the moonlight, about his senior thesis on France's decision to withdraw from military participation in NATO in 1966. She was enthralled. From Oxford, where he was avoiding his own military participation in the Vietnam War, he wrote passionate letters to her about the emerging Common Market. They were married at Christ Church in Georgetown. It was a by-the-Establishment-book affair. The secretary of state, an old family friend of Bitsey's parents, attended. The reception was at the Chevy Chase Club. The honeymoon, in Bermuda. Jobs awaited them on their return. Bitsey in the marketing and sales office of the Hay-Adams Hotel. Banion as staff aide to Sen. Germanicus P. Delph of North Carolina—fortuitously, as it turned out, just as the Delph hearings on the CIA's unsuccessful attempts to assassinate the Canadian prime minister were getting under way. It was the beginning of Banion's unlikely career as a television "personality." But then in Washington, most careers are unlikely, one way or another.

Senator Delph held his position strictly by virtue of seniority on the Senate Committee on Governmental Eliminations. He was not, as one pundit at the time put it, a charter member of Mensa. The newspapers usually described him as a man of "limited intellectual interests." Banion, bright young man that he was, made himself indispensable to the senator, and as the hearings unfolded during that long, hot summer, he became familiar to the millions of Americans watching on TV as the handsome young staff aide whispering almost nonstop into Senator Delph's ear. *The Washington Post* wrote that he "appeared not only to have the senator's ear, but to live in it."

Banion's authorship of the resulting committee report did much to enhance his new luster. It struck a well-balanced tone between righteous indignation and cautious reform, between those who thought that the United States had no business trying to poison Canadian prime ministers and those who, while disapproving of this particular instance, felt that the United States ought to reserve the right to dispatch troublesome Canadian PMs in the future, should circumstances warrant. The quality of the prose was unusually high for a congressional report, down to elegant literary quotes from Cato the Elder, Paul Valéry, and, with a touch of intellectual sauciness, Mao Zedong. *The New York Times* bestowed upon him the laurel of "young man to watch." Other senators tried to poach him away from Senator Delph for their own staff.

Banion began to appear as a frequent guest on *Washington Weekend,* one of the more thoughtful, if intolerably dull, weekend television shows. He enjoyed the sensation of being stared at on the street by people who had seen him on television, the little *ah* of recognition by a maître d' when he arrived at the restaurant. Peg Bainbridge, the *Post*'s editorial-page editor, invited him to contribute an article to her Op-Ed page. She liked what she saw and asked for more. He resigned from Senator Delph's staff—or, as he put it a bit pompously, let it be known that he was "allowing himself to be lured back into the private sector"—and set up shop as a print-and-pixel pundit, with a syndicated column in the *Post* and a regular slot on *Washington Weekend.*

He stood out on *Washington Weekend,* though, to be frank, anyone with a pulse would have, considering the other regulars: a gassy, perpetually indignant columnist who had once been ambassador to Lesotho; a woman who had been covering Washington for one of the wire services since the Truman administration, and whose favorite phrase was "on the other hand"; a woman TV reporter who was having an affair with an ancient Supreme Court justice; and an obese, lisping think tanker who had published a book passionately arguing that Shakespeare's plays had been written by Queen Elizabeth. When Roger Panter, the Australian press baron, bought the television station that owned *Weekend,* Banion made his move. He wrote him a memo proposing certain changes, beginning with making him the show's host. Panter promptly sacked the other regulars and gave the show to Banion with orders to "juice it up" and a budget to do just that.

Banion changed the format to a live, Sunday-morning one-on-one interview, introduced with a crisp taped investigative piece, and concluding with a one-minute parting thought by Banion.

It certainly beat watching a bunch of self-important talking heads sucking their thumbs and regurgitating thoughts stolen from that morning's papers, all in order to drive up their already inflated lecture fees. In a medium glutted with sound bites, people were happy to come on and have twenty minutes of national TV exposure all to themselves, even if Banion sometimes extracted an admission price by flaying them alive, on air.

His audience built steadily. His first big ratings coup came when former Secretary of Defense Robert McNamara went on the show to reveal that he had been addicted to mind-altering hair-restorative drugs the whole time he was escalating the war in Vietnam. Suddenly *Sunday* became the show to be on.

Ample Ampere, the giant electric company, signed on as sole sponsor. Banion signed a lucrative multiyear contract. The salary was nice, but the real money came from lecture fees, astronomical, bordering on intergalactic. It was amazing how much corporations were willing to pay to hear in person the same stuff they could get on TV, but such is the nature of celebrity. The historian Daniel Boorstin defined it as "being known for being known." He might have added, "being paid for being known." Banion's youthful visage was now a fixture in the media firmament. Amazonian villagers with satellite TV would recognize his face if it went floating up their tributary. Maître d's now saved tables for him on the chance that he might show up. His caricature was duly painted on the walls of the Frond restaurant, where bigfeet dined on briefcase-sized steaks and four-pound lobsters (despite the fact that younger, smaller lobsters have more tender flesh). He had to allow extra time in airports for signing autographs on his way to the gate. That is, in the event he was even traveling by commercial airline. His lecture agent, Sid Mint, now hinted strongly to his clients that their chances of getting John O. Banion to speak at their special event would be greatly improved by sending the corporate jet to fetch and return him.

And here he stood, in Val Dalhousie's Rigaud-candle-scented parlor, preparing to have his posterior caressed by the very people who ran the country. Life was good. And it had all been so effortless.

Ah, here came Bitsey and Tyler. Tyler, curator of the Fripps Gallery, was looking natty today in a houndstooth blazer, dark blue shirt, French silk tie with little framed paintings—how appropriate—gold collar pin. He wore his hair slicked back at the sides in the manner of the athletically wealthy.

"Is that blood on your shoes?" Tyler grinned.

"He'll survive," said Banion airily.

"Can't wait to see the seating plan at your dinner for him."

"If he comes," said Bitsey, looking even more alarmed than usual. "Val says they'll cook up some last-minute crisis just to cancel."

"This administration doesn't have to cook up a crisis. They come naturally."

"Here's how to solve *that*," said Tyler in a lowered voice. "I happen to know that Orestes Fitzgibbon is going to be in town that day." Orestes Fitzgibbon, the Anglo-Greek financier, now a naturalized American citizen—owing to a tax problem—had recently purchased Immensa Corporation for $7 billion. He was known to be impulsively generous with his money—in part, it was said, because it infuriated his numerous ex-wives. "He's presenting us with a third El Greco. Why don't you invite him to your dinner? I doubt the president would be late if he knew Fitzgibbon was going to be at his table. He sat next to Senator Rockefeller two years ago and wrote him a campaign check for a million—on the spot."

"Oh God, that would completely solve it," said Bitsey. "Can we get him on this short notice?"

Tyler smiled.

"I'm not really his *biggest* admirer," Banion said. "I'm glad he's giving you all those El Grecos, but I sat next to him at an Erhardt Williger dinner, and frankly I found him kind of rough around the edges."

"Oh, Jack," said Bitsey, "don't be such a *stick*." Bitsey had been to so many dos at the British embassy that she had started to sound like a subject.

"I'm sowing marital discord," said Tyler. "You two sort it out and let me know."

"It's *decided*," said Bitsey.

Clare Boothe Luce had introduced them. Tyler was originally Australian. His father had made some vast, murky fortune selling the adductor muscles of giant clams—*Tridacna gigas*—to aging, impotent Formosans who thought they would help them get the old noodles to stiffen, then laundered that ill-gotten fortune in opals, oil, ranching, and vineyards. Young Tyler was sent off to English boarding school at an early age to be sodomized and otherwise inculcated into the British establishment. He'd gone on to Cambridge and then became a protégé to Sir Anthony Blunt, Surveyor of the Queen's pictures at Buckingham Palace, Windsor, and Hampton Court, and, as it turned out, Soviet agent. It came as rather a shock that the man who had educated the monarch on the subtleties of Poussin had been whispering state secrets to the KGB's London *resident*. Tyler moved on and married the high-stepping, troubled daughter of Sir Reginald Pigg-Vigorish. Sir Reg was up for a life peerage just about the time their divorce was announced and, not eager for his daughter's shall we say *peculiar* sexual antics to become tabloid fodder, settled a few spare Cézannes on his son-in-law to ensure his discretion. The divorce was settled quietly. Tyler sold the Cézannes to L'Orangerie museum in Paris for an undisclosed sum ($8.7 million) and left for America and the curatorship of the prestigious Fripps Gallery. His social luster was enhanced by the fact that he was close to the Prince of Wales. Banion was trying to enlist Tyler's help in getting the prince on *Sunday*. What a coup that would be. Well, there was no point arguing with Bitsey over having that oversexed troll Fitzgibbon to dinner. It was, as Bitsey had made plain, decided. Had the two of them rehearsed this little dance?

But here was Tony Flemm, host of the second-rated Washington show, trying not to look jealous. "Jack. Nice show."

"Do you think? I don't know."

That's right, torture the poor bastard, make him explain, make him elaborate in front of everyone on just *why* he thought it was such a good show. But wait, here came Burton Galilee, beaming, shaking his head in mock horror at Banion's ruffling of presidential eagle feathers. And here, just behind him, came the Speaker of the House of Representatives, and behind him, the French ambassador. A triumph. Banion filled his lungs with scented candle air and exhaled the soft, sweet vapors.

Val was clapping her hands. "Lunch, everyone, lunch!"

THREE

Monday mornings promptly at ten, Banion and his secretary, Renira, reviewed the previous week's mail and the coming week's schedule. She had read the mail to decide which of the approximately three to four hundred pieces warranted personal answers and had prepared an hour-by-hour summary of the week. Renira was British, and her voice could emasculate a phone caller by the final syllable of "Hello?" As a media figure, Banion believed it was his duty to have a listed telephone number. As a practical matter, he found this a colossal nuisance.

Last week's mail contained the usual number of letters hailing Banion's brilliance; the usual number denouncing him as an intellectual bully; the usual asking for amplification on a point; the usual asking him to read "the enclosed" manuscript with a view to helping get it published; the usual asking him to speak, gratis, at an upcoming function (these were forwarded to Sid Mint, Banion's lecture agent, who would then inform them that Banion's fee started at $25,000); the usual number beginning with "You won't remember me, but . . ." (to which Renira would reply, "You are correct that Mr. Banion does not remember you"); the usual number of offers of commercial endorsement, generally for fountain pens, expensive leather briefcases, running shoes, luxurious writing paper, dictionaries, CD-ROMs, ocean liners, sports cars, and of course walking sticks, Banion's trademark eccentricity—some said affectation. (His collection included a cane made from the amputated leg bone of a Civil War soldier; it had belonged to John Wilkes Booth; another made from a bull's penis.) These received curt, offended form replies.

A clothing store chain had recently offered $100,000 if he would be photographed wearing a pair of $29 dungarees. This offer Banion had wistfully considered. Of course he couldn't go hawking clothing—much less jeans. He never ventured outside his Georgetown house without a tie—but a hundred thousand smackeroos for an hour's work was significantly better than minimum wage. He declined, coolly, with the form letter, but it left him in a foul mood all day, calculating what he could have bought with the money. Christie's was holding a wine auction, and there were a few cases of '71 Romanée-Conti that had caught his eye, but . . . no . . . mustn't start doing that sort of thing. A number of Washington media bigfeet had started down that trail of late, hawking milk, credit cards. So undignified. . . .

Finally there were the usual number of letters from prisoners, many with death-row return addresses, proclaiming their innocence and requesting Banion's championship of their appeal. It is the dream of most journalists, and the stuff of Jimmy Stewart movies, to free an unjustly accused man from death row. This fantasy had never tantalized John O. Banion. No cream puff he, when it came to capital punishment. Indeed, he had attended a number of executions and written approvingly about them in his column—except in the unfortunate case when the man exploded in the electric chair. Dreadful business. He had written forcefully about the incident in his column, denouncing the competence of the prison, saying that any nation that could put a man on the moon ought to be able to devise a decent method of frying its felons. And now Ample Ampere, his own sponsor, had taken up the challenge and was about to unveil its new electric chair. Quiet, smokeless, efficient, energy-saving.

This Monday, Renira reported that it was a moderately busy

week, schedule-wise. ("Shed-yule," she pronounced it.) Break-fast Tuesday with Assistant Defense Secretary Coyne to discuss the Russian situation; lunch Wednesday with Kurt Kendall to hear him out—yet again—on why the Fed's tight money policies were throttling the economy; breakfast Thursday with Elkan Bingmutter of the Pan-European Union, who was agitating to come on *Sunday* so that he could explain to the American people the urgency of including Albania in NATO; lunch speech Thurs-day to the American Association of Frozen Fish Producers. Renira reminded him that this might be a bit dicey, as Banion had written a column just last month taking Canada's side in the recent halibut skirmish off Georges Bank, and the AAFFP was *vehemently* anti-Canadian. Banion shrugged. Dinner speech same day to the Congress of Jewish Chairmen of the Board of Ex-tremely Successful Corporations. Might have to buff up his Mid-dle East peace process speech for this one, in light of the fact that two weeks ago Israel had annexed Jordan, on the grounds that a scholar had interpreted a vowel in one of the Dead Sea Scrolls to mean that Jordan had once been part of Israel. Um. Tricky. Perhaps something along the lines that this, finally, rep-resented *real* stability in the region. Or something like that. Fri-day morning he was moderating a panel discussion for the American Medical Association. Sid Mint had squeezed $35,000 out of them for this. What was the topic?

"Perspectives in Diminished Longevity," Renira read off Mint's briefing sheet. "Challenges and Opportunities."

Renira's assistant buzzed to say that Bill Stimple of Ample Ampere was on the line. Banion took the call.

"Jack!" Bill Stimple was the Ur–corporate relations man. Each greeting began with an exclamation mark. When the Grim Reaper came for Bill, he'd probably bray, "Death!" and ask how his golf game was coming.

Banion did not go in for the hearty salutation. The last time he had raised his voice was in college, when some football players threw him into a box hedge after he wrote an editorial for *The*

Daily Princetonian denouncing sports as a "colossal waste of time and energy."

"Hello, Bill."

"*Great* show. Boy, you really held his toes to the fire."

"Glad you liked it."

"One of your best." Bill laughed. "Don't know how you're going to get him back on, but great job. Really, really great."

"I wouldn't worry. If his numbers are any indication, we may have a new president in January."

"Say, Jack, I spoke with Al Wiley after the show. By the way, he said to tell you how much he loved the show. Anyway, about *Celeste.* I don't think I need to tell you how much we respect your integrity. In fact, we worship your integrity."

Banion's chair made a leathery squeak as he leaned back. He imagined Al Wiley, chairman of the board of Ample Ampere, down on his knees, with Bill Stimple, worshiping at the altar of Banion's integrity.

"Ample's not a big *Celeste* contractor, not if you compare it with, say, Groening or Aeromax. But we do have a pinkie in the pie, so to speak. And this launch is going to be, you know, a *major* event."

"Bill—"

"Hear me out, then I'll shut up. I'm not saying there haven't been cost overruns—but Ample's been on budget and on time. I'm not saying—look, Jack, between you, me, and the walls, I couldn't tell you if this thing is worth twenty-one billion or twenty-one bucks. Not my department. What I do know is that this launch is going to be the biggest thing since *Apollo 11,* and Al is kind of wondering if we ought to be, I don't know . . . pissing all over it."

"I'm not 'pissing' on it, Bill. I'm asking certain basic questions, like is he using a massive amount of public money as a campaign donation, and are they manipulating the launch date to coincide with the election, and is this thing necessary?"

"Not my department. You're the man. I just wanted you to

know what the big guy was thinking. I figured you'd want to know. Right?"

"Of course."

"He *loves* the show. He's always bragging on you. The other day he was playing golf with Kenzibura Motohama, and he was going on and on about it."

"That's good to hear," said Banion, yearning to be off the phone.

"What else was I calling about? Jesus, early-onset Alzheimer's. . . . Oh, right, you know we're rolling out the XT–2000 this fall at the Florida penitentiary in Starke. The governor's coming. Wondered if you wanted to be there. It was your column about the guy who caught fire that got us started on this. *What* a great column. I still have that somewhere."

"I don't do openings, Bill."

"I totally understand."

"You're going down for it?"

"Sure. It's a new product launch. A lot of other state death reps are going to be there. You know, it *reclines*? You're not sitting there bolt upright. Just like being at home watching football, only you're being electrocuted. Very humane. And *quiet*. It makes less noise than our electric shavers."

"You should include it in your next commercial. Instead of the basset hound looking at the roast in the oven, he's watching Master being electrocuted."

"I like it! I'll run it by Creative."

Banion summoned Renira back in. "Where were we?"

"AMA panel Friday."

"Managed death. This entire *week* is managed death," he said crossly." This was going to be the week I got started on the book. Don Morforken called last week to say they've scheduled the pub date." He looked at her sternly, as if it was all her fault. "If there's no book, there is no point in *having* a publication date."

Banion no longer had time to write the big, meaty policy

books that he had cranked out in his younger days, books like *Pig's Breakfast: The Failure of U.S. Foreign Policy from Cuba to Beirut* or *Colossi of Rhodes,* his admiring study of Rhodes scholars and "The World They Made"; or *Screwing the Poor,* his controversial best-seller on welfare reform. Between the TV show, his thrice-weekly column, the speeches, he simply couldn't get around to doing the longer books. Now he inclined to every publisher's nightmare: the collection, of past columns, magazine articles, even old speeches. To keep Morforken happy, he tossed him an original book every now and then, usually short, historical works, the research for which was provided by some impoverished Georgetown University graduate student. The one he was working on now—that is, *trying* to work on—involved Benjamin Franklin. Its thesis was that during his stay in Paris as American agent during the Revolution, Franklin had befriended the young Maximilien Robespierre in a brothel and urged him to start his own revolution someday. The evidence was a bit sketchy, but it was a lovely premise. The working title was *Seed of Revolution.*

"I spoke with your graduate student this morning," said Renira, "and she's coming in this afternoon with more research. You'll notice you have *all* your afternoons and most evenings free this week just to work on the book. As for guarding your privacy, Conrad Black's office called this morning asking if you could fly up to meet with him and Mrs. Thatcher tomorrow afternoon, and I told them no."

Banion said, aghast, "You told Conrad I couldn't come up for a meeting with Mrs. Thatcher?"

"You're spending weekend after next with them at the Hollinger thrash in London, so I hardly saw why you needed to gallivant up to New York for this. But if you want, I'll call them and say you *can* make it."

No wonder the British once ruled the world.

"No. All right. *Fine.*"

"Then shall we discuss Saturday?"

"*Yes.*"

"Bitsey says she's got to spend the morning with her sym-phony committee. You've got a three o'clock tee time at Burning Bush with Justice Fitch and Speaker Meeker. I thought you might want to get out there a bit early and have a few practice whacks, so I've reserved tee time for just yourself at one o'clock. Now, while you were on the phone with Mr. Stimple, Mr. Mint called with another date. American Free-Ranging Poultry Farm-ers. He says they're rather lefty."

"Left-wing chicken farmers?"

"Um. Very progressive. No force feeding, pesticides, any of that. You let them wander about to their hearts' content. Person-ally, I find them tough as nails. Give me an oppressed, caged chicken any day. It's in November, so Sid said you could just give them your postelection analysis off the top of your head. He said *if* you could possibly fit something in somewhere about how we ought to be making western cattlemen pay more for grazing on federal lands, that they'd probably carry you out on their shoulders."

"How much?"

"Twenty-five."

"Tell him thirty. Say we'll have to scramble to fit it in."

What did it work out to? Almost a thousand dollars a minute? Nice work, if you could get it, and you could get it if you tried.

FOUR

Nathan Scrubbs sat in his office deep in the rheumatic bowels of the Social Security Administration building in Washington, D.C., listlessly reading a Tom Clancy novel while waiting for his computer to advise him that somewhere in Indiana another housewife had been abducted and sexually probed by aliens in a flying saucer. Scrubbs wanted out of Abductions.

They were interesting the first dozen times. After that, it was just a job. He'd been doing them for over two years now, and he was burned out. He'd applied months ago for a transfer to Operations, where he might get a shot at flying the really ass-kicking new aircraft. It would happen. He was sure of it. He'd turned in excellent work. One of his women, Kathy Carr, had turned her abduction into a brilliant new career. She was going to be the featured speaker at this year's Congress of Alien Abductees. Her book, *Space Rape*, was a huge best-seller, and there was a TV movie-of-the-week deal in the works with Gwen Dale playing Kathy. Size-four Gwen Dale, playing size-fourteen Kathy Carr. There was Hollywood for you. Yes, his application for transfer should be gliding smoothly to approval just about now.

He was in his midthirties, tall, still basically lean, though the strain of his subterranean life—and perhaps a drink or two too many at night to banish the ennui—was beginning to take its toll. Still, he was an attractive enough fellow. His chin had the determined jut of a soldier's, but it was undercut by an antic, raccoonlike scheming look in his eyes, which overall gave him the air of someone who just missed being one of life's winners. If this feckless air weren't so transparent, he might have looked sinister. As it was, he was the sort of person one would confidently ask to watch one's bag in an airport while one used the bathroom.

Scrubbs checked his watch. They were running late. Maybe she'd put up a struggle. That could slow things down. He called up the abductee profile on the computer:

MURCH, MARGARET, 38 YEARS OLD, 5 FT 4 INCHES, 195 POUNDS.
CHILDREN, THREE. HUSBAND: HENRY. POULTRY FARMER.
ADDRESS RURAL ROUTE 1, HINK, INDIANA. CRED. RATING 2.

Scrubbs studied the chubby face before him on the screen. Another Miss America. It had been taken at the supermarket. She was wheeling a shopping cart that contained enough sucrose to sweeten the whole country's coffee for a week. The little black eyes peeked out from behind the cheeks. Poor thing. Probably didn't get much in the way of servicing from old Henry. There was one of her brood, lumbering along behind her, eating a—Jesus—was that a *raw* hot dog? Scrubbs shuddered.

"Hope it was good for you, too, Maggie," he muttered, clicking off her window and returning to Clancy, who was describing some laser weapon designed to cook an enemy's optic nerve. The boys in Mutilations used those laser guns, too. You could crank them up to full. Now *there* was a nasty job. At least he wasn't coring out cow assholes and tongues and other bovine organs in order to make people think that aliens had bizarre food cravings. Who the hell had thought *that* up? They had some sick minds in Policy and Planning. MJ-12 was one strange Skunk Works.

MJ-12, Majestic Twelve, Majic. It had started during that golden Cold War summer of 1947. It had staged the first sighting of unidentified flying objects over Mount Rainier on June 24 and followed that debut two weeks later with the Roswell "crash" of alien spacecraft. The idea was simple enough: convince Stalin that UFO's existed and that the United States was in possession of their technology. That would keep Uncle Joe on his toes.

Then, as with so many other government programs, the original plan gave way to bigger things. Majestic consisted of a top-secret twelve-man directorate (hence the name) that included CIA Director Roscoe Hillenkoetter, Defense Secretary James Forrestal, and other top members of the nation's scientific, aerospace, and military communities. They decided that as long as they were at it, MJ-12 could serve another, even higher purpose: keeping the taxpaying U.S. citizenry alarmed about the possibility of invasion from outer space, and therefore happy to fund expansion of the military-aerospace complex. A country convinced that little green men were hovering over the rooftops was inclined to vote yea for big weapons and space programs.

So what began a half century ago with the towing of some pie-shaped reflective disks behind a camouflaged aircraft over Washington State soon evolved into a "black"* program with a yearly budget running into the tens of millions of dollars. But Americans are easily bored. The problem quickly became how do we keep them interested? After a while, mere sightings of flying saucers just weren't enough. MJ-12 had to devise more elaborate entertainments: physical evidence, scorch marks in the grass, traumatized animals (easy enough), cars whose batteries had inexplicably gone dead while their occupants were staring google-eyed at the funny lights. When the thrill of disabled vehicles and freaked-out pets wore off, MJ-12 had no choice but to start providing glimpses of the alien darlings themselves. This was trickier. For one thing, it meant finding dwarfs with security clearances. For this reason, aliens have gotten considerably bigger over the years.

* That is, covert.

The public was content with these diversions for a while, even quite delighted. But soon alien visitations became a Hollywood movie cliché. Again, MJ-12 had to raise the ante. Policy and Planning (MJ-3) went to work and came back with fresh delights like crop circles, those enormous graffiti nocturnally mown into remote wheat fields, and the more crude abovementioned cattle mutilations. (Yucko.) These did the trick for a while, but before long the public was jaded again. So MJ-12 decided that something more *interactive* was called for. So began the era of alien abductions. Well, sooner or later sex enters into everything.

The odd part was that it was the abductees, not MJ-12, who initiated the business about sexual probings and egg harvesting and all that. Soon after the first abductions—simple snatching, scaring, and dropping off a few miles away—the snatchees began making extravagant claims of having been poked and prodded *down there*. It was only then that the Policy and Planning boys decided, okay, if this is what the people want, let's give it to them. Why argue with vox pop? There was this, too: it made perfect sense, from a strictly anthropological point of view. These were more than aliens—gods, come from above to provide salvation (usually from rather dreary lives here on tired old planet earth). It made the people happy to feel that the gods wanted to sleep with them, or at least have a grope. In time, of course, it led to claims of alien conception and babies, but by then there was really no stopping it.

The old-timers within MJ-12 were appalled at the sex stuff. Scrubbs used to converse with some of them, anonymously, in the MJ-12 secure cyberchat rooms that the organization provided in lieu of community. You were not permitted to discuss details of missions, but you learned to read between the lines. One old-timer, who used the code name ULYSSES, would rant on and on:

WE HAD TO MAKE DO WITH BALING WIRE, ALUMINUM FOIL, AND OUR IMAGINATIONS.
NOW IT'S ALL COMPUTER SPECIAL EFFECTS AND SEX AND BODY CAVITY PROBES.
DISGUSTING! WHAT'S NEXT I WANT TO KNOW? ALIEN BABIES?

The chat rooms helped, but working at MJ-12 was the loneliest job in the government. It made working for the CIA or even the tighter-lipped National Security Agency seem almost normal by comparison. MJ-12 was the only kept secret in the United States government. Scrubbs did not know the real name of a single other person in the organization. This was how it had managed to remain secret all these years: most people in the organization did not know the name of a single other person in the organization. Except for MJ-1, the director, whoever he or she was. All communications were via MajestNet, MJ-12's own Internet. There were some voice communications, but these were rare. It was a monkish life he led, down here in the basement of the Social Security Administration. His office was located here on the theory that no congressional investigator ever dared look into Social Security.

The hours were long. It did not make for a dazzling social life.

Hi. What do you do? I work for the Social Security Administration.

Really? That's cool. Excuse me, I have to go repark the car.

At times Scrubbs posed the question: how had he landed here, in the basement of a drab building in Washington, D.C., an invisible man, orchestrating faux alien abductions? His college yearbook had not listed him as Most Likely to be doing this sort of thing.

No, his dream, long nourished by James Bond fantasies, had been to join the CIA* and engage in foreign derring-do, helping to topple troublesome governments, parachuting into jungles, falling in love with beautiful women with foreign accents, a cyanide pill sewn into the lining of his clothing, a pistol tucked

---

*U.S. intelligence agency formerly tasked with overthrows of insignificant Central American countries, inept invasions of Caribbean dictatorships, and disastrous meddlings in Southeast Asia. Its main focus, in the post–Cold War era, has been to employ people who will sell vital classified information about it to foreign governments. Its current budget is estimated at $27 billion per year, which may seem like a lot but is still not enough to enable it to find out if countries like India and Pakistan have nuclear weapons.

into the waistband or under the pillow, able to order a perfect martini in eight languages.

None of this, with the exception of the ability to order a martini (in one language), had come to fruition. His application, marked NO ACTION, was forwarded to a post office box in Rosslyn, Virginia, across the river from Washington, and thence to another, and still another, until, via the mysterious but bureaucratically efficient circuitry of MJ-12, he received a call from a "Mr. Smith, with the government." Scrubbs was thrilled, being at the time despondent over the form letter he had recently received from the CIA thanking him for his interest and telling him to go away. They met at a Vietnamese restaurant in suburban Virginia. Mr. Smith told him that there was another government agency, even more elite than the CIA—and certainly more effective!—which was tasked with the most important national security work. Was Scrubbs interested? Was he ever! Dreams of intrigue and beautiful women danced anew.

Mr. Smith did warn him that he was signing on for deep, deep duty in the most silent service of the United States.

How glorious and cool it sounded! Where was the dotted line on which to sign?

HE HAD DOZED OFF IN THE MIDDLE OF A CLANCY ODE TO some new heat-seeking missile when he heard Mike's voice coming at him over the computer's speakers. Mike was his chief bagger.

Scrubbs blinked himself awake and entered his password for perhaps the twentieth time that day. MJ-12 was crazy for passwords. You couldn't go to the bathroom without entering your password. He held his hand on the PalmiTron scanner and simultaneously pronounced aloud the voice password so that the computer could assure itself that it really was he, Nathan Scrubbs, and not Bob Woodward, sitting at the console.

In the background he heard other voices. Jimmy, and Jake.

Jake was the low man on the totem pole, the one who had to do the actual probing. Definite entry-level job, that.

They sounded more or less normal for a postabduction brief- ing: tired, pissed off, badly in need of a beer or something stronger. He remembered his own days on a bagger team operat- ing out of Houston, Texas, snatching Vietnamese immigrant shrimp fishermen. Where *they* fit into the grand scheme of UFO promulgation, God only knew, but at least they were thin and you could lift them without herniating yourself.

"How'd it go?" Scrubbs asked.

"It *went*," said a grumbling voice.

Scrubbs heard a stretching and snapping of latex. They were taking off their bug suits. This particular mission profile called for Tall Nordics, the Aryans of alien ethnology. Tall Nordics were the most humanoid of aliens. They were less frightening than the Short Ugly Grays, who looked like the winged monkeys in *The Wizard of Oz*. One (admittedly overweight) Nebraska farm wife had a heart attack when she woke up to find herself strapped to a table and surrounded by a half dozen Short Uglies. What a mess that was. They'd had to defibrillate her and get her to the hospital. Ever since, every bagger team had to have some- one certified in CPR. They'd cut down heavily on the Short Uglies, which was just as well, since that also eliminated the dwarf security clearance problem.

"Did you return her home"—Scrubbs yawned—"or is she wandering the highway wondering what the fuck?"

"Dropped her off in a soybean field a mile from her house. She's probably doing crop circles."

"She could flatten that whole field in ten minutes," said an- other voice. "*Damn* she was big."

"Hadda *winch* her up into the ship. Man, my back."

"How much sevo did she take?" Scrubbs typed away, making notes.

"Not too much."

"*Mike.*"

"Twelve, maybe fifteen ounces."

Scrubbs whistled. "Jesus." Mike tended to go heavy on the sevoflurane—a state-of-the-art anesthetic they called happy gas—ever since Sandusky. They'd been doing some policeman's wife. They had her on the table and were getting ready to probe when suddenly she pulled out a bottle of Mace—the real stuff, not that pepper gas—and started spraying like a spooked skunk. During the debrief, Mike admitted to Scrubbs that he and the others had made some pretty human-sounding noises of distress, along the lines of "Shit!" and "Fuck!"—words perhaps unusual in your typical alien's vocabulary. For weeks afterwards, Scrubbs held his breath, waiting for some reference to this in the press. But she never went to the press. Some of the abductees were like that—afraid to say a word, for fear of ridicule. Most, however, went screaming to the nearest microphone. Wouldn't *you*?

"Nah," said Mike. "She took it on the chin. Real trooper."

"Was she conscious?"

"Yeah yeah."

"Mike, there's no *point* if they don't remember anything."

"She'll know she was probed. Don't worry about it. You want details?"

"No." Scrubbs's fingers clicked across the keyboard.

"Can I ask something?" Sounded like Larry. "How come we never get to harvest Claudia Schiffer's eggs?"*

"Yeah!"

"Yeah, how come all we get is these two-hunnerd-pound mamas?"

"I don't pick them," said Scrubbs. "The computer picks them."

When MJ-12 had decided to get into the abduction business, back in 1961, staff mathematicians devised a credibility algo-

---

*Highly desirable German model.

rithm for determining whom to abduct. The idea was that alien abductees should be just credible enough to spread the word but not so respectable that their testimony would precipitate an urgent search for the truth. They would not, for instance, want to snatch someone as prominent as, say, the chairman of the Federal Reserve. That would, in all likelihood, lead to trouble. No, MJ-1's policy directive on abductions sounded like a prospectus from a conservative financial brokerage house: "We seek slow, steady growth in abductionology rather than dramatic incrementing, with a view toward gradual accretion of phenomenological credence." (MJ-12's language, it must be said, had grown as bureaucratic over the years as the rest of it.) What this gobbledygook meant was, they were looking to make ripples, not waves.

It worked. Fifty years and more after the first UFO sightings, the vote was in: a full 80 percent of Americans believed that the government knew more about aliens than it was letting on. Better still, one-third believed that aliens crash-landed at Roswell, New Mexico. This was real growth. But this was also the result of a lot of hard, quiet, unglamorous work over the years by thousands of dedicated men and women.

Scrubbs sympathized with Mike and Larry and Jake. For some reason, the credibility algorithm seemed to have a bias toward overweight women. It would be nice if just every once in a while it picked, well, Claudia would be nice.

"Then reprogram the computer. Enter: 'tall, blonde, thirty-eight-D cup, great ass, *beautiful*.'"

"Could suck a golf ball through fifty feet of garden hose."

"Guys," Scrubbs said.

"And turns into a pizza at three A.M."

Loud, guffawing laughter. Well, let them vent.

"Good night, boys."

Scrubbs signed off, finished his report, sent it electronically along to MJ-10, with copies for MJ-7 and MJ-4. Paperwork, paperwork, it was never ending. He notified MJ-5 (Media) that there had been a level-four snatch in their area and to monitor local news. He had developed a pretty good sense by now for how loud the abductees were going to yell. His guess was Maggie would let 'er rip.

He looked up at his wall calendar from MUFON, one of the more responsible—if that was the right word—UFO organizations. They had an abduction conference coming up in October. Maggie would be able to make it in time for that. A whole new life awaited her, apart from Henry and her raw-hot-dog-sucking brood. One minute she's comparison shopping at Wal-Mart, the next she's the homecoming queen at a UFO convention, giving weepy testimony that beings from the great beyond thought she was special enough to mess with her ovaries. Her life would never be the same. Her life would never be boring again. She had purpose. She had been anointed by gods. This was empowerment. There were times when Scrubbs felt like the Holy Ghost.

When he'd finished with all his message traffic, he checked his in box. There was a message from MJ-11. Yes! Personnel! His transfer! He clicked opened the message and read:

REF: STATUS YOUR REQUEST. TRANSFER MJ-2 (OPS): **DENIED.**

SOME HOURS LATER SCRUBBS WAS ON THE COUCH IN HIS Foggy Bottom rental, so marinated in vodka that he was unable to do anything but angrily stab the channel button on his TV's remote control. It occurred to him, lying there in his underwear, that *this* was his life, vocationally and recreationally: punching buttons and watching TV screens. Blind drunk and alone on a Sunday morning. Keep holy the Sabbath. Another Bloody Mary.

Assholes! Bureaucratic sons of bitches! Small-minded dicks!

Here he had worked his ass off, giving them 1,000 percent, giving them Kathy Carr, giving them dozens of plump, juicy, media-seeking abductees, and what does he get? DENIED. Not even *REGRET* TO INFORM YOU DENIED.

More vodka. Where *was* the vodka? Where *had* the vodka gotten to? Maybe in the thing by the whatever. Empty. Damn. Wait, there was other vodka somewhere, under the whatever. Ah, here.

Uch!

He sprayed it across the shag carpet.

What the f—

Pepper vodka? Jesus. . . . Just the thing to pour into a stomach that so far that day had had styrofoam-flavored coffee and potato chips. He rummaged, finding only a stale chocolate Pop-Tart. He stumbled back to the couch with a presentiment of misery the next day. He flopped onto the couch.

He heard the words "*Sunday* . . . with John Oliver Banion."

Christ, wasn't there at least a frozen pizza in the freezer?

He went lurching toward the kitchen to the sound of the opening strains of *Sunday*'s theme music.

The president? Hm. His boss of bosses, commander in chief, the one pershon—*per-son*—who knew about MJ-12. Drunkenly, Scrubbs saluted the TV set and fell over.

He struggled back to the sofa. The president was defending *Celeste,* the space station. Word around MajestNet was that it was a boondoggle.

Banion was on his case. Banion. Pompous prick! Look at him. Bow tie. Now if you really wanted to convince the world that aliens had landed . . .

Scrubbs chuckled mirthlessly.

. . . *he* was the guy to snatch. Do a full CE-4 on John O-am-I-so-wonderful Banion. Man was so tight-assed they wouldn't even be able to get the probe in!

Scrubbs crawled over to his computer. It looked like an ordinary laptop, but it had special features. To turn it into a secure-transmission MJ-12 field communicator, you had to reach behind and press the reset button four times for three seconds each. The track pad functioned as a fingerprint identifier. There were three passwords, and they had to be entered correctly or the machine would explode. Some safety feature. It was tricky work, drunk.

FIVE

Burning Bush Country Club, ten miles northwest of Washington in the hilly, sylvan precincts of Maryland, was where the Establishment met to play the royal and ancient game. The main clubhouse looked like the set of *Gone With the Wind,* and as at Tara, you were met at the door by ivory smiles set in ebony. Burning Bush had only grumblingly accommodated the modern era. But since presidents liked to play golf here, it had little choice but to relent in its long-standing policies regarding people of pigmentation and members of the tribe of Abraham. Burton Galilee was the first son of the Dark Continent to be elected to membership. The club leadership managed to stall another couple of calendar years before opening the tent flap to the circumcised. Now Burning Bush was met on another great field of battle: whether to admit the weaker vessel. The First Lady was making the president's life hell over it.

On Saturday, just before one o'clock, Banion was changing in the men's locker room, ruminating on the *Sunday* segment he had taped yesterday with Erhardt Williger. The topic—Russia, naturally. Williger, former secretary of state, and now adviser to nations and corporations the world over, took the view that President Blebnikov's belligerent, irredentist growlings about taking Alaska back were just to placate the hard-liners in his own party. He had no intention of sending the Russian fleet willy-nilly across the water. "Anyvey," Williger said in his plummy Hungarian accent, "From vat I have seen, I am not convinced deir Navy could make it across the Volga River, much less de Bering Strait."

As Banion contentedly mused, an unseen hand reached into his golf bag outside and substituted a half dozen monogrammed balls identical to the ones it removed.

The fourth hole at Burning Bush is, in the lingo of golfers, a "bitch." The fairway is narrow, with a water hazard running the whole length on the right. On the left are deep, rough woods. Many a promising day has turned sour on the fourth at Burning Bush. It was this hole in particular that Banion had come to play in preparation for his round with Speaker Meeker and Justice Fitch. He wasn't worried about Fitch. That old boy's glory days of golf were behind him. But Banion had seen an item in the *Post* recently about Speaker Meeker attending a golf clinic in Bel Mellow, Florida, so he was wary.

He teed up and dared to use his driver. He thrilled to hear the delicious smack of the ball connecting smartly with the sweet spot. (Oh, glorious sound!) The ball soared straight and true down the fairway. *So* satisfying. Now, if he could just do that when—

What the *hell*?

The ball suddenly veered off into the woods at a positively geometric angle. It couldn't be windage. There was no wind. It was behaving like a billiard ball banking off a side. Uncanny. Inexplicable. He'd been playing golf for over a quarter century, and he had never, ever, seen a ball act like that. He watched as the ball disappeared into the woods with that discouraging rustle of leaves so familiar to golfers, that most hopeful breed.

Banion stood there for a moment wondering what freak of physics had caused his ball to carom off course at almost ninety degrees. He considered going after it but then decided to take a mulligan. Well, why not? The idea was to practice.

He teed up again, addressed the ball neatly, as he drew back, murmured that key word—*"Easy"*—to himself, and drove. Again he heard the lovely sound of precise connection of titanium and laminated rubber. The ball leapt. It wasn't as good a shot as the first, bit of a slice off to the right, but with luck it wouldn't go in the water. Stay . . . stay . . . *stay.* . . .

Seventy-five yards out, it banked left into the woods, almost exactly like the first shot. Banion watched, mouth open. He heard a distant *thok* as the ball hit a branch in the woods.

Banion examined the face of his driver, a present from Burt Galilee.

What the hell was going on?

Should he take another mulligan? The idea of two was an affront to his perfectionism. But it was too warm to go thrashing about in the underbrush, and there was poison ivy in there.

He teed up with the wary air of a man expecting his cigar to explode and drove with grim determination, forgetting the "easy" mantra.

He sliced badly to the right. Up, up, up . . . this one was going swimming . . . then zip, off into the woods at an angle not found in nature or physics.

Banion jammed his driver into the bag without replacing the embroidered "Camp David" head cover—a Christmas gift from the previous president—and stormed off into the woods, poison ivy be damned.

He was about thirty yards in, right about where his balls had vanished, when through the trees he saw in the near distance an illogical number of blinking lights. Maintenance vehicle. Odd. What was there to maintain in here? Well, maybe they'd seen his balls.

He discerned figures moving near the vehicle. They were dressed in shiny clothing. Must be—firemen?—in those flame-retardant—

Jesus Christ!

It was no more than fifty feet ahead of him, in some kind of clearing. Round, low to the ground, metallic, sort of a brushed-steel look, full of blinking lights.

His throat went dry; he could feel his heart pounding. Normally he only felt his heart on the squash courts. Maybe once or twice during sex, back when they were first married.

He crouched behind a pine tree and watched. The two firemen seemed to be examining the vehicle, whatever it was. It looked—he felt uncomfortable even thinking it—like a flying saucer. Ridiculous. Ridiculous on its face.

But there it was. Whatever it was.

Aha, he thought. There were military installations all around Maryland. Top-secret sites built during the Cold War, where they could hide presidents and congressional leaders in the event the Russians dropped the big one. Could it be something like that? A bomb shelter? Damned odd place to put it.

At that moment, one of the firemen turned to face the other fireman, giving Banion a good glimpse at him.

He cried out. He couldn't help himself. It just came out. Great merciful heaven!

They saw him! They were coming toward him!

Banion turned to run.

"*Ah!*" There was another one, blocking his way back to the golf course. It spoke.

"Alooka. Alooka walalo."

He was surrounded now, face to face with the three of them. He noticed a smell, acrid and overwhelming at first, like ammonia, with a sweetish aftertaste, like . . . cinnamon? Was this alien BO?

Things began to blur. His legs went rubbery. He passed out. Who could blame him?

BANION AWOKE TO THE TWINKLE OF LIGHTS AND AN ELEC-tronic humming sound.

"Scotch and soda," he said foggily. "What is the movie?"

He was dreaming. He was in first class. When the fog lifted, he saw a thing peering inquisitively down at him. It was about the height of an ordinary human, but with shimmery, iridescent skin. It was bald and had black, almond-shaped eyes, slits for ears.

It spoke.

"Kaloo?"

Banion stared philosophically. He was versed in every protocol. He knew the correct address for an archbishop of Canterbury, retired Supreme Court justice, wife or daughter of an earl. What was the proper form here? "How do you do?" didn't sound quite right.

"Kaloo?" he ventured. The rational thought intruded that he might well be out of his mind with fear. He felt incredibly weary, too tired to register any emotion. It reminded him of the intravenous injection they'd given him when he'd gone into the hospital for the colonoscopy.

Another one. It was speaking to him. "Mooka."

"Mooka," Banion replied. He didn't feel half bad, really. It was a pleasant wooziness, almost . . . euphoric. He tried to raise his arms, in the process discovering that his wrists were attached to the table he was lying on. His brain flashed him a panic signal. The euphoria ebbed. He rattled his wrists, feeling metal. Not good, said the brain.

"Look here," he demanded, "what's going on?"

"Wooga bakak."

"Do you speak English?"

"Kreek maku feeto."

"Do? You? Speak? English?" Useless. It was like being in the Third World, where you had to shout to make yourself understood. If they were going to travel billions of light-years or however far they'd come, to land on golf courses, they might have devoted a little of their superior technology to studying the local language. Surely they could listen to tapes on their way here. *Repeat, please: "Take me to your leader."*

"Ha. Lo."

Was it saying hello? All right, not the Gettysburg Address, but a start.

"Ha-lo," said Banion. "My. Name. Is. Jack."

"Kamu."

"You Kamu?" said Banion, now struggling to keep it together, straining at his wrist straps. "Me Jack."

Amidst this witty repartee, Banion felt a distinct chill and, looking down at his feet, noticed two things: he was naked, and his ankles were also fastened to the table, with his legs spread apart in a way that reminded him unencouragingly of a dozen movie scenes, with the sound of a cackling villain in the back-ground holding some gruesome weapon.

"Can I"—he wriggled—"*help* you in some way?"

The third thing approached toward his legs. It was holding something that did not bode pleasant. Banion stared.

"Whoa. Hold on."

Banion tried to sit up, in the process discovering there was a strap across his chest.

"Now see here—I'm an American citizen!"

Still the thing approached.

"Hey, the president is coming to dinner at my house next week!"

BANION CAME TO.

He looked up and saw the trunks of trees stretching up into a sky the color of late afternoon. The *cheep cheep* of a cricket made him yelp with fear.

He was alone.

He was dressed.

He took a deep breath. Instead of the piney scent of forest, he tasted ammonia and cinnamon.

He shuddered again, stumbled like a drunken man to a tree, leaning on it for support. He was at the edge of a clearing. He walked into it and leaned over to examine the grass. There were three circular spots where the grass was flattened, each about a yard wide. Yes, that was right. The craft had been resting on struts. These must have been where the . . .

"Easy," he told himself, as if preparing to tee off. It all had to have been some kind of neurological episode. You've been working hard. Too many synapses firing at the same time. You came into the forest looking for the balls. You tripped. You hit your forehead. Yes, that was it. And you had a weird, very weird, dream.

He felt his forehead, hoping to find a lump. He found it smooth and bumpless. And he had no headache. But, focusing on this aspect of his self-diagnosis, he became aware that he did feel pain somewhere else. A distinctly uncomfortable feeling that reminded him of how he'd felt after the colonoscopy, a feeling of stretching . . .

"Oh. My. God."

BANION BURST THROUGH THE WOODS ONTO THE FOURTH fairway and made for the clubhouse with the speed of Pheidippides carrying news of the victory at Marathon. This was an unusual sight at Burning Bush.

A foursome teeing off stopped and stared.

"Clear the area!" Banion shouted at them without breaking stride. "Run for your lives!"

"What's the matter?"

"Aliens!"

"What did he say?"

"Wasn't that Jack Banion?"

"Did he say 'aliens'?"

By the time he reached the clubhouse, he was drenched in sweat.

"Oh, Mr. Banion," said the attendant. "Speaker Meeker and Justice Fitch were looking for you. Are you well, sir?"

"Call . . . uh . . . uh . . . call . . . uh . . ."

"Mr. Banion?"

"Call . . . the . . . uh . . ."

"You better lie down. I'll get you some water."

"No water! Police. Call . . . police. Attack. . . ."

Heart attacks were not uncommon at Burning Bush, where the average member's age was well into the sixties. The manager dialed 911 and requested an ambulance.

"It'll be right here," he told Banion. "Lie down on the floor, sir."

"No no no."

"Lie down, sir." He ran off to get the defibrillator kit, berating himself for not having paid close attention during the instruction on its use.

"What's the matter?"

"Mr. Banion, he's having a heart attack. Get a blanket, elevate his legs." Or was that for shock?

The assistant dashed off. How awful. And Mr. Banion was one of the younger members.

The ambulance arrived in under ten minutes.

"No, I said *police*!" cried Banion, now in a very bad temper from arguing with the manager and his assistant, who had been trying to wrap him in blankets while hovering over him with the defibrillator kit, which Banion was not about to let them use on him. No, damnit, he did *not* have pain in his left arm. They must evacuate the course without delay! They might still be out there!

"I don't *want* an ambulance!"

People who have had cardiac episodes often say that. Two emergency medical service technicians strapped a blood-pressure cuff on his arm, lifted his shirt, and attached electrodes to monitor his heartbeat. Another held a clipboard and barked medical history questions at him.

"I'm okay. They . . . put something . . . I'm all *right*. Call the *police*. The military. Call the Air Force, maybe they're still in the area!"

"Who?"

"Them! The aliens! In the spaceship, there in the woods, off the fourth fairway."

One of the medical technicians leaned closer to sniff Banion's breath.

"I am not drunk."

"Sir, we're going to take you to the hospital now. Your blood pressure is very high."

"Of course it's high! Call the police! Clear the golf course! Oh, my God!"

"What, sir?"

"The Speaker! Justice Fitch! They may be after them! They're seizing the government! Take the cart! Quickly—tell them! They're in danger! It could be a takeover of the whole country!"

"IT WAS ABOUT FIFTY FEET ACROSS," SAID BANION, SITTING in the passenger seat, belted in by Bitsey, glassy-eyed from the sedative they'd given him at the hospital. "Maybe sixty. I ought to draw a sketch. Do we have colored pencils at home? The lights were colored."

"Jack," said Bitsey, naturally concerned for her husband, but at the moment preoccupied with what (on earth) excuse she was going to make to Tyler for their not showing up at his—lord—intimate dinner tonight for Sir Hugh and Lady Bletch, "rest. Don't talk."

"God, Bits. They *exist*. They exist."

Should she even get into it? The doctors had told her they didn't quite know what to make of it. They had taken X rays. They showed no contusions, subdural hematomas. He was not drunk. Anyway, Jack barely drank at all. A glass of wine, rarely. Hardly the type to get blotto all alone on the golf course. His blood work was normal. No family history of mental problems. The doctors told her that he had babbled at some length about being . . . how to put it . . . violated. There was no obvious, um, tearing of tissues. Bitsey shuddered. It was too disgusting.

"We'll say you had a golf-cart accident," she said.

"It changes everything. We have to revise our thinking about the universe, religion. My God, Bits."

"You ran into a tree and got a bump."

"But why the medical experimenting? They must be part of an advance team, studying us."

"A bad bump," Bitsey said.

"Advance team for what, though?"

"I'd better call Chip. I don't think you should do the show tomorrow."

"Subjugation? Colonizing? Enslavement? *God.*"

"He'll get someone to fill in."

"You should have seen the ship, Bits. It was like something in a movie."

"Maybe he can get Evan Thomas to fill in for you."

"They made my balls act in this strange way."

"Jack, *enough.*"

"They were trying to draw me in. Me. It wasn't an accident. They wanted me."

"No, not Evan Thomas. He's got his eye on your show as it is. All that angling to fill in for you last summer when we were in Turkey?"

"So why me?" Banion murmured.

"I know—Rick Simmons. I'll tell Chip to get him."

"They could have had the Speaker of the House and a Supreme Court justice. But they picked *me.*"

"Jack, stop it."

"I don't know if I can, Bits."

"Of course you can."

"I'm just one man. There might be thousands of them out there."

"We'll discuss it *in the morning.*"

"Millions."

Banion was sitting at his desk, immersed in a book by a former Army colonel who claimed personally to have witnessed alien corpses that had crash-landed at Roswell, New Mexico, when Renira buzzed to tell him that there was a reporter from the *Post* on the line wanting to talk with him about "last Sunday at Burning Bush." Banion scowled owlishly and pondered: should he take the call?

Nothing was secret in this town. So who had blabbed? Not the manager or the assistant. Burning Bush staff were as discreet as the deaf-mute slaves in the palaces of the caesars. That foursome he'd shouted at to clear the area? The ambulance crew? Someone with a police scanner listening as they radioed ahead to the hospital that they were bringing in a lunatic raving about aliens? The doctors? Surely the Hippocratic oath also extended to doing no harm to your patient by leaking embarrassing details to the press. At any rate, there was now a reporter on the line. Best just stick to the cover story.

"This is John Banion."

"Patrick Cooke, with the *Post*. How are you?" They were always so friendly, these piranhas.

"Tip-top. What can I do for you?"

"I'm following up on a report we had that you had an unusual experience at Burning Bush last Sunday."

"A very unusual experience, yes."

"How's that?"

"I bogeyed the fourth hole."

He could hear the clicking of Cooke's keyboard. *Everything you say will be used against you.*

"You're doing better than I am. So you ended up at the hospital?"

"I was in shock. I've never bogeyed the fourth."

"You, um, reported that you'd been abducted by aliens? Three of them, in a spaceship?"

Blast. He had details.

"I don't remember that part. That *would* be a story. The fact of the matter is, I was in a golf-cart accident."

"You were in a golf-cart accident?"

"I'm embarrassed to say. Yes. There's a sharp turn on the path, with a tree on the right. I wasn't paying attention, and I must have gone off the road. I don't remember much. Must have got a nasty bump. Anyway, I'm fine. A bit busy, actually, right now."

Clickety-click. It was like listening to teeth that were eating you.

"Someone at the hospital"—so they *were* the leakers. Hippocritical Hippocrats! Banion decided his next column would be an attack on the medical profession—"told me that you said you had been, this is a quote, 'raped by aliens.' "

"Ululant nonsense."

"Sorry?"

"Mr. Cooke, I happen to be a close friend of the chairman of the board of *The Washington Post*. She is coming to dinner at my house next week, with the president. My guess is that she would be possibly even more embarrassed than you to read a remark—no doubt unattributed—in her paper, whose mission, I believe, is to convey responsible information to the public and not mischievous gibberish. Or, for that matter, confidential medical data."

"So you deny having reported that at the hospital?"

"I was in an emergency room being tended to and medicated for a possible subdural hematoma, Mr. Cooke. In such circumstances, I could not affirm or deny the correct spelling of my own name. *However,* I will mention our conversation to your chairman when I speak to her later today. My wife and I are on her benefit committee for the myoplasmitis luminosa dinner in December. Good *day.*"

Banion felt a Pyrrhic sense of triumph on hanging up. Cooke would probably not run the item he had hoped to, but Banion had certainly not won him over to his admittedly intimate cult of personality. Cooke was probably telling everyone in the newsroom, *"What* an asshole." Banion knew that he was not especially popular among the foot soldiers of the fourth estate. They viewed him as an aloof, supercilious mandarin. He viewed them as a bunch of uncouth, envious hacks. The arrangement suited Banion perfectly. Let him who would turn down a guest slot on his TV show cast the first stone.

Still, it was with a squirrely stomach that he opened the next day's *Post* the moment it landed on his stoop at 5:30 A.M. Nothing. Wait—a brief item on page three of the Style section, slugged "Teed Off."

> *Sunday* Host **John O. Banion** was taken to the hospital Sunday afternoon after reportedly driving his golf cart into a tree. A hospital source said that he appeared somewhat disoriented, but was released after tests showed no serious injury. Substitute Host **Rick Simmons** filled in. Banion is expected to return to the show next week.

"Somewhat disoriented" was a significant improvement on "raped by aliens." Banion, standing in the kitchen in his bathrobe, peering down at the *Post,* let out a faint sigh of relief. He would E-mail Renira and tell her to prepare damning research for his column on the . . . let's see . . . abominable deterioration of emergency room care in America's . . . best be careful, the bastards might retaliate by really leaking everything . . .

well, Renira would find something about the medical establishment worth damning.

As he plunged the metal filter down onto the coffee grounds, Banion ruminated gloomily on the jokes about his golf-cart technique that would follow. *Jack! Running in Indy this year?* Well, it could be a lot worse.

He heated his milk and mixed it with the coffee. He shifted uncomfortably. There it was again, that pain—in the ass.

What the hell *had* happened?

"THERE'S A TREMENDOUS AMOUNT OF MATERIAL ON THIS subject." Elspeth Clark, his Georgetown University research assistant, dumped a heavy cardboard file box labeled "UFO's" on Banion's desk. Banion winced at the label. What if a reporter had seen her coming into his office with a box labeled "UFO's"?

"Are you doing a show on it?" Elspeth asked.

"No, no. Of course not. It's . . . I may . . . I don't know . . . do a column on it. Use it in a book."

"Not the Ben and Max book?" This was how she referred to the Franklin and Robespierre book.

"No. I'm toying with a book on millenarianism and the decline of rational thought. Something along those lines. Not sure yet."

Elspeth began pulling books and files out of the box. "I had a fax from Paris yesterday, from that Robespierre scholar I told you about? The one I found on the Internet, in the Sorbonne chat room? He did his Ph.D. thesis on the Revolution and says he remembers seeing a letter somewhere from Robespierre to Madame Farci, his mistress, mentioning a conversation he'd had with a Monsieur Franklin about *'mon petit probleme'** and that Monsieur Franklin had recommended *'un cours bien thérapeutique d'électricité.'*† He thinks he might be able to find the letter.

---

* "My little problem."
† "A good course of electrical therapy." What precisely Franklin had in mind is not clear.

He said we'd need to pay him for his time. Might be worth it. If we have a letter establishing that Franklin was advising Robespierre on electrical therapy for venereal disease, then it's not so far out that they would have been talking revolution in Madame Chantal's. Right?"

She was good, this one. She had enthusiasm, more than Banion would have mustered himself for the peanuts he paid his Georgetown researchers. It almost shamed him. But the chance to work for John O. Banion as a mere graduate student—who knew where that could lead? Possibly to even more low-paying grunt work as a production assistant on his TV show.

"Mr. Banion?"

"Um?" He'd been daydreaming. He sat up straight. "Yes, that could be promising. Check with Renira on what we can pay him. You have to be careful with these academic types. They go in for the old bait and switch. Tell you there's a map somewhere proving the Mesopotamians discovered America and string you along forever. Fix a price beforehand for the letter *on delivery*, and hold him to it. Don't let him sweet-talk you. Be careful—he's French. And insist on a photocopy of the document. Better get something from NIH* on what they were doing in the eighteenth century for . . . syphilis." She was pretty and young. He felt uncomfortable talking about venereal disease with her. He threw in an uncharacteristic "Fine work, Elspeth."

"Thank you, sir.

"I'm wondering what kind of treatment Franklin advised," she said. "Tying a kite string to his penis in an electrical storm?"

Banion blushed.

"This UFO material," he said gravely. "Why don't you digest it for me?"

She had come prepared. She gave him an excellent tour of the fuzzy horizon of the UFO world, beginning with the first sightings in 1947, up to the present day, when one could actually

* National Institutes of Health.

purchase an insurance policy in the event of being abducted by aliens. The first U.S. abduction had taken place in 1961, in New Hampshire. An interracial couple named Barney and Betty Hill had been in their Chevy along Route 3, stargazing through binoculars, when, bang—next thing they knew Betty was being administered what she later called "a pregnancy test," a long needle driven into her stomach. Barney ended up with insomnia and a duodenal ulcer.

They jotted dots on paper, a "star map" to show investigators where their abductors hailed from: Zeta Reticuli 1 and 2. The map had given some—if not conclusive—pause to such an eminent scoffer as Carl Sagan of Cornell University. One psychiatrist who examined the Hills opined that their experience had resulted from some unresolved conflicts having to do with their interracial status. The UFO debunker Philip Klass put it down to their having been hypnotized by some freak "plasma" that had leached off a nearby high-voltage power line, the first time in history that a religious experience had been attributed to a New Hampshire utility company.

That was the problem with alien visitations—*everyone* had a rational explanation for what had happened, except of course the people who'd been nabbed. Even Carl Jung had an explanation. He'd gone to the trouble of writing a book about the whole phenomenon in 1959. According to Jung, we were at the end of one era and the beginning of another, witnessing nothing less than a powerful mythogenesis, the birth of a new religion. Earlier generations would have called them gods—we gave them an acronym: UFO's. He said they were a phenomenon deeply embedded in the consciousness of mankind, the eternal and inexhaustible craving for "salvation from above."

Banion leaned back in his chair as Elspeth's briefing continued. Salvation from above? Okay, fine. But he, John O. Banion, personally had *no* need to be saved from above, much less by little green gods. They might do for the masses but not for a reasonably churchgoing Episcopalian such as himself. Banion didn't spend all that much time in church—Christmas and Easter were enough—but when he did get down on his knees, it was before Him who died on the Cross, not some bug-eyed albino from Zeta Reticuli l. If aliens were abducting so many Americans—one in fifty, according to one poll—the obvious question was: why did the new gods reveal themselves only to—how to put it?—the lower orders?

The Nazarene was pretty working class Himself, but He did hang out with the more respectable element as well, tax collectors, Pharisees, the odd member of the Sanhedrin, gents like Nicodemus, Joseph of Arimathea, substantial fellows.

Honestly. It was all so preposterous on its face. A few pathetic proles out to get attention make up stories about being abducted, the press duly reports them, Hollywood makes movies out of them, soon everyone wants a piece of the action and abductions are so commonplace it's no longer enough just to be abducted, now it's sexual probing—

Elspeth continued, "And a number of abductees report a strong odor of ammonia and cinnamon. Maybe they need to replace their air freshener. Mr. Banion? Sir? Should I go on?"

"I'M AFRAID I'VE GOT SOME BAD NEWS FOR YOU, JACK."

Banion sat in Dr. Hughes's office, exhausted and harried from a nightmare twenty-four hours that had included a CAT scan, MRI, blood work, and a colonoscopy (which Banion suspected Dr. Hughes had tacked on purely for purposes of revenue). But now he was about to have his worst fears confirmed—Burning Bush had been a hallucination brought on by a tumor, a dread astral cytoma that had possessed his intellectual jelly like a starfish, sinking its tentacles into the brilliant gristle of his brain, deeper and deeper until—oh God . . .

"Your bad cholesterol's up five points."

"Jesus Christ, Bill. Don't *do* that!"

Hughes smiled. "You don't have a brain tumor. Your colon's clear as a bell. You're in perfect health, aside from the slight elevation in LDL—"

"But *how do you explain what happened on the golf course?*"

"I can't. That's not my field."

"Are you saying I need a shrink?"

"You've got a lot on your plate right now. Why don't we try something?" He scribbled on a prescription pad and slid it across the polished table surface at Jack, as if it were the opening price of a negotiation.

"Prozac?"

"A very light dose, just enough to take the edge off."

"I can't take antidepressants! I need my edge! My show! I'm moderating the presidential debates!"

"From where I'm sitting, I'd say you've got edge to spare."

"All right. Let's say it *was* a reality disruption or whatever you want to call it, you supply the medical jargon. How do you explain the ammonia and cinnamon? These are not flavors normally found in suburban Maryland woods!"

Banion realized two things: he was shouting, and Dr. Hughes's face had taken on a *nurse-quickly-the-straitjacket!* look.

"There's a guy I work with sometimes. Really bright, low key. Let me give him a call. He's in the building. Maybe he can see you right now."

"You're saying you think this is psychological, is that it? After thousands of dollars of tests, you're saying I need to go rent a couch for a hundred and twenty-five dollars an hour."

"You told me yourself that you were assaulted by the crew of a flying saucer while you were playing golf. I'm trying to take this one step at a time."

BANION HAD CALLED BURTON GALILEE FROM HIS CAR AFTER storming out of Dr. Hughes's office. Banion didn't have a best friend as such, someone to whom one would turn in such situations. But he and Burt went back twenty years, and he trusted him. Everyone trusted Burton Galilee. Presidents, Supreme Court justices trusted him. The notoriously tight-lipped chairman of the Federal Reserve was even said to confide his lurid fears of inflation to Burton Galilee.

Burton had sounded a bit surprised by the urgent call but had said, by all means, come right away. He probably had to cancel something. As a senior partner at Crumb, Schimmer, Burton had most hours of his days spoken for months in advance, even at $500 per. Burton, the son of an Alabama hog farmer, had gotten his corner office on Pennsylvania Avenue by dint of charm, intelligence, talent, and the Establishment's sense that they had better admit their own African-American into the clubhouse before a less ruly one was thrust upon them, someone like the Reverend Bacon. It was a wise selection: Burton Galilee was eminently clubbable. He had a great talent: he made white people feel good about themselves. They could honestly say, *Me, prejudiced? Hell, one of my best friends is Burt Galilee.*

He rose from behind his enormous desk to greet the obviously distraught Banion.

He'd never seen Jack Banion look like this. Over the phone he'd sounded like he was calling from under ten tons of trouble and all of it concrete. So what had this prissy Princeton boy gone and done? Driving under the influence? No, not his style. Man only drank wine. White wine. Banion was the whitest man he knew. To judge from the face of woes blinking at him through spectacles, this was serious trouble, the kind keeps you from closing your eyes at night. Woman trouble? Was old Jack mustanging on the side? That English secretary of his, with the magnificent tits? Possible, possible. Someone's wife? A weird but not implausible thought occurred: had Jack knocked up some girl? Was he coming to him for advice on how to handle it? Galilee felt a little prick of anger. Wouldn't it be just like one of these Ivy League dandelions to come whimpering to him: *Burt, you're an oversexed Negro, you must know all about abortions, how do I go about this? Do I charge it on my Visa card or American Express?* If it was that, damnit all, he was going to hand him the yellow pages and kick his lily white ass out onto Pennsylvania Avenue.

Or . . . Burton continued to muse as Banion ambled, zombielike, to his seat: could this be a sexual crisis of a different sort? Twenty years earlier a prominent columnist had come to him straight from a trip to Moscow, looking like he hadn't slept in days, and told him that the KGB had taken photos of him in bed at the Metropol Hotel with one of their boy toys. They'd confronted him with the photos and told him they wanted him to take a kindlier view toward Soviet foreign policy in his writings. Burt Galilee had a moment of clarity: Banion was the lastest victim of "fairy shaking," the blackmail practiced by some D.C. cops of photographing married men coming out of gay bars and threatening to expose them. My my *my*. He could hardly wait to hear the details.

"Sit, sit," he said comfortingly to Banion, pointing out a five-thousand-dollar leather sofa behind which loomed the facade of the National Gallery.

"Now"—he smiled and spoke in the soothing baritone that set politician, criminal, and lobbyist alike at ease—their troubles were over, they were talking to the most connected man in Washington—"tell me what's on your mind and how I can help."

Suddenly Banion felt the terrible, and entirely uncharacteristic urge to burst into tears, something he had not done since scoring only 780 out of 800 on his college entrance English exam.

Steady, he told himself.

Burton Galilee did have this effect on some people. Was it his enormous, big-shouldered, black heartiness? People were always bursting into tears around him. One president of the United States, a southerner, so constantly blubbered on Burton's shoulders that he had to have his London-made suits sent out to the dry cleaner.

Banion collected himself. "Burt, this is—this is difficult for me."

All right, the boy needed a little coaxing. "I know it is," said Burton more sympathetically than any psychiatrist could have. "You just take your time."

"I called you just after I left my doctor's . . ."

Sweet Jesus. AIDS! God almighty, Jack O. Banion! He did look a little gaunt, come to think.

"I . . ." Banion looked into Burton Galilee's eyes, twin oases of understanding. Any secret deposited in them would be swallowed up and buried deep in the earth. Yes, he could tell Burt anything.

Still, Banion could not bring himself to utter the words "I have been kidnapped by aliens." It was like trying to pronounce a phrase in a foreign language in which he had no ability.

". . . wanted to discuss the presidential debates with you."

Burton Galilee's enormous eyes bulged with no less surprise than if Banion had told him, "I've been abducted by aliens."

He stared at Banion. "You came to talk to me about the *debates*?"

"Yes. I really value your input."

"Jack, after you called, I told a client who wants to pay us a great deal of money to help him build a pipeline across a country we recently bombed that I would have to reschedule his appointment. I did that because you sounded like you were ready to shit in your britches. Now what's the *matter*?"

Banion nodded, closed his eyes the way he had the first time he went off the high diving board at summer camp, and said, "Burt, where do you stand on the question of intelligent life in the universe?"

BURTON GALILEE SPENT THE REMAINS OF THE DAY TRYING unsuccessfully to focus on how to sweet-talk a maniac Middle Eastern dictator about an oil and gas pipeline, when all he could do was wonder why Banion had fed him a cock-and-bull story about aliens at Burning Bush. Aliens, at Burning Bush. Burt Galilee knew all about being an alien at Burning Bush. He'd still be one there, along with those rich Jewish car dealers, if the media hadn't made a stink out of the president playing golf at a restricted club. Was that why he came to him—some sort of psychological transference?

What the hell was he up to? What was really on his mind? But he wouldn't budge. He'd just sat there insisting that was it. For once, Burt Galilee had been at a loss for advice. All he could do was tell him he'd done the right thing in coming to him. True enough—you couldn't take a story like that to just anyone in Washington. Maybe Jack had just taken too many of those sleeping pills, the ones that had made the secretary of state collapse headfirst on the table during the GATT talks in Brazil, then wake up and ask the French foreign minister to go wash his car.

"SUNDAY, WITH JOHN OLIVER BANION, AN EXPLORATION of . . ."

Nathan Scrubbs watched on the TV in his office. He had to come in this weekend morning to supervise a triple they were staging in Ohio. (The computer, monitoring nationwide polls, had found a slippage in UFO belief in central Ohio.) The computer correlated that with an upcoming vote on the appropriations bill for the controversial new B-3 bomber—the ranking member on the committee represented central Ohio—and promptly ordered up two abductions and a cattle mutilation. The targets had cred ratings of four and five, an inspector at a poultry-packing plant and a night watchman, fairly respectable by MJ-12 abduction standards. Clearly, the computer wanted those poll numbers back up in time for the vote.

Scrubbs's baggers were grumpier than usual. MJ-12 did not pay time and a half for weekend abductions. Mike had had to cancel a fishing trip. As for Scrubbs, he would rather have been at home, drinking Bloody Marys and scratching his delicates while watching Banion go public about aliens on nationwide TV.

"Good morning. Our guest today is R. Talbott Wanker, assistant secretary of state. Mr. Wanker, you've been closely monitoring developments in the Russian situation. What in your opinion . . ."

Russia? Goddamnit, this was the third Sunday after they'd abducted him and *still* no mention of UFO's? Nothing, not even in his syndicated column, though it had crossed his mind that Banion's vituperative attack on "heartless" managed care might have had something to do with his experience in the emergency room.

Okay, pal, you want to play hard to get?

Scrubbs typed in a staccato of passwords and clearance codes on his laptop. MJ-12's mainframe computer had been programmed weeks ago to tap into Banion's home and office, turning his telephones into listening devices and his computers into tattletales. He called up Banion's schedule for the coming week.

Hmmmm . . .

Let's give him a FACE-IV* to tell his grandchildren about.

Palm Springs? That might work out nicely. Lots of clear airspace. It was hard to do a FACE-IV in a city, especially in D.C., where you ran into all the security airspace restrictions. Yes, this could do very nicely. Being Palm Springs, it fell outside his regular district, so he'd have to fill out a D-86 form and run that through MJ-9 *and* MJ-4, with copies to MJ-3. The old boys in the chat rooms were always going on about what a bureaucracy it had become. In the old days, you just jumped in your car and drove out to the nearest facility, hopped in your bird, flew off into the night, and scared the bejesus out of the citizens. Now it was as much fun as doing your taxes. But MJ-12 was like any bureaucracy, you just had to figure your way around it.

---

* Full aerial close encounter of the fourth kind, a later addition to the alien encounter classification system originally devised by Dr. Allen Hynek.

SEVEN

The driver was waiting for Banion at the Palm Springs airport, holding up one of those dippy signs with the client's name, usually misspelled. Once he arrived for a speech in Kansas City to find the driver waiting for a Mr. Bunion. His lecture agent now took pains to make sure that the car company had the correct spelling.

The driver was a burly, pleasant Hispanic fellow who introduced himself as Cesar. Normally Banion engaged the drivers in a bit of conversation. Chauffeurs perform a useful function for some media figures, providing local color without the need to do any real reporting. *Cesar Rodriguez came to this country the hard way, by swimming across the Rio Grande* . . . But tonight Banion was too tired for chitchat about Cesar's views on immigration. Anyway, he needed to collect his thoughts for the dinner speech to the car dealers.

He handed Cesar his garment bag and followed him to the parking lot, inhaling the warm, fragrant desert evening. His alarm went off at the sight of the car. A sedan? Why had they not sent a stretch limousine? John O. Banion's speech contracts were very specific, beginning with *stretch limo*.

"*This* is the car?" he said, as if he were being asked to ride in the back of a pickup truck, with pigs and chickens.

"Yes, sir," said Cesar brightly, with such evident pride that

Banion did not have the heart to complain. The car was probably his own.

It would have to do, Banion decided grumpily. It was only a half hour to the Marriott in Rancho Mirage. Tomorrow he would call Sid Mint at Enormous Talent and read him a riot act to make his head spin. Sedan. For God's sake, what were they thinking?

They drove off into the evening, the lights of expensive, gated communities twinkling in the distance. Cesar made no small talk. Good man. So many of them tried to start a conversation with a hearty "You have been to Palm Springs before?" Banion switched on the spotlight and read over his speech notes as they drove along boulevards named after comedians and singers. What a strange business it must be, giving directions in this place. *Stay on Bob Hope till you come to Bing Crosby, then take a left on Frank Sinatra. If you hit Phyllis Diller, you've gone too far.*

Tonight's event: a keynote after-dinner address to the AACA, the American Auto Consumer Association. In the best tradition of lobby obfuscation, this was the trade association representing dealers of imported foreign cars. The invitation to address them for the tidy sum of $30,000 had come shortly after the column he wrote blasting Michigan Congressman Hinkoler's "mindless xenophobia" in calling for stiffer tariffs on Japanese and German cars. The speech was AACA's way of saying *Domo arigato.*[*]

Banion was tempted to wing it and speak from notes instead of his prepared text. Despite his fatigue, he felt a bit frisky tonight. This flying saucer business had him so rattled, and that *disastrous* meeting with Burt Galilee . . . . What had possessed him to tell Burt? Would Burt tell the president?

Well, whatever had happened was over. He was back on track now, and in the mood to toss the crowd some red meat to bring them cheering to their feet. A standing ovation would be nice.

[*]Japanese: "Thank you."

He'd give them their money's worth, a defense of free trade so vibrant, so muscular, so scathing that . . .

He was aware of harsh bright lights outside the sedan. The desert around them was brilliantly illuminated. Strange.

Cesar was driving at a good clip, fifty miles an hour. Where was this light coming from? It seemed to be following them, keeping pace.

"Cesar?"

"Sir?"

"This light, what is it?"

"I don't know."

Banion rolled down the electric window and stuck his head out.

"Cesar!"

"Sir?"

"It's *them!*"

"Who, sir?"

Cautiously, as if inserting his head into a guillotine, Banion put his head back out the window. The lights hurt to look at, they were so bright. There was a soft thump on the roof of the car. It rose off the road, into the air.

HE AWOKE TO THE TASTE OF AMMONIA AND CINNAMON AND his limbs pinioned upon a table. Around him he saw familiar albino, bug-eyed faces. Again they were speaking cosmic gibberish at him. Again the hum of a moving craft. Again the blinking lights. Again the thing approaching with the—

—*oh God, not that again.*

There was another table beside him. Cesar was on it, his eyes shut.

"Cesar?"

He thought, Better try to get some dialogue going. Something, anything.

"You like be on my TV show?"

•   •   •

MOVEMENT. SHAKING. A VOICE. *MR. BANION . . . MR. Banion?* A dream, a hideous dream in which—

His eyelids snapped open. The driver—what was his name—Tiberius? Augustus? Caesar. *Cesar.* He swallowed, tasting the acrid-sweet flavors. His mouth was parched. His head throbbed.

"Mr. Banion? Sir?"

"Where are we?" he whispered, his body tensing to leap, if it came to that.

"At the hotel. You go to sleep."

Banion sat up. Had it been a dream? A flashback? Post-traumatic stress?

The pain—down there—hit him, a *stretching* feeling. It was no dream.

He clutched Cesar's arm. "How did we escape?"

"Escape, sir?"

"You were there, with me, on the table!"

Cesar's face now formed a large, uncomprehending *Qué?*

"In the spaceship!"

"Sir?"

"Don't you taste it?"

"Taste?"

"Stop repeating everything!"

Had the aliens erased Cesar's memory?

Banion slunk from the car under the confused gaze of Cesar and shuffled like a sedated mental patient into the bright marble lobby of the hotel.

SCRUBBS HAD NEVER HEARD A BAGGER TEAM SOUND SO pumped up. It was the first time in all his years at MJ-12 that he wished he could have been there for a face-to-face debriefing; for that matter, he wished he'd been there for the bag itself.

Over the speaker came sounds of Mike, Jimmy, and Jake high-fiving each other. He heard beer cans popping open. The boys loved mag-lev jobs. It was neat work, flying a heavy-lift black helicopter that was concealed from sight below by means of a suspended platform of dazzlingly bright lights. The lights, of course, were the UFO. The electromagnetic clamp was lowered from the helicopter through an opening in the light platform onto the roof of the target car. The car was lifted off the highway as the driver, holding his breath momentarily, switched open the happy-gas canisters in the passenger compartment, putting the abductee to sleep.

Jake, who had played the part of Cesar, regaled Scrubbs with a description of Banion's horror over finding that he would have to ride in a mere luxury sedan. The reason for that was entirely practical: the helicopter's lift capacity wasn't enough to heft a stretch limo into the air.

Mike did an imitation of Banion: "You like be on my TV show?"

The speaker filled with the sound of honking, snorting, asthmatic Team Banion! On to the Super Bowl!

"MR. MINT ON THE LINE."

"Jack!" said Sid Mint, whose clients included former presidents, network anchorpeople, actors, pundits, funny men, self-motivators, diet gurus, investment gurus, and people with advice on how to have better relationships with your children. "*Jeesus,* are you *okay?*"

"I'm fine, Sid." His words were measured, delivered with an almost eerie calm. For the clouds of doubt and confusion had parted now. John O. Banion saw things in a new light. He was as clearheaded as one of the apostles after Pentecost.

"I'm a little concerned. I just got off with Denny Phelps from AACA, and he's—I would describe him as a little upset. I'm sure there's another version of it, and I want to hear yours—but let me tell you what he said. He said you showed up for the speech an hour late, looking—he didn't come right out and say it, but he seems to think you were sort of, maybe, had a few drinks—and instead of talking about protectionism and foreign imports, you talked about flying saucers."

"I never used the term *flying saucers,* Sid. And I wasn't drunk. I'm a professional."

"Hey, I *know.* He said you talked about how we gotta defend ourselves against being invaded by aliens. I'm not sure that's what they had in mind by talking about protectionism. You know what these groups want. The Washington insider stuff, what it's like to have the president for dinner, what Cokie Roberts smells like. And you give them *The War of the Worlds.*"

"That's an exaggeration."

"I'm with you. But he did use the word *incoherent.* Don't shoot the messenger. I'm just quoting. He strongly suggested that I refund him his thirty thousand dollars."

"I admit that my thoughts might not have been organized. But that won't happen again, I assure you. Next time, they will be composed. Oh, yes."

"Jack, you sound . . . look, we have a *fabulous* business relationship, but you know, I also consider you a friend. Is there something going on?"

"More than we ever imagined, Sid."

"We've got you booked for fourteen speeches this fall. All of them big events. You're not going to talk to these groups about *aliens,* are you? We've got ITT, Microsoft, Aetna, Chase Manhattan, American Express, Archer Daniels. You're not *really* planning to talk to these people about little green men?"

"Sid, what could be more important than the fact that I have been abducted twice by alien creatures now, not once but twice? Social Security reform? The Middle East?"

"Jack, excuse me, but—what are you *talking* about?"

"The future, Sid. I have been over into the future. And it scared the *crap* out of me."

"Maybe you should take some time off."

"Don't worry about the bookings. You're going to have to hire extra staff just to keep up. This is a bombshell. But there's something larger at stake. They're here, Sid, and it's up to me to warn the American people."

Having proclaimed himself Paul Revere of the Milky Way Galaxy, Banion now turned his attention to how to deal with his wife.

Bitsey was having a hard time with all this. She had married him for better and worse, richer and poorer, but there was nothing in the vows about alien abduction. She had called his hotel room all night long, getting no answer. The next morning, Banion explained to her that after his speech to the car dealers, he'd been too afraid to spend the night alone in his room—what if the aliens came back for him? He stayed all night in the hotel's lobby, hovering nervously near cleaning women, night clerks, and other nonplussed security personnel, who, toward 4:00 A.M., finally alerted the assistant manager that one of the guests was acting strangely and might suddenly produce a gun and start shooting up the lobby.

"Bits," said Banion over the airplane phone on the way back to Washington, "if I were making whoopee with the local escort service, don't you think I'd come up with a more *plausible* cover story?"

She conceded the point but was still at a loss.

"I've made an appointment for you to see Dr. Offit," she said. "Burt Galilee says he's the best. He handled Bud Ferrer's breakdown." Bud Ferrer was the congressman from Ohio who, after becoming addicted to muscle relaxers, had taken off all his clothes on the floor of the House of Representatives while denouncing a bill to regulate Lake Erie polluters. (His staff tried valiantly to explain that it had been merely a gesture to dramatize the huge cost to business of the cleanup plan.)

"I'm not sure I like being compared to Bud Ferrer. I've think I've done a pretty good job of keeping it together, all things considered. Some people I know would be gibbering like chimpanzees and chewing on their socks after what I've been through. It's not much cheer to me that your first instinct is to hand me over to a psychiatrist. Would you be happier if they just shot me up with tranquilizers and dragged me off to Saint E's?"*

"I'm *trying* to help."

Banion had to face it: the only aliens Bitsey believed existed were the ones trying get into the country without proper visas.

"Mr. Banion," said Renira, "it's Patrick Cooke on the line, from the *Post*."

Oh, God.

"You gave a speech in Palm Springs two days ago to a convention of foreign car dealers," Cooke said.

"Yes."

"You told them—this is according to *several* people I talked to who were in the audience—that, quote, the most urgent priority of the federal government is preparing for a possible invasion of this planet by alien beings. Would you care to expand on that?"

Banion needed to buy time.

"Tell you what. Hold off on your story a few days. We'll talk on Saturday. I'll give you so many quotes on that theme you won't have room for half of them."

"I don't know," Cooke said. In newsroom parlance this means: no way, pal.

"All right then, but you won't have nearly as good a story. Don't you want to know what prompted the speech?"

"Let me see what I can do." Translation: you win.

"Tell Steve Coll to save you few acres on Sunday's front page—above the fold."

". . . *SUNDAY, WITH HOST JOHN O. BANION. AN EXPLO-ration of tomorrow's issues, with today's leaders. And now, your host, John Oliver Banion . . .*"

Viewers noticed a subtle difference in the show's format: the substitution of Dvorak's *New World* Symphony for the regular theme music.

---

* An insane asylum near Washington, once home to Ezra Pound.

That morning, *Sunday* had almost twice as many viewers as usual, owing to the page one headline in *The Washington Post* (below the fold):

JOHN'S GUESTS THIS *SUNDAY*:
HIS FELLOW ALIEN ABDUCTEES

"Aliens, extraterrestial beings, little green men," began John O. Banion, "call them what you will . . ."

Bitsey, at home, in bed, clutched the Pratesi sheets to her breast.

". . . most Americans believe in them. But then Americans believe in a lot of things. The eminent Swiss psychologist Carl Jung called UFO's 'materialized psychisms'—that is to say, projections of our collective unconscious. There is, of course, *another* explanation. They're real."

Burt Galilee, looking like an overweight prizefighter in his silk dressing gown, picked up the phone and dialed the special number that connected him to Camp David. A military aide answered, asked him to hold for a minute, then put him through.

"Stop whatever you're doing," said Galilee, "even if you're launching nuclear missiles, and turn on the Banion show."

"I am a rational man," Banion went on. "Until recently, I hadn't given UFO's a minute's thought, other than to dismiss them out of hand as the products of deluded minds. However, something has happened to me personally to convince me that we are, in fact, being visited by aliens."

Bill Stimple, the Washington representative of Ample Ampere, dialed the home number of Al Wiley, chairman of the electrical giant, in Woofchester, New York. It was not something he did routinely. "A.W.? Sorry to interrupt. Are you watching the Banion show? You might want to turn it on."

"My guests today. Dr. Danton Falopian. Dr. Falopian holds a Ph.D. in nuclear physics. He has worked for the U.S. government in a number of capacities. For a time he was at NASA, the U.S.

space agency. For some years now he has been president of WUFOC, the World UFO Congress. He joins us from his home near Gypsumville, in Manitoba, Canada."

Burt Galilee's phone rang. It was the president of the United States, calling back, spluttering. "A *remote* interview? I have to come to his studio on a Sunday morning? And he's doing remote interviews with UFO nuts? *Goddamnit.*"

Burt Galilee replied that perhaps it was best that Dr. Danton Falopian was not at large on American soil.

Banion himself wished that Dr. Falopian presented a less alarming appearance. With his widow's peak of jet black hair, goatee, potbelly, food-stained necktie, darting, feral eyes, enormous, beetly eyebrows, and intense manner, he gave the impression of someone who was on intimate terms with sanitariums.

"My other guest is Col. Roscoe J. Murfletit. Colonel Murfletit served with the United States Army, retiring with the rank of lieutenant colonel after thirty years. Colonel Murfletit was part of the top-secret military team that investigated the crash of an alien spacecraft near Roswell, New Mexico, in nineteen forty-seven. He is the author of the best-selling book *The Things in the Crates.*"

"Oh *dear,*" said Val Dalhousie, on her bed, surrounded by cavalier King Charles spaniels.

"He was present when government doctors autopsied the bodies of four aliens recovered at the crash site. We'll be talking about that in a moment. First, let me explain my own interest in UFO's. Three weeks ago, on a golf course outside Washington . . ."

At home, Nathan Scrubbs grinned at the television set and uttered a triumphant, sibilant *"Yess!"*

WASHINGTON DID NOT KNOW QUITE WHAT TO MAKE OF IT. There was no precedent. The city had been witness to all sorts of scandal: congressmen leaping into the Tidal Basin with strippers, third-rate office burglaries of rival politicians' offices, cabinet suicides, and the worst kind of all—sending American boys off to die in unwise wars. But, up to now, it had never watched one of its own declare so wholeheartedly a belief in the unbelievable. It was, as the head of the League of Gay Voters commented to the *Times,* "a stunning coming-out-of-the-closet moment." (Asked whether he still wanted Banion to moderate the upcoming presidential debates, he made equivocal noises.)

When Banion opened his front door in Georgetown the next morning, he found a dozen television cameras. The four-block walk to his office became an ambulatory press conference of increasingly unruliness, as reporters barked undignified questions on the order of "Did they take sperm samples?"

On rounding the corner of his office on Dumbarton Street, Banion found another clutch of cloven-hoofed beasts waiting for him with their modern instruments of torture. He had to shoulder his way through. So *undignified.*

Renira was waiting for him inside with a stern look. She had logged so far that morning over 150 phone calls.

"One-third were from what I would call reputable news organizations. One-third were from what I would call disreputable news organizations. The remaining one-third were from what I would call deranged individuals. One gentleman"—she handed him a phone slip—"says that he remembers you very clearly from the spaceship. Apparently, you met onboard."

"Was his name Cesar?"

"No," said Renira evenly, "A Mr. Hooper. He is eager to relive the experience with you. Mr. Mint called. He said it was rather urgent. And Mr. Galilee, also urgent. Mr. Stimple. *Extremely* urgent."

"You're having some difficulty with this?" said Banion, glancing at the tabloid newspaper Renira had thoughtfully spread over his desk. It showed him riding in a toy spaceship, with antennae sprouting from his temples.

None of the women in his life was taking this well. It had been a miscalculation, perhaps, to fly in Dr. Falopian after the show and to bring him, along with Colonel Murfletit, to his house in Georgetown. Bitsey, already in an agitated state, greeted them with something less than her customary hospitality. Dr. Falopian did not improve the situation by leaning over and kissing her hand moistly, in the manner of a slobbering Bavarian count. Colonel Murfletit tried to break the glacial ice by asking her if she ever went bowling. (His one pastime.) After several minutes of excruciating social intercourse, Bitsey stomped off, leaving Banion and his guests to discuss their strategy to the sound of upstairs doors being violently and serially slammed. Amidst these angry percussions, the telephone rang incessantly while outside could be heard the bruit of the encamping paparazzi.

A photograph appeared in the next morning's *Post* showing Bitsey, wearing a look of steely calm, fleeing to their Middleburg house at the wheel of her Mercedes. She reminded some of Madame Baby Doc Duvalier* driving to the airport to commence her exile.

"On the contrary," said Renira with regal British hauteur. "I'm thrilled, not to mention proud, to be so closely affiliated with someone who has just gone gaga on national television."

"So, you think I'm making this all up?"

"I'll get your tea," she huffed, exiting.

"Don't you want to discuss it?" he said to the closed door.

Maddening. Here he was, sitting on the biggest news story of the century, and what was everyone's response? Slammed doors, trenchant sarcasm, dripping scorn. He wondered if this was what the disciples went through.

But then, what could he expect? Were they supposed to run to the Nature Store and buy home telescopes? It *was* a strange tale. But it was true! And one way or the other, Banion was going to see to it that the truth got out. He was already working on that. Dr. Falopian and Colonel Murfletit assured him that the aliens would continue their contacts with him. They obviously

---

*Tightly wound wife of former Haitian dictator.

had plans for him. This was the pattern. The next time, Banion would be ready to document the experience, with a hidden camera and tape recorder. Colonel Murfletit cautioned that it was not without risk; the aliens might not like being photographed and recorded.

Banion wrote his column, an urgent call for Senate hearings on alien abductions.

He finished it, gave it to Renira to copyedit and transmit to the syndicate in St. Louis, which would send it out to the 440 newspapers. After a few minutes, she appeared in the doorway, holding the column as if it were a piece of sneezed-into Kleenex.

"Question?" said Banion.

"Yes. Paragraph three: 'There is no more urgent national priority than determining whether the thousands, perhaps tens of thousands of abductions of U.S. citizens by aliens is the vanguard of an invading force, or merely biological experimentation. Either way, this is no time for complacency.' "

"Yes?"

"Surely the Russian situation is more *urgent,* strictly speaking. I mean, there is apparently some chance of a dustup between their troops and ours. Point one. Point two, where do we get the business of 'thousands,' much less 'tens of thousands' of people being scooped up?"

"Those have been extensively documented."

"By whom, might I ask?"

"I refer you to volumes one through eighteen of the *Case Histories of Alien Abductees,* published by the Congress of Alien Abductees."

"Ah." She went off with a dubious expression, coming back a moment later to inform Banion that Mr. Stimple of Ample Ampere was on the line.

"Jack." This time there was no braying note in Bill's greeting, no slap on the back, no inquiry about golf, only a forlorn "How are you?"

"Superb. Let me guess. You're calling to register alarm about the content of the show yesterday."

"You took us all a bit by surprise there. Little green men. How about that."

"Nothing little, green, or human about them. No, these were . . ." Banion described at length the physiognomy of his captors. Bill did not sound enthralled. He emitted a occasional wan "Really?" and "Whaddya know."

Finally he said, "Everything *else* okay?"

"How do you mean?"

"Oh, you know, health-wise. What about taking some time off, work on that short game of yours?" So they were back to golf.

Banion laughed. "There's a presidential election going on, and I've been abducted—twice—by beings not of this world. At a time like this, would *you* be worrying about your chip shots?"

"You've been working yourself so hard."

"Would it help if I told you that I'm having Dmitri Shmirkin, the Russian foreign minister, on the show next week?"

"Oh, that's great! Fantastic. That'll be a great show."

"Feeling better?"

"I'm great. I was just . . ."

"By the way, you can tell the big guy that I've come around on *Celeste*."

"No kidding? Gee, that's just aces. He'll be pleased. What brought you around?"

"This is hardly the time to be cutting back on America's space program."

"You're not going to—"

"I don't know how the appropriations process works on *their* planet, but I doubt that their space programs got slashed because their toilet seats were too expensive. Assuming the bug-eyed bastards *use* toilets."

·　　·　　·

SCRUBBS WAS IN HEAVEN. TWO JOHN O. BANION COLUMNS on abductions in one week, one calling for Senate UFO hearings, the other urging swift approval of NASA's budget. He was in his apartment watching Banion interview an ex-KGB official turned Russian foreign minister about the Alaska situation. From the kitchen, where he was making himself another Bloody Mary, he heard, "Now what can you tell us about your government's knowledge of so-called unidentified flying objects?"

Scrubbs hurried back to the TV. Remote from Moscow, Minister Shmirkin pursed his lips while the question was translated for him.

The translator's voice replied, "There are no *un*identified flying objects over Russia at the present time. But we have identified all flying objects over the Motherland, especially American spy planes and satellites."

"Yes, naturally," Banion countered, "but surely you are aware that the United States government is in possession of superior alien space technology. Doesn't this *worry* your military people?"

Scrubbs stopped stirring his Bloody Mary with his forefinger.

"I have heard nothing of this business that you mention," came the response, with little pauses between words, "but I can inform you that Russia's military capability remains strong and ready in the event it becomes necessary."

Scrubbs was in the shower having a thoughtful, sobering soak when he heard the *chirrup* of his pager by the sink. He checked it, saw the number indicated—code for an incoming message of highest priority. He entered the passwords on his laptop computer, disarming the explosive within and converting it to a field communicator.

The message was signed MJ-1. In all his years he had never had a communication from MJ-1. Most people in the organization had never received a direct communication from MJ-1. It was short and to the point:

WHO AUTHORIZED CE-4 OF JOHN O BANION?

Scrubbs entered his reply, trying to make Banion's UFO con-
version sound like the Second Coming. Bypassing the question
of authorization, he dwelled at length on what a triumph the
Banion co-optation was for Majestic Twelve—a new dawn of re-
spectability (as he put it). And how about the fact that Banion
had just come out for tripling the space budget? Talk about *results* . . .

Scrubbs sent his message off into the ether and waited for a
reply.

EIGHT

Not since he had taken up collecting canes had Banion plunged so wholeheartedly into a subject. His office turned into a command center. Gone from the walls were the portraits of presidents, statesmen, and generals. In their place were charts of the solar system and distant galaxies, color photos of crab nebulae said by Dr. Falopian to be alien Canaverals. On the wall across from his desk was a huge map of the earth with color-coded pins showing the locations of documented alien abductions. Formerly, it had been his Wall of Ego, the traditional Washington space festooned with signed photographs of oneself taken with (other) important people, interspersed with handsomely framed honorary doctorates proclaiming one's superior worth. The bookshelves, once filled with the Federalist Papers, biographies and memoirs of the founding fathers, presidents, statesmen, generals, histories of civilizations living and dead, were now home to such titles as *Aboard a Flying Saucer, Above Top Secret: The Worldwide UFO Cover-Up, Angels and Aliens,* and *Blue Book Special Report Number 14.*

Banion had installed Dr. Falopian and Colonel Murfletit in rooms in his office. Renira protested their presence by pretending that they did not exist and speaking about them in the third person, creating a somewhat awkward atmosphere. Colonel Murfletit seemed content to be treated like a dead mouse on the living room floor, but Dr. Falopian, whose business card stated proudly, "Nuclear Physicist," chafed at this lèse-majesté and complained to Banion.

"Look," Banion said to Renira after she refused to help the doctor unjam the paper in the copying machine, "I'm not asking you to make him tea and crumpets, just be civil. He's a man of science."

"Science!" Renira scoffed. "Have you actually *read* his book?"

"Of course I have. Seminal stuff."

"Seminal rot. He's using you, the goateed capon. And that colonel, with his *absurd* stories about alien autopsies. Mad as march hares, both of them, and a good bit less charming."

"They happen to be top people in their field," Banion said sternly.

"I've no doubt of *that*."

"Just try to get along. Now, what do we have this afternoon?"

"At three o'clock you have the *Unsolved Mysteries* taping. I don't know *why* you agreed to this. Do you know what their last show was on? Yeti."

"Who?"

"Bigfoot. The abominable snowman."

"Well, I won't be talking about that."

"I don't see the *point*. Why do you have to give interviews to these fruity shows?"

"Because it's these 'fruity' shows that have been covering this story all along, while the so-called respectable media have stuck their heads in the sand. Anyway I *am* doing respectable media. Jerry Cramer called. He says *Time* may put it on the cover."

A look of doom came over Renira's face. "No good will come of that, mark my word."

Just once, thought Banion, it would be nice to get a little affirmation. She was becoming a magpie. But he did wonder about *Time*. So they were thinking about putting him on the cover, in the middle of a presidential campaign. Hm. He'd gotten a lot of ink lately, little of it what you'd call respectful. This was hard on someone who, up to now, had been treated with reverence and even awe by the press. Now he had to endure cruel caricatures and headlines like EARTH TO BANION, COME IN. He had become a bit prickly. The *Time* reporter who had interviewed him had tried to strike a sympathetic tone by telling him that she'd once seen "some lights doing weird things" while driving "stoned" across Nebraska as a college student. "Do not patronize me," he said icily, "with tales of funny lights in the sky. My experiences have been of another order entirely."

One aspect of the general reaction did perplex him: the amusement over how "obsessed" he had become with UFO's. His answer was: how could you *not* be obsessed after such an experience? Once you knew that the little green bastards had landed, what were you supposed to do, go back to talking about the presidential election? The weather? Did the disciples become "obsessed" when their carpenter friend began turning water into wine and raising people from the dead? Was Columbus "obsessed" by his discovery of the New World?

"Mr. Banion?"

"What?"

"Are you all right?"

"Yes, yes. Where were we?"

"Your lunch tomorrow with the CIA director—it's been postponed."

Once a month, Banion lunched at Langley with the head of the CIA, an old friend and occasional leaker of self-serving tidbits. Hm, odd. The director was regular as clockwork. He had never "postponed" before.

"They called. Apologetic. Hope to reschedule soon."

"How soon?"

"Will get back to us."

In Washington, this was a brush-off.

"You can work on your book. Miss Clark called, said she had some new material for you to look over. Something about French pox."

"The French Revolution will have to wait," said Banion, still smarting over the DCI's cancellation. Who did he think he was, anyway?

"The book *is* due in December. Mr. Morforken has included it in their fall list."

"Well, he can just uninclude it. I've got bigger fish than Robespierre to fry. You better drop him a note to that effect."

Banion had been, to use the newspaper phrase, besieged with lucrative book and movie offers. His literary agent, Simon Persimmon, a vinegary, intellectual sort of the old school, whose idea of a exciting property was a three-volume biography of George Marshall, now found himself on the receiving end of calls from Hollywood producers, talking astronomical sums of money and breathless with the news that everyone was "hot" for Banion's story. He was at pains to cope. Banion's lecture agent, Sid Mint, was better equipped to deal with such gale-force commerce, but even Sid was having difficulties with Banion's abrupt career transition. The corporate clients were calling in to express, as Sid put it delicately, "concern" about what topic Banion planned to speak on at their upcoming conferences. On the plus side, Sid said he was getting a lot of speech requests, albeit from new clients.

"Persimmon had an offer of three and a half million dollars yesterday," Banion said. Maybe *that* would impress Renira.

She tilted her head thoughtfully. "Isn't that what they gave the O. J. Simpson ex-girlfriend for *her* story?"

Why bother?

"Wednesday, interview with German television, lunch speech to the Institute of Paranormal Phenomena, it's at the Exigency. Then four o'clock at Senator Gracklesen's office to discuss your hearings proposal. His aide just called and said he might be held up by a floor debate and would you care to postpone?"

"No."

"Four o'clock, then. Don't forget you've got the symphony dinner that night. Black tie. Bitsey called to remind. You're at

Speaker Meeker's table with Mrs. Dalhousie, Mr. Pinch, and the Hinckley Eppersons. She said to remind you that they donated the half million dollars for the new acoustics."

Banion sighed. These symphony things of Bitsey's were torture. He had no ear for music. He was perfectly content to insert a "Mozart's Greatest Hits" onto the CD player and press REPEAT. To make matters worse, this new conductor was a fiend for atonality, that is, music that defied humming. Banion wondered which was worse—being sodomized by aliens, or having to sit through two hours of Charles Ives.

"Friday, breakfast speech to Aetna Insurance. Mr. Mint called and said they're expecting you to talk about the *election*. Lunch at noon, George Herrick at the Metropolitan Club. Then three o'clock, Dr. Hughes."

"Why? I'm not sick."

"He called. He wants to see you."

"What about?"

"I wouldn't know, would I? He's your personal physician."

"Well I'm fine. I don't need to see him."

"He's your doctor, and if he wants to see you—"

"*Next.*"

"Your UFO conference in Austin. Your talk's at ten Saturday morning. Topic: 'UFO's and U.S. Cold War Policy.' Your brain trust are beavering away on it."

"Anything else?"

"Miss Delmar called." The calls from Fina Delmar, movie star, had been for Renira the only welcome aspect in all this. Renira was a huge fan. Banion, no moviegoer himself, was only dimly aware of who she was until Renira pointed out that she had won Best Actress for *The Lobsterman's Wife* and *Wetly, My Darling*. Fina Delmar was a believer not only in UFO's but apparently in any paranormal phenom whizzing down the celestial highway. In her first call, she'd congratulated Banion warmly on his "coming out." She herself, she revealed, had twice been abducted, by "Nordics."

There were very distinct types of aliens, ranging from the Aryan-variety Nordics to the non-Aryan "Grays" and the even less Aryan "Short Uglies." Miss Delmar wanted it clearly understood that she had been abducted by the more urbane, almond-eyed, aristocratic alien type, and not by unchic, hirsute, ogrish homunculi. Furthermore, she had been abducted not in *this* life but in a previous one—in Paris, as it happened, in the late eighteenth century. She had been mistress to Count Bombard de Lombard, supplier of gunpower and snuff to the court of Louis XVI.

Banion told her about his Benjamin Franklin book. Indeed, Fina Delmar knew *all* about the meeting between Franklin and Robespierre, with whom she'd had a brief dalliance, *before*—she emphasized—he got syphilis.

After three somewhat endless phone conversations—Miss Delmar could talk bark off a tree—Banion delegated the Delmar detail to a delighted Renira, who could now find out what it had been like to work opposite Tony Curtis, Sean Connery, and Peter O'Toole. The two of them spent hours on the phone, somewhat to Banion's consternation.

"She's not sending me that chandelier, is she?" Banion asked suspiciously. She had told him she was sending him a chandelier made entirely of New Age crystals.

"I told her we didn't have room for it. She wants to know when you're coming to California. Wants to throw you a dinner party. Has some people for you to meet."

"Very thoughtful."

"Delightful woman. Did you know that she and Tony Curtis had a *mad* fling on the set of *Taras Bulba*? Yul Brynner was *insane* with jealousy."

"Fascinating. What else have we got?"

"We have to decide about the mail."

The mail had become a problem. It was coming in at an alarming rate, thousands of letters a day, from UFO believers, abductees, anyone who'd seen strange lights in the sky, women whose eggs had been harvested, men whose sperm had been extracted, people pregnant with alien babies, people desiring him to know that the lost continent of Atlantis was under Lake Huron, people warning him that the president of the United States had "sold out" the human race to Nordics from the planet Glibnob, people with—Banion sensed—too much free time on their hands. Only a few were skeptical of his abduction experiences. One or two inquired if he had a drug or drinking problem.

It all arrived from the Post Office in large, dirty gray sacks, delivered by bemused or surly mail carriers. The sheer bulk of it was overwhelming. Banion's previous record for mail had been after he wrote the touching column about the death of his and Bitsey's corgi, Romulus—478 letters. Now, 478 letters would be a slow day. Yesterday, Renira informed him, they had logged 4,000. Well, 80 percent of the American people believed in flying saucers, and now all of them, grateful to have such a credible champion, were writing in to express solidarity, slap him on the back, and say, "Give 'em hell!"

"I don't see, actually, that we need to answer it," Renira said.

"Why not?"

"You'll only encourage them. Do we *really* want them all writing back? They will, you know. We can't handle what we have as it is. Have you seen the upstairs lately? You can't *move*. There's over fifty thousand pieces. And I'm certainly not about to open any of the boxes. God *knows* what's inside. I have a suggestion."

"What?"

"Why not have your brain trust deal with it? Perfect application of their talents. I should think the doctor and colonel would salivate to hear all the heartwarming stories."

"You can't ask people of their stature to open mail. Hire some temps if you have to. But I want each piece answered. Do a form letter. *I'll* compose it. And I want every person's name, address, phone number entered into a database." He added heavily, "*Thank* you, Renira."

Renira huffed off.

BANION WAS SITTING ON THE LEATHER CHESTERFIELD IN Senator Gracklesen's office when the senator walked in, at 5:15, his eyes betraying a flicker of disappointment at finding Banion still there. It was the longest Banion had waited for anyone in many years.

The senator was effusive with apology. A floor debate on an amendment to make tobacco executives apologize in person to the families of any smokers who died of cancer. Senator Bore, of the great tobacco-producing state of North Carolina, was being obstinate. Pain in the ass, but you had to hand it to the old guy, never budged on principle. You look terrific, Jack. How's Bitsey? Now what was it you wanted to see me about? . . .

"Abduction hearings."

"Right." Senator Gracklesen nodded gravely, with all the enthusiasm of a reasonable man being pressed to reopen the investigation into the Kennedy assassination because someone had just found a gum wrapper on the grassy knoll.

"Right." One cheek bellowed pensively with air. "I mentioned it to Kent and John. They think it's an intriguing idea. Maybe next year. . . ."

Banion handed him a piece of paper. "This is a recent poll taken in the great state of Oklahoma. You'll note that half of your constituents feel that the government is lying to them about UFO's and alien abductions."

Senator Gracklesen furrowed his brow as he studied this unwelcome information, searching hopefully for some asterisk indicating that the margin of error for the figure was plus or minus 100 percent. He had, in fact, "mentioned" Banion's proposal to Kent and John, respectively the Senate majority leader and his chief lieutenant. Their response had been to roll their eyes rotunda-ward and change the subject to their plan to thwart the latest measure to limit political contributions.

"Jack, uh, what's going on?"

"I've been abducted by aliens, and I want to find out how much the government knows about this. Don't you?"

"Yes, naturally," the senator said, his eyes scanning the document, now desperate to find that asterisk. *This poll was conducted at the State Hospital for the Cuckoo.*

"It's your committee," said Banion. "You don't need permission from those two bad haircuts to hold hearings."

"Hold on," the senator said, now on the firmer ground of his own fecklessness. "We're all trying to sing off the same sheet of music here. The leadership's been cracking down right and left on the mavericking. We're holding on to our majority by two seats. I'm in a horse race myself."

"Yes, with a billionaire software entrepreneur whose biggest-selling computer game is about repelling alien invaders."

"I may have to concede him the stoned teenage vote. Frankly, I'm more concerned about my Hispanic numbers. They hear the word *alien* and they think I'm talking about illegal immigration."

"After the election?" Banion said.

"I don't see a problem with that."

"You'll commit to that on the show this Sunday?"

"Aw, Jack, we don't have to talk about this on TV, do we?"

"Then can I quote you in my column? 'Senator Gracklesen *will* hold hearings soon after the election'?"

"You can certainly say . . . that you've discussed it with people familiar with the thinking of people on the committee, and they are willing to debate the pros and cons of hearings along those lines. Yeah, sure, absolutely."

"WASN'T IT JUST *WONDERFUL*?" DURLEEN EPPERSON ASKED Banion in a barbecue-sauce Texan accent.

Banion's thoughts were not on Charles Ives's Second Symphony but on Mrs. Epperson's quite amazing bosoms—rumored to be genuine—a good three-fifths of which were resplendently on display. Between them, cushioned downily like a large egg, was a twenty-six-carat cabochon-cut ruby that must have set old Hinckley back a couple of tankerfuls of Permian sweet.

"Um," Banion lied through a spoonful of tepid butternut squash soup. Gracklesen's craven refusal to hold hearings, two hours of aural torture, and now a dinner conversation with the third Mrs. Hinckley Epperson—oh, for a quick death.

"Hard to believe Ives refused to attend performances of his own composition," Banion said. "Think what he missed."

Speaker Meeker, for whom the Second Symphony had lasted almost as long as it had for Banion, heard the remark and chuckled. Bitsey, looking relaxed, even radiant, here in her element, teased the Speaker that Maestro Slava, seated at the next table with the vice president, might overhear. Surely the Speaker, who was doing so much to promote the sale of American goods abroad, could hardly object to honoring an American composer. Bitsey excelled at this sort of Washington hostessing: inject a quick, knowing comment, then let the men go back to giving you their opinion. On cue, the Speaker extolled American composers. He liked Aaron Copland "especially," meaning that he had just, thank God, thought of the name of another American composer. Copland is of course big in Washington. Both political parties routinely introduce their nominees at their conventions by blasting "Fanfare for the Common Man." In a pinch, "Also Sprach Zarathustra" will do. Anything with trumpets.

Having now exhausted his store of musical knowledge, the Speaker praised Hinckley's "magnificent" gift of the new acoustics, causing a murmur of hear hears. The Speaker was hoping to hit Hinckley up later for a contribution to his political action committee, the modestly named Fund for America's Future. Tyler Pinch, curator of the Fripps, had his own designs on the Epperson mother lode—he was after Epperson to buy the gallery a Vermeer entitled *More Light Coming Through the Win-*

dow on the Left, which was about to come on the market for a
Ver-mere $28 million. For some time now he had been cooing
like a pigeon into the bejeweled earlobes of Mrs. Hinckley Epperson about the enormous status that such a "gesture" would
convey. The eager Durleen had been working on Hinckley, but it
was uphill going. He was preoccupied with trying to build a
pipeline through a particularly bellicose part of Armenia and
Urgmenistan, and a recent refinery deal in the Netherlands had
fallen through, souring him on things Dutch.

The dinner was going well, each of the men satisfied that he
had done most of the talking, when Durleen said to Banion, in a
voice that carried clearly across the $25,000 table, "Jack, my
daddy lives outside Austin, and he says it was in the paper that
you're going to a *UFO* conference there this weekend?"

Durleen's remark had the effect of dumping a large, hairy,
long-dead animal onto the table. Eyes drifted to the floral
arrangement, seeking refuge therein.

Jack looked furtively at Bitsey. For a moment, it looked as
though she would pull through, but then Durleen followed up
her innocent query by asking, "Are you going *too,* Bitsey?"

A look of horror came over Bitsey, as if she had just discovered that the dollop of sour cream in the soup was in fact a fresh
bird dropping.

"Good heavens no," Banion said, attempting a cheery tone.
"Bitsey doesn't go in for aliens. They're not PLU.* She thinks
the lower orders should be seen and not heard. Not that your
father. . . ."

Tyler Pinch tried to repair the damage by announcing that he
himself was hoping to get to Austin at the first opportunity. A
cousin of Frida Kahlo, wife of the great Mexican muralist Diego
Rivera, had lived there briefly. One night Rivera had gotten
drunk and painted a mural on her garage walls, a rather
"bawdy," as Tyler put it, allegory of U.S.-Mexican relations.

---

* People Like Us.

Hardly suitable for the Fripps, of course, but he wanted to have a look-see for himself.

Durleen, unfortunately, was not about to be diverted by talk of murals.

"Daddy's a *big* believer in UFO's," she said. "Because of his business, he's up all hours, and he says he's seen all *kinds* of strange things in the sky."

Hinckley Epperson, unhappy with the conversation drifting toward his newest father-in-law, who for a living drove chicken trucks, ventured that he would like to see even *more* American composers on future symphony programs, assuming someone knew their names.

IT WAS A QUIET RIDE HOME.

By now Bitsey had passed from the loud, viscerally remonstrative phase of her anger to frigid disdain. She had never been a hurler of objects; the slammed door was her most strident form of protest. Many WASPs are reluctant to throw things for fear of having to explain afterward to the insurance company.

In the bedroom, Banion made his plaintive case that it wasn't he who brought up the subject of UFO's. How absurd he felt. He, bearer of cosmic knowledge, millennial gnosis, secrets of the universe, reduced to pleading on the other side of the bathroom door.

By the time the door opened, Banion was in his pajamas reading the latest issue of *Foreign Affairs*. Bitsey's humor had not been improved by her half hour's unsuccessful struggle to undo her evening dress by herself.

Banion tried a last attempt to mollify, but unhooking a smoldering wife trapped inside an evening dress is, Banion considered as he fumbled like a member of a bomb squad with the abominably miniature clasp, an inherently ludicrous proposition.

NINE

Banion arrived at the UFO convention in the middle of a raging controversy over whether the U.S. government had cut its Faustian deal with the Tall Nordics aliens or the Gray Hooded Ones. His opinion on this urgent matter was sought the moment he stepped off the plane.

He had been to dozens of conventions in hotels, always as a (highly) paid speaker. He had always been well-received, but he had never been welcomed at the airport by an enthusiastic crowd waving banners. At first he thought they must be waiting for a movie star who had also been on his flight. Then he read the banners. He was engulfed by the adoring mass.

Dr. Falopian and Colonel Murfletit, on either side, tried to shield him from the crush. They too received kudos and loud huzzahs, for they had brought home this spectacular bacon. The UFO world had never before had a celebrity like John O. Banion, and the faithful had turned out to give him a conqueror's welcome. They even tried to lift him onto their shoulders, a benison Banion found both alarming and unseemly. He managed to pull himself back down, accidentally using Colonel Murfletit's large ears as grips.

He was hustled into his car, TV lights glaring, photographers snapping, women shrieking for his autograph. Through a cracked-open window, a glowing Dr. Falopian announced to the eager horde that Mr. Banion would answer all their questions after his lecture tomorrow.

On the ride in, Banion sought guidance from the doctor and colonel on this obviously radioactive business of the Tall Nordics versus the Gray Hooded Ones. First of all, he needed to know: were the Gray Hooded Ones related to the Short *Ugly* Grays? Dr. Falopian stroked his goatee and explained in a professional way the nuances of Gray taxonomy. The answer was: the Hooded Ones were an entirely different kettle of fish from the Short Uglies, and make no mistake about it. As to the controversy, Dr. Falopian and Colonel Murfletit urged Banion to take a middle position. Caution was the watchword here. There was evidence to support U.S. government collusion with both Nordics *and* Hoodeds, but there was no smoking gun as yet.

Another boisterous crowd awaited him at the Hyatt. He was escorted by husky World UFO Congress security people up to his room, which as Renira had promised did indeed have a majestic view of Lake Austin and the bridge that he was told was home to 1.2 million bats. He contemplated it in the gloaming. What a stupendous amount of guano they must generate. Surely some enterprising Texan had devised a means of collecting and packaging it as fertilizer.

Banion poured himself a restorative Scotch from the minibar, that watering hole of the lonely, and stared down on the city that he sensed was, in some ineffable way, his.

The phone rang. A woman, an admirer—a fellow abductee!—wanting to come up to his room right now and "talk." He politely begged off. But she must! No, thank you, see you tomorrow. He considered: his first groupie.

Again the phone rang. Another importunate female voice gasping to meet him, right now, immediately. She had pressing business—a message from the chieftain of the Planet Deltoid. Banion declined, then asked the operator to hold incoming calls. They were certainly more demonstrative than your average crowd at the Council on Foreign Relations, he reflected.

He ignored the repeated feminine rappings on his door. When they turned into desperate thumps, he alerted Colonel Murfletit, who posted a sentinel outside.

Steady, Banion told himself. *Don't let it go to your head.*

For all the clamor and attention, he felt lonely in a way that he had not been before. He and Bitsey hadn't been having much in the way of normal relations lately, not that sex had ever played a huge role in their relationship. Still . . .

Here he was, the John Lennon of the UFO world, sitting on top of an entire hotel full of women, eager—panting—to be probed in the Martian fashion.

No, no, no, *no*. He was a married man, he loved his wife, and that was that. End discussion.

Anyway, he told himself, the women he'd glimpsed at the airport and during that rush through the lobby were not exactly Miss America runners-up. The Girls of WUFOC, as *Playboy* magazine might friskily put it, tended to be a bit on the chunky side, with enormous hair and chewed fingernails—well, he thought with a chastening stab of sympathy, poor things, look what they've been through.

As a reward for not messing around with any of his groupies, he would watch an adult movie on the hotel TV while he went over his speech. Why not?

Vegas Vixens, starring Kimberly Kum? Well, why not?

Banion fell asleep to the sound of Kimberly's insincere moans of rapture with three Elvis impersonators. He woke up with a start when someone on the screen began shouting, "Deeper, oh God, deeper!"

BANION SPENT THE MORNING VIEWING THE EXHIBIT HALLS and attending a few workshops. Bart Hupkin, author of the best-selling abduction study *Plucked,* was giving a talk about his latest hypnotic "regressions" of abductees. It was Hupkin who had done the pioneering regression of Kathy Carr—Scrubbs's abductee. His techniques had been denounced by the American

Association of Professional Hypnotherapists for being "sugges-tive." True, some of the questions he put to abductees once they were under might be considered leading, such as *"Were you ab-ducted by four speckled, tentacled creatures from the Planet Far-ble? Yes or maybe?"*

Banion slipped in quietly just as a pallid multiple ab-ductee—the poor man had been snatched no fewer than thirty-seven times and pumped bone dry of reproductive juices—was telling Hupkin that he had reached the end of his tether. He had taken to masturbating every hour in order to deplete his supply of sperm. He might not be able to stop them from taking him, but he would be damned rather than supply them with one more drop of his sperm. The audience applauded his ingenious resolve.

Another of Hupkin's regressees shared her breakthrough of wrapping herself copiously in cellophane, which, like panty hose, made it more difficult for the aliens to drive home their vile phallic probes. She noted that this also helped with weight loss. Another abductee announced that she was depressed be-cause she missed her alien children. The father had, contrary to their joint custody arrangement, taken them off to the Pleiades with a "slut" from Aldebaran. Hupkin said that she should not take this personally. Aliens were notoriously problematic when it came to commitment.

Banion left the workshop unable to shake the feeling that there was something lacking in these people's lives. He had yet to meet someone—well, someone like him, to be perfectly frank. Even Dr. Falopian and Colonel Murfletit, with whom he had now spent hundreds of hours, were hardly ideal dinner compan-ions. They might be lions of their own savannas, but in any other setting, they were rather odd ducks. Banion had to keep reminding himself that the early Christians must have been an odd bunch, too.

He thought he should at least drop by the cattle mutilation seminar. The subject revolted him, but Dr. Falopian said it was key to UFO's, so please at least do a drop-by, especially since it was being conducted by Linda Moulton Howe, Ph.D., the grande dame of bovine mutilation. Wherever a barnyard animal was found with its innards removed, there soon would follow Dr. Howe with her camera and scientific instruments. Falopian said that her latest work on the subject was nothing short of breathtaking. Banion had seen it, a coffee table book (if you please), crammed with the most repulsive photos, and in full color to boot. Banion wondered who—on earth—would plunk down fifty bucks for a book filled with pictures of cattle with their rectums, tongues, and other delicates removed. How perfect it would look, on anyone's coffee table, next to the one on Matisse.

As he was leaving the Hupkin workshop, he heard a woman's voice say softly, "Mr. Banion?"

She was tall, perhaps five-ten, with short-cut blond hair and bright green eyes behind horn-rimmed glasses that gave her otherwise earthy, athletic demeanor the sexy, bookish look of the smart girl whose hobby was white-water rafting or jumping out of airplanes. Early thirties, handsomely turned out in a double-breasted jacket without shirt—a look Banion found much to his taste—and skintight white leggings that followed shapely limbs all the way down to perfect ankles buoyantly lofted on heels. Her smile, bookended by dimples, was radioactively warm. Her voice was husky, and she was wearing a perfume that had an intoxicating, powdery smell. Banion was utterly arrested. She seemed out of place in this oinking hog pen of perspiring Magdalenes.

"I'm sorry to bother you. You must be so tired of people coming up to you."

"No, no, it's all right."

Good God, what planet was *this* heavenly creature from?

"I heard you were going to be here, and I wondered, hoped, you might be kind enough to sign this." She held it out for him. It was *Screwing the Poor,* his best-selling critique of the welfare state.

"Of course, yes," he stammered. She'd read it, too. You could always tell by whether the pages were worn. "How should I sign it?"

" 'John O. Banion'?"

"I meant, would you like me to . . . is it . . . for . . ." Get a grip, man. "Who should I make it out to?"

"Oh," she smiled. "Roz."

"Roz. What a nice name." What an idiotic statement.

"With a *z*."

"Lovely."

"Around here, they usually assume it's with an *s*."

"Oh?"

"As in Roswell? New Mexico?"

"Yes, of course."

"I've read all your books."

"Really?"

"But this is my favorite. When I first heard the title, I thought you must be a real pig."

"Well . . ."

"Then my girlfriend told me it was really good, and I read it, and realized that you're right. Screwing the poor really *is* the only way to help them, isn't it?"

Banion cleared his throat. "What brings you here? Are you an abductee?"

"I prefer the word *experiencer*."

"Sorry."

"That's all right." She was smiling, looking right into him. "I'm not, but I'm hoping to be one. Soon."

"I'm not sure I recommend it."

"I guess," she said, twirling a pearl strand in her finger, dimpling one cheek, "it all depends *who's* doing the abducting."

Banion swallowed. His mouth had gone cottony.

Roz looked around the hall. "I hope if it happens to me, that I don't end up like that woman in the workshop, dumped for some tramp from Aldebaran." She giggled and looked around. "Does this place sort of remind you of a singles bar from hell?"

"I've never been to a singles bar."

"I shouldn't laugh. They're all so *lonely*."

"You sound as though you don't believe their stories."

"Do you?" she said.

"I'm not sure what I believe anymore. I believe what happened to me."

"But you're different. You *had* a life before."

"You look as though you have a life."

"I'm a publisher."

"Really? What do you publish?"

"You wouldn't have heard of our magazine. They're, well . . ."

"I do read."

"*Cosmospolitan?*"

"The women's magazine?"

"You're thinking of *Cosmopolitan*. This is *Cosmos-politan*. *Cosmo*, for women who've been abducted by aliens."

"Ah. Sounds . . . do you have a copy?"

"Over at my booth. I'm here on business. Would you like to . . . ?"

"Very much. Lead on."

She took Banion to her exhibit booth, where she had copies of her magazine. He examined the cover of the current issue.

"Very nice," said Banion, studying the cover photo, of a large but well-proportioned woman wearing a black leather miniskirt and leopard-skin leotard top, with a tattoo, a flying saucer, hovering over one bosom. He read the cover line:

—THE "RULES" OF ALIEN DATING
—BUT WILL HE RESPECT YOU AS A HUMAN BEING?
—STROBED, DISROBED, AND PROBED
—ARE NORDICS *REALLY* BETTER IN BED?
—IS IT YOU THEY WANT, OR JUST YOUR EGGS?

"Fascinating," Banion said. "May I have a copy?"

"You won't find it up to your high intellectual level."

"No, no, it looks very interesting."

"Our circulation has doubled in the last two years. And our demographics are getting better all the time."

Banion flipped through the issue. He saw a lot of advertisements for cigarettes, hair care, and dating services.

"How wonderful," he said, "that women who have had this experience now have a magazine they can call their own." What—he wondered—had come over him? Normally, he did not sound like the voice-over in a smarmy commercial.

"I don't suppose," Roz said, "I could do an interview with you? I hate to ask. But it would be such a coup."

"Of course. Pleasure. I was just headed to the seminar on cattle mutilation. Would you care to join me?" Now there was a come-on line for you: *would you like to go to the cattle mutilation seminar with me? I have front-row seats.*

"As a matter of fact"—she smiled—"I was going there myself."

They walked toward the Sam Houston Room, stopping every few feet as Banion signed autographs like a rock star. One pinched, fast-talking man approached to congratulate him for having the guts to tell it like it was. He had worked in Washington in the late seventies as a civilian contract employee for the Air Force. Was Banion aware that President Nixon had *personally* escorted Jackie Gleason, the comedian, to Hangar 18 at Wright-Patterson Air Force Base in Ohio to view the alien bodies from Roswell? Banion tried briskly to thank him for sharing this. He feared Roz would drift off and leave him with this lunatic. But the man had still more to share. Did Banion know who *else* from the entertainment world believed in UFO's? Jamie Farr, from the TV show *M*A*S*H*? Good to know, said Banion, trying to pull away. And Sammy Davis! Really? Oh yeah, Sammy was a *big* believer. You think he lost that eye in a car crash? No sir, that eye was *taken* from him in one of the first alien organ donations, and nothing *voluntary* about it.

"Really?" said Banion, now walking briskly.

"Yes sir, but you won't find that in Linda Moulton Howe's new book. Do you want to know *why*?"

Not really.

"Because *she's* only interested if it moos or bleats. She doesn't give a rat's ass what happens to us human beings."

"Really? Well, thanks for—"

"She's like those damn animal rights people, care more about goddamn *minks* than human people."

The man was barking mad. Banion fled.

"We need more people like you," the man called after him. "They can't ignore *you*. You've got a TV show. You give them hell. We're counting on you!"

"You're very kind with them," said Roz as they went down the escalator. "Other people in your position wouldn't be so understanding."

"I've met stranger than him in Washington." It surprised him to hear himself talking this way about the seat of his power.

"I'd love to see Nixon giving Jackie Gleason a tour of the alien bodies." She giggled.

Beauty, brains, sense of humor. He wanted to take her by the arm as they descended. With a pang, he remembered that he was a married man.

The room was dark. Dr. Howe, a well-dressed, attractive woman with the bearing of a professor, was showing slides that made Banion glad that he had not yet had lunch, and doubtful that he would today. Even worse was finding himself sitting next to an alluring young woman he had just met and watching a slide show of barnyard animals with their privies removed. Yet Roz seemed not at all discomfited by the gruesome images under discussion. Beauty, brains, sense of humor, and guts.

They sat in silence as Dr. Howe explained how the edges where the cuts had been made were eerily smooth, even more so than most surgical incisions; what was more, when the edges were put under the microscope, the hemoglobin showed evidence of having been heated to an extreme degree, as if by lasers. This could not be the work of sick yokels with crude tools. Even SRA couldn't account for the sheer volume of mutilated Elsies. (Banion worried for the future of a country where satanic ritual abuse had become so commonplace that the culture had to assign it an acronym.)

Dr. Howe had a theory as to why the mutilations were on the rise. These bovine organs were a delicacy beloved by extraterrestrials—alien sushi, as it were. Banion winced, knowing he would never again order *tekka maki*. Dr. Howe suggested that, to placate the aliens, the government might itself be playing the role of sushi chef.

Throughout the lurid seminar, Banion stole glances at Roz to see what her reactions were to these grisly hypotheses. And all he caught was a yawn.

"Would you like to have a cup of tea?" he said as they emerged blinkingly into the lights of the foyer.

"I could use something."

The restaurant was mobbed. They were quickly surrounded by more fans craving his autograph or wanting to share with him some alarming insight into the universe. Banion wanted to suggest to her that they have a quiet lunch in his suite, but he worried that it might sound forward.

Dr. Falopian and Colonel Murfletit intercepted them with frantic, exasperated looks, like nannies whose charge have given them the slip in the park. *Where* had he been? *Why* had he wandered off like that? There were *important* people who wanted to meet him.

Banion introduced Roz. They regarded her with undisguised disdain—another groupie, obviously. Only these two, Banion thought, could be immune to such dazzling female charm and beauty.

They tugged at him. He must come. Special persons were waiting.

"Would you like to join us?" Banion asked.

Dr. Falopian and Colonel Murfletit exchanged appalled looks.

The colonel whispered stiffly to Banion that the meeting was of a highly *sensitive* nature.

"It was nice meeting you," Roz said, taking Murfletit's hint.

"Join us," Banion said emphatically. "I *insist*."

"If it's not imposing . . ."

"Not at all," he said, with sharp looks at his minders.

Dr. Falopian and Colonel Murfletit sulked all the way to the colonel's room, outside which lurked no fewer than three heavies from WUFOC Security. Banion wondered what on earth they were guarding. A captured alien?

The door opened to reveal two Russians, enveloped in a Chernobyl cloud of their own cigarette smoke.

Banion coughed throughout the introductions. The older Russian was a Dr. Kokolev, the younger, a Colonel Radik. They struck Banion as Slavic versions of Falopian and Murfletit, only arguably with even better credentials. Dr. Kokolev, a father of Soviet rocketry, designer of the Pushkin-4 Booster, hero of Soviet science, holder of the Order of Lenin, had been Stalin's chief adviser on UFO's. Colonel Radik, retired from the Soviet Air Force, had shot down a UFO in his MiG fighter over Soviet airspace.

"Are you sure it wasn't a commercial airliner?" said Banion, who had never forgiven the Russians for shooting down KAL Flight 007. This attempt at levity did not crack much ice with the colonel.

Dr. Kokolev was jollier, in the ursine Russian way. He told the story of being summoned to the Kremlin in the middle of the night, several months after the Roswell, New Mexico, crash in July 1947, and being ushered into the terrifying presence of Joseph Vissarionovich Stalin. One of Kokolev's rockets had just blown up on the Alma-Ata launchpad, and he assumed that Stalin was going to shoot him personally.

Instead, the great man slid a small piece of shiny material across his desk at the young physicist and demanded to know if it was of nonearthly origin. It was, he said, a piece of the

Roswell wreckage, *obtained at enormous effort* by the KGB. Dr. Kokolev understood that much depended on his answer, most pressingly, his life. He decided to try to discern Stalin's own feelings on the subject. (Finding out what Stalin thought and agreeing with him was a popular pastime in Russia between the years 1924 and 1953.)

Stalin seemed convinced that it *was* of alien origin, if only because the American military had issued statements about the Roswell incident, saying first that it had recovered pieces of a flying saucer, then the next day retracting that and announcing that they were just fragments of a weather balloon after all.

Yes, Dr. Kokolev agreed, that was his reading as well.

Stalin wanted the analysis done immediately. Kokolev's instruments would be sent for.

When Stalin said immediately, you didn't tell him it couldn't be done until next week. Kokolev's scientific instruments were brought to the Kremlin. He made the best analysis he could under the circumstances and reported to Stalin, in artfully ambiguous language, that he could not positively identify the material and that, therefore (deep breath), it was almost certainly of extraterrestrial origin.

"So, I knew it!" Stalin said. "The Americans possess this alien technology!" He said this confirmed what they had found out from their other assets inside America. The KGB *rezident* in Washington had recently reported the existence of a secret, high-level group called MJ-12, consisting of twelve top people from the American military, aerospace, and intelligence communities, whose purpose was to advise President Truman on how to contain knowledge of alien visits, as well as to develop the captured technology, so they would have an even greater advantage over the Soviet Union.

Kokolev did not flatter himself that Stalin was sharing this extraordinary intelligence with him simply out of comradeship. Sure enough, this was the end of his career in rocket development and the beginning of another career. Stalin informed him that as of this moment Kokolev no longer officially existed. That same day, he and the little fragment of shiny material—whatever it was—were taken off by the KGB to his new home on an island in the Arctic Circle, an island so remote that even the puffins committed suicide out of boredom.

There he remained until Stalin died—six *years* on an island where the temperature plunged to minus sixty degrees, six years of trying to reproduce the molecular structure of the fucking shiny piece of wreckage. Six years afraid to tell Stalin, *Never mind—is after all piece of weather balloon!*

They released him following Stalin's death. Khrushchev apologized for the inconvenience and the two frostbitten toes and put him in charge of the Soviet Union's chief UFO project, code-named Thread Three, which spent most of the time trying to develop nontraditional propulsion fields, without success.

By now the Soviets were getting massive amounts of intelligence from their American assets indicating that the U.S. government not only was in contact with the aliens but was moving ahead with flying saucer development of its own, at an alarming rate.

Kokolev's work was carried on in the highest secrecy, but unlike his predecessor, Khrushchev had a human side. Thread Three's headquarters were outside Magnitogorsk, hardly cosmopolitan, but Paris compared with that godforsaken island in latitude 78 north. He could see his family at least. The vodka was better, and you didn't have to talk to puffins.

"What were you able to find out?" Banion asked, genuinely moved.

"Shit!" Dr. Kokolev said. They worked like kulaks, day in, day out, and in the end all they managed to produce was improved refrigerator coolant and smoother suspension for the Zil limousines.

At least the Party members who drove around in them were grateful. Billions and billions of rubles, immense resources that could have gone to feeding the Russian people, years of freezing his balls and toes in the cold—for what? Shit! And still antigravitational propulsion eluded them. All they could hope to do was steal the Americans' secrets, just as they had with the atomic bomb.

Dr. Kokolev smiled bitterly, revealing gleaming steel bridgework.

Khrushchev's successor, Brezhnev, impatient over his lack of progress in coming up with the Soviet Union's first operational flying saucer, fired Kokolev and installed his own son-in-law—an imbecile!—in the job. Kokolev was transferred to a nuclear power station in Smolensk. It was while there that he heard through the grapevine that the KGB had succeeded in planting a mole within the American UFO directorate called Majestic Twelve and had obtained a magnificent prize: actual blueprints of flying saucers!

Enormous economic resources went into developing one—Brezhnev was obsessed by the flying saucer gap—but nothing ever came of it. Though they built it exactly to specifications, spending a fortune in the process, they could never get the fucking thing to fly, even lift ten centimeters off the ground. A disaster.

After the Soviet Union finally collapsed, Kokolev was brought to the United States by U.S. intelligence. The CIA, which ran a job counseling service for former Soviet scientists to keep them from working for employers like Saddam Hussein, found him work with a defense contractor in the Mojave Desert in California. Damn hot place.

Did Banion want to know *what* Kokolev spent the balance of his career designing?

Weather balloons! High-altitude weather balloons!

Only a Russian could appreciate this cosmic level of irony.

It was, Banion reflected, an interesting story, but one with a lot of runway and not much in the way of take-off. He had been hoping for a spectacular revelation, something like: *Then I discover dat shiny material is containing traces of Assinium-5, found only one place else in galaxy—Zeta Reticuli!*

On the whole, Dr. Kokolev seemed rather ambivalent about UFO's. And yet Dr. Falopian and Colonel Murfletit were purring over his story, as if he had just provided the elusive smoking gun that the UFO world, for all its tens of thousands of sightings, still lacked.

The most interesting detail to Banion had been his reference to this Majestic Twelve directorate. Falopian and Murfletit had lectured him at length, if inconclusively, about this shadowy agency that, some evidence suggested, had been set up in the 1940s in order to report exclusively to the president of the United States. Nothing else was known about it. A few smudgy documents had surfaced in the 1980s: briefing papers for Truman signed by Admiral Hillenkoetter, then head of the Central Intelligence Agency. File a Freedom of Information request on MJ-12 and you were told no such organization existed. Same old story.

Now it was Colonel Radik's turn to speak. He had been glowering at Banion for his impertinent remark about shooting down the civilian airliner. Colonel Murfletit said something to him in Russian. He grunted and began telling his story, in a bored, mechanical way that seemed at odds with its dramatic content.

His MiG squadron had been stationed at Urmsk, yet another frigid, dreary outpost in the dreary, frigid vastness of the Soviet Union. One day air defense radar picked up the blip of an intruder. Another American U-2 spy plane, they assumed. His squadron scrambled to intercept it.

"Instead, was UFO," said Colonel Radik. He pronounced it *yufo.*

The aircraft executed a series of angular, evasive maneuvers such as Colonel Radik had never seen any aircraft perform.

"Like so." He made rapid zigzag movements with his hand. The MiGs gave chase as best they could, requesting instructions from the base commander. At first, the base commander thought they were all drunk, not uncommon among the heroes of the VVS.* But then, watching the erratic radar track for himself, he realized that something was indeed unusual. He requested instructions from his superiors, who requested instructions from theirs, all the way up, Radik supposed, to the Kremlin in Moscow.

By now they had been following the thing for almost an hour and were running low on fuel. The UFO then vectored toward a nearby ICBM base, the most hallowed womb of the Soviet Motherland. The base commander, forced to choose between waiting for Brezhnev to clear his head of too much Georgian wine and permitting an enemy craft to fly over a nuclear missile base, gave orders to shoot it down.

Radik fired two AA-6 air-to-air missiles. The first missed; the second hit. The spacecraft trailed smoke and lost altitude.

He followed it down but then was forced to break off pursuit as it neared the ground, which was mountainous and covered by clouds.

Now, he said, the story became truly strange. Did he receive a medal for his patriotic efforts? He made an obscene gesture. No! The base commander demanded that he hand over the MiG's flight recorder and told him that nothing—nothing whatever!—had happened. Understand? *Nothing! Forget entire episode. If mention one word of it, ever, to anyone, even member of the Politburo, spend rest of life in Siberian work camp watching piss freezing before reaches ground.*

So? Banion said.

So, Colonel Radik said, Russia *has* flying saucer.

I see, Banion said.

Two years later, *big* advances in MiG performance. *Huge* breakthroughs in speed and maneuverability. More zigzagging motions with his hand, this time with sound effects.

Colonel Murfletit was visibly excited. Radik's story dovetailed

* *Voenno-Vozoushmiy Sily,* Soviet Air Force.

perfectly with his own revelations, described in his best-seller, *The Things in the Crates*. It all fit—the alien craft the U.S. government recovered at Roswell had enabled all modern engineering advances, from the microchip to Tupperware. Now we know that the Russians also have their own captured craft! The implications were staggering.

"Maybe dey have *two* yufos," said Colonel Radik, crushing the stub of his cigarette out in such a way as to make Banion grateful he was not being interrogated by him.

The two Russians exchanged words. They seemed to be conferring on some minor point. Banion made out the word "Gagarin."

Colonel Radik continued. Yuri Gagarin? Cosmonaut, first man in space?

Yes, of course.

Radik blinked back tears. Greatest Soviet hero ever! His funeral in 1968—a state occasion. Brezhnev, Podgorny, all of them there on the reviewing stand over Lenin's tomb, crying like schoolgirls. The official explanation was he crashed in his MiG jet trainer.

Radik wagged a finger. Lies!

Number one, when they find his plane, all his weapons— fired. Crashing pilot does *not* fire weapons. Number two, same day, fifty miles from where Gagarin goes down, is another crash, in the village of Smelyinsk. But crash of what? Immediately area is declared off-limits, *many* helicopters, Army. Vital national security area. Everyone to turn back, go away. But what is industry in Smelyinsk? He made an up-and-down motion with his hand. What was word? When shit is stuck?

Toilet plunger, Colonel Murfletit said.

Exact! And what is the great national security value of toilet plunkers—shit sticks—to the security of the Motherland? Much better explanation—Gagarin shoots at yufo. Yufo shoots down Gagarin!

Colonel Radik leaned back, emotionally spent. He wiped his eyes and lit a fresh cigarette.

It was left to Dr. Falopian to descant on the gravity of what they had just heard. It was now beyond question that the United States government and Russia both possessed alien technology. Imagine if the current Alaskan tension turned into a shooting war between the two countries. My God. Both countries already had nuclear weapons—but what *other* kinds of weapons did they possess? There were rumors of a ghastly new weapon called a Plasma Beam Device.

Dr. Kokolev nodded darkly. Whole cities—*ffffft!*

Radik cruelly ground out another cigarette.

The important question, the key to it all was—how much did each side know about the other's ATC?

ATC? asked Banion.

Alien technology capability. This was, apart from the issue of the Nordics and Grays, the most pressing issue facing the World UFO Congress, and, to be sure, the human race. It was vital—*vital*, Dr. Falopian and Colonel Murfletit stressed—that the U.S. government be pressured to reveal all that it knew, lest the two countries embark on what would surely be the final confrontation.

"THAT WAS SOME BRIEFING." BANION WAS PLEASED AT HAVing gotten Roz access to such a high-level discussion.

"Yes. I thought they were much more impressive in person."

"How do you mean, in person?"

"I caught them on *Tales of the Weird,* a few months ago. That TV show. He told the story about shooting down the UFO a little differently, but it was better the way he told it today."

"They were on *Tales of the Weird*?"

"But I really enjoyed meeting them. It was nice of you to include me."

Banion sighed with disappointment. "I've spoken to Falopian

about this. It does the cause *no good at all* when our people go on shows like that."

"You were on *Unsolved Mysteries.*"

"That's different."

Roz smiled.

"It may not be public television, but it's certainly more mainstream than *Tales of the Weird.*"

"I guess."

"They *pay* you to go on shows like that. If those two took money, it just looks . . . It's like those witnesses at criminal trials who go and blab to the tabloids and completely destroy their credibility."

"Um."

"The *only* reason I went on *Unsolved Mysteries* is I'm trying to reach people that I don't reach with my show. It's important that we get the message out to all segments of the public. The less educated. Like your readers. I'm sorry, that came out wrong."

"You don't have to apologize."

"I'm not apologizing. I'm elaborating. Why are you smiling?"

"No reason."

"*Sunday* has very high demographics, you know. We have a very sophisticated viewership."

"I'm sure you do."

"Seventy-nine percent college-educated. Ninety percent read newspapers. Two cars. Two-point-six vacations per year. Twenty-two percent own a second home. Over seventy thousand disposable income. Okay, *combined* household income. You're smiling again. Why are you smiling?" Banion was smiling too. He couldn't help it. This wasn't like him.

"You're not like the others here," he said.

"Is that a compliment?"

"Yes, it is. Don't get me wrong. I respect these people. I appreciate what they've been through. I've been through it myself, twice. But to be honest, they're not the sort of people I usually deal with. How did you get into this business, anyway?"

"My girlfriend was abducted. She said it was the best sex she'd ever had. Sounded good to me."

Banion was staring. All background noises momentarily ceased. They had arrived at a fork in the road. One way led to a DO NOT DISTURB sign outside Room 1506, a bottle of champagne, and an afternoon of bliss such as he had not known in too many years, if indeed ever. The sign on the other said, BITSEY (YOUR WIFE—REMEMBER?)

They were in eyelock now, neither blinking. She was so desirable, the language so seemingly clear. *So, how about it?* She was playfully fingering her pearl strand.

But though his hormones roared, Banion couldn't bring himself to make the first move. Then suddenly all that remained was a numbness, a draining sensation, a leaden feeling in the bowels. The moment had passed.

"Well," Roz said, "it was a pleasure meeting you."

"We'll . . . have to do that interview sometime."

"I'd like that. Perhaps over the phone."

Banion watched her walk away until she was another head in the crowd. His misery was interrupted by a man who wanted to show him the scars on the back of his thigh, where the aliens had implanted a wire, obviously, so they could regulate his sex drive. Banion was tempted to ask if he could borrow the goddamned thing for a few hours.

THE BALLROOM NORMALLY HELD ABOUT ONE THOUSAND, BUT there were twice that present tonight. They were spilling out into the foyer. Remote TV monitors had been set up there so that the overflow could watch. It was, according to a radiant Dr. Falopian, the largest WUFOC gathering in its twenty-five-year history.

Banion entered the hall like a politician come to accept the nomination of his party. A rumble went up. "He's here! He's here!"

"Where!"

"There!"

"Oh."

"He's shorter than he looks on TV!"

On his way to the podium inside a protective scrum of biceps and crew cuts, Banion saw the bank of TV cameras and spotted a CNN producer he knew from Washington, Jim Barnett.

"Take me to your leader!" Barnett said.

"What are you doing here?"

"Covering your speech. Can we do an interview later, maybe get some B-roll?"

Yes, by all means, fine, why not? After all, the whole point was to get the message out. Banion knew Barnett for a straight shooter, and it was good to have someone from the mainstream TV media. He was still smarting from Roz's comment about his appearance on *Unsolved Mysteries*. CNN would be fine, just fine. Even if he had been rather hoping for *60 Minutes*.

Dr. Falopian, in his capacity as chairman of the World Unidentified Flying Object Congress, took the podium.

He welcomed the delegates warmly. Now, he said, they could hold their heads high. No longer did they have to be apologist UFOlogists. He denounced the late astronomer Carl Sagan, for calling him a "witch doctor" in his posthumously published book. He abjured the membership to be cautious in their comments to the press. For there was an *unusual* amount of press here tonight. The movement had come a long way from the early days. They had all worked hard to establish their organization's credibility and rigorous standards of proof.

But, he said in a lowered tone of voice, there had been problems caused by recklessness . . .

A murmur went through the crowd. They knew what he was referring to—the Milwaukee business.

The Milwaukee chapter of WUFOC had issued a press release, on national organization letterhead, without authorization from the Executive Committee, announcing that the president of the

United States had been abducted and an alien look-alike substituted in his place.

The murmur grew. It was clear to Banion that some here tonight thought the Milwaukee contingent had been entirely justified.

"This sort of thing," Dr. Falopian continued sternly, with nervous tuggings on his goatee, "is *not helpful*." He had had no choice but to revoke the charter of the Milwaukee chapter.

Boos.

The organization must be vigilant! It must be rigorous, it must be *scientific* in its discipline! Especially now, he said, looking warmly in Banion's direction, especially now that someone from the beating heart of the Establishment, the very belly of the corrupted beast, had come over to *their side*.

The crowd began to chant. "Ban-ion! Ban-ion!"

Yes, said Dr. Falopian, beaming goatishly in the spotlight, he *knew* why they had come in such numbers today—to hear from one whose credibility was above suspicion!

"Ban-ion! Ban-ion!"

For the first time he could remember, Banion felt a twinge of nervousness before a speech.

As it happened, someone else present was also nervous about Banion's speech. A dozen rows back, Nathan Scrubbs sat miserably between two large, unshowered devotees, one of whom was clutching Linda Moulton Howe's expensive, glossy, new coffee table book. Until now Scrubbs had never rubbed so closely up against this world that he had helped to create, and he was not finding it much to his liking.

He had come because it was the only thing he could think to do. And because this was probably the last place where they would think to look for him.

His superiors at MJ-12—whoever they were—were upset with Scrubbs, very upset. When he'd shown up for work the day after Banion's Palm Springs abduction, he'd found everything normal in his basement office in the Social Security Administration building—except for his computers. When he keyed in his password, the screen lit up with a voluminous listing of disability benefits paid to retirees in Georgia, Oklahoma, and Delaware.

At first he assumed it must be a glitch.

Two days later, after tapping his fingers on the keyboard so repeatedly that he got digital neuropathy and only more pension, disability, and Medicare records, he came inevitably to the conclusion that he had fallen into disfavor with his anonymous masters.

The trouble was, there was no one to call. After all these years in the organization, he still didn't know the name of a single other human being in Majestic Twelve. That was the organization's genius, its infinite compartmentability.

Then something else happened to make his liver quiver. In the midst of his feverish tappings, a Social Security Administration security guard opened the door. Scrubbs bolted out of his chair like an electrified lab frog.

"Didn't mean to disturb you, sir."

In all his years in this office, no guard had ever ventured in. And there was something about the guard—he seemed a little too crisp and businesslike and physically trim, somewhat different from the uniformed somnambulants he routinely passed in the corridors on his way to his subterranean lair. Being a security guard at Social Security was arguably the least exciting job in law enforcement. Why, then, did the one who had stuck his head in look like a stand-in for Clint Eastwood?

That evening, back in his apartment, Scrubbs got out his laptop computer. He entered the first two passwords. Halfway through entering the third and final password that converted the computer into a secure MJ-12 communicator, something made him pause. His brain went clammy.

He considered: surely the protocols that deactivated the explosive booby trap within the computer could—in theory—be reprogrammed remotely to do the exact opposite: blow it up.

Slowly, Scrubbs closed the laptop's lid. He spent the next few hours staring at the machine.

He did not sleep. Finally, around four in the morning, he carefully wrapped the laptop in cellophane. He drove to Theodore Roosevelt Island in the Potomac, across from the Kennedy Center, parked, crossed the footbridge, and buried it, behind a granite slab engraved with a TR exhortation to live the manly life and not to take any shit from anyone.

Back home, he slept fitfully. The larger problem remained—what now?

One by one, Scrubbs had eliminated possibilities, and so he had arrived at his present situation, wedged between malodorous UFO believers, trying not to breathe through his nose, about to hear a keynote speech by the Frankenstein monster that he had, in a moment of weakness, created ex nihilo out of pixels on a television screen. On the whole, he would rather have been in Philadelphia.

"Ban-ion! Ban-ion!"

At the podium, Dr. Falopian, who had implied that he was Banion's sole mentor—occasioning a pouting lower lip from Colonel Murfletit—was finally coming to the end of his triumphant introduction. (Dr. Falopian was not one quickly to yield a microphone.) He congratulated Banion on his courage for coming forward, when more timorous souls would have clung for dear life to the concealing shadows.

The crowd were on their feet again. They began to clap in unison, like Mediterraneans at a soccer match.

Give us what we came for! Give us Banion! We want Banion!

Banion had never heard anything like it, other than the single Rolling Stones concert he had been forced to endure when he took a godson—the son of a U.S. president. He could feel the blood pumping through his temples, and for some reason a mischievous synapse in his brain kept repeating, "Deeper, oh God, deeper!" as he walked to the podium.

It took nearly five minutes to get the crowd to sit down and be quiet.

On the spur, Banion decided to chuck his prepared text, "UFO's and U.S. Cold War Policy." Tonight he would wing it. Tonight, he would speak from the heart.

"My name," he began, "is John O. Banion . . ."

Roaring, applauding, stomping the floor. Only Scrubbs remained sitting, drawing scornful looks from his mephitic neighbors. Dr. Falopian gaveled them to order. Banion waited for them to be totally quiet.

". . . and I am an abductee."

Rhetorically, it was a cross between an Alcoholics Anonymous declaration and John F. Kennedy's *Ich bin ein Berliner*. The media marked the similarity. The headline in one tabloid newspaper the next day declared: ICH BIN EIN KOOK.

But here, there was no derision. The crowd, overcome by emotion, poured forth from their seats and began to surge toward the stage.

Colonel Murfletit squeaked orders to his crew-cut hearties to hold the line. Some in the audience managed to gain the stage, climb up, and hurl themselves at Banion. His glasses were knocked askew and taken for souvenirs. His boyish mop of hair was violently tousled by a large-breasted, prehensile woman from Oklahoma named Viola, who later breathlessly told CNN that she had seen a "shimmering like heat waves coming off his head." Barnett, the CNN producer, was trampled by the adoring, pachydermal herd and had two fingers broken. The thing had taken on an untidy, religious aspect.

Finally order was restored by Dr. Falopian, who himself got knocked about in the fracas. Sternly, he warned the crowd that if this continued he would call down the ultimate authority—the fire marshals. They quieted and let their new champion speak.

Even those mainstream observers who had already concluded

that John O. Banion had gone stark, staring cuckoo, admitted afterwards that it was a stirring speech he gave that evening. He had always spoken well in public, but now he spoke with something that he had, up to now, lacked—passion.

He described his ordeals on the golf course and in Palm Springs, glossing over certain intimate details. He was nothing special, he told them. After all, how many others in this very room had undergone similar trauma?

Loud murmuring, hands raised. Yes, they too!

Now, he said, listen to me, people. He held no animosity toward the U.S. government.

What was this? But the government *was* the enemy. The government was in cahoots with the extraterrestrial swine! What was he talking about?

This government, he said, is for the most part run by decent, hardworking, able people, who do not get large limousines, Air Force jets, and unlimited cellular phone service. They are in it for the simple, honest satisfaction of public service.

Groans. Disappointed looks. The crowd had not come for *this*.

And yet, said Banion. And . . . *yet* . . .

Pin-drop silence.

. . . and *yet* . . . certain . . . *quarters* within this government, unelected, unaccountable, *unresponsive* quarters, had determined, somewhere along the line, that the people of the United States could not be *trusted* . . .

Stirrings, rumblings.

. . . were not *worthy*.

Rumble, rumble.

These *elements* within the government were like the high priests of the ancient religions. They wanted to keep the knowledge to *themselves*.

Now he was talking. *This* was more like it. The crowd purred.

Sightings! Encounters! Abductions! Every *day* we see them with our own eyes, endure them with our own bodies. And yet these *priests*, these techno-shamans tell us, Oh no, that was nothing, just a bit of *swamp gas,* a bit of light reflecting off a lenticular cloud. Go back to your lives. Tend to the machinery of production. *Don't worry your pretty little heads!*

They were on their feet again now, but eerily silent.

People! Do you know what we are?

Tell us! We want to know! What are we, anyway?

Mushrooms!

From the sea of perplexed looks, it was clear that Banion's metaphor was not immediately apparent.

You know what you do with mushrooms, don't you? Stick 'em in the dark! Feed 'em a lot of shit!

Ah! Yes, now we get it! It's a metaphor!

Mushrooms! That's all we are to them!

Right!

Are you *happy,* being kept in the dark and fed a lot of shit?

No! Let us out! Light, we want light! And we won't be fed any more shit! For one thing it tastes like shit!

So began what was dubbed by the media the Revolt of the Mushrooms.

The whole room was shaking now.

Looking out on the crowd, Banion realized that he had total power over them. He could order them to march right off the bat bridge into the lake. How did the saying go? "When Aeschines speaks, the people say, 'How well he speaks!' But when Demosthenes speaks, they say, 'Let us march!' "

He held up his arms for quiet.

Are we not a democracy?

Yes!

Are the people not sovereign?

Yes!

Will we be lied to anymore?

No way!

Open the files!

Yes!

Unlock the files!

Yes!

In 1812, did the United States not declare war on Great Britain because its citizens were being abducted on the high seas?

Yes! We sort of remember that from high school!

And are not U.S. citizens—our very selves—once again being abducted and pressed into durance vile?

We're not sure what that last part means, but yes! Anything you say is okay by us!

Are we not being taken, against our will, aboard foreign vessels, and submitted to horrible, personal violations?

Yes! Though some of us kind of enjoy the probing part!

Banion lowered his voice: And what is our government *doing* about it!

Nothing! The lying, miserable, bureaucratic bastards! String them up!

Not only are they keeping us in the dark and telling us lies *but they are handing us over to the enemy for unspeakable purposes*! As breeding stock for Short Uglies! Or Tall Nordics, if we're *lucky*.

Hang the government bastards! Shoot them! Do something terrible to them! Campaign finance reform!

Even our cows, our poor, defenseless, stupid cows, are not safe from their ghastly depredations! Slaughtered, gutted, and served up as gruesome canapés! Alien sushi!

The man standing next to Scrubbs clutched his cow mutilation book and began rocking back and forth, humming in a way that made Scrubbs feel distinctly nervous.

No more! No more! To the castle, with our pitchforks and torches!

Now, said Banion, two great countries, the United States and Russia, both of them possessors of alien technology, the new fruit of the tree of the knowledge of good and evil, stand poised on the verge of Armageddon.

Armageddon! Sounds great!

The crowd hushed. All that could be heard was the click of camera shutters.

Banion stood aloft, supreme, haloed by spotlight.

If these two powers clash and use their secret weapons against each other, what dire forces will they unleash? What terrible genii will be loosed upon the cosmos?

No! We don't want that! We can't have that!

Can we allow this to happen?

No *way*!

Is not the Congress of the United States servant of the people?

Right! We definitely remember that from high school!

Now it must *serve* the people!

Absolutely! Whatever you're driving at is fine by us!

I call upon the Congress of the United States to come clean, to open the UFO files, to hold hearings—open hearings—*now*!

Now is too late! We want hearings yesterday!

I call upon Sen. Hank Gracklesen to hold abduction hearings now!

Gracklesen! Give us Gracklesen! Grrrrrrrrrr! Rip him to shreds!

A half continent away, a young aide opened a door and said, "Senator, you might want to turn on C-SPAN."

TEN

"Mr. Stimple on the line," Renira announced.

Banion frowned. He was working away on the word processor, banging out a column on the latest photographs from *Loiterer One,* the U.S. space probe currently orbiting Neptune and sending back photographs. One of these showed a mountainous rock formation on the planet's surface that, from 270 miles up, vaguely resembled human faces. Dr. Falopian seized on it as evidence of alien life on the planet and pronounced it a Neptunian Mount Rushmore.

Bill Stimple did not ask Banion about the status of his golf handicap.

"The big guy is unhappy, Jack. Really, really unhappy."

"Oh? Why?" Banion continued typing: *Increasing numbers of abductees, when hypnotically "regressed" by Bart Hupkin about their experiences, reveal that their captors telepathically communicated to them that they are using Neptune as a staging area for their exploration of earth. . . .*

"The show you did from that UFO conference. Jesus, why didn't you tell me you were doing that?"

"Didn't know I was supposed to clear my programs with you, Bill." *These developments, together with the stunning Loiterer photos of the Neptunian "Mount Rushmore" suggest that alien colo-*

nization of our solar system may already be more advanced than previously . . .

"*Sunday* is supposed to be a public affairs program, not a *freak* show."

"And just what did you find freakish about it?"

"Everything! There wasn't one person on there wearing matched socks. Falopian, your so-called nuclear physicist? I wouldn't trust him with a toaster oven! And that chinless colonel who saw alien bodies from Roswell, in bottles? Jeesus. What planet is *he* from? And those Russians. Where the fuck did you find them? On the Internet, under fraud.org? Plasma Beam Device? Shooting down flying saucers? My daughter says she saw the fighter pilot on *Tales of the Weird* a couple of weeks ago. Jack, your show was like the bar scene in *Star Wars*."

Informed sources within the UFO scientific community now say that NASA should concentrate Loiterer*'s cameras on the area 750 kilometers southwest of the humanoid rock formation . . .*

"Jack?"

"I'm listening."

"Am I getting through?"

"You saw the Nielsens?"

"Yes, I saw the Nielsens."

"Then no doubt you remarked that we were up five points. We had the highest rating since the Monsoone show."*

"Great," said Bill acidulously. "We're doing wonderfully in households with no teeth and combined household income of three thousand dollars. *Exactly* the sort of people Ample Ampere is trying to reach."

"That's a very outdated demographic model of the UFO community. We're mainstream now. Just look at me."

"Jack, the closest your new viewers will ever come to one of

---

* Susan Monsoone, Hollywood actress who defected to Hanoi during the Vietnam War to protest U.S. policy. Married Ho Chi Minh. Returned to the United States after his death. Now married to a multibillionaire Silicon Valley entrepreneur, she is active in veterans' causes.

our refrigerators is using the packing box for an addition to their home."

"Are you saying that Ample Ampere has no interest in being on the cutting edge of the biggest story in history?"

"The only cutting edge at Ample right now is the ax that Al Wiley, chairman of the board, is sharpening. He tested it on me this morning. He chopped off the tip of my dick with it."

"Have you packed the extremity with ice?"

"Jack, goddamnit, this is serious. The next call is going to be one you don't want to get."

"He's going to cancel my show?"

"Not the show. *You*."

"Bill, not to sound like the Sun King, but I *am* the show."

"You're not the only warm body in Washington. If it came to that."

"You were thinking perhaps—Evan Thomas?"

"Not my department. But we're not there yet. Look, we're a two-hundred-and-eighty-billion-dollar company. The chairman of the board does not want to hear people sniggering behind his back when he's trying to sink a long putt at Pebble Beach. My advice, and I'm saying this as a friend, is—lay off the aliens."

"Lay off the biggest story in history?"

"Jack, I'm not going to get *into* this with you."

"Not going to get into the fact that aliens are abducting U.S. citizens—"

"I'm going to hang up the phone now, Jack. Good-bye. I'm hanging up."

Bill Stimple's call annoyed Banion. It was all he could do to concentrate on the Neptune rock formations. He didn't want to lose his TV show, but what was the point of having one if the bastards weren't going to let you use it to expose the really Big Story? Perhaps there was a middle way.

He decided to call his producer, Chip, and tell him to line up Secretary of State Slippersen for this coming Sunday's show. That should please Ample Asshole. They could talk about Russia and North Korea and whether to give Most Favored Nation to Iraq, now that Saddam Hussein had become a born-again Christian. And if the conversation should . . . *drift* into alien abductions, well, it couldn't be helped. To hell with it, he'd call Slippersen himself. They were close friends.

"It's John O. Banion. I'm calling for Secretary Slippersen."

"Oh," said the secretary, with unsuccessfully disguised alarm. "Could you hold a moment?" She came back on. "I'm sorry, Mr. Banion, but the secretary is unavailable."

Unavailable? When John O. Banion called, minions rushed to pull their principals out of meetings with prime ministers.

"I see."

"Is it something I can help you with?"

The cheek! He never should have placed the call himself. "I'm calling to ask if he'll be our guest on the show this Sunday."

"I'll certainly pass that along."

In gloom, Banion returned to his Neptune column. When it was finished, he gave it to Renira to copyedit, fact-check, and transmit to the syndicate in St. Louis.

A half hour later, Bob Newcombe, the head of the syndicate, was on the line.

"You son of a gun," he said in his hearty, broad-shouldered way. "You really had us going!"

"How's that?"

"With this column about Neptune. Mount Rushmore! I almost fell out of my chair."

"Yes?"

"We're gonna put it in *Clippings,* our in-house newspaper. Funniest thing I've ever read. You ought to do more of this. I never realized you had this side."

"Side?"

"Comic side."

"How do you mean, 'comic'?"

"To come up with something like this."

"Bob, that is my column. It is not 'comic.' 'Comic' is not what I do."

After a longish pause, Newcombe said, "Jack, we can't run this."

"Why not?"

"I haven't said anything up to now. You've done eight columns on alien-related topics in the last three weeks. That's a lot. Time to get back to meat and potatoes. Who's gonna be the next president, are we going to war with Russia. Inconsequential things like that. Enough aliens, please. I gotta run. We need the new column in an hour. Say hi to Bitsey."

Gotta run? Bob Newcombe had something more important to do than continue a conversation with his leading syndicated columnist? Banion sat holding the uncradled phone, listening in amazement to the dial tone. Send *another* column?

When he had calmed down, he fired off that staple of newspaper columnists who have nothing else to write about that day—700 words of diatribe about his latest commercial airline ride. He had to fudge a little, since he had been seated in first, but he did a reasonable job of pretending he'd been in the back, along with the rabble. He rationalized it by reflecting that even in first these days the food would gag a ferret and you sometimes had to drink your Scotch and soda out of a plastic cup, not that these were privations to bring tears to the eyes of people reading your column while riding to work on an overheated subway train, face to face with someone with a wracking wet cough.

Moreover, the phones they provide these days on planes seem programmed automatically to cut you off in the middle of an important point. . . .

A couple of paragraphs into this jeremiad he hit delete and started over, with a blistering attack on the Federal Aviation Administration for not proceeding more swiftly with installing wind-shear detectors at regional airports. Probably wise, even if it was the dullest column he had filed in ten years.

Newcombe rang back fifteen minutes later on a cell phone. Banion refused to take the call. Renira passed on the message: "You at your best! Keep it up!"

Amazing. Here he had been over into the future, and all they wanted from him was white noise about wind shear. He groped for an analogy: Lewis and Clark, returning triumphant from the Pacific with marvelous tales of the newest world, only to be told, Never mind, tell us about the streetlights of St. Louis! Philistines!

"A Mr. Barnett on the line, from CNN."

Banion took the call. Barnett's piece on the UFO conference had been skeptical but not snide, which was about all he could hope for.

Barnett's question hit him pretty hard. But then this was the Washington way: even at the White House you were apt to find out that you had just been fired by hearing it on TV. The League of Gay Voters had dropped him as moderator of the presidential debates.

"I'm sorry," Barnett said. "I hope you're not hearing this from me first."

"No, of course not."

"I'm really sorry. Would you like to comment?"

"Obviously, I'm disappointed. I was looking forward to moderating the presidential debates. However, I certainly respect their—oh, to hell with it. What did you hear?"

"They were worried you were going to spend the whole time grilling the candidates about aliens. It's their first time sponsoring a presidential debate. I guess they were counting on a more—maybe the word is *mainstream*—moderator."

"I *am* mainstream!"

"Would it be all right if I sent a crew over? It wouldn't take much time, I promise."

Banion was rehearsing his sound bite: magnanimous, yet cutting: *I'm only disappointed because UFO abductees and the gay community have so much in common, the struggle for acceptance amidst bigotry and prejudice*—when Renira walked in with a face like a funeral parlor.

"Yes?" Banion said cautiously.

"Mr. Mint on the phone."

"Hello, Sid."

"Jack!" Good old Sid—he was never one to let bad news deprive him of an exclamation mark. "Howyadoin'?"

"Never better," Banion lied.

"Sorry about the presidential debates."

"I'll survive."

"Oh yeah. It's just, it would have been so great for the bookings. You hate to lose that kind of TV exposure. But no sweat, I'm with you all the way."

"I appreciate that, Sid."

"So, the ITT date."

"Good."

"Not so good. They just canceled. They feel—what am I going to do, lie to you? It's this UFO stuff. It scares some people, like large insurance companies. Banks. Wall Street firms. Forbes Five Hundred corporations."

"Your biggest clients, in other words."

"Yeah, basically. But now listen, I got one for you, and you don't even have to travel far. It's in Pennsylvania. King of Prussia."

"Yes?"

"It's supposed to be the big annual conference on crop circles. I'm not—are you clear on what these things are?"

"We don't know exactly, but they appear to be alien semiotics. Large-scale alien hieroglyphics mown into agricultural fields. Very precise and elaborate. Wheat, corn, soy." Banion sighed. "Sorghum."

"They really, really want you to speak."

"How much?"

"I'm trying to get them up. Their opening offer was totally unacceptable."

"How unacceptable?"

"I'm not even going to tell you. I'll get 'em higher. Don't worry. But I gotta wonder."

"About what?"

"You know more about this than I do. But if there's intelligent life out there, what's it doing making graffiti in wheat fields in Nebraska? Don't they have anything *better* to do?"

Banion did not have the heart to go into what he knew about this admittedly recondite extraterrestrial manifestation.

An hour later, Secretary of State Slippersen's press officer called to say, in a decidedly unapologetic tone, that the secretary had a "previous commitment" on Sunday morning. For a moment Banion wanted to ask what it was, but he decided not to, for fear he would be bluntly told: a secretarial bowel movement.

It was only four o'clock, yet Banion found himself craving a martini the size of a swimming pool.

Burt Galilee called.

"What is the difference," he said in his deep voice, "between a woman and a computer? A woman will not *accept* a three-and-a-half-inch floppy." Booming laughter.

Burt, who had better antennae than AT&T, had heard from an Ample Ampere lobbyist that Big Guy Al Wiley was "quote going ape" over the UFO show and was threatening to pull the plug on *Sunday*. Banion told him about his conversation with Bill Stimple. Galilee told him not to worry about Stimple, he was just Al Wiley's "butt boy." Good old Burt. Always so upbeat. Burt said he and Wiley would be playing golf next week, and he would put in a soothing word. Everything would be fine. Not to worry.

"Why don't you come to dinner Saturday?" said Banion, feeling relaxed already. "We'll round up the usual suspects."

"Isn't that the night of Erhardt's dinner for Prince Blandar?"

Erhardt Williger was former U.S. ambassador to the Soviet Union, former head of the U.S. delegation to the United Nations, former secretary of defense, former everything except shadow of his former self. He was now a "strategic planner," the phrase preferred over "influence peddler," used by former government officials who negotiated advantageous trade deals. He was a figure of some controversy outside Washington—his thick Hungarian accent made for easy parody—but within the town he was esteemed for having managed to rise above a government career that featured a disastrous war, somehow earning him a reputation as the wisest of the Wise Men. He was certainly the most expensive of Wise Men. But he did not always charge for advice. Since he had perpetuated catastrophe when he was in charge of U.S. foreign policy, presidents now turned to him to advise them on how to perpetuate catastrophes of their own. His very presence in such situations was deemed by the press to be encouraging.

All this he had accomplished by untiring and dexterous stroking of the most susceptible egos in the culture, that is, the ones belonging to the people who owned and ran its newspapers and television networks. (He did not slum to flatter mere radio broadcasters.) In social Washington, he ruled supreme, thanks to an impeccable and, by common consent, superb trophy wife. He was ruthless in the continual revising of his A-list. Banion and Bitsey had long been members in good standing. Now it dawned on Banion with a chilly presentiment of social ruin that he had, evidently, been dropped from it. He could practically hear the thud. He'd better get home quickly and keep Bitsey from drinking furniture polish.

"Saturday," Banion temporized. "Saturday. Of course. Well, what about the following Saturday?"

Banion heard a flipping of thick, English diary pages. "That's Nini Ferguson's thing for the Organgorfers."

"Umm. So it is," said Banion, regarding the blank Saturday in his own diary.

"What are you doing later tonight?" Burt said.

"Tonight?"

"After the sun goes down. Celestial phenomenon, repeated daily."

"Nothing, far as I know. Just me and Bitsey. Bitsey's deep into that twelve-parter of Eleanor Roosevelt on public TV. Thought I might work on my Franklin book."

"I'll swing by around six-thirty, pick you up, we'll have a drink at your place."

"You don't have to do that, Burt."

"I *want* to!"

Banion hung up feeling good about Washington for the first time in a while. That imperious Magyar Williger might dump him, but he still had friends like Burt Galilee.

At six-thirty on the button, he heard the moneyed honk of Burt's Mercedes. He had replaced the radiator ornament with a miniature Negro jockey of the type once commonplace on American lawns—Burt's little joke, a thumb up the ass of the Establishment. They drove over bumpy cobblestone streets and the remnants of trolley tracks to Banion's house on Dumbarton, the former residence of a distinguished, if ineffectual, secretary of war.

Banion's first inkling that something was amiss came when Lucretia, the maid, met him in the vestibule and announced that the *"invitados"* (guests) were in the living room.

What *invitados*?

He rounded the corner into the step-down room and saw, sitting in a hushed semicircle, as if at a wake: Tyler Pinch, Bill Stimple, Bob Newcombe (no wonder he'd had to run), Val Dalhousie, Karl Cuntmore (hugely successful writer of technothriller novels), Sid Mint, and a man he did not recognize. He felt Burt Galilee's large hand on his shoulder and heard the deep molasses voice say, "Jack, we're here because we love you."

THERE'S REALLY ONLY ONE WAY TO FACE AN INTERVENTION— with a stiff drink in your hand. Under the glum stares of the assembled, Banion calmly walked to the bar and, taking his time, mixed himself the mother of all martinis. No one spoke as he shook and poured the gelid liquid into a glass and, with a certain melodramatic air of defiance, dropped one, two, and three vermouth-soaked olives into it. He took a sip, feeling the divine vibrato up and down his cortex. This, he knew, would be the only moment of pleasure this increasingly gruesome day was likely to afford him.

"So," he said, not moving from the behind the foxhole of his bar. "To what do I owe this *pleasure*?"

"Jack," Bitsey said, "don't be angry. Burt's right. We're here because we love you."

"I'm grateful to be an object of such mass devotion. Does this gentleman"—Banion motioned with his drink in the direction of the unknown man sitting on a chintz armchair—"also love me?"

"This is Dr. Blott," Bitsey said, "from Well Haven."

"Aha. Of course. Rancho Risible."

"What?"

"The funny farm. How do you do, Doctor? Do the men with steel nets lurk behind the arras, or are you packing a tranquilizer gun?"

Dr. Blott, a mild, balding man with a forehead creased by perpetual empathy, said in a soothing voice that would have cajoled King Kong down from the Empire State Building, "Mrs. Banion asked me to come tonight because she's concerned about you."

"Of course she's concerned. Erhardt Williger just dumped us. Um," said Banion, "now *that's* a martini. Dad used to say you could always tell when an angel had been to visit because there would be a faint whiff of vermouth in the air. So, who wants to register concern next?"

"Jack," Bitsey said sharply, "this is important." Tyler Pinch, curator of the Fripps, was, Banion thought, sitting rather closer to her than he would have thought necessary.

"Comfy, Tyler?" Banion said.

"Bitsey asked me to be here, Jack. There are a dozen places I'd rather be right now."

"Philadelphia?"

"Don't be hostile," Bitsey said.

"*Cet animal*," Banion said, "*est très méchant. Quand on l'attaque, il se défend.*"*

The remark left a third of the assembled looking perplexed.

"But I speak in tongues. Well, enough sparkling repartee. You've come to tell me that I have gone mad and am making a spectacle of myself. Or, more to the point, of *you*."

"No one doubts that you underwent some kind of traumatic event," Dr. Blott said.

"Like being kidnapped by aliens?"

"All right, let's talk about that."

"Don't try to teach a pig to sing. Wastes your time and annoys the pig. No comparison intended, Doctor."

"Why don't we talk about the affairs you've been having?" Bitsey said.

"Oh, Bits, puh-leeze."

"Every time I call your hotel room you have some *bizarre* excuse why you're not there. Spending the night in the lobby with janitors so aliens wouldn't get you? You expect me to believe that? I don't want to get some *disease,* Jack."

"I'm not having sex with them." He didn't have the heart to point out in front of everyone that she wasn't likely to get a disease from a husband she hadn't slept with in quite a while.

Into this momentary vacuum lumbered bullish Karl Cuntmore, techno-novelist supreme. And yet, for all his tens of millions, he still looked like a man who had just been told there was a dead porcupine in his water tank.

"To date, there's no credible evidence that aliens have landed on earth. NORAD† can track anything bigger than a football. I know Bud Walp personally. He's the four-star in charge of the whole show. He's as straight as they come, and he's one of your biggest fans. I talked to him at oh-eight hundred this morning, and he told me there is just no way José any flying saucer could

---

*French sign: "This animal is very naughty. When you attack it, it defends itself."
†North American Aerospace Defense Command. The military headquarters that operates America's radar and satellite warning system.

get through his net without his knowing it. He'd blow 'em out of the sky like clay pigeons."

"Well, Karl, then I'd say we're in very deep poo-poo, because these spacecraft were significantly bigger than footballs. Though they were slightly smaller than your ego."

"Back off, Mister," Cuntmore snarled.

"Oh, don't play soldier with me. The only uniform you ever wore was a Cub Scout outfit, with a merit badge for pulling the legs off insects."

There was this to be said about an intervention: you learned who among your friends you really didn't like, after all. But now it was Val's turn. Poor Val, they must have had to drag her here, screaming.

"Darling Jack, I couldn't care less *what* happened to you on the golf course. Jamieson used to come back from Burning Bush and Augusta with the most outrageous stories."

"About being abducted by aliens?"

"No, no. Of shooting under eighty. I never believed a *word*. He was an appalling golfer. Men lie about golf scores, women about their age. The first kind is *far* the more serious."

"Val, I appreciate your concern, I really do, but I'm not sure Jamieson's lies about golf are in the same league as being kidnapped by creatures from outer space. Or am I being obtuse?"

"The *point,* sweet, dear, darling, *adorable* Jack, is that you've become a dreadful *bore*."

"You're right. Touché. But what am I supposed to talk about? Medicare? NATO expansion? The Middle East peace process?" He looked about the room at all the earnest faces. "Does this remind anyone of the play scene in *Hamlet*?" He picked up a miniature plastic cocktail sword from the bar. "So, who wants to hide behind the arras and get run through?"

Sid Mint spoke. "Personally? I don't give a shit what happened on the golf course. But we're losing a fortune! We're getting more cancellations than bookings! You know what the ITT vice president said to me? 'We hear he's gone nuts! We've got major clients coming to this conference. We can't have him up there at the podium chewing on his necktie.' "

"My ties are too expensive to eat." Banion turned to Stimple. "Bill? Doubtless you have something lugubrious to add."

"We're taking the show away from you, Jack. Al Wiley called me an hour ago. I can't tell you how I regret this."

"I know. You fought for me tooth and nail. You even offered to resign. To ritually disembowel yourself, right there, in the big guy's office."

"Jack—"

"Not your department."

"Burt?" Banion said, "any grace notes to add? Personal message from the president? Ultimata? Bottom line? Balm in Gilead?"

"I'm just very sad, Jack. That's all I have to say."

"An honest statement. Accepted at face value."

"Suppose," Burt said, "it did happen the way you say it did."

"For the sake of argument."

"So here you are—we are—at the fork in the road. The road in the dark forest in the middle of your life. You know your Dante. Now you have to ask the question: Am I going to let this ruin my life?"

Banion looked around the room, slowly, from face to face. "I suppose I could say it was all a bad reaction to some medication, right?"

They looked like faces in a crowd below, willing the man on the ledge to jump. But the moment came and went. The next step had obviously been rehearsed.

"Jack," Bitsey said, "I'm going to leave you if you don't agree to be treated by Dr. Blott."

The two of them looked at each other as privately as they could in the amphitheater of eyes.

"I was never one for epiphanies," Banion said. "If it had been me, two thousand years ago, I'd probably have gotten back on my horse, gone on to Damascus, and hanged a few extra Christians just for good measure. I mean, bad enough to have an epiphany in the desert when no one's watching, but on a golf course? Or in Palm Springs, on your way to make Japanese car dealers feel better about themselves."

He sighed. "But, you take these things as they come, even if they come in the form of little green men. I don't know what happened out there. But it happened. And your response to my telling you that there is something very strange going on is to pack me off to Well Haven to mainline Haldol and do origami. Don't you *see*? This is big! This is the biggest thing that ever happened! You all ought to be helping me find out what it is. And all you can do is wring your hands about how it might affect your seating at Erhardt Williger's next dinner party."

And so Banion left his house in Georgetown. Outside, on the sidewalk, he started at a car noise, half-expecting to be wrestled to the ground by men, not in black but in white.

PART
TWO

SEPTEMBER

ELEVEN

"... Saturday, *with John Oliver Banion ... a discussion of millennial issues, with top leaders from the UFO world ...*"

Except for the name, time slot, announcer's voice, theme music, set, graphics, guests, and sponsor, Banion's new television show was just like his old one. The press was treating it with whooping derision and Prozac jokes, but this Saturday, even as the general presidential campaign was ending its second week and all the talking heads in town were getting ready for sweaty pontificating on the weekend shows, a number of TV sets in town were tuned in for the debut of *Saturday,* out of curiosity. Self-immolation makes for fine viewing.

"*... brought to you by Gooey-Lube. When your car starts to make that grinding sound, drive on into Gooey-Lube. They'll grease your moving parts so fast your wheels will spin! And now, the host of* Saturday, *John Oliver Banion.*"

The Washington Post had run an article about the new show illustrated with a caricature showing Banion dressed in a pointy-shouldered robe of the kind associated with intergalactic shamans, but the John O. Banion who appeared on the screen was every bit the old John O. Banion, owlish in his horn-rims, still boyish, and yet—viewers noted—less solemn. Instead of the usual dark suit, he wore a sports jacket, with a little green ribbon pinned to the lapel. He seemed buoyant, sprightly, almost—one Georgetown dowager remarked—happy, if that was the right word.

"Good morning, everyone, and welcome to *Saturday*. My guest today—Fina Delmar."

Washington gasped.

"Miss Delmar is of course best known as the Academy Award–winning actress. Her films include *The Lobsterman's Wife* and *Wetly, My Darling*. She is less well known as a multiple alien abductee. It is both a pleasure and an honor to have her on this show. Welcome to *Saturday*."

"Thank you, John." Fina Delmar looked quite dazzling, no less so for a woman of her certain age. If they expected her to be encrusted with New Age crystals, they were mistaken. She wore a flattering, jewel-toned shantung silk pantsuit and simple gold earrings.

"How many times is it now?" Banion asked.

"Six."

"All by Tall Nordics?"

Fina Delmar smiled coyly. "Darling, I don't *go* with Short Uglies." A star is a star, whatever the firmament.

"I want to talk about that. But first, I want to ask you if you've picked up anything from your captors about their motives, plans for increasing abductions, invading the earth, and such. What intelligence can you share with us on this?"

"You're trying to get me in trouble, aren't you?" She smiled.

"No, I'm trying to find out what you know."

"What I know. Where do I *begin*?"

"How about at the beginning?"

"There was this map. It was the time before last. No—it wasn't. It was *three* times ago."

"Yes?"

"They came for me at the Golden Door.* I'd just finished

---

* A fashionable spa in Arizona.

shooting *Going Postal,* with Burt Reynolds. My God, that was an interminable shoot. Burt kept—"

"Tell us about the abduction."

"After they got me inside, and I was strapped down—and you know what that's like, these freezing cold tables, you'd think they'd at least cover them—and, so, they're doing their little things that they do, down there. Maybe after it's all over, we'll find out it was all training for alien proctologists and gynecologists. I mean, *Who knows?* I was trying to distract myself by singing show tunes—maybe Ethel Merman would get their attention. Can you imagine abducting *her?* That would have been one short abduction, let me tell you."

"Yes? And?"

"I look up and I see this map over the control panel and it was of the United States of America, and I'm thinking, This isn't random. This is all part of a *plan.*"

NATHAN SCRUBBS WAS WATCHING FROM HIS ROOM IN THE Hotel Majestic, in a part of Washington that politicians periodically denounced as a national scandal, situated as it is only a few blocks from the White House. He had been living in various cheap locales for several months now, having decided that it would be unwise to continue living at his apartment until he received some kind of communication from MJ-12 as to his status, such as it was.

The room smelled of a half century of cigarette smoke, loneliness, and bad karma. It was the kind of room one read about in the newspapers following a terrible crime: the lair of the perpetrator, where he had lived in wanky squalor, eating only cat food or other vile nourishment while hatching his outrage. The bed sagged like a sinkhole; the porcelain on the sink was rusted through—what horrible things that sink had endured, Scrubbs did not want to think about—the faucet dripped, and emitted chthonic rumbling from the hotel's no doubt hellish bowels; the fluorescent light buzzed like a bug zapper; and lately he had begun to hear nocturnal scratchings that sounded like rodent quality time with the whole family. But the room was seventeen dollars a day and came with cable TV to while away his long, bleak hours.

Miserably, he viewed his Frankenstein creation. Fina Delmar was now elaborating on her insight that aliens traveled "interdimensionally" rather than, "you know, vertically." This would explain, she said, why they did not appear on military radar screens. Assuming the military wasn't lying through its teeth, of course. Scrubbs thought he detected the beginning of glaze starting to gel on Banion's eyeballs.

Scrubbs calculated. Had the moment of maximum danger passed? Banion's bracing *J'Accuse!* at the Texas UFO convention had not resulted in the hoped-for Senate hearings. Indeed, the U.S. government had not collapsed from exposure and embarrassment. The Russians had not admitted to possessing alien death technology. (Plasma Beam Device? Where did they *get* this stuff?) Indeed, the only Russian reaction at all was conveyed by a junior embassy press officer, who publicly and somewhat humiliatingly dismissed Banion's allegations as "intellectual hooliganism" and "brazen hysterics." The Revolt of the Mushrooms had wilted, and now Banion, the former lion king of Washington punditry, was reduced to Saturday morning with an over-the-hill Hollywood diva who seemed genuinely to have convinced herself she had had sex with aliens as well as eighteenth-century French nobles. Under these circumstances, it was possible that his superiors at MJ-12 might incline to letting bygones be bygones. He had kept his MJ-12 pager, having dismantled it to check for explosives. Yet MJ-12 had made no effort to summon him electronically. It was, as John Wayne used to say, quiet out there—too quiet.

He bit on another Cheezo. Really, he had to watch the junk food. He'd put on almost ten pounds since going into hiding. He brushed yellow chemical crumbs from his lips and watched.

"Let's take some calls," Banion said. "Elbo, Texas, you're on the line."

"Yeah, I'd like to ask Miss Fina—hello? *Hello?* I can't hear nothing."

"Yes, you're on."

"Okay. Is it *true* that you and Tony Curtis had a thing on?"

"I didn't ask Miss Delmar on to talk about that," Banion said stiffly. "This is a public affairs program."

Washington choked on its brunch.

"She said she'd slept with aliens and that two-hundred-year-old French duke or whatever he was. I don't see how it's different asking what it was like having sex with Tony Curtis. And I *admire* Tony Curtis."

"Let's take a call from someone with a substantive question for Miss Delmar. Sump, Arkansas, you're on the air."

"I have a question for Miz Delmar. I have been kidnapped many, *many* times by aliens. I don't *use* the word *abducting* because kidnapping is what it is, and they ought to be hung or fried in the electric chair for what they done to me. It's shameful. My husband, Euple, he won't have sex with me no more. He says—"

"What is your question, madam?"

Scrubbs shut his eyes. It was too painful. Banion might be a pompous asshole, but Scrubbs couldn't help but feel a wring of sympathy for the man. He had, after all, destroyed his life. A copy of that morning's Style section of the *Post* lay inside the sagging bed crater, open to the headline

BITSEY BANION, COPING, PINCH BY PINCH

"I'm taking things as they come," **Bitsey Banion** said at last night's "Salute to Rich People" at the Fripps Gallery. If she didn't arrive on the arm of curator Tyler Pinch, she certainly spent a lot of time holding on to it during the festivities. The two of them have been spending a lot of quality time together since she separated from her TV-host-turned-

UFO-abductee husband, former *Sunday* big **John O. Banion**. During the dinner, Pinch told the 500 attendees, each of whom had given $5,000, that they were "the best human beings who have ever lived."

Scrubbs wondered if it would cheer Banion to know that Scrubbs's own life, too, had taken a grim turn.

He gazed out his window, with its panoramic view of the back of Uncle Big Busy's Fried Chicken and twenty-four-hour XXX ADULT VIDEOS. Last night he had gone to sleep to the sound of gunfire and police sirens.

So, he mused, what shall we do today? Stay in and lidocaine the brain with daytime TV, or will it be another fucking museum? He felt safe in museums, since they had guards who might, in the event he screamed, prevent MJ-12 agents from kidnapping him. At least if they got him, he would know more than before about the Bronze Age, the Dawn of Steam, and Fra Angelico, which up to now he'd thought was a liqueur.

How long would his cash last him? He had cleaned out his bank account when he went on the lam. He was reluctant to use his credit cards, since they could use those to trace him in a flash.

Suddenly he felt sticky and claustrophobic inside his squalid cell. He forlornly checked the newspaper for his entertainment alternatives, a Hobson's choice between the only unexplored aesthetic experiences left to him in town: a Jean-Michel Basquiat* retrospective on the artist's "Middle Period" or thirteenth-century Korean porcelain. MJ-12 wouldn't have to bother killing him. At this rate, they'd find him dead on a park bench, of boredom.

Scrubbs peeled off twenty dollars for food, stuffed his diminishing wad of cash underneath an ancient floorboard that he had pried loose beneath his bed, and ventured blinkingly into the unartificial light.

---

* Andy Warhol protégé who died of embarrassment at the age of twenty-seven when his paintings began selling for hundreds of thousands of dollars.

· · ·

"MR. CROCANELLI ON THE LINE, FROM GOOEY-LUBE," Renira announced. Renira, who had once told a president of the United States that Banion was not available at the moment, was now fielding calls from the president of Gooey-Lube, his new TV sponsor. Banion wondered why she had stayed on through his career transition. Brits could be magnificently stubborn when they wanted. Just look at how they held on to India and all the other pink bits on the map for so long. For all her apparent disdain for this brave new world of his, he suspected that she might actually, deep down, believe in UFO's, though as a correct Englishwoman she would never admit to it. There was this, too: she was from Devonshire, scene of the infamous "Devil's Footprints" in 1855, when mysterious unhuman tracks were found in the snow extending forty miles. Or perhaps it was her new friendship with Fina Delmar that kept her here. The two spoke on the phone incessantly.

"Jackieeeee! Have you *seen* these numbers? They're fucking incredible!"

Despite the man's deplorable vocabulary, it was, Banion reflected, a pleasure to have such an earthy and straightforward sponsor. Andy Crocanelli, president of Gooey-Lube, the national chain of automotive lubricating centers, was not one to bore you witless with brayed insincerities about the excellence of your golf game. The man came to the point like a lathe drill.

"I wanna expand the show to two hours."

"It's not that sort of program, Andy."

"Are you kidding? A fuckin' twelve, with a sixteen share?* I wanna run this show twenty-four hours a day!"

"It's very gratifying."

"You fucking WASPs, you get some good news and you go, *'Oo, oo, I am so graaaatified. Maybe I will have another cup of teeee.'* Jesus Christ, Jackie, you oughta be celebrating in Atlantic

---

* A Nielsen rating point equals about 980,000 households. *Share* indicates the percentage of homes with television in use.

City inna fuckin' penthouse suite, Jacuzzi filled with Dom Pérignon, smokin' pre-Castros and gettin' a blow job from a five-hundred-dollar hooker. From *two* five-hundred-dollar hookers. You want? It's on me."

Coarse as it sounded, it was certainly more alluring than the kind of blandishments Ample Ampere used to offer him, such as celebrity golf tournaments at Bel Mellow.

"Thank you, Andy. Let me get back to you on that."

"We're turning people away! Coast to coast, we got *lines* outside, customers killing themselves, for a lube job. I'm gonna have to start buying my own tankers."

"I'm very pleased. The important part is, we're getting the message out."

"I want this show on network television. Next *week* I want this show on network TV. I already called Shick Farber at VBS. I told him, 'You got dick on your Sunday morning lineup. Bible thumpers—all of em' fuckin' ex-cons on parole. I got a hot show for you.' By the way, Jackie, I wanna move you back to your old Sunday slot—I want *Saturday* on Sunday. I guess we better change the name, huh?"

"Let's take this a step at a time. But I really do appreciate your support and enthusiasm—"

"There you go again with that WASP shit! *I really fucking appreciate your enthuuuuusiasm.* Pull that fuckin' tea bag outta your ass. Talk to me! *We got a hit show!*"

True enough, *Saturday* had had a huge debut. Banion was vindicated in his decision—over the growls from Dr. Falopian and Colonel Murfletit—to have had Fina Delmar on the first show, instead of someone of more, well, scientific background. Renira, whose loathing of the two had increased to the point that she now treated them with open, dripping contempt, said they were obviously jealous of Miss Delmar. *Miss* Delmar, she called her.

At any rate, the response to the first show was, as WASPs would say, gratifying in the extreme. *The Washington Post,* tail between their legs, phoned to ask meekly if they might send a photographer. Banion instructed Renira to tell them he was "too busy." The headline nonetheless told the story: NEW BANION SHOW SCORES RECORD RATINGS. Banion's office phone, silent for so many months now—other than with calls from the more lurid of the tabloids—began to ring again. Amidst the torrent of interview requests came this:

"Someone named Roz to speak with you, from *Cosmospolitan* magazine? Says she met you at the Austin thrash."

"I'll take it." Banion dove for the phone.

"I hope I'm not bothering you," Roz said. "I had to tell you how fantastic the show was."

"Where are you?"

"As a matter of fact, I'm in Washington."

"Really? Can you have dinner with me?"

"I'd love that."

What had come over him? He felt like a teenager. He was grinning, his pulse was racing, he felt, he felt . . . *wonderful.*

"Renira!"

"Are you all right?"

"Fine! Great! What am I doing tonight?"

"Eight o'clock dinner at Le Chat Énorme, with that alleged scientist Falopian was so avid for you to meet, the expert on swamp gas."

"Cancel it."

"I didn't want to make the reservation in the first place."

"Are there any romantic restaurants in Washington?"

"I assume."

"Where? What's a romantic restaurant—the *most* romantic restaurant?"

"Well, I suppose it rather depends."

"Don't give me that WASP shit, Renira."

"I beg your pardon?"

"Romantic! Don't you speak English? Not tragico-comico-historical-pastoral. Romantic!"

"There's Swann's Way. It's a bit far, and you usually have to book weeks ahead, but—"

"Call them. Offer them—how much do I have left in the bank? Offer them all of it. Renira—get me a table."

"Will you be . . ."

"What? Out with it."

"Spending the night. It *is* an inn."

"Yes! Maybe. I don't know. See if they have a room. A suite. With a Jacuzzi."

"It's not Las Vegas. It's a quaint spot in the Shenandoah foothills. The chairman of the Federal Reserve got married there. I gather the food is—"

"*Ask.*"

What had gotten into Mr. Banion? So unlike him. She wasn't hugely looking forward to asking them if (a) they had a room, in a hurry, and (b) did it have a Jacuzzi? But it was good to hear Mr. Banion sounding happy. It had been a while. In fact, Renira couldn't really think *when* she'd heard him like this. Maybe she could help make it more romantic.

IF ROZ HAD LOOKED GOOD BACK IN TEXAS AT THE ALIEN CORral, she looked dazzling standing outside the Hotel Importance when Banion pulled up in his foreign convertible. She was wearing an iridescent blue-green silk dress suit, cut high on the thigh, and Manolo Blahnik stiletto heels at the end of endless long legs. Within seconds of her getting in the car, her perfume filled the inside. It was all Banion could do not to begin baying like a bloodhound as they crossed over the Theodore Roosevelt Bridge, heading west. He must get a grip. But it was so good to see her.

It was good to see him, too.

What brought her to town?

Sales conference. Had to meet with marketing people. Trying to reposition *Cosmos*. Going more upscale. The advertisers, of course, still balked at the abductee market, still stuck in the old demographic model. Yawn. Sorry, long day. Smile. *Really* good to see you again.

How long is the conference?

Wrapped up today.

Oh.

Um.

What time was she leaving the next day?

No particular time. Thought she might stay on a day or two, see the Basquiat.

The what?

Art show. Might as well. Didn't get to Washington that often. Smile.

"Roz?"

"Yes, Jack?"

"I'm so glad you called."

"Me too."

"In Austin, when we met, it was . . . I was married and . . . But that's over now. Not technically yet, but—"

"I know. I read about it. I'm sorry."

"No, it's—she's really better off without me at this point. She wasn't cut out for life as Mrs. Prominent Abductee."

"It's so difficult. Our readers tell us that all the time. Imagine if your spouse came home one day and said, 'Hi, honey, I've become a Jehovah's Witness. So, what's for dinner?' "

"Roz?"

"Yes, Jack?"

"Are you . . ."

"Yes?"

"Are you seeing anyone?"

Roz leaned over and kissed Banion on the ear.

A moment later she said, "Jack, you're going eighty-five."

THEY SAT AT A CORNER TABLE, A FEW FEET FROM A WAR-bling caged finch, sipping champagne out of flutes and eating caviar and scrambled eggs out of eggshells nestled in cups. The room had been extravagantly decorated by a London stage designer: florid Edwardian wallpapers, velvety chairs, tasseled lamps casting soft, focused light on the culinary prodigies that emerged, dish after dish, from the kitchen. The room was hushed, the diners emitting a collective *uuummm* as they gave themselves over to the food. A fire burned. A large bust of a splendid Nubian noblewoman perched majestically on a marble mantel. A Dalmatian lay at the entrance, forepaws dangling over the step, as decorative as a porcelain figure. Waiters and sommeliers glided by silently, like synchronized swimmers.

Banion felt himself being borne aloft on a mist of well-being. Normally he would be inwardly fretting. Did enough people in the restaurant recognize him? Did he have as good a table as the chairman of the Federal Reserve? Was the service sufficiently deferential? But now all he could think of was this exquisite, unlikely creature before him, editor of a magazine for the female abductee, delicately spooning Caspian beluga onto her tongue in a way that made his heart and other organs swell and ache. Through his tunneled vision, she appeared as an eighteenth-century cameo—perfect, voluptuous, luminous. All else was excluded. *Stay this moment . . .*

She almost startled him when she spoke, as if the jewelry had come suddenly to life.

"Do you think it might have been a hallucination?"

"I think I *am* hallucinating."

Two waiters arrived simultaneously with the next dish on the tasting menu.

"This is the monkfish in a pistachio crust, on a puree of whipped parsnips with a suggestion of coriander."

"I hate to admit this," Roz said, "but I've sort of started to wonder if some of my readers really were abducted. Visions, hallucinations, whatever, can be a reaction to some kind of trauma. Or, you can just want it to happen. The Germans have a word for it. *Wundersucht*. It means a thirst for miracles."

"The Germans," Banion said, dabbing at his lips, "have a word for everything. How's your monkfish?"

"Delicious. Do you think everyone you've met in the UFO world is on the level?"

"Do we have to talk about aliens tonight?"

"No." She smiled. Their fingers interlaced across the table-cloth. Did the Germans have a word for *this*? He wanted to take her into bed upstairs, remove her silky netherthings, and ravish her until the cows mooed.

"Let's talk about you," he said. My God, what *had* come over him? No Washington alpha male had ever uttered those words to a woman. "Who are you, Roz? Tell me your story."

She reached across and caressed his cheek with a finger. Her hand smelled of perfume. Roses. *Heaven; I'm in heaven. . . .*

"I'm a government agent sent to seduce you."

"I knew it. How's your mission going?"

"Contact is established. It's not a difficult assignment. I've had tougher."

"I could make it harder."

"I bet you could."

Banion blushed.

"Maybe I'll have to go to Plan R."

"Plan R?" Banion swallowed dryly.

"It's very extreme."

"How does it work?"

"You lean forward across the table, like this, look the target right in the eye, and whisper, '*I don't think I can wait any longer. I've got to have you* now.' "

Banion had to shift in his chair to release certain pressure. "That's some plan, your Plan R."

"It never fails."

There were still five courses to go. If only he hadn't ordered the tasting menu. More waiters arrived with more exquisite food, all of it now wasted on Banion, who yearned only for dessert.

"Venison mignonettes," the waiter announced, "in blackberry reduction, accompanied by truffled risotto."

"What," Banion asked in a businesslike way, as if he were doing a TV interview, "would the ultimate purpose of this seduction be?"

He looked up from his truffled risotto to a pair of golden dimples.

"To replace one obsession with another. You see, Jack, you are making the government very worried." She leaned forward, her breasts almost grazing her venison—oh lucky venison! "You know too much."

"Ah," Banion said, swirling the remains of his Châteauneuf-du-Pape in the glass, plum-colored vortex, "then there's no use struggling, is there? What can one man do, against the power of the entire government?"

"It's no use. We have you surrounded. Surrender."

"Yes," Banion croaked. "I guess there's no way out."

They sat, finishing their wine, unspeaking, playing fingertips until the waiter arrived, carrying what looked like a chocolate cake with a little plastic dome on top and legs sticking out underneath.

"This," he said as he set it down with quiet flourish between them, "is from Renira. Normally we would call this our Chocolate Decadence. But tonight we're calling it an Out-of-This-World cake. Renira said you would understand. She also sent this." The sommelier arrived with a bottle of vintage champagne.

"And she said to tell you that she didn't want you driving all the way back after dinner, so if you want to stay, she's reserved a room for you upstairs. One of our nicest ones, with a Jacuzzi."

"That was smooth," Roz said after the waiter had left.

"I . . . honestly . . ." Banion flushed.

"I'll take the Jacuzzi. You get the couch."

SCRUBBS RETURNED TO HIS ROOM AT THE MAJESTIC HAVING failed to achieve aesthetic epiphany, and with indigestion from the two half smokes he had consumed al fresco at a hot dog stand on Constitution Avenue.

The Basquiat exhibit brochure, gravid with proclamations of the painter's importance in the scheme, strove to make it sound as though dying of a heroin overdose at age twenty-seven had been a sacramental act, yet Scrubbs still scratched his head. But the visit to the Fripps Gallery had not been altogether a failure, for there, standing amidst such perplexing genius, Scrubbs had experienced an epiphany of another sort. He had resolved to get out of town and start anew. A little plastic surgery, a new Social Security number, new surroundings. Miami, he thought. Yes, Miami was a good place for exiles. What better shade for the shady than palms? Warmer climes, employment opportunities for the creatively inclined. Why wait? He could be there this very night.

He turned on the television as he gathered up his possessions. There was a report on the big *Celeste* launch a month from now. The president would of course attend, and would personally press the ignition button to launch the crown in the jewel of America's space program, leaving his opponent to rail on about how it was more urgent for America to build high-speed trains. The campaign had boiled down to: *My millennium is brighter than your millennium.*

Take your millennium and shove it. Scrubbs would take his to Miami. He felt good for the first time in weeks. On hands and knees, he pried up the floorboard over his wad of cash. He stared incredulously at the unlovely sight.

His wad of cash was no longer the tightly rolled little log of hundred-dollar bills. Now it resembled sofa stuffing. Crisp currency of a proud nation had been ignominiously used by rodents—a family of them—as a gnawing post and litter box. Scrubbs peered dismally at a shredded visage of Ben Franklin— thrifty Franklin!—embedded with pellets of rat crap. Over two thousand dollars, and not a single bill presentable as legal tender.

Scrubbs indulged in the kind of release of emotions that modern therapists say is healthy. When rats have dined on your life savings, why keep it in? Cursing violently, he ripped up a few more floorboards. The rats, of course, had retreated elsewhere to digest their rich meal in peace. He gave the wall a kick that made the mirror over the sink fall off and shatter.

He counted his uneaten money. Nine dollars and change. That would get him to the airport. But then he would have to present a credit card and photo ID.

"Checking out," he said to the night clerk sitting behind the bulletproof glass in the Majestic lobby. You can tell a really first-class hotel by the bulletproofing around the front desk, and the buzzer locks on the double doors to the lobby. Scrubbs slid his room key and credit card through the slot with a show of nonchalance.

The clerk was a chain smoker; he was enveloped in a miasma of his own smog inside the Plexiglas booth. He looked like an exhibit at a tobacco trade show. All that was missing was a sign: IF SMOKING IS SO BAD FOR YOU, WHY IS THIS MAN STILL ALIVE?

Without taking his eyes from his TV, which was showing a documentary about sharks eating unsuspecting seabirds, the clerk pointed to a sign that said, PAYMENT BY CASH ONLY. NO CREDIT CARDS, CHECKS, FOOD STAMPS, PERSONAL EFFECTS. NO EXEPTIONS.

"Oh," Scrubbs said, affecting mild surprise, "then I gotta go to the cash machine."

The clerk, absorbed by a great white shark's attempt to fit an entire Tasmanian muttonbird—or was it a tawny frogmouth?—into its mouth, said, "Lemme see yo' cash card."

Scrubbs held it up to the glass, as if displaying travel documents to a twitchy border guard with a machine gun.

"Leave yo' bag and wallet here."

The problem with this arrangement was that the ATM machine would only laugh hysterically if Scrubbs asked it for money. He had cleared out his account. He was therefore reluctant to part with his last remaining personal effects—how far can one go in life with the clothes on one's back and nine dollars?

"Is the manager around?"

He realized immediately that his petition to a more exalted member of the Majestic's managerial hierarchy had been an error, for now the clerk turned his attention wholly back to the shark and the unfortunate pelican.

"Uh uh."

Scrubbs examined his options. Alphabetically, they ran the gamut from abominable to atrocious.

"That's okay, I'll have the money wired to me in the morning. Just give me my room key back."

The clerk shook his head. "You already checked out."

"Yeah, and I'm checking back in."

"Nope."

"Why?"

"Room's taken."

"What do you want me to do?"

"Pay fo' yo' room."

There was one other option: wait for the clerk to die of lung cancer.

"Lemme make a call," Scrubbs said. His training was kicking in. *Faced with an intractable situation, create a diversion to buy yourself time to evaluate alternatives.*

Scrubbs went to the pay phone, dropped in coins, and punched the number for the time recording. He listened. Nothing. Not even a dial tone. No matter. He went through the motions, speaking loudly for the benefit of the clerk.

"Fred? Yeah, hi, it's Nate. How are you? Listen, I'm in a ridiculous situation here, can you bring, hold on"—he called out to the clerk—"how much do I owe you?"

"Two hunnerd fo-teen dollars."

"I need two hundred and fourteen dollars. Could you bring it down? I'm really sorry to do this to you. You can? That's great. The Majestic, on tenth, between E and F. Can't miss it. It's got a huge Mobil Five Diamond Award outside. The Queen of England stays here when she's in town. Thanks, you're a pal."

Scrubbs hung up and with an air of aggrieved triumph announced, "He's coming with the money. Okay?"

"Phone's broke," said the clerk, not looking up from his TV.

BANION AWOKE ON THE COUCH WITH A CRICK IN HIS NECK and a hangover. He hadn't drunk that much—since college, probably. Outside he could see the Shenandoah frosted with moonlight, but he was more interested in another sight, through the opened door to the next room: Roz, asleep, alone, on the bed. She looked like a partially unwrapped alabaster statue, lying there in a tumble of sheets. He yearned to be there in bed with her. But he had hopes. Apart from the disastrous appearance of the waiter, it had all gone so well, even afterwards, in the suite, as they talked—through the door—while she soaked in the Jacuzzi. Maybe it was even better this way, he mused, more romantic not to have . . .

He heard the voice of Andy Crocanelli saying, "You fuckin' WASPs! You get a babe like this in a hotel room and say to yourself, *Oo, how romantic not to fuck her!*"

"I WASN'T TRYING TO RUN OUT ON MY HOTEL BILL," SCRUBBS said as he sat in the back of the police car, handcuffed. "I was trying to get to the cash machine."

"I told you to shut up."

"You should be arresting that asshole clerk. It was his rats that ate my money. Two thousand dollars. It's there, in my room. It's proof."

After hours of enduring the night clerk's baleful glare, punctuated by occasional taunts of "Yo fren' with the money musta died on his way here," Scrubbs couldn't stand it any longer. When the clerk buzzed someone in, he made his move, a bold lunge for the opened door. Unfortunately, the person coming in turned out to be not a resident of the Majestic but a narcotics detective.

"If you don't shut up, I'll spray you in the eyeballs with pepper gas and say you resisted arrest."

Scrubbs had never had the pleasure of being thrown into the Central Detention Facility. He had read that the best thing you can do, on finding yourself in a holding cell with a dozen or so of the most frightening human beings on the planet is—*show no fear!* Viewing the minatory specimens circling him, who appeared to be calculating which of Scrubbs's bodily orifices to make merry with first, this advice seemed impractical.

"Yo, whitemeat, get over here and suck my dick."

Show no fear!

"I *said,* get over here and *suck* my dick."

Scrubbs knew some rudimentary karate, a neat, two-fingered stab to the Adam's apple. He could probably incapacitate the man currently extending this thoughtful invitation. It was the dozen others chortling who worried him. They might take exception to Scrubbs's leaving their friend choking on the floor. On the other hand, Scrubbs thought, perhaps being swiftly beaten to death by a savage mob was preferable to the looming evening of amorous rapture.

"Fuck *you,*" Scrubbs said.

Show no fear! Nothing to it.

THEY HAD BEEN KICKING HIM IN HIS KIDNEYS AND OTHER sweetbreads for what seemed a very long time when Scrubbs became aware of electrical sounds and shrieks as the guards broke up the soccer game.

"You Scrubbs?"

He made a gurgling noise.

"You're free to go."

As, hunched over in pain, he retrieved his possessions from the desk sergeant, Scrubbs was informed that the charges were being dropped. He was handed a manila envelope. Scrubbs opened it. It was a page from the day's newspaper, the stock market report. No note was attached.

"Who gave you this?"

"He didn't say."

Scrubbs examined the stock report. Various letters and numbers had been circled in blue ink. It took him a few minutes to figure out the sequence

ⓜ ⓙ ① ② ② ④ ④ ② ⓪ ④ ④.

A phone number.

He made the call from an all-night coffee shop a few blocks from the station.

A cheery female voice, entirely out of place at this time of night, answered. "Creative Solutions, how may I route your call?"

"It's Scrubbs."

"One moment please," she chirped. Scrubbs waited. MJ-12 did not entertain callers on hold with classical music or the weather station. She came back on. "What number are you calling from?"

Scrubbs gave the number on the pay phone. He heard clicking over the line.

"Hang up please, and stand by."

Less than a minute later, the phone rang. It was a male voice, tired, unhappy at being awake at this hour, but in command, a voice accustomed to giving the orders.

"Is this Agent Double-O Seven?"

"Who is this?" Scrubbs said.

The voice yawned. "Two unauthorized abductions of a leading media figure, unauthorized removal of official equipment, absent without official permission, and now this career capper—arrested for trying to run out on the bill at a fleabag hotel. We're all real proud of you, Nathan."

"You shut me down. I thought—"

"No, no, no. Do not use the words *I* and *thought* in the same sentence. They don't go together in your case."

"What was I supposed to do?"

"Don't get me started. Let me see. Contact us on your field communicator, your laptop computer. Speaking of which, where is it? You don't have it with you."

How did he know that?

"You didn't pawn it or anything stupid like that, did you? Scrubbs, you with me?"

"No, I still have it."

"Where?"

"At my apartment."

"Negative that. We'll get along a whole lot better if you don't blow smoke up my ass."

So they had been to his apartment.

"Why are you so interested in the computer?"

"Another brainteaser. Because it's government property. It's not a piece of equipment that should be floating around in the civilian world. And I'm conducting the interview."

"It's in a safe place," Scrubbs said.

"You know, we could have left you in lockup with your boyfriends. There were some who wanted to do that."

Okay, he had something they wanted. It was a start. "Then why didn't you?"

Another yawn. "We're going to bring you in."

"Bring me in? Is that normal procedure?"

"Nothing in your case qualifies as 'normal,' Nathan. But you've made such a pig's breakfast of everything, the only thing to do is stick you somewhere where you can't do *too* much more damage."

"Like where?"

"One of our desert facilities."

"Nevada?"

"What did you have in mind? Paris? I guarantee you it's an improvement over that Hotel Majestic—Majestic, Jesus,

Scrubbs—and jail. I need you to bring in your computer. We can't leave that on the outside. So where is it?"

"I buried it in a public park."

"Man, it's one thing after another with you."

"I didn't want it in my apartment. I thought you were going to set it off."

"If we wanted to, we could have done a CE-Six on you at any time."

"CE-Six?" The MJ-12 Close Encounters Playbook only went up to five—rough sex with aliens.

"Close Encounter of the Final Kind. Where's the computer?"

"Theodore Roosevelt Island."

"At least you didn't bury it at the Lincoln Memorial. It's five-ten now. Go to the island. You have nine dollars, that's enough cab money to get you there. There's a parking lot and a bridge to the island. Retrieve the machine, walk back across the bridge to the parking lot, there will be a car waiting for you."

"How will I know which car?"

The voice sighed. "I'll have your driver hold up a sign with your name on it. How many cars are going to be in the Teddy Roosevelt Island parking lot at six o'clock in the morning? I don't think you're cut out for fieldwork. To be honest, I don't know what you're cut out for, at this point. Maybe washing aircraft in the desert. The car will take you to the safe house in Virginia. From there, you'll proceed to an air base where we can fly you out west to the facility. Prior to that, I will debrief you. I'll see you at the safe house in one hour and a half. Try not to get arrested for something stupid."

DAWN WAS JUST STARTING TO BREAK WHEN SCRUBBS reached the entrance to Theodore Roosevelt Island. The gate at the end of the pedestrian footbridge was locked, so he had to climb around it, which made him feel like a criminal for the second time in twelve hours. No one watching his awkward, crablike exertions—due to his still aching kidneys—would have mistaken him for a professional cat burglar. Mr. Majestic had been right about that: Scrubbs was no field man. He thought about his future as he finagled his limbs around the gate spikes, trying to avoid Bobbitting* himself on them. What dreary job in the Nevada wasteland were they preparing for him? UFO groups had romantic names like Dreamland for the mysterious installations out in the desert, where the U.S. government was supposedly reverse-engineering captured alien spacecraft so that they could build their own. But these sites, from the inside, were anything but dreamy. Security was so intense you weren't allowed to leave, except for two weeks a year. It was the worst post in the organization. In the MajestNet chat rooms, people spoke with shudders of the stints they'd served in these top-secret Potemkin villages, where all they did, day in, day out, was turn lights on and off and drive mock-ups of flying saucers around on the sizzling tarmac in order to keep Russian spy satellites and UFO nuts with telescopes goggle-eyed with excitement. Maybe, Scrubbs thought, almost impaling his calf on a nasty spike, if he worked hard and kept his nose clean, they'd transfer him after a decent interval. After all, Banion *had* been promoting interest in UFO's.

What a mess.

The woods were lonely, dark, and deep, but there was sufficient light to find the spot where he'd buried his laptop, fifteen or so feet from the stone tablet engraved with manly exhortations from the twenty-sixth president. He got down on his knees and began to claw at the damp, leafy earth, grumbling over his lack of a shovel, feeling distinctly unlike James Bond. For one thing, Bond would have managed to make it out of the Hotel Majestic without getting himself arrested. In his moment of extremis, Scrubbs finally came to terms with his rejection by

---

*Neologism derived from the surname of a wife batterer whose Latin spouse settled the score by severing his penis with a kitchen knife. The penis was famously reattached, providing its owner with gainful, if undignified, employment as a celebrity penis reattachee.

the CIA: it was probably the one thing the agency *had* gotten right.

A few minutes of digging with blackened fingernails, and the laptop, wrapped in plastic, revealed itself like a treasure chest. Almost there.

He was about to lift it out of the hole when he heard something to his left. He looked.

He saw three shadows approaching. This was not part of Mr. Majestic's program. They didn't look like bums or bagmen, unless the bagmen who inhabited Theodore Roosevelt kept themselves well groomed and in athletic trim, in deference to TR.

What the hell?

They must have been dispatched by MJ-12 to ensure the safety of the valued object. Then why weren't they greeting him with cheery hellos and a grande latte? Could they have some murkier agenda?

"Hello?" Scrubbs tried. No answer. Not especially reassuring. There was something inherently *un*reassuring about a trio of crew-cut trolls pretending to be pine trees, unless this was some local amateur theatrical troupe rehearsing the final act of *Macbeth*.

"Hello?"

Something definitely unwell here.

His brain shouted, Abort abort abort.

Scrubbs saw a hand appear from behind a thick tree twenty feet away. There was something in the hand, something small and metallic, with a tiny rubberized antenna. A walkie-talkie? Then why was he aiming it directly at Scrubbs, and why was a thumb closing down on a button?

What would Bond do?

Scrubbs picked the laptop from its hole and heaved it through the air in the direction of the hand.

The blast knocked him back several feet and rolled him over. When he had cleared his head, he tasted earth in his mouth, and his ears felt like Quasimodo was inside ringing every bell. Gradually he made out other sounds: men shouting. Angry men shouting. Extremely angry men.

The voices apparent belonged to the remaining two, both of them staggering like drunks, weaving into tree trunks, holding their ears, while their shredded clothing smoldered. Their partner, the one who had been holding the remote detonation device, seemed to have disappeared, in the way people do when bombs have gone off in proximity.

Scrubbs lurched to his feet. Quasimodo ringing in Easter Sunday. He stumbled into a tree trunk, hurting his shoulder. He was eager for this wretched day to be over, and it had just begun.

The two smoldering goons had now produced what looked like—yes, those were definitely guns, and they were pointing them in Scrubbs's direction, if unsteadily. It was time to be away from this unhappy bower.

New explosive sounds filled the woods, puny by contrast with the previous big bang, but argument enough to get the adrenals pumping.

Scrubbs began to run, briskly, in the direction of the Potomac River.

"DO YOU HAVE TO GO BACK TO CHICAGO RIGHT AWAY?" BANion asked moonily over his untouched panfried trout and hash browns. Nearby, the finch chirped sweetly in its Victorian bamboo cage. Through the open door to the garden came the trickling of water. For someone who had spent the night on a couch in a state of advanced sexual frustration, he felt oddly relaxed and happy.

Roz looked back at him through eyeglasses over the rim of her coffee cup and smiled. "Not right away."

"Do you have to go back at all?"

"How's that?"

"Why don't you stay here in Washington?"

"Woo. *That's* sudden."

"I'm serious."

"What would I do in Washington?"

"Work for me."

Roz frowned. "You want me to give up the editorship of the leading abductee magazine to get you coffee and do your filing and give you blow jobs in the office?"

An older couple nearby stared. Banion blushed.

"I already have someone who takes care of that."

"Sure you do."

"Renira would probably bite it off." He took her hand. "I'm serious."

"I worked very hard to get where I am."

"I know you did. And I respect that. It's a terrific magazine. Your last cover article on whether Short Uglies make better lovers was the best of its kind I've read. But you've done that. Take on a challenge. The new show's taking off like a rocket. This is exciting. Come on."

"I don't know."

"There's something else."

"Yeah?"

"I think I, well, love you. I'm not very good at this sort of thing."

"Falling in love?"

"I don't have a baseline on which to make any definitive assessment, or . . ."

"I love it when you talk about me like I'm a fiscal outlay." Roz put a forkful of trout in his mouth. "You're married."

"It's nothing six months of expensive lawyers screaming at each other can't fix."

She was smiling. Yes! She was so beautiful! He loved her!

"What would my title be?"

"Executive Assistant."

"Please."

"Executive Director?"

"I was thinking Chief Executive Officer."

"Whatever."

"I'll think about it."

"Oh come on," Banion said. "Say yes. It's the most beautiful word in the English language. West Saxon, originally."

"How does it pay?"

"Oh, *very* well."

"Benefits?"

"Many."

"Medical?"

"Major."

"Vacations?"

"Frequent."

"So." She smiled, taking his hand. "Do I apply for this position in person?"

"Um. You do have to pass a physical exam first."

"What sort of physical?"

"Pretty rigorous, from what I hear."

"I'll . . . think about it."

SUBMERGED UP TO HIS CROTCH IN THE FRIGID POTOMAC River, Scrubbs hid behind a large rock on the eastern bank of the island, directly across from the Kennedy Center. Early-morning commuters were driving in to work. He was hiding from assassins. Another day, another dollar.

They were getting closer. Soon, he guessed, the police helicopter would appear. An amplified voice would bark at him to put his hands in the air. The rest was predictable. He would be taken into custody. In the car he would feel the jab of a hypodermic needle. Or perhaps they'd use sevoflurane on him, straight, without the ammonia and cinnamon flavoring. He would fall into a deep, untroubled sleep for, oh, ever.

He peered over the top of the rock. They were a hundred feet away and closing on him, sweeping the bank, guns at the ready.

The river was cold and dirty, but it beat getting shot. Scrubbs slipped in, gasping, up to his neck, and pushed out until he felt the current start to carry him downriver. It was swift.

As he was passing the southern tip of Theodore Roosevelt Island, moving swiftly now toward God knew where, he saw a fishing boat, about fifteen feet long, anchored in the lee of the island. A number of fishing rods were deployed in holders. A man was sitting in the boat, leaning back. He appeared to be asleep. Scrubbs began to drift toward the lines. He tried to kick away, but the current was drawing him in.

Fifty feet past the boat, he felt a sharp pain in his leg.

In the distance, he heard the distinctive and normally cheering *zzzzzzzzzzz* of unspooling fishing line.

The pain in his leg—*ahh!* He thrashed against the current, trying to reach the boat. The fisherman was now standing, holding his rod.

With enormous effort, Scrubbs reached the boat. He grabbed the transom, spat water.

"Morning," he said.

The fisherman was a black man in his early sixties, roly-poly in the belly, with a finely trimmed mustache. At the moment, however, his most prominent feature was his mouth, which was hanging open.

Scrubbs coughed up more Potomac water. "Sorry to disturb you, but your line hooked my leg."

"*What,*" the man said, "are you *doing* in the water?"

Scrubbs was too tired for invention. "There are some men with guns on the island trying to kill me."

"Police?"

"Sort of. Not really."

"Well, which is it?"

"They're with the government." Scrubbs gasped from the exertion required to hold on. "They want to kill me because I know about flying saucers."

Well, there—the ball was now squarely in the man's court.

"Mister, are you *drunk?*"

"No. They're going to see us any minute. Do you suppose you

could pull in your anchor so maybe we could drift out of their range while we talk?"

"Oh, *man* . . ."

Scrubbs sympathized. Here you come out on the river for a nice, peaceful early-morning bit of fishing, and you catch a man who tells you he's on the run from the UFO police. What would *you* do?

The man was shaking his head, as if trying to make Scrubbs vanish mentally. Just then the first shots zipped into the water a yard away.

"Sweet Jesus!" the man said. Quick as a flash he sliced the anchor line clean with a razor-sharp fillet knife and ducked under the gunwales. More shots were fired. Scrubbs heard one connect with the side of the boat, eliciting a "Damn!" from the crouching fisherman.

But the boat, borne by the current, was drifting rapidly away from the island, and in minutes they were under the Memorial Bridge and out of range.

"Thank you," Scrubbs spluttered. "Appreciate it." He was exhausted, frozen, and bleeding. He began to slip under. As his head went in, he felt arms pulling him into the boat.

Next thing he knew he was lying in the bottom of the boat, smelling gasoline and fish. Above him, he saw a 727 landing at Reagan National Airport.

The fisherman started the outboard. The boat buzzed south.

"Scrubbs," he said, wincing as he tried to pull the hook out of his thigh. "Nathan."

"Did I *ask* to know that? Do I *want* to know that?"

"You can drop me near the airport if you want."

The man shook his head again.

"Look at you," said the fisherman with a mixture of disgust and concern. "You're wet, stuck full of hooks. I've seen better looking *roadkill*. You're gonna get far."

"Ow!"

"And now you just sat on another of my seventy-nine-cent triple hooks. I'm going to have to ruin that hook to get it out of you. Plus you're sitting on my *fish*. Nothin' much going right for you today. Now what's this you telling me, about UFO's?"

"The government is afraid of what I know about UFO's." No sense in hitting him with the entire history of MJ-12 at this hour of the morning.

"Hm." The man snorted. "You from Saint Lizbeth's?"

"No. I know this must sound strange."

"It *does*."

"I'm too tired to lie."

"Hm." But it was a gentler *hm*.

"I seen a UFO once. In the Chesapeake Bay. *Three* of 'em. One red, one blue, one sorta yellow. Crisscrossing like fireflies, except they weren't no bugs. I could see that. Know what I'm saying?"

"I do."

"I told my wife about it, and she said, 'You been *drinking*.' I said the only *drinking* that was going on was in those UFO's, from the way they were driving. Never seen such a thing. Never have since."

He was warming to the subject. "What I don't *get* is—if they so damn intelligent to come *all* the way here from wherever it is, how come they don't just set down on the president's lawn over there like they do in the movies and say, 'Okay, we're here. *Deal* with the situation.' Know what I'm saying? Make a hell of lot more sense than drunk drivin' over the Chesapeake. What is *that* supposed to prove? That they're *intelligent*? If that's all they got to do, they aren't no more *intelligent* than humans." He stared at Scrubbs. "But they may be one up on *you*."

"Don't doubt that."

"Do you have money?"

"I'll give you what I've got. It's not much."

"I didn't say I *want* your money, did I? There's easier ways of making money than catching fugitives in the Potomac."

He shook his head again. He seemed to be trying to reach a decision. Scrubbs knew that much depended on whatever it was.

Suddenly the man turned the outboard throttle to the right, angling the boat east, away from the airport.

"Where we going?" Scrubbs asked.

"We are *going* to get you some dry clothes. Then we'll *see* about getting you some running money."

"Thank you," Scrubbs said.

"Don't think you're getting something for nothing. So you know about UFO's. Do you *know* about hanging Sheetrock?"

"Huh?"

"Well, you going to *learn* about Sheetrock."

TWELVE

Heads turned as Banion and Roz strode through the stony corridors of the U.S. Capitol. Roz's heels clickety-clicked with executive staccato.

A few courageous souls greeted Banion with brief handshakes. Most gave fleeting glances and noncommittal nods of recognition and hurried on, despite their curiosity over why Mr. UFO was now prowling the halls of Congress. What on earth did *he* want here?

He was a celebrity again, but of quite a different sort. *Saturday* had become the number 11 show in the country. *TV Guide* had put him on its cover, dubbing him Mr. Millennium. In New York and Los Angeles, TV networks were holding meetings to explore how quickly they might mount their own UFO-related talk shows. Meanwhile, Gooey-Lube was lubricating as fast as it could. Millions of American automobiles hummed frictionlessly along the highways.

In the newspapers, pundits and critics were scratching their heads over the show's success. One *Times* columnist, quoting heavily from Yeats's "Second Coming"—things falling apart, the center not holding, mere anarchy being loosed upon the world, etc.—called it "ultimate PMS—PreMillennial Syndrome." The news sections of the papers showed that, indeed, the country was having difficulty adjusting to the new time zone. More nutty cultists were taking the plunge. Most recently, three dozen people, convinced by their leader that apocalypse was imminent, had committed mass suicide by holding hands and leaping off one of the more popular tourist vistas in the Grand Canyon, creating a nasty cleanup job for the poor Park Service. (The cult's leader decided at the last minute not to take the plunge and was later arrested in the first-class lounge of the Phoenix airport.) Everywhere, fundamentalist preachers were discerning portents that God's patience with mankind's villainy was finally exhausted; the only question was, what form would His wrath assume? A murderous, tsunami-causing asteroid? Massive volcanic eruptions ushering in permanent atmospheric winter? Or did He have something more . . . lurid up His sleeve, some pestilence, perhaps, that would make the biblical plague of boils look like a mere case of teenage zits? It didn't help that Southern California chose this moment to have one of its semi-spectacular earthquakes.

"Shouldn't we have called him to ask for an appointment?" Roz said.

"He wouldn't have given us one if we had," Banion said. "And this will give us the element of surprise." A senator he knew well pretended not to notice Banion as he breezed by.

"They used to hurl themselves at me when I came here, all of them begging to be on the show. Now look at them, rats. Scurrying."

They had arrived at a doorway with a proud, unambiguous sign above proclaiming SENATORS ONLY.

"This is where they put their coats?" Roz asked.

"It's just called the Cloakroom. They used to hang their cloaks there. It's where they hang out and devise ways of thwarting the will of the people. Where they discuss their deals. Their little *deals.*"

"You're Mr. Banion, aren't you?" It was a uniformed Capitol Hill policeman.

"Yes," Banion preened.

"I saw your show on TV. The one with that lady who takes pictures of cows with the—that was *nasty*."

"It's a nasty situation."

"What they ought to do is take all those hamburgers that are making people sick, and feed them to the aliens."

"I'll pass that suggestion along. We're looking for Senator Gracklesen."

"He's on the floor. They're voting."

Banion and Roz stood awkwardly outside the Senate Cloakroom while people came and went, giving Banion surprised looks.

"I feel like a lobbyist," Roz said. "I've never met a senator before. A congressman once made a pass at me."

"We'll use you as bait. When Gracklesen comes out, undress and hurl yourself at him."

"Is he going to talk to us?"

"I doubt it. But I want to be able to say on the show that I gave him every chance. Before"—Banion grinned evilly—"I ruin his life."

"Why is everyone going to drop everything and march on Washington? Not that you aren't persuasive. I mean, here I am." True enough, Roz had given up her job as editor of *Cosmospolitan* to become executive director of 4-A (Americans Against Alien Abductions). She had become indispensable to him, much to the jealous consternation of Dr. Falopian and Colonel Murfletit. They spent all day with each other. If only, Banion yearned, she would spend the rest of the time with him. But despite the inklings he had that she was fond of him, Roz insisted that their relationship be strictly professional. He was hopelessly in love, but too correct to press the point. There were times when he wished he had not been brought up so well.

"They'll come," he said confidently. "Think about it. If they've got nothing better to do than watch television on Saturday mornings, they have time to spare a few days to come to Washington to scare the crap out of their elected representatives."

"Maybe. But wouldn't it be embarrassing to threaten Senator Gracklesen with all these barbarians at the gate and then have no one show up?"

"I have twenty-five million regular viewers. How many regular hitters are we getting on the web site?"

"Four or five million."

"So thirty million. If half of one percent show up, that's a hundred and fifty thousand people. That's a lot of Porta Potties on the Mall. Why, hello, Senator."

"Jaack Baanion, you son of a gun! Lemme lookatcha!" Sen. Raysor Mentallius of Wyoming was, at age ninety-two, the eighth oldest member of the United States Senate, ancient, perhaps, but enormously influential by virtue of being chairman of the Senate Hindsight Committee, always referred to in the press as the "*powerful* Senate Hindsight Committee."* He and Banion went back many years. He had been a regular and, by virtue of his engaging, folksy manner, highly popular guest on *Sunday with John Oliver Banion*. In additional to his other charms, Senator Mentallius was a keen appreciator of feminine beauty, a trait he expressed by groping every woman he met. In the old days, this was of course standard practice among senators. In the era of political correctness it was not, but he managed to persist in his tactile enthusiasms by pretending to be functionally blind. His manual explorations of the opposite sex appeared to be nothing more than a harmless form of full-body Braille. The fact was that, in private, he read without glasses.

"They told me they put you in a *loony* bin!"

"They had to let me out." Banion smiled. "I made too much noise banging my cup against the bars."

"*That's* the way!" the senator said, embarking on a free-ranging, five-minute reminiscence of arguable relevance about his experiences in boot camp in the Army in the 1930s. He had

---

* Established when it was determined that there were more committees than there are members of Congress.

taken part in the Normandy beach landings and could recite from memory the whole of the "Once more unto the breach" soliloquy from *Henry V*. Indeed, he frequently did recite it. During his famous filibuster in the early 1950s he had read aloud to the Senate the whole of Shakespeare. It took a while.

"And who is this dee-*lightful* creature?" he said, fastening Roz's upper arm in a bony death grip. Banion had to admire the man's Jurassic libido.

"This is Miss Well, my assistant."

"*That's* the way!" he winked.

"He means executive director," Roz said. "I'm pleased to meet you, Senator."

"Not half as pleased as I am to see *you*. Shall I compare thee to a summer's day?"

Roz blushed.

"Jack, don't you be selfish. You bring this majestic young lady to see me sometime, you hear? I will explain to her the ways and means of this *august* body. You been in the papers too much lately, Jack. You need anything? You all right?"

"As a matter of fact, I do. I need Hank Gracklesen."

Senator Mentallius snorted. "I've heard of higher aspirations than that." He turned his attention back to drooling over Roz. "I knew a Roz. Rosalind Russell. Actress. *Fine* woman. She paid me a visit. Must have been back in . . . where does the time go?"

"What I need," Banion pressed on, "falls under the purview of his committee. But he's in the middle of a vote."

"Then let's do you *and* the Republic a favor and get him off the floor." With that Senator Mentallius reached out and grabbed the ID neck chain of a passing aide, nearly strangling him in the process. The aide started to protest, until he realized who it was who was garroting him.

"Sir?" he said, rubbing his throat.

"Go in there and fetch Senator Gracklesen and bring him out here. Quick, now."

"But they're voting on—"

"Just *do* it, son. I'm timing you with my watch here. You *hurry.* You bring him right here to me. You tell him I want to see him."

The aide scurried off.

Senator Mentallius took Banion's hand warmly. "I'm tempted to stay just to see the look on his face, but I got to go meet with the Joint Chiefs. They're trying to talk me into giving them a coupla new aircraft carriers." He chuckled. "Now you come see me if they try to put you back in that loony bin, you hear?" He took Roz's hand. "Young lady, I expect to see more of you. Good-bye, now. Good-bye."

"Well," Banion said after he had gone, "now you've been groped by members of the lower and upper house."

"He's a piece of work," Roz said.

A few minutes later, Sen. Hank Gracklesen appeared in the doorway with a look of votus interruptus, accompanied by the fretful aide.

"What's the meaning of this?"

"I want abduction hearings, Hank."

A look of outrage spread like fire across the savanna of Senator Gracklesen's face. "Just *who* are you to pull me off the floor in the middle of a vote and make demands?"

"A taxpayer?" Banion said.

"I'm going back in there."

"With a hit TV show and twenty-five million viewers."

"Bully for you."

"And I'm going to tell them to march on Washington if you don't hold hearings."

Senator Gracklesen's progress back to the floor was momentarily arrested. Banion could see the harried cogitations taking place inside the senatorial cerebrum: UFO convention . . . Revolt of the Mushrooms . . . nothing happened, some mail, no big deal, bunch of losers grousing about being diddled by aliens . . . a nutcase . . . new TV show? . . . about flying saucers? . . . so what . . . he's bluffing.

A smile appeared on the legislative visage.

"Jack, I'm going to say something to you that I don't get many chances to say, as a United States senator—fuck off."

"Shall I put you down as undecided, leaning against?"

"Go *away*."

"All right, Hank, but don't say that you weren't warned."

Senator Gracklesen then reached out, took Roz's hand as if it belonged to an admiring constituent, shook it, and said, "Good to meet you, thanks for coming by."

"Are they all like that?" she said after he had stormed off.

"Let's see how he feels when he looks out his office window onto the Mall and sees a hundred and fifty thousand people chanting for his head."

CIGAR-CHOMPING ANDY CROCANELLI PACED IN A SWEATY fret at the edge of the set.

"You can't smoke that in here," a technician said.

"Do you know who I fucking am?"

"No, who the fuck are you?"

"Andy," Banion said, sitting in his chair going over his notes. "Relax. It's going to be fine."

"Fine? The fucking lawyers say we could fucking get indicted for inciting violence."

"Try that sentence again, but this time leave out the word fucking. You'll get twice as much said, in half the time. I'm not going to tell them to attack the government with pitchforks and torches. I'm calling for a march. If you can't march on your capital, then what's the point in having one? There are precedents. So relax. Think about all the money you're going to make when they drive to Washington in their lubricated cars."

"I gotta go sit down. I don't feel good."

"Why don't you watch from the Little Green Room?" Banion said.

"Thirty seconds," the technician called out.

Roz, lovely in a green mini, came forward and brushed his mop back with her hand.

"Give 'em hell." She winked.

"Five seconds . . . three . . . two . . . one."

The music was cued. Banion introduced himself. He decided that, given the importance of what was about to follow, he would dispense with the usual "But first, this word from Gooey-Lube." Instead he said, "But first, this message."

The commercial ended, and he began his carefully prepared text for the day, a brilliant précis of the government's more than fifty years of denials and dissemblings about UFO's. He recounted his own attempts to get Senator Gracklesen's committee to open hearings, including accosting him outside the Senate Cloakroom. (He graciously left out the senator's crude valedictory.)

As he was talking about the great protest marches of the past, he realized that something was amiss. The director's face had taken on a look of grave concern bordering on panic. He had sneaked off to a far corner of the studio and was talking excitedly into his microphone. The two cameramen, normally the most stolid inhabitants of a TV studio, were exchanging nervous glances and wheeling their cameras to and fro, as if the sedentary Banion had suddenly become the lead car in the Indianapolis 500 race and they were at pains to keep up with him.

What on earth? It didn't make his job any easier. Banion did not speak from prepared texts and disdained TelePrompTers. It was all he could do to keep from losing the thread of his talk, but he managed to press on: a show of force, massive crowds, that was the thing. Only if they—the people—demanded action would the government act. Nothing less would do than a Millennium Man March on Washington! Who was a "Millennium Man"? Everyone who had seen a UFO, who had been abducted, probed, terrorized, or otherwise affected by alien beings. The time was—now.

"And so," he concluded, "until we meet two weeks from now on democracy's front lawn, the Mall in Washington, D.C., this is John O. Banion."

The theme music started up. He sat back in his chair while the credits rolled, eager to find out what the problem was, impatient to find out what the problem was. From the back of the studio he heard raised voices and the phrase "chest pains" in connection with Andy Crocanelli. The director approached at a pace suggesting that he was not eager to bear this news.

THE HEADLINE GLOWERED UP AT HIM FROM THE FRONT PAGE of the Sunday paper. Variations on it adorned every paper spread out before him.

CLOSE ENCOUNTERS OF THE KINKY KIND
VIEWERS OF BANION UFO SHOW
EXPRESS OUTRAGE OVER AIRING
OF ADULT MOVIE ON MORNING UFO SHOW

Banion forced himself to read the article one last time.

The Federal Communications Commission is investigating complaints from thousands of viewers of John O. Banion's popular new TV show about UFO's, after yesterday's live show transmitted graphic clips from an adult movie called *Space Bimbos from Planet Lust*.

Banion and his producers strenuously denied that it was deliberate. At the time of the broadcast, the movie was being shown on the Yearning Channel, a twenty-four-hour pornographic movie channel. Producers of *Saturday* were at a loss to explain how sections of the movie, featuring naked astronauts having sex in weightless environments, ended up on their program.

"We are pursuing our own investigation into this," Banion said, "but at this point the indications are that this was an act of sabotage aimed at stopping me from forcing the government to reveal what it knows about the continuing abduction of American citizens by aliens."

He wondered if the quote made him sound like a paranoid loon. Its only advantage was that it was true. It had to be sabotage. If it wasn't, then it was clear evidence that God hated him. This was not a possibility that Banion, a practicing Episcopalian, was prepared to admit, at least for the time being.

Yesterday should have been a triumph. Instead, it had been hell. He spent most of it fielding furious calls from various UFO groups. Andy Crocanelli was still in the hospital, having had some kind of cardiac "event," as the doctors called it. His hysterical wife was shrieking that they had tried to kill him in order to get rid of him as a sponsor. If he died, she said she was going to quote "sue" Banion's "nuts off." Bimmerman, the producer, was trying to find out how the Yearning Channel's broadcast of unspeakable goings-on aboard a space shuttle had found itself on *Saturday*. Their satellite distributor didn't know. No one knew. The FCC was playing it bureaucratically straight-faced, focusing on the complaints rather than the cause.

Once more, Banion found himself besieged by reporters, who were swarming anew like reënergized locusts. Once again he was the stuff of hooting headlines. Crews from disreputable tabloid shows were camped out on the sidewalk in front of the house. Tomorrow, Monday, the first tabloids would hit the stands. There he would be, on the covers, no doubt, sharing scandal space with overweight and over-the-hill actors, unhappy royals, and plastic-surgery accidents. He could hardly wait. He wished now that he hadn't left the studio with his head slunk down like a mafia don entering the courthouse to be sentenced for shooting his former mentor outside a restaurant.

John O. Banion had a headache.

Roz called. She was at the office, spinning the media as hard as she could, telling them that this only strengthened the resolve of Americans Against Alien Abductions. But to Banion she admitted that it was tough going. Jokes were going around, and once you were the butt of those . . .

"I'm *sorry*," she said. "This should have been such a triumph for you. Do you want me to come over, bring you some chicken soup or something?"

He did. But he didn't want a photo of his attractive executive director entering his house to appear on the cover of some tabloid with some screaming headline like BANION'S REAL-LIFE BABE. But he wanted nothing more than for Roz to come over. Maybe she'd even sleep with him, just to make him feel better.

"Better not." He sighed.

NATHAN SCRUBBS WAS LEARNING ABOUT HANGING DRY-wall. So far, he had learned that he did not want to hang drywall in his next career. However, it did provide an atmosphere free of people trying to kill him.

Bradley, the man who had rescued him, lived near the river in Anacostia, a part of Washington that white people by and large tended to avoid, and where, paradoxically, Scrubbs now felt safe. Bradley was divorced and lived alone. Scrubbs had use of a mattress on the floor of a spare room. It wasn't the Ritz, but it was shelter in this strange storm.

True to his promise, Bradley woke him out of a sound sleep at five o'clock the next morning and put him to work with the rest of his crew, installing Sheetrock in a town house in a part of town hovering on a thin wedge of gentrification.

Scrubbs had been taken aback when Bradley introduced him to the other members of his work crew as a fugitive.

Stunned, Scrubbs accepted high fives and hearty congratulatory hellos from his new colleagues.

When opportunity presented itself, he took Bradley aside. "Why did you tell them that?"

"You the only white man on the crew, aren't you?"

"So?"

"Don't you *want* to be accepted?"

"What if they turn me in? Jesus."

Bradley chuckled. "I don't think any of *them* is going to be calling the police. And leave the Lord out of it. A man on the run makes a sad blasphemer. Now get back to work. I'll *tell* you when the coffee break is."

At the end of the first day, when they got back home, Bradley handed him a ten-dollar bill.

"Ten bucks? For busting my hump all day? That won't cover the aspirin I need for my back."

"I deducted your expenses."

"What expenses?"

"The hole in my fishing boat from your friends' bullets. The hooks I ruined pullin' them out of you. Rent on the room. And your donut and coffee this morning."

"God bless the cheerful giver," Scrubbs grumbled.

" 'Rejoice in the Lord, O ye righteous: For it becometh well the just to be thankful.' "

"Whatever. Thought they abolished slavery."

"Not so's I noticed. But if you can do better at McDonald's, be my guest, and while you're *at* it, you can bring me back a couple of Quarter Pounders. With fries and a large Coke."

"SOMEONE WHO SAYS HE HAS IMPORTANT INFORMATION about the satellite business," Renira said. "He won't say who he is."

There had been a lot of these calls the last two days. The angry calls had almost stopped entirely. The ones coming in now were almost all sympathetic.

Dr. Falopian and Colonel Murfletit were in his office with some former military type who did satellite security, going over preparations for ensuring the electronic integrity of next Saturday's broadcast, assuming there was one. Andy Crocanelli had pulled through his cardiac event, but his wife was adamant that he could not have stress and was threatening to pull Gooey-Lube's sponsorship if Banion went ahead with his call for a march on Washington. Banion's lawyer, Barrett Prettyman, Jr., was threatening Mrs. Crocanelli with head-spinning breach of contract. The once happy *Saturday* family now resembled most other families: dysfunctional, miserable.

Banion decided to take the call.

"I cannot discuss how I know what I am about to tell you," said the caller, an intelligent-sounding male in his forties or so. But then most nuts, including presidential assassins, are forty-ish, intelligent-sounding males. "If you have caller ID you will already have determined that I am calling from a pay telephone in Los Angeles. That narrows your search to three and a half million people. That is all you will find out about me, so just listen to what I have to say."

"Fine," Banion said, doodling the word ROZ on a notepad.

"I am an admirer, Mr. Banion. You are doing important work. That is why I have compromised a Yankee White security clearance to place this call. So much for my bona fides. Now as to the purpose of my call. Last Saturday, a jamming signal was directed at the Geostar satellite carrying your television show. It came from another satellite designated *Thruster Six*. It uses an EHF—that is, extremely high frequency—relay system called Polar Adjunct. But never mind all that. The point is that *Thruster Six* blocked the signal of your show and substituted the signal of the sex movie. Not a bad movie, I must say, as those go—no reflection on your own show."

Banion was paying full attention. "And who operates *Thruster Six*?"

The voice laughed softly. "Who do you think has the capability to operate such a satellite?"

"The government?"

"Don't ask me for further details. I'm not in a position to provide them. They are trying to silence you, Mr. Banion. They are afraid of you. Fight them. You have friends in many places. We are with you. Good-bye, sir. Good luck!"

Hours of heated debate in Banion's office followed the call. Dr. Falopian and Colonel Murfletit were of divided opinion. Falo-

pian thought the man was a fraud. In his view, the satellite sig-
nals could only have been tampered with by one source—the
aliens. They had motive—to stop Banion's call for the march.
They had know-how—for them, it was a local telephone call.
And they had, as he put it with a flourish of his bushy eyebrows, the wit. Time and again, the aliens had shown themselves
to be adept manipulators of public opinion.

Colonel Murfletit was less sure. He was intrigued by the man's
mention of his Yankee White security clearance, one of the very
highest in the military—the same one given to pilots entrusted
with flying the president of the United States. Could it be, he
wondered, that the man piloted the black helicopters that the
military used to enforce control of the civilian population?

Of course, there was no way of establishing, much less con-
firming, that the satellite jamming had been the work of a black
gang from NSA.* And what folly it would be to charge them
publicly. They had means of retaliation at their disposal.

Falopian and Murfletit went at it like medieval scholars arguing over the metallurgy of the Holy Grail. Banion listened until
he went back to doodling Roz's name. He concluded that (a) the
caller was for real, (b) his show had been sabotaged, and (c) there
was nothing he could do but push ahead, assuming (d) that anyone out there still cared.

Falopian and Murfletit finally arrived at a synthesis: the government had effected the sabotage, in *collusion* with the aliens.
The two had been working together for years as it was. It made
perfect sense that they should combine resources at this critical
juncture.

But they had to have someone on the inside. Thus Dr. Falopian and Colonel Murfletit planted the tumorous thought that
there was among them a spy.

Banion said nothing. The clear implication was that it was

---

* National Security Agency, the government agency that listens in on all your phone
calls.

Roz. Inwardly, he scoffed. It was hardly a disinterested conjecture on their part. They had both taken a dislike to her from that very first moment at the UFO convention in Austin. They looked upon her as a cosmic Yoko Ono, ruiner of cozy male comradeship. She'd been nothing but trouble from the start. Her suggestion that their pair of eminent Russians were nothing but post-Soviet con men—what cheek! Then, too, Banion mused, there was the pantingly obvious fact that these two space muffins yearned to have sex with her. No, it was ridiculous.

He dismissed them, saying that his headache had reached violent proportions and he was going home. He would, like Scarlett, think about it tomorrow. Roz was going to cook dinner for him, her specialty, macaroni ai quattro formaggi, his favorite, the perfect Italian dish for a blancmange WASP appetite: macaroni and four cheeses.

"Jack! Over here! Jack!"

The lens- and microphone-wielding horde was waiting for him on the red-brick sidewalk outside his office. He forced his zygomatic muscles into an approximation of a smile—what effort it took—and stepped into their range like a man bravely baring his chest to the firing squad. He leaned on his cane, a light malacca that had once belonged to Fatty Arbuckle.

"And what can I do for you gentlemen today?"

"What's the latest?"

"Our switchboards are flooded. They want to know if we're showing the rest of *Space Bimbos* next Saturday."

The paparazzi laughed. There. They had their bite. They were, for the time being, defanged. He stood with his chest bared while they fired away at him until they were out of bullets.

"Thank you," he said, walking away, knowing that they would not bother to follow now.

He walked, unhindered and alone, to the little house on Dumfiddle Street that he had moved into. A light rain slicked the bricks. He became so lost in troubled thoughts that he took a wrong turn on N Street. He couldn't shake the nasty suggestion that Falopian and Murfletit had dumped on his desk. Had he, who so yearned to penetrate, been penetrated first?

He found his way home. Warm, delicious cheesy smells embraced him, shortly followed by Roz, in white leggings and sheer top that showed off her breasts in heartbreaking detail. He could not persist in this insistent chasteness of hers much longer. She kissed him with wine-wet lips.

She stood back and examined him. "Oh baby, you look *awful*."

Banion tossed his coat at the rack. "Long day. Spent the whole afternoon with the brain trust listening to conspiracy theories. I need . . . ibuprofen."

"An afternoon with those two would give anyone a headache. I'm sorry. I know Dr. Falopian is a nuclear scientist and Colonel Murfletit was in the Army for thirty-five years and saw the Roswell aliens, but they just seem so off-the-wall. Renira agrees with me, you know. She says they're 'off.' It's Brit for food that's gone bad. Hungry? It's all ready, I just need to stick it in the oven for twenty minutes."

"*Oh* that feels good," said Banion. "Rub lower."

"There?"

"Um. Roz?"

"Yeah, honey?"

"Are we ever going to . . . you know . . ."

"Do it?" she said cheerfully.

"Yes."

She kept rubbing and gave the back of his neck a brief kiss. "Like that?"

"It's a start. It's just that every time we do start, you say 'not yet.' When are we going to get to 'yet'?"

"Have you been watching porno movies again?"

"I'm serious."

"Why do we have to rush?"

"I may not be Leopold Capriano—"

"Who?"

"The one in that movie, *Titanic*."

"Leo DiCaprio."

"Whatever. I may not be a nineteen-year-old movie star—"

"No, you're not. You're a middle-aged, Episcopalian UFO wonk."

"Stop interrupting."

"But *I* think you're sexy."

"Then why—oh never mind. I'm not going to plead. It's undignified. The point I was trying to make was that I feel very close to you. I enjoy being with you. You make me laugh. I seem to afford you *some* enjoyment, or at least that's the indication you give."

"I love it when stuffy WASPs let down their hair."

"I assure you there's nothing awkward about me in the sack."

"Why does that sound like a George Bush acceptance speech?"

Banion realized with some dismay that in fact it *was* a paraphrase of George Bush's 1988 acceptance speech at the convention. He was hopeless as a lover. Perhaps with time. He turned around to face her. God, she was lovely, and she was smiling.

"What I meant was, I love you and I want to marry you."

The smile froze on Roz's face and melted. Then it came back at about one-third its previous strength. "That was sudden," she said.

"I propose to all women who make me macaroni with four cheeses. So how about it? Or do you want to see the size of the ring from Tiffany first? Actually, I don't have one on me. This wasn't really planned."

He knew he wasn't very good at reading women, but she did seem to be reeling. "I'm very fond of you, Jack."

"Now that's the sort of thing a WASP would say instead of *'Marry you? Are you nuts?'* Oh well." He reached over and kissed her, chastely, on the cheek. "Just something I needed to get off my chest. There's something sexy about sleeping on the couch, even if it's tough on the back."

Now she kissed him, and there was nothing chaste about it. It was, he reflected later, the longest kiss he had ever had. By the time it was over, both their eyeglasses were on the floor, his hair looked like a tornado had moved through it, and his lips were numb. His vision was blurred, but perhaps that was from the glasses.

They sat up and looked—as best they could—into each other's eyes with that unembarrassed intensity lovers exchange after the first caresses. When the silence was finally broken, it was by Roz, who said, "Well . . . maybe we should move into the kitchen. I'll fix you some—"

The word dinner was preempted by another kiss, this one even more confident and exploratory, ranging from one earlobe to the other. There was also some whistling of air in and out of the ear, generally a prelude to more ardent goings-on elsewhere. When they came up for air, they were on the floor next to the couch.

"Dinner first." She smiled. "Then . . . dessert."

She rearranged herself and padded off on bare soles to the kitchen. Banion, utterly content, remained on the floor, sipping the remains of her wine. He listened to the comforting sounds of food being prepared for him. At heart, all men want to be cooked for. But first, there was business.

"I have to go out later," he called to her.

"How come?"

"I got a call today. Out of the blue. Someone who says he works for the government and can provide me proof that they tampered with the satellite transmission. He sounded for real. We're going to meet. He says he'll provide me with proof that I can take to the media."

Roz appeared in the kitchen doorway, holding a wooden salad spoon. Her short blond hair was mussed. Her glasses made her look schoolgirlish. He had never desired a woman this much. *Please give the right answer,* Banion said to himself.

"What makes you think it's for real?"

"Just a hunch, really. He sounded for real. Sometimes you can just tell about people"—he smiled—"even if you're a dull old WASP."

"I don't think you should go."

"Oh, I'm going. If this guy has proof, I want it. Wild horses couldn't keep me from going."

"I think it's a setup."

"Why?"

"I just do. Why would someone from the government want to help you?"

"Good question. Guess I'll find out."

She went back into the kitchen. "What time are you meeting him?" she called out.

"Eleven oh-three," he said. "That made me think he's for real. Military and intelligence types set precise appointment times to eliminate confusion and ambiguity. Nothing ambiguous about eleven oh-three."

"Where are you meeting this guy?"

"National Cathedral. Gazebo in the Bishop's Garden. It's a pretty spot. I used to go there sometimes just to clear my head, or if Bitsey and I had had a dustup. It's made from the stones from Grover Cleveland's house there."

"*Shoot.*"

"What's the matter?"

"I forgot the Pecorino."

"What's Pecorino?"

"A kind of Romano. One of the four cheeses."

"So *make macaroni ai tre formaggi.*"

"No such thing."

She emerged from the kitchen, slipped on shoes, and took her jacket and purse off the rack.

"Won't take two secs. I'll just walk over to the Griffin."

"I'll go with you."

"No." She leaned over and kissed him. "Go take a nice hot shower." She smiled. "Or a cold one. Be back in five minutes. Dinner in fifteen. Open another bottle of wine."

She was out the door in a flash. Banion went into the kitchen. He stepped on the foot pedal of the trash bin. The lid flipped open. He rummaged. He found what he was looking for under the empty bag of pasta—a discarded piece of plastic wrapping with a Sutton Place Gourmet cheese section sticker on it with yesterday's date and the words PECORINO ROMANO.

"DELICIOUS," BANION SAID. THEY WERE AT THE TABLE; THE candles were lit. He'd drunk most of the second bottle of wine to get up the courage and to deaden certain parts of his brain and body.

Roz smiled curiously at him. "First thing you've said."

"How long have you been working for them?"

She didn't look up. "Working for who?"

Banion reached into his pocket and passed the cheese wrapping, neatly, WASPly, folded to show the labeling, across the table to her.

"I *knew* I'd bought some. I must have tossed it out with the—"

"Don't. You went to phone them about my rendezvous."

She put down her fork. She dabbed at her mouth. Her head was down, avoiding eye contact. "I thought you were walking into a trap," she said quietly and deliberately. "No one from our—from this side would have called you today. I was worried for you."

"I see you only like it when I walk into one of your traps." Banion drained what was left of his glass. "Have you been working for them from the beginning? Or is this more along the lines of a betrayal?"

"I can't go into it, but don't leap to conclusions. You can't possibly have this figured out."

"So, what branch of government is it that discredits UFO believers? CIA? FBI? Or are we dealing with some more exotic acronym here?"

"Sweetheart—"

"*Please.*"

He saw tears in her eyes. Good.

"It's not what you think."

"Well, that's a relief."

"I can't go into it. You're not cleared."

"Cleared? *Cleared?*"

She said hotly, with what seemed to be genuine professional concern for ethics, "Do you want me to commit a security violation?"

"Oh no. We can't have *that!*" He stood, suppressing the strong urge to smack her and start hurling objects. He reeled with wine and rage. He wandered over to the fireplace, where men feel comfortable indulging in philosophical outburst, a nice roaring fire at their backs. "So the government and the aliens *are* in it together," he muttered. "Of course. The government had to know, after all. How could they *not* know?"

"Jack, I swear, you've got this wrong."

Banion laughed bitterly. "So your job is to discredit people who make too big a deal out of it. Who threaten the *arrangement*. But how does editing a magazine for women abductees come in?"

Roz started to answer.

"No," Banion interrupted. "Let me figure this out for myself. To manipulate public opinion with respect to UFO's. Gain the readers' confidence, steer them in this or that direction, as the situation requires. It's all about *management,* isn't it?"

"I'm not in a position to talk about it."

"I go down to a UFO conference. And what do you know— there you are. Looking quite the dish. Boy meets girl. And what's the first thing the girl does? Discredits the Russians. Of course."

"Those Russians are frauds."

" 'Oh, Mr. Banion, I'm so thrilled to meet you! I can't wait to be abducted myself.' What a crock."

"I was doing my job."

"Oh, well, fine, never mind. Next thing—surprise!—you show up in Washington after Bitsey and I split, and nature almost takes its course, except that your contract doesn't call for you to sleep with me. But I respect that much. Then tonight. Tonight it started to get more interesting. Did they change your orders? Tell me one thing—what escort service did they recruit you from?"

Roz looked at him with wet, angry eyes. "That wasn't part of the assignment."

"I'm flattered."

She went upstairs. A door slammed loudly.

"If there's any storming off to be done," he yelled up at her, "it's going to be done by *me*. This is my house, and *I* will storm out of it."

So for the second time in almost as many months, John O. Banion stormed out of a house in Georgetown into the night.

He marched down the street and spent a fitful, sleepless night at the Four Seasons Hotel.

When he returned the next morning, she was gone. On the pillow was a note.

> *Too late for a lecture about poking around in the garbage, but you really do have it wrong. And last night wasn't part of the assignment. Sorry it turned out this way. I really was looking forward to dessert.*
>
> *Love, still*
> *R*

THIRTEEN

Scrubbs's interest in hanging drywall was rapidly approaching endgame.

When Bradley's back was turned, he ducked out early for his morning coffee break to hazard a phone call to the office. He walked to the nearest Metro station, took the subway halfway across town, and from a pay phone three blocks from the station dialed the number, his only connection to his former life.

"Creative Solutions," came the cheery female voice, "how may I direct your call?"

"It's Scrubbs."

"Stand by, please."

A male voice came on, the same one he'd spoken with before, Mr. Majestic.

"Nathan?"

"You double-crossing rat bastard."

"Are you all right? We've been worried."

"Don't give me that. And don't bother sending more of your goons. I'm going to hang up in one minute. I just want to tell you that you're a piece of—"

"Calm down. Take a deep breath."

"You tried to kill me!"

"Negative, negative. That was not us."

"*Bull.*"

"No. Believe me. Dark forces are at work here. Things are not what they seem."

"You've got forty-five seconds."

"We've been compromised. Another element has become involved."

"Speak English."

"Another agency of government, also not chartered by the founding fathers, has become involved. They monitored our phone conversation. They got their people to the island before ours. That was their man you blew up, not ours. By the way, they're very upset with you for doing that."

"*They're* upset? They tried to kill me."

"Write a letter to your congressman. Meanwhile, they're looking for you, and they're looking hard. And they think you're still working for us, so now we're in the middle of a shooting war with them. All because of your Banion stunt. It's like a mafia feud. It's embarrassing. We're supposed to be above that. We're the government. Do you have any idea how this could impact our budget request next fiscal year?"

"Screw your budget. I'm out on the street."

"Exactly why we have to bring you in. Stay by that pay phone. I'll have a bagger team there in ten minutes."

"*Negative.* I'm hanging up in fifteen seconds. Mail me some money and a passport. You'll never hear from me again. I promise."

"It doesn't work that way, Nathan. We have to bring you in, for your safety, and ours. If this other group gets to you . . . I don't even want to think about it, and you don't either. These are not nice people."

"Stop being mysterious. Who are they?"

"I can't get into that, not over the phone. The situation is very volatile."

"I'm hanging up. Maybe I'll call again, maybe I won't."

"Don't—"

Scrubbs hung up.

He rolled his work bandanna down over his forehead, adjusted his dark glasses, looked over his shoulder, and caught the subway back to the job site.

On the train, in a funk, he processed this new information, trying to decide what other government agency could be after him. Or was this a trick on Mr. Majestic's part, to get him to come in, so that they could silence him once and for all? If he was telling the truth and two highly covert government agencies were shooting it out like New York City mob families breaking each other's legs over who got the garbage hauling contracts for the Bronx, with Scrubbs in the middle . . . Oh man, what a mess. The sooner he was out of Washington, the better. But they'd be watching airports, the train station, the bus station. And Bradley wasn't about to hand over the keys to his car.

The woman next to him was reading the paper. He hadn't seen one in days. His eyes strayed to it. There was a photo of Banion standing in front of a bank of microphones.

BANION ALLEGES "SABOTAGE" OF TV SHOW

"Do you *mind*?" the woman said.

"Sorry." Why do people mind your reading over their shoulders? Are you stealing the ink?

He got off the train at his stop and bought his own copy of the *Post*. He read:

> UFO talk show host John O. Banion charged today that the U.S. government "sabotaged" his live TV broadcast last Saturday using a top-secret military satellite, jammed the normal transmission, and substituted pornographic images as part of an effort to discredit him and prevent him from announcing a UFO protest march on Washington.

The article ended with a spokesman from the Pentagon refusing to comment on the existence of a satellite designated

Thruster Six while emphatically denying that it would ever be used to broadcast dirty movies.

Scrubbs scratched his head. Millennium Man March? Accusing the government of trying to discredit him? The man was like a dog with a bone. He wouldn't let go. As for the government trying to discredit him—if only he knew. They must be freaked out about this march to pull a stunt like jamming him with space porn. He reread the paragraph that quoted some of the more memorable lines of dialogue from the movie: *"Houston, we have an erection!"*

Who had done this to Banion? MJ-12? Or this other agency Mr. Majestic was talking about?

He thought, It was smart of Banion to go public with this. Now they can't just make him disappear. The newspaper article said that the Pentagon was being "deluged" with phone calls from outraged UFO believers protesting the government's treatment of him. This thing was not going to go away. And that didn't bode well for Scrubbs. Ultimately this was all his fault, a point sure not to be lost on them. A transfer to a desert facility was probably not what they had in mind for him now. And yet, despite his intimations of doom, he couldn't help but cheer Banion on. *Go for it, pal. Give those bastards hell!*

"*Where* have you been?" Bradley said. "Coffee break is ten minutes. You been gone an *hour*."

"Hadda check in with the people trying to kill me."

"*And?*"

Scrubbs picked up a trowel, plunged it into a bucket of joint compound, and started smoothing. "They're still trying."

THE PRESIDENT OF THE UNITED STATES CLICKED OFF THE TV set in the Oval Office. No one said anything. It was, to be sure, an unusual situation. There were no precedents. Finally the president said, "Is he drinking?"

The chief of staff said, "My information is, no."

"He looked sober to me," the press secretary said.

"It's got to be a psychological breakdown of some kind," the chief of staff said. "Delusional paranoia. Burt Galilee says they tried an intervention on him, even had a shrink standing by to take him off to someplace, and he bolted. You almost feel sorry for him."

"I wouldn't go that far."

"How many calls did the Pentagon get from these people?" the president asked.

"Thousands."

"White House?"

"Thousands."

"E-mail?"

"Hundreds of thousands. They believe him."

"So what?" the press secretary said. "These people are nuts. They'll believe anything."

"And there's nothing to this satellite business he's talking about?" the president said. "You checked?"

"Spoke with General Tunklebunker personally. *Thruster Six* is highly, highly classified. He didn't even like saying its name out loud."

"These military guys." The press secretary snorted. This drew a sharp look from the president, himself a former military guy.

The chief of staff continued, "The general said he would prefer it if the president did not speak publicly about *Thruster Six*. But he did emphatically deny that it's being used to show porn movies. He almost laughed at the idea, except that I don't think the general is a laughing type."

"So Banion is just plain crazy?" the president said.

"Certifiable."

"Is it some manic-depressive thing?"

"I'm not a psychiatrist. If you'd like, I can have someone from Bethesda Naval give us an opinion on that."

"No, no, no. Thank God he's not moderating the debates. Can you *imagine*?"

"I'm glad I was able to get that stopped," the press secretary said.

"I thought the League of Gay Voters stopped it."

"Well, I did talk to—"

"Okay," the chief of staff said, "we really need to decide how we want to handle the *Celeste* launch."

"Flickery's been hitting us hard on it," the campaign manager said. He read from notes. " 'Horrendous cost overruns' . . . 'shameless opportunism' . . . 'debasing the entire space program' . . . 'using billions of taxpayer dollars for cheap political—' "

"I saw his comments," the president said.

"He's backing us into a corner. If we don't attend the launch, it looks like he scared us off. If we do attend, we look like we orchestrated the whole thing for a photo op one week before the election. I'm lying awake at night waiting for some unnamed source within NASA to be quoted saying, 'We moved up the launch date to accommodate the White House.' "

"That won't happen," the chief of staff said. Just that morning he had had a very discreet heart-to-heart with Hedgepath, chief administrator of NASA, on this very subject: If anyone in your shop tells the press that the White House asked you to move up the launch date, you will find yourself on the street, designing balsa wood gliders.

The president puffed out his cheeks in thought. "Maybe we should give the launch a pass. It's the last week of the campaign. It's a busy time for someone running for president. The people understand."

"Disagree," the campaign manager said. "Strongly. No one is so busy that they don't have time to attend the 'crowning moment of the millennium.' You did call it that. You have to be there."

"Millennium. I'm sick of that word. It's a year with zeros in it. What's the big deal?"

"There were those," the chief of staff said, "who didn't think we should make a big deal out of it."

"Let's move forward." The president said this whenever the chief of staff subtly pointed out that the president had, in fact, created the present predicament.

The campaign manager said, "There are practical considerations. Hambro's people say if you don't go, it will look like you're insulting Florida."

"Oh for God's sake."

"We're seven points down in Florida. Do you want to risk twenty-five electoral votes?"

"What if I have to be somewhere else that day?"

"Kissing pigs in Illinois?"

The president's eyes narrowed. "I'm sure my handlers could find something better for me to do."

"I see Sid's point," the chief of staff interjected. "Even if you're addressing the UN General Assembly on world peace, it's still small potatoes next to being there when they're launching the final stage of the space station that's supposed to usher in the new—I know, I know—millennium."

"All right," the president said, "we'll do the launch."

"But we need cover," the campaign manager said. "It'll come up in the debates, for sure. Oppo says Flickery's planning to sock you hard. Ugly allegations about"—he cleared his throat—"manipulating the *Celeste* budget to . . . well, the old charges."

"Why don't I just say that, as commander in chief, I have an obligation to be there?"

"It's not a military deal," the campaign manager said. "It's a space station. It's about peace. That's what you've been emphasizing."

"It's *about* twenty-one billion dollars, most of which went to Texas and California. That's why this thing is such a hot potato."

"A space station with two-million-dollar toilet seats," the press secretary said. "What could be so complicated about—"

"Taking a crap in weightless environment? You try it."

"I still don't see why they cost two million dollars. You could crap in a coffee can for—"

"I didn't design it."

"I'm not saying you did."

"All right, all right," the president said, "let's stay focused, people. Just get me to the launch without making me look like a twenty-dollar hooker."

The Oval Office was silent for a moment.

"I say we just go and to hell with it," the chief of staff said. "Balls it out. Take the position, This is a great day for America, for the millennium. Whatever. And I as the president of the United States am damn well going to be there. Fuck you, strong letter follows."

The president raised an eyebrow.

"Here's how we handle it," the campaign manager said with a smile indicating that his brilliance had attained new heights. "We leak it that you're not going to attend. Why? Because your opponent has used the launch to score points for his own political gain. He has dragged the integrity of the U.S. space program into the gutter. And you, as president, will not let him get away with it. You are determined to keep the exploration of space above politics. This was a wrenching personal decision for you. You agonized over it. Your place is there with the brave American astronauts. But in the end, you didn't want to detract from the, the . . ."

"Grandeur."

"Grandeur of the occasion."

"So we don't go?"

"No, we do go. But you decide to go at the last minute, after . . . you read an interview with one of the astronauts, where he says—she says—that she wishes the president of the United States could be here to share this moving, patriotic moment."

"Hm," the president said. He turned to his chief of staff and said, pregnantly, "What are the chances an astronaut might say that during an interview?"

"I would guess"—the chief of staff scribbled a note: *Hedgepath—need interview with girl astronaut*—"astronauts do a lot of interviews before the launch."

"It could be poignant," the press secretary said.

The president looked out the French doors into the Rose Garden, where squirrels were foraging for fall nuts. "I think, under such circumstances, I'd really be obliged to go. Wouldn't I?"

"No question," the campaign manager said.

FOURTEEN

MASSIVE CROWDS EXPECTED IN CAPITAL
THIS WEEK FOR "MILLENNIUM MAN" MARCH
Hotels, airlines, trains, buses
report "record" bookings

Police, Park Service, Cancel Leaves
National Guard May Assist with Logistics

Scrubbs was now following the newspapers with keen interest. He took another long coffee break—Bradley docked him five dollars' pay every time—and rode the Metro to a distant part of Washington, where he placed another call to Mr. Majestic.

"Nice move with *Space Bimbos*. Seems to have backfired."

"Your guy is creating a real clusterfuck." The voice on the other end of the line sounded tired and strained.

"You wanted publicity," Scrubbs said, savoring his pain. "Isn't that what our shop is supposed to provide?"

"Our mission is to stimulate interest. We're way beyond that now. Things are getting out of control. I may not be in a position to extend assistance to you much longer."

"Don't break my heart."

"I hope for his sake this doesn't get out of hand."

"How do you mean?"

"I mean, this can't be permitted to go on. They're going to do something."

"They?"

"The ones you met on the island. Our information is they may be planning to remove your friend."

"Take out Banion? What good would that do? They'll create a martyr, a messiah. He'll be the UFO Jesus."

"How do you know that's not exactly what they're after?"

"It'll look kind of obvious. The Senate will have to hold hearings then."

"They aren't going to nail him to a cross while he's addressing the crowds. It'll be subtle. A bad oyster, a car accident, an embolism. Man's under a lot of strain. His heart could just *go*. So he becomes the UFO Jim Morrison. Who cares?"

"Who are these people? Assuming they exist."

"I can't tell you that. But they do exist, believe me, and you better pray that you don't meet them. That can't be allowed to happen. They will squeeze you until your head bursts. That's why, for the eighteenth fucking time, you need to come in where we can protect you."

"Send me dough and a passport and I'm out of here."

"You really have balls, you know that? You create this, this *pig's breakfast* of a situation and then you demand money. Have you stopped for one second to contemplate how unethical that is?"

Scrubbs looked at his watch. They were trying to keep him on the line.

"I love it when you talk ethics," he said. "I see the newspapers are estimating as many as a million marchers. Go rent some outdoor toilets."

"Scrubbs—"

On the ride back to work, the thought chewed on him: What if there was another group and they were planning to kill Banion. It was one thing to ruin a man's life, but this . . .

He put the thought out of his mind. There was no other group. It was just Mr. Majestic's ploy to get him to come in.

M³HQ, MILLENNIUM MAN MARCH HEADQUARTERS, HUMMED with activity. Dr. Falopian was coordinating the myriad UFO groups. Colonel Murfletit was in desk colonel heaven, organizing logistics. The challenges were, in all fairness, enormous. Banion had galvanized every UFO group in the country. They were angry, they had rallied, and they were headed this way. The attendance estimate was now over one million people. Banion worked the media, whose attention he now not only had but commanded. All three network television anchors were coming to Washington to do live coverage of the event.

Renira came in. "Here's the sketch of your trailer."

Banion's trailer, containing his command post, dressing room, cot, bathroom, would be behind the main stage in front of the Capitol. It was the shape of a flying saucer.

Banion examined the drawing. "Where are the lights?"

"Lights?"

"Blinking lights. The real things have blinking lights." He sketched in lights. "Amber, red, and green. Some blue would be nice."

"By the way," Renira said, "Miss Delmar called. She's arriving at Dulles at four P.M. I suggested to her that's cutting it a bit close, as she's scheduled to address the mob—"

"Stop calling it a mob."

"Convocation. Whichever. She's speaking at seven in the evening, before the Tall Nordic Singers go on. I assume we'll have a trailer for her backstage."

"Talk to Colonel Murfletit. That's his department."

"She *is* a major star. She should really have her own trailer."

"She can hang out in my trailer. Also, some orange lights, the kind that pulse."

.   .   .   .

NATIONAL PARK SERVICE
SAYS IT WILL NOT ISSUE
PERMIT TO MARCHERS

"WHY IS THIS ON MY DESK?" THE PRESIDENT ASKED TESTILY.
The day before, his opponent had called him an "ozone hugger,"
in reference to his environmental views. They had woken him
up in the middle of the night to tell him that an F-14 fighter had
disappeared off the radar in the Bering Strait. Then they woke
him up two hours later to tell him that they had found it, and
everything was all right. He'd planned to spend the morning cramming for his upcoming presidential debate, and now
this . . . irritant.

"Sorry, but it's your front lawn," the chief of staff said, nodding toward the Washington Monument and the Mall. "There's a
very real chance of this thing getting unpleasant if the UFO people don't get their march."

"Let the Park Service deal with it."

"That's the problem. They want to deny the permit. On the
grounds it wasn't filed in time, excessive numbers, inadequate
planning, et cetera."

"So? End of problem."

"Do we want a headline that says, GOVERNMENT DENIES PERMIT
TO UFO MARCHERS?"

"No, we want a headline that says, PARK SERVICE DENIES PERMIT
TO RAVING LUNATICS. I want this off my desk."

The chief of staff shifted in his chair. "I'm getting some vibra-
tions on this."

"From where? Pluto?"

"Gracklesen's people call me every ten minutes. They're pissing down their pant legs. They think these people are coming
here to burn him at the stake."

"Not a bad idea."

"They've requested we give him Secret Service protection."
The president looked up from his briefing book. "In his

dreams. Everyone wants Secret Service protection these days. It's just about status. Absolutely not."

"I turned them down. But it's Gracklesen who got the permits killed."

"What? How?"

"He told Bimmins, the Park Service director, to refuse them."

"Why is Bimmins taking orders from a numb nuts Oklahoma senator?"

"Because Gracklesen told Bimmins if he issued a permit, he'd have his good friend and colleague Senator Grooling hold hearings on the Mount Rushmore renovation disaster."*

The president nodded appreciatively at this neat parliamentarian blackmail. "Why not get the District government to develop a permit problem of their own? If it's a *District* problem, then our hands are tied."

"No go. The mayor loves this march. He told Burt Galilee he can't wait for a million white people to come make jackasses of themselves."

"Aren't there any black UFO believers?"

"I don't have numbers on that. Burt says there aren't any, to speak of. Blacks have a hard enough time of it already without worrying about aliens. My general sense is UFO's are for people with extra time on their hands."

"Where does that leave us?"

"I've been thinking, why not give them their permits? Hang out the welcome banner. What harm can it do? They'll come, let off some steam, have a few beers, piss in the Reflecting Pool, and go home with hangovers."

"I suppose."

"You'll be at Shangri-la.† Let the Congress deal with it.

---

* An experimental cleaning fluid used during the monument's renovation reacted chemically with the granite and turned the presidents permanently pink, causing a furor, especially among right-wingers.

† Franklin Roosevelt's code name for the weekend presidential retreat in the Catoctin Mountain Park in Maryland near Washington. President Eisenhower renamed it Camp David after his grandson. For some reason, they are using its old name.

They're the ones these people are gunning for, not us. As a matter of fact, I was thinking you might want to do a little satellite linkup Friday night, you know, welcome them to town."

"Address a UFO convention? I'll look like I'm pandering."

"Not at all. Just a little neutral hello, welcome to town, you having a good time? Perfect chance to remind everyone that you've been a ceaseless advocate of open, responsive government all your public life. Who kept pressing to open the assassination files?"

"I don't know. Alien abductees?"

"Let me give you numbers I do happen to have: Over one-third the American people think aliens landed at Roswell in nineteen forty-seven. Eighty percent—eighty—think we, the government, know about aliens and are hiding it."

"How is this possible?"

"Seventy-five percent think JFK was killed by the government. Okay, so they're a little flaky upstairs, but they vote, a lot of them."

"Sure, for Perot."*

"So we show a little sensitivity. We might even pick up some support. This thing is getting massive media coverage. The anchors are flying in."

"That'll *help*." The president snorted. "All right, but a short greeting. And nothing in it that's going to come back and bite me in the ass."

"I'll have a draft for you tomorrow morning."

BANION WAS SWAMPED. THEY ALL WANTED HIM ON, AND all at the same time, it seemed. The morning shows, the all-day shows, the evening shows, the late-night shows, the late-late-night shows. He had dragooned Elspeth, his graduate-student Robespierre book researcher, into temporary duty as a press sec-

---

*Ross Perot, erratic billionaire populist candidate for president in 1992, 1996, and 2000. Eventually moved to Central America, where he purchased and ruled his own republic, Rossta Rica.

retary. She was doing a good job in the face of demands by imperious producers.

Time magazine was preparing a cover story. Banion was negotiating the terms of the interview with him when Renira, appearing unusually impressed, came in to say that the White House was on the line. It pleased Banion to tell the managing editor of *Time* that he had to hang up on him because the White House was on line 2. Just like the old days.

"Please hold for the chief of staff," the White House operator said.

Banion counted. After ten seconds, he hung up. *Just* like the old days.

A minute later, Renira reappeared to say that the White House was again on the line. This time, they did not keep him waiting.

"Jack, Bill Dibbish. Long time."

"So it is." *My army is headed your way . . .*

"This march of yours is coming along nicely."

"How about that?" *They are going to burn your house, ravish your women, pillage your land.*

"If you'd like, I might be able to arrange for the president to speak to your people by remote from Shangri-la."

"Is that a fact?" Banion leaned back in his chair. At times like this, he wished he smoked cigars. "And what would the president like to tell my 'people'?"

"You know, welcome to the capital, hope they get what they came for, that sort of thing."

"What they're coming for, Bill"—Banion chuckled—"is your ass. Sure you want to wish them well?"

"My ass?" The chief of staff laughed nervously. "Whoa. *We* didn't have anything to do with your satellite mix-up. To be honest, Jack, we have better things to do. We're in the middle of a campaign, you may have noticed."

"So I did. Eight points down. Not so good, for an incumbent."

"It's not easy campaigning in the middle of a recession caused by reckless policies of the previous admin—"

"Yeah, yeah. Spare me."

"So, would you like the president to address your event?"

"We'd love it."

"Let me see what I can do. I think I can sell it."

"Of course, we would want him there personally."

"That's not—the Secret Service wouldn't go for that."

"Then tell them, tough tamales, you're calling the shots. Now, we do have a very full program. So what I would suggest is he make a short statement apologizing for the fifty-year-long UFO cover-up, then announce that he is personally directing that all government files on UFO's be opened."

"We're getting ahead of—"

"Then we can open it up to questions. You're always saying how he loves a good town meeting exchange with just folks. I can guarantee you a lively exchange."

"With all respect, Jack, your people aren't just folks. They're—"

"Careful. You called to kiss my ass, not to make me mad. Now I'll admit, privately, that some of them are a little, well, rough around the edges. But then you probably seem weird to them." *Then we are going to cut off your head and play polo with it. What fun we'll have!*

"Jack—"

"Bye bye, Bill. Give my best to POTUS."*

Yes, just like the old days.

"CREATIVE SOLUTIONS, HOW MAY I—"

"It's Scrubbs. Put Asshole on."

"Stand by, please."

"Scrubbs, where the hell have you been?"

"This other group you keep talking about. Tell me who they are, or this is my last call to you."

"I'm a little busy right now. They're estimating two million of

---

* Acronym used by White House staff for President Of The United States.

these people. So right now I don't really give a rat's ass if I never hear from you again."

"You say they might take out Banion?"

"I'd say at this point that is a very real possibility, yes."

"You can't let that happen."

"Don't download your bad conscience on me. None of this was our creation."

"Suppose I get Banion to back off."

"How are you going to accomplish that, exactly?"

"I'm not going to tell you that. But suppose I can get him to turn this around and send them home. Would that make this quote, unquote other group cease and desist?"

"I have no way of predicting that." His hesitation said otherwise. "But that might help. Yes. It might be a start."

"Why are we still pretending there's another group out there?"

"Because the world runs on arrangements like that."

"What if I do this?"

"Then your friend might not end up with a blood clot."

"What's in it for me?"

Mr. Majestic laughed bitterly. "You expect a reward?"

"Safe-conduct and money. Get me a severance package—and I'm not talking about having my head severed."

"We might be able to work something out. But we'd have to see concrete results first."

"All right." Scrubbs sighed. "Stand by."

BANION, DR. FALOPIAN, AND COLONEL MURFLETIT WERE AT HQ going over the final schedule of events with the M³ marshals, event coordinators, and security staff. Colonel Murfletit was wearing the uniform he had designed, a military jumpsuit with ascot and swagger stick. With his bald pate, thick, tinted eyeglasses, permanently wet, protruding lips, and general lack of chin, he looked slightly less formidable than General Patton. Dr. Falopian's eyes had taken on an alarming aspect. He looked like an unwashed Bolshevik revolutionary who had spent the week sleeping on a bench at the Finland Station waiting for Lenin's train to pull in so that they could start executing anyone who owned land. He had taken to chain-eating donuts—for energy, he claimed—which left his Falstaffian abdomen covered under a permanent snow blanket of confectioners' sugar. (Renira referred to his stomach as *le grand massif*.) Banion, too, was showing the strain. He had dark circles under his eyes and had lost almost ten pounds, he nonetheless presented a more reassuring image than his two top lieutenants.

Colonel Murfletit reported on his progress. The stage was being erected at the head of the Mall, in the shadow of the U.S. Capitol. It would make a splendid backdrop. The stage itself was in the shape of a large flying saucer, with a Plexiglas dome suspended overhead like a giant cockpit canopy. Huge speakers would broadcast cosmically themed music, the soundtracks from *Star Wars, Star Trek, 2001, The Day the Earth Stood Still, My Favorite Martian,* and other classics.

"Is it going to be finished in time?" Banion asked. Colonel Murfletit gave a weary nod. He might be a bit of an odd duck, Banion thought, but the Army got the job done.

Kathy Carr, who until Banion's abduction had been the nation's leading abductee, would kick off the Friday-night program by singing the national anthem. It had taken a lot of stroking on Falopian's part to get her. She chafed at no longer being number one.

"Do we know"—Banion rubbed his temples—"if she *can* sing?" The entertainment committee chair said she could probably get through it without making people wince. She said Kathy wanted to substitute some lyrics: "saucers flying through air" for "bombs bursting in air."

"No, no, no, no, no," Banion said, "we do *not* rewrite the national anthem. Please make that pellucidly clear to Ms. Carr. We are gathering as patriotic Americans petitioning our elected representatives. If I hear her sing one word I don't recognize, I'm going to cut off her microphone."

Fina Delmar, Hollywood star, would then welcome the assembled. Renira, in her cherished capacity as liaison to Miss Delmar, said that the actress would make brief remarks about how her abduction had changed her life.

"Brief, please," Banion said. "No endless reminiscences about everyone being pushed in Darryl Zanuck's pool."

"It was Jack Warner's swimming pool."

"Whatever. Okay, what's next?" He looked at the lineup. "Tall Nordic Singers. What are they going to sing?"

"We Are the World," the entertainment chair said. They'd been rehearsing all week. It promised to be very moving. Later in the program they would come back on and do a haunting vocal accompaniment to "The Ice Forests of Orion." That would be even more moving, she promised.

Next, Dr. Falopian would speak. Glancing over at his crazed-looking colleague, Banion could only hope that the good doctor would shave, comb his hair, and wipe away the blanket of sugar on his belly before standing up to address a crowd that was now estimated at over 2 million, to say nothing of a live television audience expected to be in the hundreds of millions.

"What themes will you be striking, Danton?" Banion cautiously inquired.

Dr. Falopian went into a long, not altogether linear tirade about the U.S. government's evil connivance in this new form of slave trade. Banion collegially urged him to try to keep it to five minutes. We have a long program, folks.

Next was Darth Brooks, the Grammy-winning sci fi/country-western singer. He would sing his golden oldie, "Momma Don't Go with Little Green Men"—always a crowd pleaser, then his popular sing-along number "Ammonia and Cinnamon."

Next would come the film. It was a documentary featuring an actual alien named Freepo. It was controversial even within the

UFO community. In it, Freepo declared that he had met with top U.S. government political and military leaders to warn them about El Niño's impact on global weather patterns and that they had ignored his warnings entirely. After watching a rough version of it, Banion pointed out that Freepo had a pronounced southern accent. Dr. Falopian, who staunchly championed the film, argued that Freepo hailed from the Ulnar-5P galaxy, where vocal patterns were, in fact—how astute of Banion to point it out—remarkably similar to those of the U.S. rural South. He insisted that they show it. Finally, he said, we have one of them on tape! The footage was too hot to hold—why wait until after it had appeared on *Tales of the Weird*? Banion was too tired to argue, but he did put the kibosh on the revolting cattle mutilation video they wanted to show.

Colonel Murfletit would speak next. He would describe how he had been personally ordered by shadowy Pentagon brass to change the fluid in the tanks where the alien corpses from Roswell were preserved, not a pretty story either. Banion urged him not to dwell in too great length on the details. His headache throbbed.

Much discussion had been given to who should introduce Banion. Murfletit and Falopian had both been jockeying fiercely for the honor. Yet Banion felt—without putting it directly—that it should be someone of greater, well, stature. He had settled finally on Romulus Valk.

Dr. Valk was the father of the halogen bomb, whose development had changed the course of the Cold War. The halogen weapon had so alarmed President John F. Kennedy that he had Dr. Valk himself classified, causing the dwarfish, beetle-browed Czech émigré no little inconvenience. He was finally declassified by President Nixon, enabling him to use credit cards and telephones and other services Americans take for granted. Nixon and Kissinger consulted with him regularly on how to scare the shit out of other countries.

Valk had come late to the belief that dared not speak its name.

One day, looking out his office window at the Valk Institute in Ojo, California, while calculating how many halotons it would take to incinerate the Chelyabinsk Red Army base, he saw funny, blinking lights, and that was it, he never looked back. Unfortunately, his health was now far from robust. He was in his late eighties and had a tendency, in conversation, to begin speaking in Czech. Banion earnestly hoped that Dr. Valk would not lapse into his natal tongue halfway through his introduction.

"Should we have a translator standing by, just in case?" Elspeth suggested.

"Excellent idea, Elspeth," Banion said. "All right, then I come on. I'll speak for fifteen minutes, max. I'll try to get the chant going. How does it go again?"

"Wee-ooo, wee-ooo, how much does the government know?"

"Right. Okay, then the Tall Nordic Singers come on, and we'll segue right to the fireworks. How are we coming with the fireworks permits?"

They were working on it. The Park Service, cheesed about having been overruled on the march, was being pissy about certain details, such as the possibility of undetonated ordnance landing on concentrated masses of people, or on the White House for that matter.

"Okay"—Banion yawned—"let's quickly run through Saturday's program."

IT WAS ALMOST THREE IN THE MORNING BY THE TIME HE GOT home. He had just thrown himself onto the bed, too tired even to take off his clothes and get under the covers, when the phone rang.

"Yes?" he growled. It had better not be Falopian or Murfletit, trying to persuade him again to turn the march into a sit-in surrounding the Congress. The maniacs wanted to turn it into Bunker Hill.

"It's me."

Banion sat up.

"What do you know. Mata Hari."

"I wanted to thank you."

"For what?"

"Not blowing my cover at your press conference."

"Don't flatter yourself. That wasn't for your benefit."

"How so?"

"You think I want Falopian and Murfletit to know how easily I was suckered? Everyone thinks you had to go home on family business."

"Well, thanks anyway. How are you doing?"

"Are you on duty, or is that a personal question?"

"I'm worried about you."

"I know you are. I'm about to pry open your can of worms. My people are going to put such heat on the Congress that you and your alien-protecting colleagues are going to be running for—"

"Jack, you've got it very wrong. Trust me."

"Trust you? What a joke."

"You're making a mistake."

"Fine. I'll tell my two million marchers, 'Never mind, go home, Roz says I have it all wrong.' Fat chance. My advice to you would be, get a good lawyer for when you're subpoenaed to testify before Congress for crimes against the American peo——"

"Jack, shut up. Listen—there's more going on here than you know."

"Look, toots, I'm not Horatio and you're not Hamlet."

"What?"

" 'There are more things in heaven and earth, Horatio, than are dreamt of in your philosophy.' Anyway, I'm supposed to be Hamlet here, not Horatio. I'm the one whose life got turned upside down by weird apparitions."

"I majored in Poli Sci, not English."

"Never mind. It's too late for a Shakespeare seminar. It's after

three. I'm tired. I have a headache. I spent the whole day with
Falopian and Murfletit."

Roz giggled.

"You're amused?"

"Can't help it. Every time I think of those two. They're such
dorks."

"You wouldn't laugh if you knew what those 'dorks' are trying to turn this march into."

"Oh?"

"Never mind. I keep forgetting I'm talking to a spy."

"They're trying to push it, aren't they?"

"Danton keeps muttering about 'convergence.' They think it's
nineteen seventeen and we're about to march on the Winter
Palace. I feel like Kerensky."*

"Keep it together. If this thing turns ugly, it's not going to do
your side any good. And someone's going to have to pay. Like
you."

Banion yawned. "So what are you doing these days, aside
from calling me on a tapped phone to find out what I know?"

Silence.

"I know. You can't go into that." He wanted to hang up, but
he couldn't.

"Are you back in Chicago, editing *Cosmos*? 'Pleiadeans Are
Lousy Lovers'?"

"I've moved on. Jack, I wish you'd believe me. That night—I
really did think you were being set up. I was trying to protect
you."

"It doesn't matter now, Roz."

"I care. It's gotten out of control. We're trying to—"

"Who is 'we'?"

"All I can tell you that you have got this—through no fault of
your own—one hundred and eighty degrees backward."

---

*Leader of the Russian Duma at the time of the Revolution who tried to keep things
from getting out of hand, with spectacular lack of success.

"Well, that clears up *everything*. I've got to get some sleep. I've got a real bitch of a day tomorrow."

"Be careful, baby."

"Good-*bye*."

He feel asleep wondering what she'd meant by "through no fault of your own."

"YO, SCRUBBSY, WAKE UP, MAN. WAKE *UP*."

Scrubbs opened his eyes. Bradley was hovering over him. It was pitch black outside.

"What time is it?"

"Time for your ass to rotate out of here."

"Why?"

"The man. He's here."

"What?"

"I went down to my boat. I was gonna do some fishin' before we went to work. There they were."

"Who?"

"The *man*. Come on, get dressed, keep movin', take your clothes. I ain't no *butler*."

Scrubbs sat up, rubbed his eyes. His mouth tasted of Sheetrock dust. Bradley had made him work late last night to make up for his long coffee-break phone call. He pulled on his jeans.

"What man?"

"Three of 'em. They had badges."

"What kind of badges?"

"Couldn't tell. Too dark. They asked me if it was my boat. I played dumb nigger. 'No sah! Dis heah ain' *my* boat. Dis boat belong to my man Bernard. Sometimes he loan it to me so I can go catch me a *catfish*.' Come on, *move*."

Scrubbs was pulling on his clothes. "Where are they now?"

"On their way to *Bernard's* place. Bernard ain't going to be happy to see them. Shit is going to *fly* when they knock on his door."

"Who's Bernard?"

"Drug dealer. *Major* drug dealer."

"Jesus Christ, Brad."

"Going to be *loud*. Come on—you waitin' for breakfast in bed?"

They drove through dark streets from Anacostia to Union Station. It was busy even at this early hour. Crowds carrying UFO signs were milling around.

Bradley said, "They won't find you in this mess of people. You'll be a needle in a haystack."

"What are you going to do?"

"Going fishing. Got a cousin in Pennsylvania."

Bradley handed Scrubbs a wad of cash. "That's your retirement fund. I been putting some of your pay aside."

Scrubbs counted it. There was five hundred dollars.

"Thanks, Bradley."

"Can I give you some *advice*?"

"Yeah, okay."

"Don't apply for no job hanging Sheetrock. You got no *ability* for it."

They shook hands and parted.

FIFTEEN

The National Park Service had long since stopped giving out official crowd size estimates, since groups had begun suing them if they didn't like the estimates of their turnouts. The media, however, were under no such restraint. From the Capitol two miles down the Mall to the Lincoln Memorial, their helicopter cameras showed a solid, impacted mass of humanity. By Friday noon CNN pronounced it the largest gathering in the capital in the nation's history. The Millennium Man March was on.

"We were thinking," the chief of the staff said to the president as they glumly watched TV in the Oval Office, "that it might make sense for you and the First Lady to go to Shangri-la by limousine."

"Why?" the president said suspiciously. He loved his helicopter, *Marine One*.* What better way to commute to your weekend home than to have a military helicopter land on your lawn to pick you up and whisk you away?

"The Service is nervous about your flying out over the crowd."

"What are they going to do, shoot me down?"

"Those are three million very strange people out there. I'm not sure I'd want to fly over them."

*Who wouldn't?

"I used to fly over the Ho Chi Minh Trail in unarmored Hueys. I'm not worried about dusting off over picnicking weirdos."

"Your call."

The chief of staff left the Oval Office and called the First Lady. A few minutes later, the First Lady called the president and informed him they would be traveling that afternoon to Shangri-la by limo. The president called his chief of staff and bellowed at him for going to the First Lady.

The change of routine was duly reported to the White House press corps. They badgered the press secretary into a statement that made it sound as though the president of the United States was afraid to fly over the Millennium Man Marchers. The press secretary later took issue with this interpretation of his remarks. The president, he said, was bound by Secret Service recommendations.

AFTER HOURS OF SHOULDERING HIS WAY THROUGH THE dense masses, Scrubbs managed to reach the perimeter of the stage area at the head of the Mall. It was guarded by Colonel Murfletit's security people, wearing their military-style jumpsuits with ascots and batons. All in all they looked like gay storm troopers.

"I have to speak with Mr. Banion," Scrubbs said, presenting himself to the least intelligent-looking one he could find.

"So does everyone."

"Son, I have a Priority *Five* message for Mr. Banion." Sounded official, anyway.

The guard stiffened. "Sir, I am not authorized to handle Priority Five–level message traffic."

"Well, who the hell around here *is*?"

"You'll have to check with Commo."

"Right. Commo."

"Communications. Over there, sir." He pointed to an unpromising looking area full of even more butch-appearing guards with ascots and batons.

• • •

BANION WAS INSIDE THE COCOON OF HIS SAUCER-SHAPED trailer, trying to go over his speech while being interrupted every three minutes by someone urgently needing something. Yet for all the frenzy swirling about him, his fatigue, his lonely turmoil over Roz, he felt a strange serenity. He had worked hard for this moment, against enormous odds. They had tried to silence him, and they had failed. Now he was about to address his followers—his army, 3 *million* strong. It occurred to him that he had more people on his side than the U.S. armed forces had in uniform. Now he was about to poke a large forefinger in the eye of the Establishment that had dismissed and ostracized him. He saw himself in a long, historical context of revolutionaries, truth seekers, and—

"*Yes,* Renira?"

"I've spoken with the Virginia Highway people. They say the roads are impassable between here and Dulles. We'll have to arrange for a helicopter to fly Miss Delmar in from the airport."

"Whatever."

—visionaries who were willing to take on the orthodoxies of—

"Come *in.*"

His heart sank at the sight of Dr. Falopian and Colonel Murfletit. Falopian was avid to storm the heights and encircle the Capitol with a sit-in. He said that he had spoken with no less a personage than the head of the International Congress of Abductees, who reported that his people were for it. If this was war, let it start here.

Colonel Murfletit, his lips moister than usual with excitement, concurred. He had taken to quoting his hero of heroes, Patton. History might not afford another such opportunity for a thousand years! The diem must be carpeed! Colonel Muffin—as Roz used to call him—had never fought in a real war, only bureaucratic skirmishes. Here at last was his chance for martial glory.

Banion sighed and told them no, no, no, under *no circum-*

stances would there be a sit-in, or any other kind of confrontation. Now please, leave him, go, attend to their details. Surely they had work to do. He must have the cone of silence in which to compose thoughts.

They murmurously withdrew. The phone rang. Elspeth answered. "One moment, please. Burton Galilee," she announced, "for you."

Well, well.

"Hello, Burt."

"Is this Mr. Millennium?" came the rich, chocolaty voice. "I was here with Martin in 'sixty-three. I thought *that* was a crowd! You got everyone running in circles." He lowered his voice, "You got them squealing like scalded hogs at the White House. They don't know whether to shit or go crazy." He laughed.

"What can I do for you, Burt?"

"Just calling to see if there's anything I can do for you. Want me to make some calls up to the Hill? See if we can't set up some meetings with some of the committee chairmen? Get you those hearings you want?"

"Burt"—Banion smiled—"are you proposing to lobby for me?"

Burt laughed. "Now, Jack, you know I don't lobby. I just like to help my friends."

"So what's Bitsey up to this weekend?" Banion changed the subject.

"She and Tyler decided to spend it in the country. The *English* country."

Banion laughed.

"They're with some duke or other, scaring hell out of pheasants. One of those house-party deals. Prince of Wales was supposed to be joining them, with whatsername, woman caused all that fuss. Tyler likes to have a few royals around, you know, for *tone*. Bitsey still goes white as a sheet when your name comes up. And she's pretty white to start with."

"I have to go, Burt. My people beckon. Good of you to call."

"I'll make some calls for you. I'll be in touch."

Banion went back to his speech.

The first Americans to land on the moon brought a message from the American people: "We come in peace for all mankind." So, too, do we. But we come, also, for the truth. "Ye shall know the truth," says the Bible, "and the truth shall make you free." . . .

"SERVICE ADVISES THAT ALL ROADS ARE BACKED UP SOLID," the chief of staff said. "They say it would take 'extraordinary measures' to clear the way for a motorcade. By that I think they mean bulldozers."

The president was already in a foul mood from having heard on CNN that he—and not the Secret Service—was "nervous" about flying over the marchers.

"Where does that leave us?"

"I was thinking we might seize the opportunity and stay here for the weekend. Prep for the debate."

"I will not be a prisoner in my own house! Get me *Marine One.* I want my helicopter. Get a gunship escort if you have to."

"Now how's that going to look?"

"I don't care how it *looks!*"

"I HAVE AN ANNOUNCEMENT," THE PRESS SECRETARY TOLD the reporters in the White House Press Room. "The president has a cold. He and the First Lady have decided to remain here for the weekend."

IT WAS GETTING DARK. SCRUBBS HAD PROBED THE ENTIRE perimeter of the backstage area. Short of digging a tunnel underneath, there was no way in.

He saw from the program that Kathy Carr, his other prize abductee, was going to sing the national anthem. Banion was scheduled to go on last. He had to get to him before he spoke. He studied the program. Tall Nordic Singers? The program had a picture of them in their costumes.

He presented himself to a guard.

"I'm with the Tall Nordic Singers. I got separated at the bus station. Where are we supposed to change?"

The guard looked at his clipboard. "Tent F, that way."

Scrubbs found his way to a large tent to the side of the stage area. It was outside the security perimeter, so he did not have to present a pass. He took a deep breath and went in. About fifty people were inside, some of them already wearing their Tall Nordic outfits, consisting of silvery body stockings and face masks with almond eyes, gilled ears. It was a look Scrubbs knew well. He had worn this uniform himself years back, when he was just starting out.

He looked for someone approximately his size who hadn't yet changed into his costume. He found one, circled him a few times until he was able to read the name on his pass, then approached.

"You Rob Farbert?"

"Yeah?"

"You got a phone call."

"I do?"

"They said it's urgent, something about a fire at your home. Phone's at the Commo desk, all the way the other side of the stage."

"My God!" He ran off.

"Don't mention it."

Scrubbs scooped up Rob Farbert's changing bag and made his way out the opposite end of the tent.

"SENATOR GRACKLESEN, LINE TWO," ELSPETH ANNOUNCED.

"Hello, Hank. Did you just look out your window?"

"Jack, let's just start over."

"Little late for that. My speech is already written."

"We can work together on this. Put our heads together. Reach some kind of consensus. I hadn't realized the extent of this abduction phenomenon, in terms of the sheer numbers."

"So I can go ahead and announce tonight that we have your promise—let's make that solemn promise—to hold hearings? Right away?"

Banion heard senatorial dry-swallowing.

"I can't have it sound like I just caved to pressure. That wouldn't work for either of us."

"It would for me."

"Let's let this evolve. Gradually. You and I, we sit down, talk it over, give the press to understand that we're getting closer and closer to an understanding, then announce an exploratory review . . ."

"And then do nothing. By which time my people have all gone home. No, I don't think so."

"I'm trying to meet you halfway, Jack."

"I'll go with my speech the way it is now. Then we'll see what evolves."

"What are you going to say?" the senator asked nervously.

"Let's see . . . hm . . . hm . . . *hm*."

"What?"

"I'm not sure you want to hear this, Hank. It's kind of *harsh*."

"Jack, we go back a long ways—"

"Course, it's only a speech. Still, you might want to leave the country for a while. Go to South America. Have some plastic surgery, change your name . . ."

"It's against the law to incite violence, especially against federal officials."

"I'm well aware of it. But some of my people are little excitable, and when they hear that one senator in particular despises them and holds them beneath contempt—who knows what they might do. But there's nothing in my speech that specifically urges them to make your life a living hell."

"All right, you got your damn hearings."

"Why, thank you, Hank. Mighty democratic of you."

"But I want to hear you say loud and clear in your speech that we worked it out amicably, or it's no deal. I don't want any of your freaks coming after me."

"I don't see a problem. I've always been a process guy. Would you like to attend the speech? I'll get you a seat in the VIP section, you want."

"No thank you." Senator Gracklesen slammed down the phone.

SCRUBBS'S TALL NORDIC SINGER COSTUME WAS A PRETTY good fit, if a bit tight in the crotch. He made sure to stick close to the other costumed Tall Nordics. Through his mask he could see the hapless Rob Farbert looking in vain for his purloined duffel.

"My bag. Has anyone seen my bag?" he cried. At one point he looked directly at Scrubbs. Scrubbs shrugged.

Finally a marshal appeared to lead them inside the perimeter to the backstage area. Scrubbs kept close to the other singers.

Damn. The guard was checking passes at the rope.

"Where's your pass?" he asked Scrubbs.

"Huh?"

"Your pass. I need to see your pass."

"Oh, gee, I had it right here."

"You can't go in without a pass."

A marshal appeared. "He's okay, he's with the singers."

Scrubbs was in.

BANION WAS MAKING HIS FINAL CHANGES TO HIS SPEECH when a guard rapped on his door.

"It's one of the Tall Nordic Singers. Says he needs to speak with you."

"What does he want?"

"He says it's real important."

"Tell him I'll see him afterwards."

"Says it can't wait."

"Oh yes it can."

Banion went back to his speech. A moment later he heard shouting, the sounds of a scuffle.

He went and opened the door. Two guards had one of the Tall Nordic Singers pinned up against the curved side of the saucer with their batons. They looked ready to administer earnest bastinadoes.

"What's going on?" Banion demanded.

"Mr. Banion," said the Tall Nordic Singer, "I really, really have to speak to you."

"This better be important," Banion said, motioning the guards to release their prisoner.

They were alone inside the trailer.

"Well?"

Scrubbs peeled off his Tall Nordic face mask. "I'm the one who abducted you."

"What do you mean?" Banion said with annoyance.

"The golf course, the speech in Palm Springs. That was me. Us. I work for a government agency called MJ-Twelve. It's a covert program to promote belief in UFO's so's to keep up military and space funding."

Banion stared. Scrubbs felt somewhat ridiculous standing there in his silver bodysuit.

"Go *away*," Banion said. He turned back to his speech.

"You've got to believe me."

"Will you go sing, please? There are three million people out there. Get a grip, man. This is no time to lose it."

" 'You like be on my TV show?' "

Banion stood still.

"What you said in the saucer in Palm Springs. Those weren't aliens, Mr. Banion, and that wasn't a flying saucer any more than this thing we're standing in is."

Banion's face went as slack as ebb tide. He had never, for obvious purposes of dignity, told anyone about his desperate attempt, in a moment of extremis, to try to mollify the aliens with the offer of a guest slot on *Sunday*. Whoever this man was, he . . . knew something that no one else did.

"Not a flying saucer?"

"No sir. It was a model. Kind of like this. I see you took some decorating clues."

"*Not* aliens?"

"Costumes. Like this thing I'm wearing. The aliens are humans. They work for me. We call them baggers. You got bagged. Twice. Sorry about that."

"*Sorry?*"

"Yeah, see, it wasn't authorized. I sort of did it on my own. I see you've got Kathy Carr on the program singing the anthem. She was one of mine, too. You all right, sir? Do you need a drink of water or something?"

Banion was croaking. Scrubbs decided he might as well tell him everything while he was in a state of shock.

"MJ-Twelve, Majestic Twelve, Majic. I don't really know too much about it—which is the whole idea, it's compartmentalized for security reasons—but it was set up during the Cold War to convince the Russians we knew about UFO's. Then one thing led to another, and it became sort of a tool for fund-raising, you might say—military, space budgets, the whole nine yards. The sightings, abductions, what have you, that's all us. There's a computer somewhere that generates names of people to abduct. Obviously, you don't want to snatch people too prominent, like yourself. I decided more or less on my own to grab you. It was sort of a protest, you might say. Not such a great idea, huh? Anyway. MJ-Twelve wasn't happy about it, and they tried to, well, kill me, basically. Only now they're telling me it wasn't them, it was some other secret government agency that did it. Which is bullshit, of course. To be honest, I really don't know *who's* trying to kill me. Someone is. But the reason I need to tell you all this is . . . You with me, Mr. Banion?"

Banion was staring at Scrubbs.

". . . is that you're now in danger yourself." Scrubbs chuckled. "I mean, I gotta hand it to you, sir, you really ran with this ball. I'm downright proud of you. Three million people. That's impressive. But now you've got them shitting bricks. This is just way too much UFO belief. So unless you cool it, right away, they're going to take you out of the picture. I figured I owed you that much, to tell you. Can I get you something? Mr. Banion? Sir?"

HE HEARD A VOICE, SUMMONING HIM BACK TO THE SUR-face.

"Mr. Banion? Don't crap out on me now. There you go. Breathe into the bag. Deep breaths. That's it . . ."

Banion shoved away the paper bag that Scrubbs was holding to his mouth.

"What . . . ?"

"You fainted. Don't be embarrassed. I'd have done the exact same thing, it was me."

Banion blinked up at the ceiling. He took stock. He was lying on the floor. He sat up, groped his way to the chair.

"This . . . *grotesque* story you have just told me," he said. "It's *true*?"

"I'm afraid so."

"You wrecked my life. And you didn't even have *permission*?"

"I was going through a bad patch. Personally speaking."

"And now this, this, this agency is going to kill me?"

There was a knock on the door. The stage manager put his head in. "Fifteen minutes, Mr. Banion."

"And you're telling me all this . . . *now*?"

"I realize the timing's a little awkward. But it wasn't easy getting to you. I could have telephoned, but I wasn't sure I'd get through. Plus, I figured you'd want to hear this in person."

Banion was staring like a tranquilized mental patient. Interesting thoughts were going through his mind.

"Three million people are waiting for me to speak to them."

"Quite some crowd. I understand the biggest ever. Helluva job you did."

"I wasn't looking for a compliment. What am I supposed to tell them? That their whole world, their entire cosmology, everything they believe in, is a total fraud?"

"Kind of like finding out about Santa Claus, huh?"

"It is fucking well *not* like finding out about Santa Claus! It is fucking well on an entire different *order* of disillusionment than finding out about *Santa Claus!*"

"Maybe you shouldn't be shouting so soon after fainting. Let's focus on the practical problem first, then we can deal with your feelings of anger, which are understandable."

Banion felt another tingling under his scalp, the presentiment of oxygen saying ta-ta to the brain. He put his head between his legs and took deep breaths.

"I'll expose you," he gasped. "I'll tell the world. You'll go to prison. You'll—"

"Let's talk about that. You could get up there and say, 'Okay, people, it's all a fake, it's the government.' Fine. But one, you're going to have three million extremely confused people on your hands. Who could turn very angry on you. Two, how are you going to prove it? By pointing to me? While I was on the run, I got arrested for trying to beat the bill at a fleabag hotel. MJ-Twelve can make me look like a total flake. My credibility rating is zero. Three, you've worked hard to get this kind of following—three million people. Is this any time to be telling them, 'Never mind, go home'? We're up against the U.S. government. Three million people could come in very handy."

"My head. I hope they do get you. I'll tell them everything."

"I feel your pain, sir, but think about it. You get up there and start spouting this, and they'll haul you off to Saint Elizabeth's, where they'll keep you so doped all you'll be able to do is sit in a corner and drool into a Dixie cup. MJ-Twelve is the best-kept secret in town. These people do not leave fingerprints. Trust me.

I don't know the name of one other person in the organization. And if you go on with this Millennium Man show and force them to hold Senate hearings and make a pain in the ass of yourself, they're going to have to get rid of you and make it look like natural causes. They mentioned blood clots. I imagine they have access to pretty much anything they want in the biochemical area."

"God."

"I know the way it looks now, you're sort of screwed no matter what."

The stage manager called out, "Five minutes, Mr. Banion."

"I was thinking we should join forces," said Scrubbs. "Pool our resources, so to speak."

Banion could hear the roar of the crowd outside. Half an hour ago, he was a conquering hero preparing to take his place at the head of his army. Now he was a millennial patsy, at the center of crosshairs.

"So," Scrubbs said, "maybe we should be thinking about your speech?"

SIXTEEN

"You've just heard the keynote speech by the leader of the three million Millennial Marchers, John O. Banion. Let's go now to the Mall, where our correspondent Ann Compton is standing by. Ann, what's the reaction down where you are?"

"Peter, people here seem generally *pleased* by what they heard tonight from John O. Banion. I have to say, from where I was, his speech seemed somewhat *listless,* almost lacking in *passion.* This is a very enthusiastic crowd, and I think if he had asked them to march all the way to California, they would have. Instead, he seemed very *deliberate.* At times he seemed stunned. But this *is* the largest gathering of people in the nation's history, so perhaps he was just taken aback by the enormity of it all. He kept repeating the phrase 'this majestic situation,' a number of times. And there *is* a sort of majesty to the occasion, all these people, who have come from all over the country. We're hoping to speak to John O. Banion later. Meanwhile, I have with me Dr. Danton Falopian, who is Banion's top scientific adviser on UFO's. . . ."

BANION AND SCRUBBS WATCHED ON THE TV MONITOR IN HIS trailer. Banion sat, a wet towel over his forehead. On his lap, cradled in both hands, was a large glass filled to the rim with Scotch.

"I thought you were great," Scrubbs said. "What did she

want you to do? Rip your clothes off, set yourself on fire? These TV people, they drive me nuts sometimes."

A moan came from under Banion's wet towel.

"She picked up on our signal, anyway. And if she did, you can bet they did. Now they know that you know. That buys us some time."

There were frantic knockings on the door of the trailer, people demanding admittance. It was Elspeth. .

"She says Tom Brokaw wants to interview you," Scrubbs said. "Shouldn't you go talk to him?"

Banion took huge swallow of Scotch.

"Are you going to drink all of that at once?"

"Yes. Then I'm going to drink another. And another after that. And then," he said, "I'm going to kill you. And the jury will let me off because I was drunk."

"That's how all this started, me knocking back Bloody Marys one Sunday morning. I was mad because they'd turned down my transfer out of Abductions. So I'm not sure booze is the answer."

"You ruined my life because you got drunk one morning?"

"You gotta go talk to Tom Brokaw. Hey, there's your pal Senator Gracklesen."

Banion lifted the cloth. Gracklesen was being interviewed by CNN, trying his best to sound thrilled that his committee would be holding abduction hearings without leaving quotable footprints.

"This isn't to say that I personally am convinced that these entities, or whatever you want to call them, are engaging in the kinds of activities that are being alleged here. That said, I am enormously impressed by the energy and commitment that I have felt from the people who have come to Washington for this event. Thank you very much, thank you . . ."

Banion replaced the cloth over his eyes. Scrubbs was holding something out to him.

"What's that? Cyanide?"

"Breath mint. You can't talk to Tom Brokaw smelling like a distillery. Come on, time for phase two."

"JOHN O. BANION, THANK YOU FOR JOINING US."

"Pleasure." Banion burped.

"Senator Gracklesen has now agreed to hold hearings on alien abductions. That's what your people came here for. Now you have it. You must be feeling pretty good."

"Um. Much better."

"Were you surprised by the turnout?"

"Hm?" said Banion.

"Did the fact that three million people came surprise you?"

"Oh. Yes. Lovely."

Brokaw's producer said into the anchor's earpiece: "Jesus, he's drunk."

Off to one side, Scrubbs trying to signal Banion. *Get it together.*

"This must be a very emotional time for you."

"Yes, Tom. A lot of emotions are going through me right now. It's been a very . . . strange year. But, here we are. All three million of us. In this *majestic*"—he cleared his throat—"situation."

"What's next on the Millennium Man agenda?"

"Survival."

"How do you mean?"

"Staying alive."

"In what way?"

"Not dying. That's at the top of my own personal agenda."

"Is someone out to do you harm?"

"Not to sound too paranoid about it, but when you go poking about in Uncle Sam's sock drawer, you never know what you might stir up."

"He's plastered," Brokaw's producer said.

"Put it this way," Banion continued, "in the event I'm run over by a car, or contract some strange, fatal disease, or slip and break my neck in the bathroom, or get a blood clump—clot—then I think you and other members of the press would certainly want to investigage-*gate,* whether I died from natural causes."

"Why would the government want to get rid of you?"

"Well, Tom, I—along with over eighty percent of the American people—have come to the conclusion that the government knows much more about UFO's than it is letting on. Indeed, I think the government has a *majestic* amount of knowledge about flying saucers. But getting back to the issue of my personal shafety, I've taken certain precautions. I've left documents behind in a secure place, which, in the event something happens to me, like so much as a severe head cold, will be opened and made public. You can see over my shoulder that there are three million people who would be very, very upset if anything happened to their leader. Who knows *what* they'd do."

"Are you saying they would turn violent?"

"Well, they're reasonable people . . ."

The producer cut to show a marcher holding up a sign: JFK KILLED BY ALIENS.

". . . but you wonder if the next march would be as peaceful as this one."

"John O. Banion, thanks for being with us."

"Pleshure."

"I THOUGHT YOU WERE GOING TO FALL OUT OF YOUR CHAIR," Scrubbs said when they were back in the flying saucer trailer. "But I think you bought us our insurance policy."

Banion drained the rest of the Scotch. He let out a belch. "I've got insurance. You have nothing. Squat. You think they'd march on account of you? Ha."

"This isn't the time for personal considerations. We have to work together."

"Oh? Why?"

"Because we need each other."

"I was doing fine by myself. I had a life, a wife, a syndicated column, a top-rated TV show. The president came to my house for dinners. I moderated the debates. I had millions of respectable, thoughtful readers and viewers. Now look at me. Moses, to a flock of fruitcakes."

"Yeah? How many of your respectable, thoughtful readers and viewers would have marched on Washington for you?"

"What does that have to do with anything?"

"I'm sure they all worshiped you for your suave delivery and keen intellect and rapier wit, but did you ever change their lives? I gave you an issue as big as the millennium! You want to go back to arguing about Social Security reform and who should be in NATO?"

"That's not the point. I had a life."

"I didn't."

"Who cares?"

"Let me tell you something—you've abducted one Indiana housewife, you've abducted them all. Then you came along. It definitely got more interesting."

"I'm truly gratified. I'm thrilled that wrecking my life made your job more stimulating."

"Maybe if you'd been a little less hysterical about it, your life wouldn't have gotten ruined. You know, we abducted a lot of people who didn't make a federal case out of it. There was this woman in Kentucky, we did her *three times* before she even mentioned it, and that was only to her pastor. You—you were Chicken Little. *The aliens have landed! The aliens have landed!*"

"Oh sure. How hysterical of me to mention the fact that I was being *routinely* kidnapped and personally *violated* by aliens. Which—by the way—makes you and your accomplices disgusting *perverts.*"

"Hey, don't look at me. The probes weren't our idea."

"Well *I* certainly didn't ask for them!"

"It was the abductees who started talking about how they'd been probed."

"Revolting, all of you." Banion groaned. "How do I get back to my own world?"

"This is no time to lose it. Keep it together."

"Oh, shut up." Banion stood, went to the window, looked down on the clutch of paparazzi. "Roz—she worked for you?"

"I don't know. Possibly. Probably. They might have put her in to do damage control. I caught her on TV. Quite the looker. Have you heard from her?"

"She called me. To apologize. Just like you. I must say, for a rogue government agency, you're all so polite. Is that part of your training?"

There was knock on the door. Dr. Falopian and Colonel Murfletit appeared, smiling luminously. They stared questioningly at Scrubbs, still in his Tall Nordic bodysuit, sans face mask.

Scrubbs looked at Banion. Banion looked at Scrubbs. This would be the moment to toss him to the mob to be torn to pieces. One word, and Colonel Murfletit's ascots would be on him, pulping him with their batons.

"This," Banion said, "is Mr. Dick. He's going to be helping us."

The brain trust collectively frowned. No sooner had they gotten rid of one Banion groupie than another appeared. At least this one looked like someone they could do business with.

They reported that the first TV network viewer polls had come in. The people were with them! Overwhelmingly! More than eighty percent supported the Millennium agenda! Especially the provisions calling for tax breaks for abductees.

The two scuttled off to be interviewed.

"Mr. Dick?" Scrubbs said.

"*Fits.*"

"I'M NOT GOING TO READ THAT," THE PRESIDENT SAID. "I don't care how many telegrams we got in support of these yo-yos, I won't do it."

"All it says is—"

"I know what it says. I read it. It says I support them. Well I don't. And I think Hank Gracklesen is going to look like a gold-plated jackass by the time he's finished. Abduction hearings! He never should have given in to them. I won't have anything to do with it. I won't be associated with it. I won't be the first president in history to have a position on flying saucers."

"You were willing to welcome them to town."

"Your brilliant idea. And what did it get us? Insults."

"You'll get questions on this."

"I welcome them. I'll tell them that I'm just a little more concerned with the real issues facing America in the new century."

"You can't say 'real,' " the campaign manager said.

"Why not?"

"Eighty percent of the American people think these are real."

"Eighty percent of the American people," the president said, "have snakes in their heads."

"You want to tell them that right before an election, eight points down?"

"Blebnikov called me last night, drunk as a porcupine on brake fluid, to tell me he can't control his own army. I told him, It's no damn wonder, you haven't paid 'em in over a year. He says, Well, they may mutiny and take over and what is he supposed to do? Meanwhile, my Supreme Court justice just got arrested for drunk driving, son of a bitch, and the CBO is about to release figures blaming this recession on me personally, and the IMF is bellyaching that if we don't send Mexico another forty billion by next *Tuesday,* the whole place is going to blow like a toilet, and Flickery is eating my lunch in states that I bought and paid for. I have enough on my plate right now without worrying about flying saucers!"

"Blebnikov believes in flying saucers," the chief of staff said "It was in that CIA profile."

"All right, he's got snakes in his head, too."

The chief of staff nodded to the campaign manager, who handed the president the summary of a tracking poll done among undecided voters. "Over seventy percent think that the government—that's us—is lying about UFO's and support Banion and his marchers."

"How did we get to this pass?" the president asked, shaking his head. "Doesn't anyone have imagination enough *not* to believe in something?"

"No one's saying we should jump in headfirst," the chief of staff said. "Just a brief statement reiterating our support of open government. We could put it in the context of civil rights."

"Civil rights? These people ought to be locked up in mental institutions. No, and that's final. We're going to do the right thing for once."

"What?"

"Ignore this whole business. Now what else you got for me?"

After the meeting, the press secretary whispered to the campaign manager outside the Oval Office, "Let me work on it."

STAKES HIGH IN TONIGHT'S DEBATE
RUSSIA, UFO'S, ECONOMY EXPECTED
TO DOMINATE AS CANDIDATES CLASH

"THANK YOU, GOVERNOR. MR. PRESIDENT, YOU HAVE ONE minute to respond."

"Thank you, Jim. My concern over the possible abduction of American citizens by these . . . whatever you want to call them, is a matter of public record. Not that you would know that from listening to the governor's distortions, if I may with all due respect call them that. When I was in the Congress, I introduced legislation time and time again calling for declassification of a vast number of government documents, many of which surely touched, directly or indirectly, on this issue. Now, if the governor wants to engage me on matters related to space, I *welcome* him. I have pushed for Project Celeste's completion practically from the first moment I took office four years ago. And I am *proud* to note that this historic event will take place on my watch. *Over,* I might add, the constant naysaying of people like Governor Flickery, who would rather spend the money on questionable highway projects than on forging boldly ahead into the future. I would add, if I might, that I won't be there personally to witness the launch, since my opponent has seen fit to impugn—"

"Your time is up, Mr. President."

". . . my motives and charge that I would be using it for tactical political advantage. I only regret that it had to come to this."

BANION LISTENED WEARILY TO DR. FALOPIAN, COLONEL Murfletit, the head of the International Congress of Abductees, the head of the World UFO Congress, and the chairman of the Presidents of Major Paranormal Organizations argue loudly over which of them would have the honor of presenting the opening statement at the Gracklesen hearings. A trio of appalled aides from Gracklesen's office were present, doing their best to cope.

Banion did his best to appear interested, but it was hard going. He felt ontologically stuck. He couldn't go back, and he wasn't sure how to go forward. The head of WUFOC and Falopian were arguing fiercely. The fault lines within the UFO community were showing: the purists held that the abductees were flakes and that the hearings should concentrate on forcing the government to reveal what it knew about UFO technology. Banion now found himself in the unwanted role of mediator between competing groups of maniacs. It took willpower not to stand up and start screaming.

It was getting ugly. The head of Experiencers Anonymous, the abductee support group, had just called the vice president of the Area 51 Investigative Association a "dupe." It reminded Banion of the French Revolution tribunals. The only thing missing was a guillotine. Someone stood up and announced that they had been penetrated. Government agents were among them!

Banion thought, Oh you lambs, you poor, bleating stumblers in Plato's cave, bumping into your own shadows on the wall, if only you knew. . . . As the dissonant rumble grew louder, he wanted to shout: Go home! Hug your children, fix yourselves a drink, take up chess, knitting, woodworking, crossword puzzles, kinky sex, anything, but *get a life*! But the show had to go on. The play was still the thing, in which to—what? Scrubbs had no plan. Banion's head throbbed.

He stood up. No one noticed. They were too busy shouting at each other. Gracklesen's aides watched him with silent alarm: *You're not leaving us alone . . . with* them? He shrugged in their direction—*Have fun, guys*—and left.

Reporters were waiting for him outside his Georgetown office, clamoring for interviews. Let Elspeth deal with them. Inside, Renira was on the phone to Miss Delmar, who was complaining bitterly over having had to share a trailer with Kathy Carr. Between um hums, Renira handed him a half-inch-thick wad of phone slips. As he walked somnambulantly to his office, Banion flipped through them, discarding them one by one onto the floor like love-me-love-me-nots. He closed the door behind him. He was about to hurl himself onto the couch—and maybe, just maybe, have a good cry—when he saw that it was occupied by the recumbent form of Scrubbs, a newspaper spread over his face like a death shroud.

"There's a couch in the other room, you know," he said. "This is my office, not a bedroom."

Scrubbs stirred. "It's not as comfortable. How'd the meeting go?"

"The techies and the abductees have 'issues' with each other. At least take your shoes off. Damnit . . ."

"Your dedicated techie," Scrubbs said, going back to reading his newspaper, "has no use at all for your abductee."

"Tell me about it."

"He'd rather talk about the hieroglyphics on the Roswell wreckage than alien date rape."

"My God," Banion said, "I used to moderate presidential debates. Now I'm refereeing hissy fits between paranoids and paranormalists." He looked at Scrubbs. "God hates me. That's it. There's a higher meaning to all this."

"I thought we were finished feeling sorry for ourselves."

Banion sighed. "I'm too tired to be angry. I only have the energy for self-pity."

The phone rang. Renira said over the speaker, as if she were announcing the queen of England, "Val Dalhousie."

"What kind of name is that?" Scrubbs said.

Banion put the call on the speakerphone. "Hello, Val."

"*Darling* boy, what have you gone and done? Everyone is *bouleversé*. It's too delicious for words. How are you? I know you're gaga with work, so I won't keep you. Are you in town Saturday? I'm having a completely informal brunch, all your favorite people, Henry and Nancy, Polly and Lloyd, the Galilees, Burts, Organgorfers, Hynda and Tucker, Eela Dommage, Knatch and Penny Wemyss, oh, and Nicholas and Sveva Romanov—I *adore* her, one of her ancestors is in the *Inferno,* Ugolino something-or-other, he's supposed to have eaten one of his relatives or something macabre, but *how* chic to have an ancestor in Dante . . ."

"What the hell was that all about?" Scrubbs said after Banion hung up.

"It appears"—Banion sighed—"that I am back on the A-list."

"You don't sound very happy about it."

Hearing Scrubbs point it out made Banion conscious of the fact. True enough, he felt curiously indifferent to his reëlection to the innermost circle. Only a few months ago he had gone to pieces over his ouster. Now, really, he couldn't care less.

He became intrigued by this transition he had apparently made, without so much as realizing it. Why did he feel so— oblivious? He couldn't quite put his finger on it. Was it some still-glowing ember of resentment over having been dumped by his former friends? Or was it simply that all his former glories and laurels—the plaudits, the invitations to dine with kings and princes—now seemed somewhat . . . dull beside this gaudy existential drama into which he had been freakishly drawn? What thrill was there left in watching the peacock pageant when you stood at the head of an army on the march?

He was on the phone to *Newsweek*—also doing a cover story on him—when Scrubbs bolted from the sofa and held out his folded newspaper to Banion, urgently tapping a story headlined SHOOT-OUT IN S.E. LEAVES TWO DEAD.

"Excuse me," Banion said, cupping the phone. *"What?"*

"This."

Banion scanned the story. "Happens every day in Washington."

"Hang up. We gotta call the office."

SCRUBBS'S BRIEFING ON THE BRADLEY BUSINESS LEFT BANion numbly contemplating the Dorothy Parker line "What fresh hell is this?" The shadowy feds—identified in the newspaper story as Drug Enforcement agents (Scrubbs assured him they were not in fact DEA)—had apparently knocked on Bernard the drug dealer's door at an inopportune time, but then what hour of the day is appropriate to call on a drug dealer? The unexpected fusillade of machine-gun fire that greeted them was described by one Metro police officer as "impressive."

Scrubbs dialed the number and put the call over the speaker.

"Creative Solutions, how may I direct your call?"

"It's Scrubbs." He whispered to Banion, "Creative Solutions. Cute, huh?"

"Hello, Nathan," said the familiar voice. It sounded tired and somber and all business. "I was wondering when you'd call."

"I've been kind of busy."

"I see you're not calling from your usual pay phone. Sharing an office, huh? Is Mr. Banion with you?"

"He's here."

"May I speak with him?"

"He doesn't want to talk to you. He's kind of upset."

"That makes everyone."

"You got his message? In the speech?"

" 'Majestic situation'? Yes, I got that. About a dozen times. You can tell him he doesn't have to say that anymore in all his public statements. We all understand where we are and where we stand."

"So, we're square?"

"Hardly. The arrangement that we discussed did not happen. And the present situation is untenable. It has been elevated beyond proportion. It is a very unmajestic situation. And a murder warrant is about to be issued for you."

"What are you talking about?"

"You know very well what I'm talking about. Two law enforcement officers are dead, another is wounded."

"Law enforcement officers, my ass. Assassins."

"We know about your friend Bradley. And we *will* find him." Banion saw Scrubbs recoil.

"I was the one who sent them over to Bernard's house," Scrubbs said.

"I don't think so. Not from the description the wounded agent gave, unless you're now black and in your early sixties."

"What do you want?"

"You know what we want. You need to come in. And your friend needs to call all this off. He can issue a statement to the effect—well, he's good with words. Delusions can result from any number of causes. Medication, alcohol, bipolar disorders. There's no dishonor in it. But it needs to be an emphatic, and immediate, public rejection and denunciation of his recent activities. The situation is too highly charged. It needs to be unplugged. If these two things occur, tomorrow, if not sooner, then your friend Bradley is a nonissue."

NOW IT WAS BANION'S TURN TO ASK, "ARE YOU GOING TO drink all of that at once?"

Scrubbs sat on the edge of the sofa, silent, hunched forward over the remains of enough vodka to stun a Russian. Finally he spoke.

"Shit."

"That's not a particularly penetrating analysis of the objective situation," Banion said.

"Fuck off."

"Don't get bilious with me."

"I've gotta do what he says."

"And me? What about me?"

"You'll be all right."

"I'm so reassured."

"Just what he says. Say you went nuts on medication or something. Disband the marchers. There's only one problem. If you do that, you won't have any leverage left. They'll be able to do anything they want to you."

"Then I'm not about to announce that this was all just some midlife crisis."

"Yeah. I guess I'd hold on to the army. Oh, *man* . . ."

Scrubbs picked up the phone.

"What are you doing?" Banion asked.

"I'm going to call him and tell him I'm coming in."

"Why?"

"Bradley. He saved my ass. Twice. They'll find him. I can't let that happen."

"Wait," Banion said.

"I have to."

"And what am I supposed to do?"

"You'll be fine."

"As long as I remain leader to three million kooks? This is the rest of my life? The Lonely Messiah? No thanks."

"Where do you get off feeling sorry for yourself? I'm the one who's going off to get killed."

"Talk about self-pity! Well see here, pal, this is not Paris, and you are not Sydney Carton, so you can stuff the 'It is a far, far better thing that I do, than I have ever done' speech."

"You got a better idea? Asshole?"

"Yes, as a matter of fact." Banion reached for the phone.

"Who are you calling?"

"Rule number one: start at the top, and work your way up from there."

"White House," the operator answered.

SEVENTEEN

IN REVERSAL, PRESIDENT WILL ATTEND CELESTE LAUNCH

SPECIAL TO THE WASHINGTON POST

The White House today announced that the president will be on hand after all for the launch of the final stage of Project Celeste, the controversial space station.

The announcement came following emotional remarks at a press conference by Amber Lamb, a female mission specialist who is a member of the *Celeste* crew. Lamb, a fitness instructor who will study aerobic exercise in space, said that she felt it was "totally not fair that the president can't attend just because of politics. *Celeste* was his deal all along."

Press Secretary Fred Tully said the president was "deeply moved" when he read Lamb's comments and had "decided it was his duty" to attend, whatever the political costs."

Mona Moyst, spokesman for the Flickery campaign, said the president's decision came as "no surprise." She denounced *Celeste* as a "$21 billion orbiting pork barrel."

"Hello, Burt."

"Jack O-mighty Banion, how are you? We going to see you at Val's?"

"Don't think so. I need your help."

"Anything."

"I need a meeting with the president."

"Hoo! You do need a favor. What's up?"

"Probably better if you don't know."

"You got to give me some idea."

"Little green men, Burt. It's about little green men."

Burt Galilee laughed. "You don't give up. I admire your pertinacity. But look now, Jack, the man's busier than a one-legged Cajun in an ass-kicking contest. The campaign, Russia, now he's decided to go to the *Celeste* launch. Did you see that? It's in the papers this morning. Maybe after the election, we could—"

"No, no, I need to see him today."

"Jack, this is the *president*. I know you're operating in a different universe now, but the old one's still working according to the rules."

"You know me, Burt."

"Let's be honest. You have been going through some significant changes . . ."

"Have I ever wasted your time?"

"You're a down-to-earth sort of fellow, for someone who believes in flying saucers. But I can't do what you're asking."

"Do you want the president to have a second term?"

"Come on, Jack. Don't talk shit to me."

"If I don't get this meeting, I promise you, his photo op at the *Celeste* launch is going to be the mother of all nightmares."

Burton Galilee pressed the record button on his telephone console.

"Jack, do I understand you to be threatening the president of the United States?"

"So you're taping? Testing, one, two, three. You getting this? I'm saying, if you don't want a disaster on your hands down there, get me my meeting with him. By the way, nice move with the stress specialist. 'Gee, like if only the president could like, wow, be here.' "

"You want me to go to the White House and tell them Jack

Banion is going to throw a wrench into the *Celeste* launch unless you get a meeting with the president? Now how's that going to sound?"

"Convincing, I hope, for your sake."

"Why?"

"Flickery says he's going to crack down on influence peddling in Washington. It'll be slim pickings for you if he gets in."

Burt laughed. He pressed the pause button. "They all say that when they're running. Then they get to town and see how it works and we all become best friends."

"Sure, but it'll take him a year or two to figure that out. Meantime you're out on the sidewalk. The quid pro quo for this is you get to keep the status quo. It's a pretty sweet status quo. You're the First Friend. West Wing access, state dinners, sleepovers in the Lincoln Bedroom, golf at Burning Bush, clients lining up around the block outside your office because you've got the president's private number on your speed dial. You really want to risk all that by *not* getting me ten minutes with him in the Oval? Think about it. I'll expect a call within an hour."

The call came forty-five minutes later, from the White House chief of staff. His voice was two degrees above freezing.

"Burt Galilee called. He said you called him, making threats. Extremely unwise, and possibly criminal. What do you want?"

"A meeting with your boss, this afternoon."

"Out of the question."

"Now you're being unwise. You haven't even heard what it's about."

"I assume it's about flying saucers. We tried to meet you halfway on that. You were unreasonable, to say nothing of ungracious. So let me explain reality to you. You've had your moment in the sun. You got your hearings from Gracklesen. If you're looking for sport, go frighten some more senators. This is the White House. That crap doesn't play here."

"You saw what three million people look like, packed into the Mall?" Banion asked. "Okay, now imagine them camped out at

Cape Canaveral, screaming that the president of the United States is about to bring about the end of the world."

"You're insane."

"Not really, but that's another conversation. That's exactly what they will do if I tell them that launching *Celeste* will provoke the aliens into attacking the United States."

"You need a psychiatrist, not the president."

"You're taping this, I assume? Well, why not, everyone does. All right, here's the deal . . ."

Banion glanced over at Scrubbs, who gave him a thumbs-up.

"We have received a communication from the aliens—"

"I don't have *time* for this, Banion."

"Two minutes. See, they know that the military payload module aboard the *Celeste* shuttle is a . . ."

Suddenly Banion's mind went blank.

"Plasma Beam Device," Scrubbs whispered.

". . . Plasma Beam Device, designed as a first-strike weapon against them."

"Get *help*."

"All right, it sounds a little far-fetched. But I assure you the aliens are taking it very seriously. And they have communicated, through me, their, if you will, ambassador here on planet earth, that they *will* initiate all-out war on the United States if *Celeste* is launched. Now, if I tell my people about this, they are going to go bananas and do everything in their power to prevent the launch."

"If they set one toe on government property, they will be arrested and charged. And you with them. You'll spend twenty years in federal—"

"You want to make me into the Millennial Gandhi, go ahead. Do you really have jail space for three million people? And what becomes of your triumphant preëlection photo op? The word catastrophe comes to mind. Is that the photo op you're looking for on the eve of the election?"

"I'm going to hang up."

"Bill," Banion said, "if you doubt my ability to muster a crowd, just remember the scene outside your window last weekend."

Silence. Gotcha.

"I'm asking for ten minutes with the president. What's ten minutes, next to pandemonium, right before the election?"

"What do you want to talk to him about?"

"You don't really want to know that."

"I have to know that. Goddamnit . . ."

"Okay"—Banion cleared his throat—"I have a plan to stop the aliens."

"For God's sake—"

"Three million people, Bill. Three million really strange people, chanting 'We Shall Overcome.' What a visual, eh?"

"All right, all right. Four-thirty. But ten minutes, that's all."

"Four-thirty's bad for me. Can you make it two?"

BANION HADN'T BEEN IN THE OVAL OFFICE IN ALMOST A year. The Secret Service gave him a thorough going-over with their metal-detector wands and even took apart his fountain pen. Scrubbs had never been to the White House, much less the Oval Office. His clearing-in was complicated by the fact that he could produce no photo ID or, for that matter, valid Social Security number. (MJ-12 erased you from federal records when you joined.) They wanted to arrest him. It took the chief of staff, already deeply unhappy about the meeting, to intervene. Finally, they were ushered in and found themselves with the president of the United States and his chief of staff.

"This is Mr. Scrubbs," Banion said. "He works for you."

Banion related the whole story, with corroboratory grunts and nods from the awestruck Scrubbs. (Many first-time visitors to the Oval Office tend to clutch.) The president listened in silence, which he seemed at pains to maintain. His eyes widened slightly when Banion got to the part about Bernard the drug dealer greeting the MJ-12 assassins with a hail of machine-gun fire. It took more than ten minutes to tell the whole story, but the chief of staff did not interrupt.

"So," Banion concluded, "you need to call these people off, right now, before they harm this Bradley person, the man who rescued Mr. Scrubbs."

While the president and chief of staff were chewing on this large radish, Banion continued, somewhat airily, "As for me. I have been put through unmitigated hell by the United States government, and I will require redress. Large redress. To begin with, I want, on an exclusive basis—naturally—the goods on this rogue agency. Details. Everything, especially who's in charge. If I'm going to try to get my old life back, I'm going to need a Pulitzer Prize–winning scoop, for starters." Banion sat back. "Quite a story, don't you agree?"

The president looked down at his desk, pursed his lips, looked at the chief of staff, looked back at his visitors, unreadable as the sphinx. Finally he said, "Well, we'll certainly look into it. Thanks for coming in."

"Thank *you*, sir," Scrubbs said eagerly. Banion thought, Novice.

"Excuse me," Banion said. " 'Look into it'? What does that mean?"

"It means," the chief of staff said starchily, "that we'll let you know."

"Well, screw that," Banion said.

"Jack," Scrubbs hissed, "the *president*."

"There seems to be a misunderstanding," Banion said. "I'm not some supplicant from a Middle East sheikhdom come to beg you to sell me F-Sixteens. And I didn't grow up on a pig farm. You're not going to get rid of me with 'We'll get back to you' and a presidential tie clip. I've just informed you that a rogue agency of the government is going around kidnapping U.S. citizens and is at this moment on its way to kill this Bradley person, unless Mr. Scrubbs hands himself in to them. God only knows what ghastly plans they have in store for me, but I certainly have no intention of waiting for them to inject my arteries with an air bubble. So you're going to have to do better than 'We'll get back to you.' I'd suggest you pick up that phone, dial that number Mr. Scrubbs gave you, and issue a cease-and-desist order. Unless," he said, "you want a millennial *zoo* at your precious launch."

"That's it," the chief of staff said. "This meeting is over."

"Jack," the president said in a not-unfriendly voice, "you're only going to look like a maniac if you do this."

"Mr. President," Banion said wearily, "I already look like a maniac. I've lost everything I cared about. You, on the other hand, still have something to lose."

"How am I going to lose the election just because a bunch of nuts show up at my launch? How is that going to make me look bad? Unless"—he smiled—"your aliens do retaliate and launch an attack on the U.S."

The chief of staff chuckled mirthlessly.

"I think," the president said, standing up behind his desk, "I can live with that possibility. Thanks for coming in, Jack. Take care of yourself." He came around his desk and extended his hand.

"Well," Banion said to Scrubbs when the two of them had reached Pennsylvania Avenue, "that was a success."

"SORRY TO PUT YOU THROUGH THAT," THE CHIEF OF STAFF said, "but I figured, better give him his meeting. A lot's riding on a smooth *Celeste* launch. No point encouraging him to turn it into a freak show if we can avoid it."

The president was contemplating the phone on his desk.

"Sir?"

"Who," the president said, "would theoretically be in charge of this Majestic Twelve? Assuming."

"Assuming what?"

"It exists."

"Sir, at the risk of stating the obvious, Jack Banion is not playing with a full deck these days. You heard what Burt Galilee said. The man's had a breakdown. To put it in clinical terms, he's nuts."

"He seemed pretty lucid to me."

"A lot of nuts do. Look at Perot. You didn't *believe* what he said?"

"Look, I never could stand the arrogant son of a bitch, but if this is some sort of midlife crisis, it's a lulu. I think something happened to him. Some kind of trauma, maybe. I'm not a doctor, but I'm telling you, a man—especially a snob like him—doesn't throw away everything that he had to go hang out with UFO loonies because of some 'nervous breakdown.' I've known a lot of people who had nervous breakdowns, psychotic episodes, reality disruptions, whatever hundred-dollar name you want to put on it, posttraumatic stress—saw plenty of *that*—and I never knew any of them could sit here like he did, cool as ice. All right, maybe I'm wrong and he is nuts. Fine. Find out. So you call George Herrick right away and tell him to have CIA look into it. Or would this be more of an NSA deal? I wouldn't know who'd be in charge of this worm farm. Anyway, start making inquiries."

"Mr. President . . ." The chief of staff only called him that when he was about to not do what he was being asked. "Poor Ike," Harry Truman said before handing over the reins to Eisenhower. "He'll sit there and say, 'Do this,' and nothing will happen."

"Damnit, Bill, don't you give me that 'Mr. President'—"

"This is the figment of a deranged mind."

"Then let's find out for sure."

The chief of staff was silent a moment. He said gravely, "Let's for the sake of argument say that there *is* something odd going on here. Now let's pose the critical question: Do you *want* to find out?"

"Damn straight. It's my job."

"Your job, if I may quote the oath of office, is to preserve and protect and defend the Constitution of the United States—"

"I *know* that."

"—not to light a match to it."

"I haven't heard one word of sense from anyone today."

"Suppose we ascertain that, starting in nineteen forty-seven, the U.S. government has been behind every UFO in the sky. For God knows what reason—spooking the Russians, for starters. For fifty years, every blinking light in the sky, every scorch mark in the desert, every—my God—abduction . . . why don't we just call it kidnapping? . . . has been brought to you courtesy of Uncle Sam. Your tax dollars at work. How is this going to play on the evening news? It would make everyone's worst Kennedy assassination theory read like Mother Goose. No one would trust the government ever again. And who would they blame? The handiest person around—you. I can't wait to get to work on your TV address from the Oval Office. 'Guess what, I just found out that for the last half century we've been making funny lights in the sky and kidnapping your womenfolk, plowing crop circles. Did I mention the cattle mutilations?' Never mind reelection. Let's skip directly to impeachment proceedings."

"Hold on. *I'm* the one blowing the damn whistle. I'd be a hero."

"No one," the chief of staff said somberly, "remotely associated with the United States government would be in the running for the title of hero. Do you have any concept of the chaos such a revelation would create? At a time, let me point out, when we face the prospect of war with a country that still has sixty-eight hundred nuclear warheads, under the control of a man who, CIA tells us, brushes his teeth in the morning with vodka and instructs his mistresses to address his penis as Peter the Great. Is this really a good time to bring the government crashing down?"

"We're getting ahead of ourselves here," the president said after a reflective pause. "Banion probably is haywire. It's probably nothing."

"Exactly. Then why go poking into it?"

"It's ugly, coyote ugly. Makes me want to chew my arm off."

"All I'm saying is that if it is true—which it isn't—there's no way you can reveal that it is. And if it isn't—which it can't be—then there's no need to do anything. When you come right down to it, it's a no-brainer."

The president frowned. "We still have a Banion problem. He's going to piss on my parade if we don't do anything."

"What's Banion going to do? Announce that the aliens are going to attack. What'll that do to his credibility? The moment he announces that, no one has to take him seriously anymore."

"What about his three million followers marching down to Canaveral to crap all over my moment? *My* moment."

"Bring them on. You emerge as the strong leader who stood up to the forces of cuckoodom. The more I think about this, the more I like it. This may be the best thing that could have happened to us. This could be our margin of victory."

"It's going to be a goddamn mess."

"It'll be a triumph. Unless . . . ," the chief of staff said darkly.

"What?"

"The aliens attack."

For a brief, unusual moment, the Oval Office filled with laughter.

UFO BIG IN KINK STINK
BANION LIKED TO DRESS UP AS ALIEN AND HAVE PROSTITUTES "PROBE" HIM

"IT'S ONLY THE *BLARE*," SCRUBBS SAID FROM THE SOFA.

Banion sat at his desk staring down at the headline in the nation's largest-circulation supermarket tabloid. The escort service girl with whom he had purportedly "holed up" in the Hay-Adams Hotel, right across from the White House, for several weekends of "sextraterrestrial" whoopee was attractive enough, in an overrouged sort of way. What branch of the government was *she* employed by, he wondered. Inside were four full pages of color photos. The one that would probably go out to the wire services and be reprinted in *Time, Newsweek,* and other glossies showed Banion wearing nothing but Martian antennae. It was a good job of Scitexing. In the digital age, photos lied all the time, through their teeth. You could put Mother Teresa in a bordello, Hitler in a synagogue. Should he even bother issuing an outraged denial? In the outer office, he could hear Renira's phones clamoring. Outside, TV trucks disgorged camera crews like soldiers deploying from a troop carrier.

Renira walked in to say that *The New York Times* was on the line demanding comment. Banion said to Scrubbs, "You were saying how the mainstream media wouldn't pay any attention to this?"

Scrubbs shrugged. "I was only trying to cheer you up."

"You failed." Banion told Renira to tell the *Times* he'd call back and returned to his tabloid. In a lurid sort of way, he was fascinated by this fictional fantasy they'd concocted for him.

"What an idiot," he muttered. "To think that I could walk into the Oval Office and start issuing demands." He shook his head. "But I didn't expect them to hit back this way. I thought, well, I thought he was above this sort of thing." He read aloud, " 'While we were doing it, Jack liked me to make these noises like a spaceship. Like this: Wee-ooo-wee-ooo—you know, just like they did at that march last weekend?'

"The government's got no class anymore," Banion said.

"There's plenty of reporters outside. Tell them the White House is trying to make you look like an asshole because they're scared of you."

Banion looked at Scrubbs sourly. "I'm not sure you're cut out to be a spin doctor."*

"It's true, isn't it? Unless it was MJ-Twelve again."

"This is no time for earnest denials, especially honest ones. It's

---

*One who lies for a living, usually for a politician.

time to take the fight to them. But when you strike at a king, you must kill him."

"What?"

"Emerson. In a way, this might work to our advantage."

"You being an alien sex freak?"

"When you're hot, you're hot. It's not like I'm going to have a hard time getting on prime-time TV tonight, is it?"

"OUR GUEST TONIGHT, JOHN O. BANION. WELCOME BACK ON *Larry King Live*."

"Thank you, Larry."

"This story in the *Blare*, the tabloid, about you and this woman. Want to comment?"

"I could deny it, Larry, and say that powerful forces are out to discredit me, but why bother? I'm sure the young woman in question is a patriotic-minded person just following orders, the way all those Germans did in World War Two. Maybe she even thinks she was doing the right thing. I hope so. But I didn't come on your show tonight to talk about the government's latest clumsy attempt to force me to look like someone who's overdosed on Viagra.* I have something much more important to talk about."

"What's that?"

"I have received a communiqué from the alien high command."

Larry King arched his eyebrows and nodded. "No kidding."

"It's a very serious situation, I regret to say. I hope people listening tonight will pay very close attention, because this affects every man, woman, and child in this country."

"They're listening. Believe me."

"Well, Larry, the aliens are going to attack the United States

---

*Erection pills. Introduced in 1998, until protests from exhausted women pressured Congress to get the Food and Drug Administration to ban them. Now sold at higher prices on the black market.

with everything they've got if the president insists on launching the final stage of Project *Celeste* this week."

"That *does* sound serious. What's their problem?"

"Their intelligence apparatus here—as you know, Larry, the aliens have an extensive intelligence operation here—well, they have to, don't they? Anyway, their information is that the payload aboard this shuttle, bound for *Celeste,* is a first-strike weapon. A Plasma Beam Device. This is potentially devastating to the, uh, alien fleet. A dagger, if you will, Larry, aimed at their heart."

"Who did you speak to about this?"

"Their leaders. I only deal with the top echelon."

"And you've told this to our leaders?"

"I revealed this to the president, in the Oval Office at the White House, just a few days ago."

"Oh, *Goddamnit,*" the president said. He and the First Lady were watching in bed.

"What was his reaction?"

"I'm sorry to report, Larry, that his attitude was one of complete denial. As you know, his poll numbers are way down, he might lose, the election is right around the corner. He needs all the publicity he can get. He seems to think that a photo opportunity at Cape Canaveral is more important than total annihilation at the hands of superior alien firepower. A sad situation, Larry."

"Right."

"You read in the papers this morning that he's going to be the one to personally push the launch button?"

"Yeah, I saw that. Let me ask you, doesn't this all sound kind of—to be honest—nuts?"

"It won't sound 'nuts,' Larry, to the majority of the American people. Let me remind you that eighty percent of the American people believe that the government has been lying to them about UFO's for over half a century."

"Yeah, but—"

"So why would they start believing the government now—when the stakes are so high? That's why I'm here tonight, to announce that unless the president agrees to halt the *Celeste* launch and agrees to inspection of all future space payloads by certified UFO organization inspectors, then the Millennial Man Militia will have no choice but to halt that launch."

"Millennial Man *Militia*?"

"Yes, Larry. The military arm of the Millennium Men."

"Get me the attorney general," the president barked into his bedside phone.

EIGHTEEN

CANAVERAL AUTHORITIES BRACE AS 500,000
"MILLENNIUM MILITIAMEN" ARRIVE AT CAPE
TO HALT LAUNCH OF CELESTE'S FINAL STAGE

PRESIDENT IS REPORTED "DEFIANT"

ATTORNEY GENERAL VOWS
MASS ARRESTS IN EVENT
PROTEST TURNS VIOLENT

With the *Celeste* launch less than forty-eight hours away, the media had all but abandoned the presidential election, only one week away. Beside the surreal tableau unfolding at Cape Canaveral, the campaign paled. Banion's call to arms, Dr. Falopian's perfervid networking, and Colonel Murfletit's deft logistics had produced a crowd of a half million, and growing. Traffic on Interstate 95 was backed up two hundred miles, to the Georgia border. Only the 1969 launch of *Apollo 11*, which had carried the first Americans to their rendezvous with the surface of the moon, had drawn such numbers, but those viewers had come in peace. Local and state authorities were overwhelmed. The government called up the National Guard and then mobilized regular airborne units to parachute in, if it came to that.

The mood inside Banion's flying saucer command trailer (trucked down from Washington) was as defiant as that in the White House. Banion paced in front of a large map of the area, a pointer tucked under his arm like a swagger stick. Dr. Falopian had just informed him that a self-styled guerrilla UFO group had arrived. Its specialty was staging incursions into Area 51 in Nevada, where the government was supposedly reverse-engineering the captured alien spacecraft. The complicating factor was that members of Group 51, as they called themselves, were dedicated gun enthusiasts, and they had been observed toting large, bulgy duffel bags.

Banion summoned Colonel Murfletit and instructed him to convey to Group 51 that there was to be no plinking at *Celeste* on the launchpad. He had been doing his best to sound Gandhiesque, harping incessantly on the nobility of civil disobedience, millennial *satyagraha*. (The trick was not sounding like a weenie.) The emphasis was to be on tactics such as lying limply across the roads, preventing ingress to or egress from the Space Center; a little harmless chaining of limbs to fences, gates, that sort of thing. So far, the National Guard had carted off more than 5,000 superbly limp militiamen. Having filled all the local jails within fifty miles, the authorities were now having to bus them to a federal detention center in a swampy, godforsaken part of the state where several thousand extremely undesirable Cuban illegals were still being held. What the long-incarcerated Cubanos would make of their new fellow inmates remained to be seen. Lunch, probably.

Banion now turned his attention to the Millennial Man Militia Auxiliary Air Force, or MMMAAF. It consisted of four single-engine planes, nine hang gliders, two motorized airfoils, three hot-air balloons, and one motorized parachute, an odd little craft consisting of a sort of fan-driven, four-wheeled scooter with a parachute attached. The original plan was for them to overfly the launch area. But the real Air Force, alerted to this stratagem, announced that it would summarily shoot from the sky, with aircraft far more fearsome than MMMAAF's, any airborne contrivance that transgressed the exclusion zone surrounding the launchpad. Banion caught Colonel Murfletit giving one of his pilots a surreptitious pep talk about the greater good of going down in a blaze of glory and emphatically reasserted his authority over the auxiliary. As for Dr. Falopian, God knew what phlegmy fomenting he was up to. He had brought in a pallid, twitchy homunculus by the name of Fidge who claimed to be able to jam *Celeste*'s guidance system by means of a mysterious "ultratransistor."

Banion posed the question he would have thought obvious: was it wise to cause a 4.5-million-pound rocket ship, full of the most combustible solids and liquids known to science, to go belly-up and plunge, flamingly, onto 500,000 people? (For that matter, was it fair to the poor seven astronauts aboard?) Though privately Banion wondered if America's collective gene pool might be better off, in a Darwinian sense, if it were purged of the population cohort that comprised the Millennial Militia.

"I have the distinct feeling," he announced to Scrubbs when they had a moment alone, "that this is going to end in tears."

Renira informed him that Deputy FBI Director Bargenberfer was on line, and that he did not sound happy, amused, or otherwise felicitous.

"It's come to our attention," he said, forgoing the usual howjados, "that some of your people are armed." A reference, obviously, to Group 51. Clearly, the FBI had copiously deployed undercover agents among the Militiamen. (Who could blame them?) Banion feigned ignorance as best he could but pointed out that the gun laws in Florida were notoriously liberal. The state legislature had recently repealed a measure that, during its brief time in force, had barred Floridians from owning twenty-millimeter cannons. Deputy Director Bargenberfer darkly warned that at the first sight of anything more threatening-looking than a slingshot, the Four Horsemen of the Federal Apocalypse would descend mercilessly upon him and the Militiamen, and grind their bones into plant fertilizer. Yet the very fact of the warning revealed its impotence. Was the government likely to provoke a clash with a crowd that equaled in size one-third of its armed forces? Banion could take comfort from the enormity of his army, however much it gave him the willies.

POLL: 56% SAY CELESTE LAUNCH
RUNS RISK OF ALIENATING ALIENS

"SECRET SERVICE FEELS—"

"I'm not pulling out, damnit. I am going, and that's final."

"FBI feels—"

"Does anyone in this room understand the English language?"

"NASA feels—"

"NASA? Those yo-yos wouldn't *have* a space station if I hadn't gotten it for them. *NASA* better damn well be good to go, is all I can say."

"The First Lady feels—"

"Meeting concluded."

"We've received over twenty-five thousand letters from schoolchildren begging you to stop the launch—"

"Schoolchildren don't vote."

"This one is from a Caitlin Gregg, age nine—"

"I *don't* want to hear it."

" 'Dear Mr. President, please don't make the aliens angry and wreck—' "

"Meeting concluded! Out!"

The chief of staff went to his office in an attitude of misery to coordinate with the Secret Service and military the plans for getting the president to and from Cape Canaveral, preferably alive.

Alone in his office, the president pondered for a moment, then picked up his phone and dialed.

"Creative Solutions," the cheery female voice announced, "How may I direct your call?"

•　　•　　•

THERE WERE PROBLEMS WITH THE CANDLELIGHT VIGIL, LIKE coming up with half a million candles. Finally a New York billionaire who still preferred to remain anonymous, heir to one of America's oldest fortunes and an avid amateur UFO enthusiast, announced that he would airlift several tons of them in his fleet of private jets. In the midst of this, Renira announced that the president of the United States was on the line.

"Classy move with the hooker," Banion said icily. "Prick."

"That wasn't us," the president said, somewhat unused to this form of presidential address.

"Oh, please. What do you want? I'm busy."

"This is strictly between you and me. I called that number you gave me."

"That's a start."

"I spoke to your guy, Mr. Majestic, whatever his name is."

"And?"

"He knew from his caller ID it was me. Meanwhile, I had our people trace his number."

"And?"

"I told him about your visit to me. I instructed him to cease and desist whatever the hell he was doing with respect to whatsisname, Bartley, Scrubbs's friend."

"Bradley."

"Whatever."

"And?"

"He told me I didn't have the authority to issue that order. I said, 'You hold on a goddamn minute, this is the president of the United States speaking.' Then he said that under the charter of MJ-Twelve—which he said was classified and wouldn't read to me—the president has no authority over it."

"He did?"

"Then the sumbitch hung up on me."

"That's it?"

"FBI says the phone company doesn't have any record of the number. They're looking into it. Point is, I tried. I can't do any more, least not for the time being. Now will you call off your damn freak show?"

Banion considered. "The president of the United States can do better than this."

"They shut down the number! It's gone dead. They've gone to ground. What do you want me do?"

"You're the most powerful man in the world. Do *something.*"

"Now listen to me. You've got to stop this carnival right now. You tell those people whatever you need to. Tell them the aliens decided they like us after all. Tell 'em whatever you want. But you tell them to go home. Someone's going to get hurt."

"That sounds like a politician's promise."

"We'll get to the bottom of this Majestic business. I promise you. But we all need time to cool off."

"I'd like that in writing first."

"Damnit it, Jack, I said I'd work with you. Now call off your nuts. Do it now. We'll deal with your rehabilitation later."

On another phone, across from Banion, Scrubbs was trying to reach the MJ-12 number. He held the receiver to Banion's ear. "The number you have reached is no longer in service."

"I don't care about the exclusive," Banion said. "There are my cards on the table. You're the president, you tell the people. But I want the truth of this grotesque situation exposed."

"Look, if we, and I'm perfectly willing to share credit with you, can defuse this situation, everyone'll come out of this looking good. My pollster says I could get a bump of ten points if we have a nice, happy launch without any of your dogs howling at the moon. I could use that about now. Then—I promise you—we will get to the bottom of this hair ball. We'll make you whole again. I'll give you an exclusive interview, right here in the Oval. Televised live, just the way you like it."

"No," Banion said, "it would be better if it came directly from you, without me there."

He hung up.

Scrubbs said, "You just gave up a hell of an interview there."

Once again, Banion had no explanation for how he felt, but, having just forfeited a career-remaking opportunity, he was surprised by how at peace, even good, he felt. Perhaps, in a strange way, Scrubbs's abductions had served some purpose.

"LISTEN UP, EVERYONE," BANION ANNOUNCED. HE'D BRIEFED Dr. Falopian and Colonel Murfletit and told them to round up the leaders of the various UFO groups. Fifty or so of them stood inside the large tent, listening, awaiting the word from their commander to storm the gates. If this was war, let it begin now!

"I have spoken with the aliens," Banion announced in appropriately portentous tones.

A murmur rippled through the small crowd.

"I told them that I have spoken personally with the president of the United States. He satisfied me that there is no payload aboard *Celeste* hostile to aliens. They have accepted my assurances. And they have withdrawn their threat to destroy us. Let the launch go forward!" he cried exultantly.

The crowd's response was rather subdued, considering that he had just informed them the United States had been spared alien annihilation. In fact, they merely stood and stared at him blinking, twitching.

"I *said*," he tried again, "that everything is all right. The threat is over! We can go home now! Our work is done!"

Off to the side, Dr. Falopian gave a nod to Colonel Murfletit, who in turn signaled several of his ascots, who moved in toward Banion, surrounding him. Then Dr. Falopian took the microphone and announced that he was relieving Banion of his authority over the Millennial Man Militia, on grounds of treason.

"WE GO LIVE NOW TO KEN WENTLEY, WHO IS AT CAPE Canaveral. Ken, what's going on down there?"

"Tom, the situation here now could best be described as *confused*. We've had a report that John Banion, the leader of the Millennial Man Militia, is in the midst of some kind of power struggle with others in his organization. Some tell us that he's still in charge, others say that he is no longer calling the shots. We are unable to locate him for comment. As you can see behind me, the crowd is still very much here in force, protesting tomorrow's launch. We are told that elements of the Hundred and First and Eighty-second Airborne Divisions are in a state of high readiness. Earlier this afternoon the Air Force forced down a hot-air balloon that was flying over the launchpad."

"Is the president still planning to attend the launch tomorrow morning?"

"Tom, we're told that he is determined to be here. *Celeste* has been his pet project from the start, as you know. The details of his visit are being kept from us for security reasons, but I'd told that they plan to fly him from Washington to Patrick Air Force Base near here. Tomorrow, shortly before the launch, he will be flown in by *Marine One,* the presidential helicopter. I'm told it will be escorted by a *number* of helicopter gunships. It's a *very* tense situation here. Almost a war zone. Tom?"

"Thank you, Ken Wentley, at Cape Canaveral. We will of course be providing live coverage of the *Celeste* launch, starting at two A.M. Eastern time."

THEY WERE HOLDING BANION IN HIS FLYING SAUCER, ALONG with Scrubbs, Renira, and Elspeth. Falopian had told the assembled that the perfidious Banion had cut a deal with the aliens and the government to sell out the Militiamen, who would be taken off to the mines of Noomuria in the Anthrax-14 galaxy. With the Militia out of the way, the aliens and the U.S. government would proceed with their fiendish plans to turn the earth's population into an interplanetary sushi bar and breeding facility. Banion had sold them out. Colonel Murfletit's unsmiling, ascoted myrmidons stood outside the door with strict orders not to let anyone in or out.

"I told you from the start those two were trouble," Renira said, playing solitaire.

Banion was on the floor, leaning against the wall, resting his head in his hands. He stifled a yawn. Scrubbs was rummaging around, trying to find a cell phone so they could call the president and advise him of the slight change in program. Elspeth watched the proceedings outside on a small TV. Dr. Falopian was being interviewed by one of the blonder network TV correspondents. He was telling her that there had been an attempt on Banion's life by government agents, and that they were keeping him in a safe place. This vile attempt to silence him, he said, had only strengthened Banion's fierce resolve to stop the launch, at all costs.

"Oh, *God*." Banion groaned.

The correspondent, in the best tradition of the media's calming influence in any crisis, asked Dr. Falopian, Was the Militia determined to stop the launch *by any means*? Dr. Falopian would not say exactly but conveyed his earnest hopes that it would not . . . come to that. And yet, alas, the government seemed *bent* on initiating intergalactic war.

Scrubbs gave up his search for a cell phone and sat down next to Banion. "You think Falopian and Murf are going to order an assault?"

"No," Banion said. "They don't want to die. They just want to be in charge. He'll give a big, rip-roaring speech tonight, claim the mantle of leadership of the UFO movement, then, after the launch, declare moral victory, denounce me, go home, and start collecting fat lecture fees. He's probably on the phone to the president right now, cutting some deal."

"What are they going do with us?"

"Just keep us here until it's over. After tomorrow, we're has-beens. It's their show. And there goes my leverage with the president. I doubt he'll be addressing the nation from the Oval Office to tell them about MJ-Twelve."

"I've been thinking," Scrubbs said. "You think Falopian could be MJ-One?"

"It had occurred," Banion said.

"Murf?"

"MJ-Two? But I have to say, if those two are running the show, it doesn't speak very well of your agency. It's a wonder you got anything done. We were almost home free."

"I thought you said you didn't want it back."

"Well," Banion said, looking around, "it would have been an improvement on this."

"GOOD MORNING, PETER. THE SOUND YOU HEAR IS THE president's helicopter escort. As you can see, it is quite an *impressive* display of firepower, eight gunships. There are literally hundreds of Secret Service agents at the launch facility. The perimeter is being patrolled by scores of armored vehicles. Three divisions of elite, battle-ready troops have been mobilized and are standing by. We also understand that Special Forces paratroops are circling in C-One-thirties in the event rapid response is called for."

"Brad, are the Militiamen expected to *do* anything at this point? The launch is only twenty minutes away. What are their intentions? Have they said?"

"Peter, last night Dr. Danton Falopian, one of the Millennial Man Militia leaders here, gave a speech in which he urged *restraint* on everyone's part."

"What's happened to Jack Banion, whose idea this all was?"

"We're *told,* Peter, though we cannot confirm it, that Banion was *relieved* of his leadership role in some kind of palace coup. Sources close to the leadership tell us that Dr. Falopian and Colonel Murfletit felt that his approach was too, quote, confrontational and dangerous. Falopian is seen as a moderating influence."

"I'd say," Banion said, watching in the trailer, "that they have struck their deal with the White House."

"Thank you, Brad. Let's go now to the helicopter pad at the Kennedy Space Center. As you can see, they are keeping us back quite a ways. . . . *Marine One* is landing. The President and First

Lady disembarking . . . being met by NASA administrators . . . surrounded by security agents . . . moving briskly into the building. Brad, apart from all the drama going on, I would think that this would have to be a very satisfying moment for the president. He has pushed very hard, as you know, for *Celeste* funding, taking a lot of criticism for it. Even for the timing of the launch itself."

"That's right, Peter. *Celeste* was originally supposed to be completed next January, but then the date was moved up."

"Good timing for the president's reelection?"

"NASA has said that it had nothing to do with it, but it certainly does seem like a lift for the president, coming just a few days before the election."

"The president is now in the launch facility . . . he is shaking hands with the mission controllers. . . . Do I understand he will speak to the astronauts?"

"That's right, Peter. Of course, they are already *aboard Celeste,* but he will speak to them by phone and extend his wishes for a successful mission. We understand he will thank Amber Lamb, the fitness instructor on *Celeste*'s crew. She was the one, you'll recall, who urged the president to attend this launch at a time when he was taking political heat for it."

"Brad, is the plan still for the president to press the ignition button?"

"That's right. That is a presidential first, of course. We do have a close-up of the ignition button on the console. The red button there . . . that ignites the three million pounds of fuel in *Celeste*'s booster rockets, sending her on her journey skyward, on this historic journey, completing America's platform for the twenty-first century, as it has been called. Just two minutes from lift-off. Peter?"

"The president has now taken his place at the console . . . smiles all around . . . he's putting on his headset so he can communicate. . . . This is always a tense time in the control room, as it of course must be for the astronauts. John Glenn, first American to orbit space, once said, 'How reassuring to think that everything underneath you came from the lowest bidder.' . . . Here we go."

"We are go for launch."

"Ten seconds . . ."

NINETEEN

The explosion, which could be detected as far away as the Florida-Georgia border, could certainly be felt inside the Banion flying saucer trailer, where it wreaked havoc. By now, Scrubbs was an old hand at being hurtled through the air by percussive blasts. But for Banion, as well as the other occupants, it was a novel experience. After colliding with a bulkhead, he found himself supine, looking up at the ceiling, trying to take in what had put him there. Renira, to judge from the indignant noises she was making—the word *bloody* featuring prominently in her commentary—was all right. Elspeth, too, seemed alive. To judge from the groaning coming from whatever part of the trailer his head had embedded itself in, Scrubbs would survive, with medical attention.

The TV, bolted down, continued to emit images and sound.

"Peter, there's been a *tremendous* explosion . . ."

Well, Banion thought, that much was obvious. He craned his head, ever so gently, lest he find that it had separated from his neck, so that he could see the screen. It showed—well, it showed a large cloud of smoke, with little trails going off in different directions, eerily reminiscent of another explosion that had once taken place here. The anchorman was making inquiries of his reporters as to the disposition of the astronauts. As yet there wasn't much information, but now the focus of attention was shifting to the president.

"Let's look at the tape," the anchorman said.

The tape showed an exuberant president, proudly wearing his white engineer's gown and colorful *Celeste* mission vest.

"Ten . . . nine . . . eight . . . ." The camera closed in on the presidential index finger pressing down on the red ignition button. There was a moment's hesitation, and then—*boom*—the camera went wobbly. When it got back into focus, the presidential visage could no longer be called a beacon of national pride. Most commentators described it as looking "stunned." And well they might have. Three million pounds of combusting solid rocket propellant does have that effect, especially on the features of the person who, however blameless at the technical level, ignites it.

The images on the screen then became frenetic as the Secret Service grabbed their principal by the arms and torso, and, forming a protective scrum around him, got him the hell out of there, knocking down NASA technicians like tenpins at a bowling alley. To judge from the number of machine guns the Secret Service displayed, they seemed to be under the general impression that the *Celeste* explosion was the preamble to a spectacular attempt on the president's life by NASA technicians. But then, in this harried atmosphere, who could have blamed them?

The next images showed even greater heights of security, with Special Forces commandos, bristling with even greater firepower, rushing to surround the presidential helicopter, whose blades were already rotating, amidst a whining of turbine engines.

"The astronauts!" The anchorman was thumping his desk. "What about the astronauts?"

"We don't know," his correspondent on the scene replied.

"Well find *out!*" He thumped again.

Banion was riveted, but at this point his viewing was interrupted by the FBI paramilitary unit that burst into the trailer, shouting bloody murder, and arrested him and the others.

THE WORST PART, ASIDE FROM THE FOOD—IF IT COULD TECH-nically be called that—was the isolation. They gave him no papers, no TV, no phone. He had to wear a ridiculous orange jump-suit that felt like it was made of paper. They'd taken away his watch, presumably so that he couldn't hang himself with the wristband. He didn't know how long he'd been there, or whether it was day or night outside. It occurred to him that, after twenty-four hours, habeas corpus ought to kick in and they should charge him formally with some crime or let him go; at the very least, they should have let him make his phone call. God only knew what statute they were holding him under. Terrorism? Threatening the president? All he knew was, *Celeste* had blown up and they were treating him as if it were his fault.

In the midst of these joyless ruminations, the bars opened and several grim-faced men entered, the grimmest of the lot identifying himself as FBI Deputy Director Bargenberfer. He announced that Banion was being held on charges of conspiracy to incite violence; further, that he was under investigation for willful destruction of federal property and conspiracy to commit murder using a weapon of mass destruction. And that was just hello. It took the deputy director several minutes just to cover everything that Banion was alleged to have done, by which point, the merits of their case notwithstanding, Banion decided it was prudent to tell them to piss off and talk to his lawyer.

ASTRONAUTS ARE "SHAKEN BUT SAFE"
AFTER CELESTE BOOSTER ROCKETS
EXPLODE AS PRESIDENT PRESSES IGNITION BUTTON

BANION'S ATTORNEY, BARRETT PRETTYMAN, JR., HAD brought as many newspapers and magazines as he could carry.

Banion was almost as eager for news as he was to discuss how to make it more difficult for the government to send him to the electric chair.

The cover of *Time* showed *Celeste* blowing up. *Newsweek*—whose coverage had favored the president's opponent—showed a grainy close-up of the presidential finger on the ignition button, accompanied by the cover line WHOOPS. Banion drew some sustenance from the fact that the other person the media were most avid to blame for this catastrophe was—the president.

THE WHITE HOUSE BRIEFING ROOM HAD NOT BEEN THIS lively since the day a president had announced that he had not had sex with a twenty-something White House intern.

"Did the president hit the button before he was supposed to?"

"Of course not. The president was just following orders. Let me rephrase that—"

"What about this report that the White House told NASA to move the launch up to before the election?"

"That is . . . there's no . . . I have nothing on that."

"Sources within NASA are saying that."

"That may be, but I still don't have anything on it."

"Does the president feel remorse about what happened?"

"Of course not. Let me rephrase that. Of course he feels badly for those who were killed, and his thoughts go out to their families. But I would emphasize to you this was not his fault. The president did not cause the explosion. I want to emphasize that. Everyone needs to be very *clear on* that point. . . ."

"We have a source inside NASA who says the White House secretly directed them to move the launch date up before the election, despite certain safety issues NASA had."

"I'm still not going to categorize that beyond saying . . . what I've already said to you on that."

NASA NOW SAYS WHITE HOUSE
MOVED UP LAUNCH DATE

"GOOD EVENING. IT HAS BEEN A DAY OF CHARGES AND COUN-
tercharges between an *embattled* White House and NASA. As
the investigation into the *Celeste* explosion continues, both parties are trying to distance themselves from the disaster by pointing fingers at each other. Contrary to earlier denials, NASA now
says the White House *did* exert pressure on them, as far back as
last summer, to move the date of the launch up to *before* the
presidential election. The White House maintains that is not
true. But the *Celeste* blowup may already have had a catastrophic
impact on the president's reëlection campaign. We go now to the
White House, to our correspondent, Sam Donaldson . . ."

"Peter, the question they're asking here today isn't whether
the president can now win reëlection but whether he might have
to resign *before* the election . . ."

U.S. IS PREPARING TO INDICT JOHN BANION
FOR CONSPIRACY TO INCITE VIOLENCE;
POSSIBLY SABOTAGE, WRONGFUL DEATH

THE FOOD HAD IMPROVED, ANYWAY. THEY HAD MOVED HIM
closer to Washington, to a federal detention facility where most
of his fellow prisoners were white-collar criminals of varying
distinction, and decent conversationalists. He could watch television to his heart's content. Barrett sent over all the newspapers
and magazines each day so that he could have an informed wal-
low in how his predicament was playing out there. His mood
was, surprisingly, not too bad. Perhaps he had been so buffeted
by vicissitudes that he was by now inured to horrible news. Barrett said not to worry about the death penalty—that it was just
the AG showing off. But it was clear from the media that the
country was in a hanging mood. The papers were reporting the
latest Internet dirt. Pierre Salinger,* who had made a sensation
with his report that the U.S. military had shot down TWA Flight

---

*Increasingly obscure figure, believed to have been JFK's press secretary.

800 with a missile, was now alleging that Banion had been paid by the government to stir up trouble in order to provoke a military takeover of the space program. If only Roz were around. She'd have enjoyed these ironies.

Barrett reported that the book offers were coming in at the rate of several a day, the latest being $7 million. This was about what Banion figured it would cost him in legal fees just to avoid the electric chair—though Barrett had decently not yet brought up the subject of money.

A guard announced that he had a call from a Mr. Stimple, of Ample Ampere. What could Bill be calling about?

"Jack! How are you?"

"I'm in prison, Bill, and they are talking about executing me. How are you?"

"We're all pulling for you, I want you to know that. From the big guy on down."

"Thanks. I feel much better now."

"Jack, this is a long way off, and we're all really, really hoping that it would never come to this, but let me just put it on the table. They use our product down there, as you know . . ."

"Product?"

"The XT-2000."

"Yes?" Where was this headed?

"If it ever came to that, not that it will, I want you to know—this chair is just state of the art."

"Yes, I was under that impression."

"Nothing at all like your standard model, where people were catching fire and—well, you wrote about it."

"Um."

"This one is painless, noiseless, smokeless. It's really—our engineers just surpassed themselves."

"Bill, is there a point to this? Or did you just call to console me?"

"Let me just plant a thought, all right? If it does come to that, in return for a substantial—and I'm talking seven figures—do-

nation to your estate, to a charity of your choice, heirs, whatever . . . would you consider making a statement at the time
about how—maybe pleased isn't the right word—relieved or reassured you are that the technical aspect is being handled by
Ample?"

"That I'm being electrocuted by one of your products?"

"It won't come to that. But I just wanted to plant the idea. I
mean, better to bring it up now than when everything's . . ."

"Emotionally fraught?"

"Exactly. Still the word wizard!"

"Thanks, Bill. You've really lifted my spirits."

"Hey, that's my department."

FLICKERY WINS LANDSLIDE VICTORY; VOWS NEW ERA OF HONESTY, OPENNESS

PRESIDENT'S CELESTE WOES SEEN AS KEY FACTOR IN STUNNING LOSS

BARRETT'S NEWS WASN'T VERY GOOD. BARRETT SAID THE
feds were going to indict him the next day for incitement of violence among other charges.

Banion decided he might as well tell Barrett about MJ-12 and
all the rest of it.

Barrett listened attentively, nodding here, frowning there.
When Banion finished, he kept nodding, as if lost in thought.

"Well?" Banion said.

"You know, Jack," he said, "we really ought to consider the
merits of a psychological defense."

TWENTY

ONE YEAR LATER

If his life weren't hanging on the outcome of the trial, Banion would certainly long since have died of boredom.

He did his best to appear interested as his lawyer, the flamboyant, silver-maned westerner Jasper Jamm, methodically labored to besmirch the reputation of the forty-eighth aerospace engineer he had thus far called. (Only twenty-three to go.) At moments Banion wondered if a quick death in Ample Ampere's noiseless, smokeless, energy-efficient electric chair wouldn't be preferable to this water-drip torture.

The day before, he had drifted off during some mind-numbing testimony from a hydraulics engineer, occasioning a severe lecture from Jamm. "I need you to make *love* to this jury," he said gravely, "not to look like you don't give a possum's ass. Where do you think you are? Back in one of your Princeton eating clubs?"

Banion looked up at the stern face looming over him—Jamm stood six feet six in his cowboy boots.

"Don't you think *they're* bored too?" Jamm demanded.

"Is this your strategy?" Banion said. "Boring them into letting me off?"

Jamm was halfway into quoting another apothegm from Running Water when Banion wearily held up his hand to indicate that he was just not in the *mood* for another wise saying from Jamm's favorite nineteenth-century Shoshone philosopher-warrior, however fucking sagacious he was. Jamm made much of his partial Native American ancestry, despite his distinctly Caucasian looks. In place of the traditional necktie, there was a string bolo tie fastened with a silver-tipped bear claw. He wore a Stetson hat and Lucchese boots made from the skin of Gila monsters. He kept a pet cougar at his home in Idaho, and hunted elk in the Rocky Mountains with bow and arrow, using flint arrowheads made by his voluptuously attractive wife, Bliss. It was rumored—and never quite denied by him—that he had Custer's scalp in a secret compartment in his study. Before each trial, Jamm fasted and went naked into a sweat lodge in his backyard, there to prepare himself for the coming battle.

There was some feeling, within the criminal legal community, that all this colorful juju was for the benefit of the media, whom he assiduously courted. They of course gobbled it up. Given the choice between a lawyer who quotes Justice Brandeis and golfs, and one who claims to be related to Sitting Bull and slays large, antlered animals in his spare time, the press will usually go for the latter. Jamm's undeniable charisma and folksy sound bites eventually landed him his own television show, immodestly titled *The Best Defense,* but it had been canceled due to poor ratings, and he wanted it back. Fewer people had been stopping him for autographs in the street.

For all the grousing from other top criminal lawyers, Jamm was acknowledged to be among the best. Whether in a moment of weakness you had blown away your loved one or embezzled a few million dollars, betrayed your country, dumped toxic waste into the water supply, whatever, Jasper Jamm was the man to see. He had a way with juries. Who but Jamm could have convinced the Tracy Lee Boodro jurors—or at least enough of them—that his client was being controlled by the Central Intelligence Agency through the pacemaker in his chest at the time he dynamited the nuclear power plant in Jerome, Tennessee? When it came to imputing government conspiracies, Jamm was without peer. There was no telling what he might be able to do when handed a real one.

The trial was now in its eighteenth expensive week. Other than a theatrical opening statement—hysterically protested by the prosecution—in which Jamm hinted that the government itself had blown up *Celeste* in order to provide continued work for the military-industrial complex—*Objection!*—the trial had so far yielded little in the way of drama. (Banion wondered, Where *did* the courtroom drama genre ever originate?)

Jamm's strategy, apart from his customary "breaking" of the jury down into brain-dead zombies so that he could remake them to his will, was to (a) disagree with everything the prosecution said, including "Good morning, ladies and gentlemen of the jury," (b) demolish the wrongful death charge, and (c) produce reasonable doubt in the minds of the jury that his client was guilty of the odious charge of treason. This last was the most troublesome of the numerous charges against him, fifty-eight in all, inasmuch as it carried the death penalty.

NASA had yet to determine what exactly had caused *Celeste* to explode. There weren't many pieces of the rocket left much larger than a thumbnail. The investigation was at this point focusing on the rocket's self-destruct mechanism, normally designed to go off in the event something went wrong and the craft began heading murderously into a populated area. It was not designed, so far as anyone knew, to detonate when the president of the United States pressed the ignition button.

The fallout from the *Celeste* explosion had been radioactive. The ex-president, who had lost his reëlection, was now embroiled in a world of legal hurt of his own, stemming from the revelation that he had secretly ordered NASA to move up the launch date. Top NASA officials had been forced to resign in disgrace. Now it was Banion's turn to pick up his share of the tab.

Originally, the government had been able to indict him on

only a plethora of charges ranging from demonstration permit violations to incitement to riot, reckless endangerment, et cetera, et cetera, and wrongful death. A Mr. Newbert Figg, aged seventy-two, a retired citrus farmer from nearby Onanola, Florida, had driven to Cape Canaveral just to "see what all the fuss was about," according to the testimony of the lachrymose widow Figg. When *Celeste* blew up, Mr. Figg, beholding the spectacular fireball, suffered his third and final heart attack. The United States—as in *United States vs. John Oliver Banion*—being avid to throw everything at him that it could, leapt to link Banion to this cardiac event. They charged that Banion, by convening his Millennial Man Militia, had created an "attractive nuisance" and was thus directly to blame for the demise of Mr. Figg.

Jamm was confident of convincing the jury that Banion had not conspired with half a million of his followers merely to bring about the death of a curious septuagenarian with a history of heart problems.

But then a larger difficulty presented itself, in the persons of Dr. Falopian and Colonel Murfletit. Banion's former brain trust, fleeing federal authorities for their role in this millennial ka-ka, had turned up in Moscow, where they were publicly embraced as heroes by the ever-belligerent Russian government and given state jobs advising the Kremlin on Inoplanetnye Dela.* Banion was left to look like the Third Man who had not managed to escape. (Scrubbs made the Fourth.) The government was thus handed the golden opportunity to divert some of the public heat from its own flaming hide. It promptly added treason—18 United States Code section 2381, providing aid and comfort to the enemy—to the groaning board of charges.

As their cases were so intricately intertwined, Scrubbs was to be tried separately. He had valiantly resisted the government's repeated attempts to get him to incriminate Banion and cop to

---

*Literally, "extraterrestrial affairs."

the much lesser charge of conspiracy to impede traffic. Fine, said the government—then he too would stand trial for treason.

Jamm promised it would get more interesting when they came to this portion of the trial. Meanwhile, there were another twenty-three aerospace engineers to discredit in an attempt to persuade the jury that far from being the cream of American aerospace technicians, they were nothing but imbeciles and incompetents who could not be trusted with fixing a leaky faucet, much less overseeing a $21 billion space station.

So Banion sat, a rictus of ersatz concentration frozen onto his face, forbidden by Jamm even the consolation of doodling on a legal pad. For a while he had sought mental relief by filling up pads with every list in his memory: names and dates of U.S. presidents, Jesus' genealogy going back to King David, the kings and queens of England, the handicaps of Supreme Court justices, and the names of the 711 survivors of the *Titanic,* which he had memorized on a bet as a child at Camp Ear Wig.

"Mr. Crummekar," Jamm said, leaning companionably on the edge of the witness box. "In nineteen seventy-four, while you were attending Oklahoma Tech as an undergraduate, you belonged to a *fraternity,* is that correct?"

"Objection."

"Sustained."

"I apologize, Your Honor. I will rephrase that. Mr. Crummekar, did you ever participate in a 'toga party' at Delta Kappa—"

"*Objection.*"

"Sustained. Mr. Jamm, I have spoken to you about this before."

"Your Honor, there is no margin for error in aerospace technology. I am merely trying to establish that—"

"Get *on* with it, Counsel."

BY THE TIME JAMM HAD FINISHED WITH THE LAST AERO-space engineer, in the twenty-seventh week of the trial, Banion was personally convinced, by the looks of hatred coming from jurors 6, 9, and 10, that they not only were itching to send him to the chair but would vote for putting him to death by the slowest means possible. Jamm, however, appeared quite satisfied, even exultant over having established that one of the technicians had filled a prescription for an antidepressant two weeks prior to the launch. That night he went on seven TV shows and declared, "One of the key members of the launch team was on drugs. It is the government that should be on trial, not Mr. Banion."

Weeks 22 through 27 were consumed with the less than riveting testimony from eighteen cardiologists as to whether Banion had the blood of Mr. Figg on his hands. Jamm was prepared. His investigators, a nasty pair of high-priced Washington ferrets, had established that Mr. Figg had a copy of *Juggs** in his pickup truck at the time of the launch. Jamm had charts ready to go showing the heartbeat of a seventy-two-year-old male during arousal. Much as he felt innocent of the death of Mr. Figg, Banion privately expressed his earnest hope to Jamm that he would not have to play the *Juggs* card.

At a certain point in the proceedings, it occurred to Banion that he was seeing more of Jamm on the television set in his cell—he was allowed one—than he was in court. He began to drop hints that since he was paying $475 an hour, it might be nice actually to lay eyes on Jamm every now and then.

One morning Jamm showed up looking exhausted. Banion inquired if he had been up burning the midnight oil, poring over the law books. Not exactly. Jamm yawned. He had stayed up late in order to appear live on the British morning television program *Wakey, Wakey*.

"Why," Banion said, "are you jeopardizing my defense in order to impress people eating bangers in Luton?"

---

* A glossy magazine devoted to large-breasted women, begun as a color insert in the *Atlantic Monthly*.

Jamm replied that he was as alert as a falcon soaring above the forest and then proceeded to doze off during the prosecution's admittedly protracted exploration of the viability of Mr. Figg's myocardium.

The next day Jamm was not present in court, leaving the cross-examination of the current cardiologist to one of his assistant attorneys, an attractive redhead thought to inspire lubricious thoughts in male juror number 2, since he kept shifting in his seat whenever she was on display. Jamm was absent for the following three days. Where was he? Banion was unable to get a straightforward answer from the assistant attorneys, other than that he was "tracking down some important leads."

One morning, while waiting for the court to convene, Banion read in the paper that Jasper Jamm had just sold the rights to his story for "seven figures" to Big Pictures, the Hollywood movie studio. Banion wondered what exactly was meant by that "his." He reached Jamm by phone at the Beverly Hills Hotel and suggested that he take the next plane back.

He was not in a receptive mood when Jamm finally showed up the next morning, bleary-eyed and yawning from having caught the red-eye. He blandly assured Banion that Ms. Plumm, his deputy, was perfectly competent to handle the cross-examination of the cardiologists and said that his presence in California had been a necessity because "Warren" wanted to meet him before closing the deal.

"Warren?"

"Beatty. He wants to play me in the film."

"Ah," Banion said. "And who do they have in mind to play me?"

"That's one of the things I want to discuss with you after today's session. I'm not at all satisfied with their casting suggestions so far."

"Isn't this *my* story? Or am I missing something?"

"I absolutely think that you *should* sell your story. If you want, I'll pursue that when I go back out there tomorrow."

"Tomorrow?"

"Nothing much is happening here, just more heart stuff. Warren is giving a dinner. Under the circumstances, I think I should probably be there. Don't you?"

So as the trial moved into its most critical phase, it did Banion good to know that his lawyer's attention was equally divided between keeping him off death row and negotiating with Minnie Driver to play his wife.

IT WAS NOT GOING WELL. THE PROSECUTION HAD MANAGED to make Banion's interview with Dr. Kokolev and Colonel Radik at the UFO convention sound like a meeting of the Committee to Overthrow the U.S. Government. In the general atmosphere of continued hostility between the two countries, trying to halt the launch of a rocket that was also carrying a military payload—what hay the prosecution made of that inconvenient fact—looked downright unpatriotic. One of the jurors was recused for high blood pressure. A week later a paperback entitled *Juror Number Five: Why John Banion Must Fry* appeared under his name; in it he announced his conviction that Banion had been working for the Russians—and aliens—all along. He was invited to share his insights on all the evening news and talk shows.

Morale on Team Banion was not running high. Crowds outside the courtroom held up signs for the cameras saying TRAITOR! For the first time, it dawned on Banion that the day might in fact dawn when the prison barber appeared in his cell to shave a contact spot onto the top of his head. He found himself musing on famous last lines of people who had been handed the traditional blindfold and cigarette, and even began rehearsing a few of his own.

When one night, musing on these pleasant thoughts, he looked up at the TV bolted to the wall and saw the debut of a new late-night legal affairs program called *The Offense Never Rests—With Host Jasper Jamm,* he wondered if it wasn't perhaps time for a change in legal representation.

• • •

"MR. BANION," THE JUDGE SAID IN CHAMBERS, "THERE IS AN axiom of the law that says—"

" 'He who defends himself has a fool for a client.' Yes, Your Honor, I am aware of it. But there is another axiom."

"What is that?"

" 'He who pays himself four hundred seventy-five dollars an hour will soon be rich.' "

"Very well," the judge said.

On his first day as his own counsel, Banion called Roz as a witness. There was only one problem: Roz had vanished without trace. All he could do was put himself on the stand and describe the night she had betrayed him. After that, she became known in the tabloid press as the "Missing Macaroni Woman."

He called the ex-president. This took some doing, since the former president was in the midst of motions preparing for his own trial. But Banion's old nemesis seemed to be in an agreeable frame of mind when he arrived to be interrogated one last time by his old nemesis.

"Mr. President," Banion said, "thank you for being with us this morning."

"My pleasure."

"I know you're busy, so let me get right to it. Does the name MJ-Twelve, or Majestic Twelve, mean anything to you?"

"It's a lubricant, isn't it? You spray it on squeaky hinges."

"Now, Mr. President, you do recall that I came to you in the Oval Office and informed you that there was a secret agency within the government—"

"Oh, that." The ex-president smiled at the jury. "The one that launches UFO's and abducts people?"

"The same. The one that Mr. Scrubbs worked for—"

"Objection."

"Sustained."

"Your Honor."

"Proceed, Mr. Banion."

"And what did you do after I informed you of its existence?"

"Nothing."

"Well, isn't that a bit strange—"

"Objection."

"Sustained."

"Honestly. All right, I will rephrase that. Why didn't you do anything?"

"For two reasons. First, I assumed since I was president, I'd have heard of such an agency if it existed. And second, by that point I was personally convinced that you were working for the Russians, so—"

"Objection." Banion said.

"Overruled."

"Your Honor—"

"The witness may answer the question."

"Your Honor, *really*."

"Mr. Banion, this is not your talk show. This is a court of law. If you persist in this unproductive way, I will appoint a lawyer for you. You may continue, Mr. President."

"Thank you. I thought you were working for the Russians. Under those circumstances, I wouldn't have divulged any national security information to you."

"And what made you think I was working for the Russians?"

The president smiled. "Because, Jack, you were trying to stop the launch of an American space vehicle carrying a military payload specifically designed to assist in the defense of our country, which was then, as it is now, facing a serious external threat from Russia. To be honest, I didn't believe you when you said you were doing it because aliens had instructed you to." He turned to the jury. "Not that I don't keep an open mind on these things."

"Well"—Banion sighed—"you're wrong—"

"Objection."

"Oh, shut up."

"Mr. Banion!"

"But I have to say, I see your point, Mr. President. I have no further questions."

"WE'RE JOINED NOW BY OUR CHIEF LEGAL ANALYST, JEFFREY Toobin. Jeff, how does it look to you?"

"Peter, if I were Jack Banion, I would be seriously be considering trying to negotiate an eleventh-hour plea bargain. But it may be too late for that. I think the prosecution's biggest challenge at this point is trying not to appear overconfident."

"Why wasn't Mr. Banion allowed to inform the jury that the former president is himself about to be tried for conspiracy to commit reckless endangerment in the *Celeste* case?"

"Under American law, Peter, juries are not allowed to have relevant information like that. That's why, for instance, if you're being tried for murder, it's not relevant that you've previously killed twenty people. Under our system, the more ignorant the jury, the better. This is either the great strength of our system or a mind-boggling defect, depending on your point of view."

"Jeff Toobin. We will of course be providing continuing coverage of the Banion trial in the days ahead as the case prepares to go to the jury . . ."

BANION WAS IN THE PRISON LIBRARY WORKING ON HIS CLOSing statement when a guard notified him that he had a visitor.

"Who is it?"

"Reporter."

"I'm not giving interviews," Banion said.

"From *Cosmopolitan* magazine."

Banion started. "*Cosmos-politan* magazine?"

"Whatever. Fifteen minutes."

The person sitting on the other side of the glass partition was not immediately recognizable. She had dyed her hair jet black, and the clothes, to the extent they made any statement at all, announced "Frump." A dazzling creature had managed to turn herself into something you might find waiting on a bench in a bus station.

They both picked up the phones on either side of the partition.

"Is this my conjugal visit?" Banion said. "It's going to be tricky, with this glass between us."

"Hello, Jack."

"Nice outfit. You might want to rethink the hair."

"You okay?"

"Oh fine. About to be found guilty of treason. Because I couldn't locate a key witness. How are things with you?"

"I wanted to help, but I couldn't."

"Right."

"Testifying wouldn't have done any good. They'd have discredited me."

"The same way they did me? 'John couldn't have sex unless he dressed up like a Martian.' Thanks so much. It's fun being made out to be a pervert."

"I tried to stop that."

"Stop *who*?"

"MJ-One."

"Look, I have fifteen minutes. I don't have time for Twenty Questions."

Roz spoke in a whisper. "I was in MJ-Eight—Publications—editing *Cosmos*. After your second unauthorized abduction, I received a Pri-One—Priority One—message, right from the top. I was brought to Washington to meet with MJ-One. My instructions were to get close to you. Observe, defuse, at least control the situation. Then things got complicated."

"You mean, we almost had sex on the floor."

"Jack, they blew up *Celeste*."

Banion leaned in to the glass. "Why?"

"You and Scrubbs went to the president and told him about Majestic."

"How did you know that?"

"Because he tried to call us on the hot line, from the Oval Office."

"He did?"

"Yes. After that, he had to go. He couldn't be allowed a second term to go poking around. He'd have found us, sooner or later."

"So you . . . blew up the rocket? To make him look like an asshole?"

Roz nodded. "And organized the leaks about moving up the launch date to before the election."

"MJ-Twelve could do that?"

"Sure. We have assets all through NASA. In every agency of the government. You really have to, to run an outfit like this one."

"Why are you telling me this now? To make me feel better about going to the electric chair?"

"I'm trying to help."

"Well help harder. Who's MJ-One?"

"You know him. He's actually a fan of yours, but he's not about to let that get in the way of the job."

"Roz—who *is* it?"

She said in a rangy accent, " '*Jack, you bring this majestic young lady to see me sometime, you hear?' *"

"Mentallius?"

"Who better than the chairman of the Senate Hindsight Committee? That's how they set it up back in nineteen forty-seven. The idea was to ensure continuous funding. Put in charge the one senator all the other senators are scared to death of. Are they going to complain when he attaches a rider to some agriculture program? Not if he has the power to veto their pork without even giving a reason. He's only the second MJ-One in the agency's history. He's been running it for over thirty years. And he's *good*. He brought it into the modern era, upgraded all the equipment. The stuff they used to use was like out of bad sci-fi movies. He set up the abductions program. Area Fifty-one—his baby. Now he's old, and some of the others, especially in MJ-

Two, have been trying to move him out, but he can't be budged. He loves it. It's what he lives for."

"How," Banion said suspiciously, "do you know all this? Scrubbs says it's all tightly compartmentalized so no one knows too much."

"I made it my business to get close to him."

"You *slept* with that old goat? Disgusting."

"Of course I didn't sleep with him. He's past that, even if he swallowed a whole bottle of Viagra. He just likes to have me around." She looked at him the way she used to. "I have that effect on people, you know."

"Yes," Banion said wistfully. "I remember that part."

TWENTY-ONE

Banion's closing argument was in its fourth day, and His Honor was not pleased. It was an unprecedentedly lengthy close. One commentator proposed that Banion was attempting to put everyone in the courtroom to sleep and then escape.

The nation was fascinated, if not exactly spellbound. He had quoted Catullus, Robespierre, John Lennon, Dickens, Oliver Wendell Holmes, Origen, Suetonius, Merle Haggard, Jefferson, Mencken, Balzac, Gibbon, Dante (three times), the Book of Job, Pliny the Elder, Montaigne, Diderot, Thomas More, Yogi Berra, Dean Acheson, William Dean Howells, and Hoagy Carmichael. He even, apparently unable to resist, quoted himself. "A new height of vanity, perhaps, but let me just read you what I wrote in my column eight years ago when . . ."

His Honor, who had begun scowling openly the second day, had clearly, to judge from his continuous scribbling, begun writing his memoirs. The prosecutor and his team were at pains to conceal their pleasure, for it was plain from the faces of the jurors that they were going to make Banion pay dearly for this last torment he was putting them through. Legal experts were unanimous in pronouncing Banion's filibusterlike performance, for all its occasional true eloquence, a tactical disaster. "It's as if he's saying to the jury: 'The only way you're going to shut me up is with a thousand volts.' "

"Now," said a visibly exhausted Banion, flipping through the multivolume, 50,000-page trial transcript in front of him, "I would draw your attention to page thirty-six thousand, seven hundred seventy-eight, . . . where Rudolph Fribblemeyer, the . . . solid-fuel engineer . . . *admits* . . . in his own words . . . that . . . if you subject fuel to extremes of . . . temperature . . . well, I believe it was Montesquieu, the eminent French philosopher, who said . . . *Ce n'est que la vérité qui blesse* . . . or possibly Rochefoucauld . . . ."

Spectators began to give up their hard-won seats.

Then, shortly after three o'clock on the fourth—and, His Honor swore, final—day, the television networks interrupted the broadcast.

"I JUST DON'T UNDERSTAND," THE NEW PRESIDENT SAID TO the director of the National Reconnaissance Office* in the Oval Office, "why these pictures haven't surfaced until now. And who the hell in your shop leaked them. My God, these are KH-Eleven photos. They're supposed to be top-secret. Why are they on the front page of today's *Washington Post*?"

The photos spread out on the president's desk showed an aerial view of the *Celeste* launch. Clearly visible, above the *Celeste,* was an object that looked like a flying saucer. Also visible was a thin beam of light emanating from it, aimed down toward *Celeste.*

"Sir, at this point, we're not sure. All we know is that these are in fact Keyhole photos. You can see that from the identifiers there, down in the corner. At this point, we're looking at CIA. They're the ones who had requested Keyhole tracking of a Russian SSN submarine off Florida at the time of the launch, which would explain why Amethyst—that's the code name of this particular satellite—was positioned over Cape Canaveral at the time of the launch. Coincidence that would seem to indicate that this

---

*Government directorate tasked with coordinating aerial and satellite intelligence between agencies that hate each other and keep the juiciest parts for themselves.

was CIA's photo session. As to why these photos surfaced now, we're not—I assure you that we're in an evidence-gathering mode at the present time."

"You don't *know,* in other words." The president snorted. "Well, what do your people say? Is this thing"—he pointed at the flying saucer—"What the hell is it?"

"Sir, we're unable to make an evaluation at this time."

"Well, who *is*?"

The president turned to a general whose chest was a valorous rainbow of ribbons. "What do your people say about it? Was there a radar track?"

"No sir. Nothing at all."

The president studied the photos on the gleaming surface of his desk, once used by President Kennedy. "It *looks* like one. What's this beam coming out of it"

"We don't know, sir."

"Your budget's twenty-seven billion dollars a year, and you don't *know*?"

"It would be consistent with a high-energy beam, such as a laser. But that's only speculation."

"All right. Everyone out." The president looked at his attorney general, who had been sitting on the sofa, studying one of the photos while puffing on an unlit pipe. "*You* stay."

When the admirals and generals and others had left, the president grumbled, "Experts! Couldn't even tell me Brazil was about to set off a nuclear blast. Now this." He sat down on the sofa. "All right, what do we do?"

"I don't know what to make of it. It does *look* like a UFO, I have to say, even though I don't believe in UFOs. And, according to NASA, this beam or whatever is aimed at the area of the booster where the self-destruct mechanism was housed."

The president said, "There's got to be some explanation."

"I'd love to hear it."

"Point is, where do we go from here?"

"Your call."

"My call? You're the AG."

The two men stared at each other. The president flicked on the television set. It filled with pictures of swelling crowds outside the jail where Banion was being held. There had been a shift in tone among the banners: BANION SAVIOR OF HUMANITY! FREE BANION! BANION SCAPEGOAT!

The attorney general said, "FBI says the Millennium Man people are gearing up for another march."

"Oh *God,* not again. Where to this time?"

"White House."

EPILOGUE

The house was a vacation home on the Shenandoah River, a few hours west of Washington, that Renira had rented under another name, to throw off the media. Banion and Scrubbs had done little the last two days other than stuff themselves with nonfederal prison food and drink pricey French wine.

Around them, scattered like masticated hamster bedding material, newspapers were piled and strewn. One headline read:

BANION FREED AS U.S.
DISMISSES CHARGES

WHITE HOUSE VOWS TO CONTINUE
INVESTIGATION INTO SAUCER PHOTO

It was dusk. They were sitting on the wooden deck with a clear view of the sky, working on a second bottle of Château Latour '82, a celebratory gift from Barrett Prettyman. Jupiter, Venus, and Mars blazed brightly against the crepuscular blue. Hundreds of miles above, a satellite blinked placidly as it made its transit.

"One of yours?" Banion asked. He was half in the bag, and well past caring about the provenance of any blinking lights other than the ones inside his own brain, and, for that matter, he didn't much care about those.

Scrubbs, also feeling no pain, belched.

A rising smallmouth bass pimpled the flat surface of the river. They heard the sound of heels on the wooden deck behind them.

"Hello, boys."

Her hair was back to blond, and she was back to dressing sharp. She walked over to the rail and looked up at the stars. "Beautiful evening."

"Where have you been?" Banion asked.

"Had a few details to attend to. Mentallius wanted to have a good-bye lunch."

"After your telling him you had him on tapes implicating himself as the head of MJ-Twelve and were going to mail them to the Justice Department and the media? He still wanted to have lunch?"

"He's an old sweetie at heart."

Banion grunted. " 'Old sweetie.' Fucker tried to send my ass to the electric chair."

"You talk differently than you used to, Princeton boy," Roz said.

"That's because I've been hanging out with Harvard types. Prison's full of them." He sighed. "What the hell took you so long?"

"You might show a little appreciation."

"I'll send you a thank-you note."

"Hey—I had to get him on tape, present him with the situation, then fix it with our people to come up with a satellite photo, and get it into the system so it would look like an accidental U.S. intelligence picture. What did you expect? This isn't like ordering take-out pizza."

"You might have told me I was going to have to stall for four days. I thought the judge was going to have the bailiffs strangle me."

Roz said to Scrubbs, "We're history, as of sixteen hundred hours. Majestic is shut down. The message went out to all divisions: 'Mission Complete. All operations terminated immediately. Signed MJ-One.' "

"End of an era," Scrubbs said.

"I actually got kind of choked up," Roz said.

"*Spare* me," Banion said.

They watched the stars.

"Has it occurred to either of you," Banion asked, "that none of us has a life left?"

"Two days ago," Scrubbs said, "I was wondering if I was going to make it through the day without someone shanking me for my morning donut. This is life."

"Doesn't take much to make you happy." Banion snorted. "What are you going to do when the 'eighty-two Bordeaux runs out?"

"Thought I'd take another crack at applying to the CIA. Bet they'd take me now."

"What harm could it possibly do?"

"What are you going to do with your three million followers?" Roz asked. "They think you're God. Not that those of us who know you agree."

Banion looked thoughtfully into his wine. "Yes, an awesome responsibility. Look what happened after I called Jasper Jamm an asshole on *Nightline*."

"What's the latest?"

"He's still in hiding in the hills, with his rifle. Barrett had a cell phone call from him this afternoon, offering to cancel the three point whatever million dollars I owe him if I'll issue a public statement instructing the Millennium Marchers that he should be allowed to live."

"That's a tough call." Roz smiled. "Don't know what I'd do, it was me. What are you going to do?"

"I thought of adding on punitive charges, for pain and suffering. I suppose I should be magnanimous in victory, but I must

say I'm tempted to let them tear him limb from limb. It's not a problem I've had up to now, figuring out what to do with three million adoring followers that I don't want anymore."

"There's a rock band called 10,000 Maniacs." Scrubbs said. "You could start one called Three Million Lunatics."

"I was thinking of telling them that I've received new instructions from our friends up there."

"No," Roz said. *"Please."*

"That our time is not yet at hand, and that they should go home and not say another *word* about UFO's, to anyone, until they receive further instructions, directly from me. That way, if I need them . . . well, you never know when you might need three million devoted followers. Good to know they're there, just in case."

Roz stood. "Well, take care, boys. Don't go starting any new religions without checking with me first."

Her heels left a faint echo on the wooden planks.

BANION CAUGHT UP WITH HER AS SHE WAS GETTING INTO the car. "Where you headed?"

"Thought I'd spend the night at Swann's Way. Remember, where we stayed that night, on our first date? It's not far from here. Food's good."

"I'll drive you there."

"I can manage," Roz said.

"These are lonely roads at night. There have been reports of alien activity in the area. You might get abducted, and subjected to strange sexual practices. You know, *probing.*"

He could make out a dimple in the light of the opened door.

"In that case"—Roz laughed—"maybe you better come along."

AUTHOR'S NOTE

I am, as usual, grateful to the usual suspects, especially to my editor at Random House, Jonathan Karp, not only for his excellent suggestions and guidance, but also for (*finally*) coming up with a decent title. Martha Schwartz and her able copy team did another fine job. Thanks also to John Tierney and to Greg Zorthian for their eagle eyes. Doctors David E. Williams and William S. Hughes were standing by with their *PDRs* at the ready. Amanda Urban of ICM saw the green in the little men. My wife, Lucy, was, as always, a devoted encourager. Certain people within various UFO organizations were welcoming and helpful. They would probably, under the circumstances, prefer anonymity. I am grateful to, and commend to anyone interested in this subject, Keith Thompson's book, *Angels and Aliens*. It was amidst those wise and excellent pages that I first came across Majestic Twelve. It provided an irresistible cue ball, needing only a bit of English. And finally, thanks to the forty-second president of the United States, who during a chance encounter expressed an interest in this project that seemed to go beyond the merely polite. I understood why when, a few weeks later, I came across the newspaper story that provides the second epigraph at the front of this book. I hope that he found his answers.

—*Blue Hill*
August 18, 1998

ABOUT THE AUTHOR

CHRISTOPHER BUCKLEY is a novelist and editor of *Forbes FYI* magazine. He lives in Washington, D.C., with his wife and two children and dog, Duck. In 1998, he was inducted into the Légion d'honneur by the president of the Republic of France for "extraordinary contributions to French culture," despite the fact that his French is barely sufficient to order a meal in a restaurant. He has been an adviser to every president since William Howard Taft, a remarkable achievement, since he was born in 1952. His next book, a refutation of the theories of the physicist Stephen Hawking, will be published this fall by Princeton University Press.